DRAKON

Book II
UNCARVED

C.A. CASKABEL

ISBN 978-1541163713 (paperback)
ISBN 978-0-9906150-1-9 (e-book)

This is a work of fiction

Contents

BOOK II: UNCARVED

"And the day dawned blue."

www.caskabel.com

XVII.
I Seek Only One

Fourteenth spring. Uncarved—Starling.

This I know, now that I am older and have seen many winters come and go: there are some wounds that never heal. Even when the flesh breathes again, the mind keeps rotting. Memories torment every day and consume every night.

During my winters with the Uncarved, the Guides would give me the only treatment they knew: yet another brutal trial. Every new trial that awaited me was so much worse than the last that my mind had no time to get stuck in the mud of the past. The nose smelled; the head obeyed and moved arms and legs to save my life. Only now that I am here with the monks within the stone walls of the Castlemonastery, can I ponder the wounds of my soul.

The Sieve ended on the fortieth morning. Reghen and Keko were leading us northwest. The night was descending fast, and we were much closer to the Endless Forest.

"Where in the Demon's name are we going?" I asked.

Defeat had loosened my tongue, and I was in no mood to obey anyone.

"We've passed all the grazing meadows and training fields of the warriors and the young Archers. We'll deliver you to the camp of the

Uncarved. It is in the northwest corner of Sirol."

"Is it deep in the Forest?"

"No, next to it. You will hear the wolves sing," said the Reghen.

"And the Reekaal…but they don't sing," added Keko.

That was his last word. *Sing.* A word so out of step with the murky-eyed, shit-mouthed Guide. When we arrived at the camp of the Uncarved, Keko turned around and started galloping back to where we had come from before the Reekaal caught his scent. He said no goodbyes, and I never saw him again. Much later, I heard that he died of the plague, though I believe that the rose-colored worms had been eating his body from within for a long time. His mouth always smelled of death, whether he was talking or breathing.

"Two more youths from this winter's Sieve," said the Reghen, pointing to Malan and me. Across from us stood a tall and broad-shouldered man, not as old as our Guides, with deep scars on his cheeks.

"This is Chaka, Leader of the Guides of the Uncarved. For five winters, you will be in his hands," added the Reghen.

Five winters. What was this? In forty days of the Sieve, almost half the children I knew had died. I couldn't even imagine my bare bones in five winters.

At his heels were four children I had not seen in the Sieve. Three of them were my height. One of them was huge, at least two palms taller than me.

"Stand next to them," Chaka told us.

"We will bring seven more," the Reghen said to Chaka. "That makes thirteen in all for this spring."

"I seek only One."

That was the only thing Chaka said to welcome us. He said it first looking at me and then at Malan, not the Reghen. And that was enough.

"How many Khuns does the Tribe have?" the young Reghen turned and asked me with wide eyes.

Another fool to torment me, that's all he was. I didn't answer. I'd had enough for one day.

I knew all this already. Only one Khun. He was seeking only One Leader. I wouldn't have any friends or brothers here. Had I wanted any, I should have gotten a carving on my left arm.

Chaka smacked me hard, a suitable greeting for what I'd face over the next five winters.

"You rat, you answer when the Reghen asks you something. Are you the one who dared go into the wolves' tent? The two rabbits?"

News of Malan's brave deeds had traveled faster than we had. I was not the one. I exhaled again, bored stiff. He smacked me again on the same cheek. It was a strong one this time.

More twelve-wintered Uncarved boys kept coming from the other packs of the Sieve over the next few days, and I met them all with a bruised right cheek. When all thirteen of us arrived, Chaka and the rest of the Guides called us in the middle of the camp to speak to us.

"Starting tonight and till next spring you will sleep in that hut," Chaka said, pointing to a wooden structure at the eastmost corner. "Go in there, wear the clothes of the Uncarved and come back, I have a lot more to say."

We all ran to the hut, pushing and shoving to make it there first. We rushed in like a herd of animals, searching for the clothes, each one of us wanting to grab the best pieces. A Guide was waiting there for us, and we stopped at our heels when we saw him in front of the thirteen piles.

"Boots, hides, trousers," he said. "Undress, wear them, and then we go back outside for weapons. Keep the breeches, and this thing for later."

This thing was a linen tunic, one of the rarest that only the othertribers south of the Blackvein could make. It was the softest thing I'd touched until I first embraced a naked woman.

When we all dressed, I started looking around the hut more carefully. Wooden poles, holding hide covers aloft, reached to the top of the log-built walls and joined only at the center, making a tall roof. I had never slept in anything other than a tent. We stepped out of the hut where four more Guides were waiting for us in a row, each one in front of a pile.

"Form a line and go to each one of them one by one."

Once more we started to push and shove to get ahead of the others.

"Short blade," said the first Guide as he gave me a sword the size of my forearm.

"Long blade," said the next and gave me a sheathed sword almost twice the size of the small one.

"Double-curved bow. The rage of Enaka."

"Rider's quiver, hunter's quiver."

Our eyes wide, we started talking about all these precious gifts.

"Hey, we'll go hunting! I grew up with the Hunters," said the one called Balam. He was cocky, strong, and stupid.

"Rider's quiver, we are going riding!" said Anak. That one was as much a hairy, ugly oaf as any twelve-wintered could be. But he proved to be a great rider later.

"No one is going riding for another two springs," said Chaka. "If you lose any of these weapons, you will sleep with the fish gutters or the Tanners. Got it?"

Each boy strapped his blade tighter or gripped his bow with all his strength.

The kid next to me was sweating in the middle of winter. Fear does that. "Redin…from the Archers," he whispered to me. He was holding his shaking left hand with the right one.

You shouldn't be here, Redin. It was my only silent thought.

Chaka was facing all of us. He grabbed a boy by the back of the neck and pulled him closer.

"Who are you?" he said.

"Urdan," the boy said. He was my height, with oily hair.

"Urdan of what?" an angry Chaka asked.

"Urdan of the Archers," he said.

"Archers? Urdan of what?" Chaka asked again hitting the boy in the head.

"Urdan of…the Uncarved," the boy said.

"You're smart, Urdan. How smart are you?"

The boy didn't reply.

"If you are very smart, you'll leave the Uncarved now. Those hands of yours… They are not warrior hands. You'll have better luck at the Tanners, seaming the hides," Chaka lifted the boy's hand. He had long, delicate fingers.

"I want to stay," the boy said.

Chaka was towering above the boy. He pointed with his fat arrow finger at Urdan and said to the rest of the Guides. "Brave, not smart." He then turned to Urdan. "We'll keep you. Here, you will have meat almost every night, more than in the Sieve. You'll need stronger bones," said Chaka slapping Urdan in the back of the head one last time.

Meat every night.

"When do we eat?" asked Gunna to my left. He was a head taller than all of us.

"The Carriers will bring meat," said one of the Guides.

"So, listen carefully. This is the rider's quiver. The true Archers call it Skyrain." Chaka lifted the large, deep bag over his head. It didn't look like a quiver. "You put the reed arrows in here, those with the narrow-shoulder head. And this one with the clasp is the hunter's quiver. Or Selene. You fill it with the birch arrows, those with the hooked-shoulder head. Got it?"

Thirteen heads nodded, uncertain.

"I know all this. Reed to travel far and fast, birch with wide head to kill. You try to pull one of those out of the guts, it makes a mess," said Lebo. He had the hungry eyes of a mauler.

There were six more around me. Three not even worth mentioning; they would join Enaka early. Malan the only one I knew from before. And two more who were talking and laughing in a corner.

"And who are you two, shitheads?" said Chaka. He had the same question as me. "Let me guess; you are the best of the Blades' children," he said.

"Yes, I am Akrani," said the first. He ended up being a coward, but it would take me a long time to find out. He didn't even know it.

"Noki," said the second. That one had caught my eye from the first moment because he didn't run or push anyone to get first in line. He moved around us all day, calm and smooth, as if he had been there for many winters.

"Akrani the shithead, and Noki the featherbrain," said Chaka. "I seek only One, and you, scum of the Blades, are not going to be that One. This camp here is a nest. One Khun to nourish, One Leader to hatch. The rest are his food, the eggshells, and bird shit. So, you two, enjoy the meat, learn to shoot a bow, unlike your fathers who ended up Blades, and don't give me any trouble. Now, you can go eat."

Our own quivers, bows, and meat. This was too good to believe.

"The Carriers couldn't find enough meat," said one of the Guides with a grin. The rest of the Guides curled up laughing.

"You'll eat later, boys. Some of you. Undress, you know the trial," said Chaka joining the others in roaring laughter.

Oh, not again.

The sun's warmth was dying out, and we were once again suffering the usual standing trial of the Sieve. They did it only that first day, once, to mock us. To remind us. To laugh. To suck the air out of us before we got too full of ourselves. Once was enough. They left us standing in the soupy mist. The Forest demons, hanging from the naked branches, were our only companion. They came to watch the ones who never fall. Deep in the night, we were all still standing. The Guides took us all back to our hut, and Chaka said we were all winners. No one slept a winner that night.

Each one of the thirteen of us, or maybe twelve, was boiling hard in his chest, restless, certain that he was already the chosen One Leader of the Tribe. Each one of us. Balam, Lebo, Gunna, Malan. Any day now, he thought, they would carry him to his wooden throne to rule. Victory sneaks in and becomes a curse when it fills a young head.

There was only one problem: the other twelve boys were certain of the same destiny. Maybe eleven. There was a smart one among us, one who didn't care to be Khun. Not I. Noki.

"How can we ever beat Gunna?" Akrani asked when the giant boy went out of the hut to take a piss.

"He can bring down a horse with one punch," Lebo said.

Redin had fallen exhausted in his corner and was sleeping.

"I heard that Redin is the son of Druug, the Leader of all the Archer warriors," said Anak.

That was the first thing that worried Malan.

"No one knows his father," said Malan the orphan.

"Almost no one. They say that Redin would fall many times before sundown during the Sieve but would get up in the middle of the night, go back outside, and stand alone. His father told Redin that if he didn't become the next One Leader, he would skewer him alive on the stake if he ever saw him again," said Lebo.

"I see a stake that has his name on it already," said Gunna.

"Don't say that. All the Guides keep an eye on him and protect him. Druug commands all the Archers. He is the most powerful man of the Tribe after the Khun."

Malan was pumping his clenched fists. He talked with slow, clear words, staring at the dirt. "No one knows his father," he repeated as if he wanted to drive a stake through his fear.

"As I said. Almost no one. Sometimes the powerful escape the rules," said Lebo.

Someone must have told him that word for word. Lebo didn't look so smart.

Those first days of training were the last and worst of the winter. We rarely went outside and had endless time for Stories. A snowstorm started soon after we got our bows and lasted for four nights. The snow covered all of Sirol and was up to my waist outside our wooden hut.

"I have never seen this before. The end of the world," Chaka mumbled to himself, angered that we couldn't begin our training.

The rumor I liked the best was the one about Noki. Noki didn't care about any of us. He was the most handsome, with a long mane of the blackest hair. The sun had baked his skin darker, and he was the fastest of all of us. I believed that Noki was a more difficult opponent than Gunna.

"He's a mad stallion, that one. Don't fear him. He will never be Khun," said Lebo the windbag.

Akrani, who had gone through the Sieve with Noki, told another Story from their old camp.

"Noki never fell on the Sieve. One night, he was the last one left and started to mock the Guides by dancing around while everyone else was already as dead as a log. He sang to the stars to bring the rain to wash him. The Guides became furious. Instead of taking him to the Wolves' tent, they left him out all night with a mauler for company."

Akrani would have continued, but I stopped him.

"And he remained standing all night," I said.

"How did you know?"

"I just do."

I dreamed that same dream once in the Sieve. It was a clear night, so many stars, not a single Guide or kid around. Silence. Only the two of them were watching from above as I endured throughout the night. Enaka. Elbia.

"Yes, that's how it happened, and it is no lie. He was still standing in the morning when we went back outside. But now here is the really crazy thing: he kept standing all the second day too, and that afternoon he finally got his meat."

Never did I dare dream that.

"What tents did he come from?" asked Redin.

"The Blades."

"Shitheads and vultures, all of them!" said Redin, the son of Druug, the Leader of the Archers.

Noki had just walked into the hut, but Redin had his back on him and hadn't seen him.

"What were you saying, Redin?" Lebo asked with a grin.

"Rats, jackals, Blades. This whole bunch of scum."

Everyone looked at Noki for a reply, but he didn't care.

I stayed silent, with pursed lips after the end of the Story. I would beat everyone in the end, I knew that much, but it wouldn't be easy. It was those first nights that I was so certain before I saw the older boys of the Uncarved.

It was a small camp, with few horses that we were not supposed to ride for two more springs. It seemed larger because we had to move around on foot. It was enough for the forty Uncarved, the thirteen of us and the older ones who had joined winters prior. They lived in huts close by. Smaller huts, as there were fewer children from the previous winters. The Guides, a few tents farther down, had five carvings and wouldn't dare sleep in a hut. During the first days, they kept us away from the older boys, to protect us. Later, when we started mixing, the beatings came heavy and frequently.

The snow melted when the cursed day of my ninestar birthday came. I was one of the few who knew the exact date of his birth: nine days after the first full moon of spring. They took us out for training the next morning, and from then on, it was the same ordeal day in and day out. We would go out in the clearing before the Endless Forest and empty quivers of arrows one by one into the targets, as fast as we could. I carried bow and quivers until nightfall.

"Where do we aim?" I asked the Guide on the first day. Across from me was only a lifeless meadow.

"Straight ahead."

I waited for him to stop teasing me. He waited too.

"You should have known these things from your tenth winter," he said.

He took a closer look at me, and his hand passed through my hair.

"Ninestar? In the Uncarved? What demon spat on me this winter? To freeze my ass in the snow for a ninestar."

He spat on the ground with disgust. When he saw that I wasn't moved or the least bit scared, he smiled and parted his hair with his hand to reveal the hollow triangle behind his ear.

"Yep, I am a ninestar too. My name is Bera," he said. "Well, I never became Khun, or even made Chief of a Pack, but I'm still alive."

"Can you tell me where to aim?" I asked him again.

I should have learned these things from my eighth winter, but Greentooth, the old crone who had raised us at the orphans, had not cared to teach me anything more than to carry the sweet-smelling buckets of horse piss.

"Do you see the clearing before the trees and after the stream? Aim at that. Between the two banners. There."

"You mean the whole field?"

"You see a field in front of you, right? No grass, no rocks. Sixty paces ahead? It is a hundred paces wide and fifty deep. I am sure you can see it."

"But I can hit that blindfolded."

"Good for you. Because when you ride to battle in the dust storm or under the thundering rain, you will be as good as blindfolded."

The Guide took my bow and the quiver and loaded five arrows between the fingers of the bowgrip hand and one in the bowstring hand.

"Redin, shoot. Malan, shoot. Gunna, shoot. Lebo, shoot. Anak, shoot. Noki, shoot."

He shouted the six names, exhaled quickly six times, and shot all six arrows, one after each name.

"You will grab six arrows at a time—one on the string, three between pointer and middle fingers, and two between middle and third fingers."

He continued with the next six names. After he said all twelve children's names three times, he had emptied a whole quiver. One quiver which had more arrows than three times the fingers on my two hands. And every single one of them had gone into the target field. None in the stream—or left, right, or beyond the trees.

"Three Packs of Archer riders. Forty men in each Pack. By the time they shout a dozen names three times, each of them empties one quiver. There, in that field. Count them if you can.

"They shoot half of the half of those arrows galloping backward, away from the enemy. As the Archers fall back still throwing arrows, three new Packs come in. Each rider empties one more quiver. Yet another three Packs refill all the way back to attack again. Nine Packs altogether. They'll ride back and forth nine times, never too close to the enemy, always changing direction.

"The othertribers stand in the clearing. Eighty men wide, twenty deep. They have wood and leather shields, and they stand in formation. They want a man-to-man, blade-on-blade battle. They will never get it. How many othertribers will survive the rainfall of arrows until you can say nine times the names of the three-times-three Packs?"

Bera was funny.

"None?"

"None will survive. They shot six dozen arrows, two quivers on each othertriber. How many of our Archers will die?"

"None?"

"None. And when you learn to count—because you will learn to count Packs and men here—you will know that in this Story you just heard, the othertribers were four times more than our Archers," added

Bera.

"And why don't the othertribers shoot back at us?"

"They don't have this bow, they don't have stirrups, they can't ride and shoot holding shaft to ear with both hands. They can throw a spear, but not far enough to reach a horse."

"Got it."

"Rain of arrows from the sky. Rain without mercy. Master the bow this spring. Nothing else. Blades and horses are for later."

"I aim straight ahead, on that field."

"And learn the names of your twelve comrades by sundown."

I was a miserable sight when I tried to grab the arrows and nock them with the same speed as Bera. The first days, I couldn't even shoot half of the arrows into the target field, even though it was right in front of me. Some fell on the trees, others in the stream, and others didn't even make it that far.

As soon as we shot, we had to run and gather the arrows. If they fell into the stream, then we had to dive in. The closer we came to the afternoon, the harder it became as I lost my strength. My fingers would bend like iron claws, and I would pull them open one by one when the day was over. Some boys were better than I. And some were worse, thankfully. But I kept getting better. Every day, one day at a time.

The Goddess of Spring finally awakened in a dazzling brightness, as if she hadn't heard anything about the countless deaths that had marked the winter. Spring didn't care about Elbia, or the plague, or anyone else. Spring came and warmed the Blackvein, greened the fields. The lands rejoiced. The maulers rode the bitches, and the stallions mounted the mares in the camp. Life would no longer mourn. The Endless Forest had begun to burst into color. The red flowers in the tree branches were trying to lure me into the Forest, the demons' lair. But it was so dense and vast that from a distance, the Forest still looked black most of the time.

We celebrated the full moon by roasting lambs outside, in front of our huts, together with the older boys and the Guides. They had placed sticks around the fire to make small fences. The fences surrounded the fire, and we skewered the lamb pieces on them to grill slowly.

My training to become a man and a warrior would last five times spring, and that was the first day that I saw everyone at the Uncarved camp together, their faces not hidden under thick fur hats and hides. The older boys were fewer.

My Pack were all in their thirteenth spring, but I was one winter older, although no one else remembered except me. I had entered my fourteenth spring.

Our Pack was the one with the youngest Uncarved, and they called us Starlings.

Our closest elders, in their fourteenth spring, were nine children, and they were called Owls.

Those in their fifteenth spring were eight, the Maulers. May they die terrible deaths.

In the next Pack, there were only six left, and they were called Eagles.

And the last, those in their seventeenth spring, were called Wolves. Only four of them were still Uncarved. If our Khun died that spring, one of the four of them would take his place.

We were the many, the thirteen, the greenhorn, the frail Starlings.

"Why do they call us that?" I asked.

"Because you still fly together as a flock," said the Reghen.

"Because the Eagles are hungry!" Bera roared.

All of us together were exactly forty children, and that was as far as I could count back then. At night, when we finished with the bows and arrows, the Reghen would teach us how to count.

"*I seek only One*," whispered Malan. He was looking at me, pointing, and counting heads instead of caring about the sticks with the roasting lamb cuts.

"And the others? What do you think will become of them?" I asked.

"Pack Chiefs, Archers…" Lebo jumped in.

"Blackvein's vultures need to feed."

"All true." Chaka, who was standing behind us, said only that and waited for us to put down our cups and listen to him carefully. The lamb's juices were feeding my belly.

"Those who survive the five winters of training will become something. Ask what happened to those who aren't here anymore." Chaka pointed toward the four older boys who were eating. "You see those Wolves there? A few winters back, they were thirteen. Proud and tall. Now four are left."

Anak was staring at them.

"Don't stare," Lebo said.

It was too late. The Wolf had smelled the prey.

"Time to pluck their feathers," shouted one of the Wolves as he came and sat next to us. He grabbed the cup of Anak the Oaf. The hunt had begun, and we were the prey. When Anak tried to push him away, the Wolf emptied the cup of milk onto his head and then grabbed him by the neck with one hand and locked Anak's wet head. The Wolf's knuckles struck and repeatedly rubbed like a flint rock against Anak's skull. It might have hurt a little but it made Anak suffer much more in humiliation. Anak knew he wouldn't make Khun ever. Right then, right there.

"Don't eat so much. The horse will die carrying you. Do you want to be Khun, you swine?" the Wolf said loudly for all to hear. "Listen, little Starlings, and clear your little bird heads. To become the Khun of the whole Tribe…" He made the biggest circle with his hands and roared a laugh. He stopped with his hands still in the air so we could all swallow his truth. "The whooooole…" He dragged the *o* every time. "Sah-Ouna must name you the First Wolf of your piss-poor hut. And that might be easy with the weaklings like you that they brought this winter. But you will have to be a Wolf standing, on the last Pack, the oldest in the Uncarved, on that one winter when Khun-Taa finally dies. Not one winter before or one after. Khun-Taa has to die when your moment comes. And that just won't happen. It hasn't happened for thirty winters. And before that, another thirty winters passed with the same Khun. So…never. And something even more difficult has to happen: you have to stay alive till then."

"If Khun-Taa dies tomorrow, only one of those four Wolves could become Leader of the Tribe. No one else from the whole Tribe. Not you," said the Reghen, who had also come to stand by us.

"But if Khun-Taa dies the next winter, none of those four will be able to become Khun," said Malan, probably talking to himself.

"Yes, so it is. All four will get their carving as soon as they pass their seventeenth winter."

"So," continued the Wolf, who had understood long ago that he would never become Khun, "forget it."

He remained quiet for a while so the words could sink deep inside our souls. But only for a while—he just couldn't stop. He enjoyed this so much that he wanted to soak our heads into whole winters of blind misery.

"None of you will become Khun. Not one. But many will burn in the fire like those lambs in front of you," added the Wolf.

"What happened to the other nine of you?" asked Gunna.

"Two were carved early by the Guides and left for other camps."

"And the rest?"

"Like the lambs."

'How did they die?" asked Malan.

"Bleeding. They bled to death. All of them." The Wolf who had smelled us first started to laugh loudly again and added his tale, his eyes fixed on Anak. "Wait for the night of the Bear's Sleep full moon. Then we'll hang the fattest and slowest Starling from a tree upside down, and the dogs will pull bloody chunks from his face and tear him apart before the sun rises," he said.

Wolves and Maulers drowned out all the other sounds of the camp with their barking laughter. The Eagles and the young Owls were screaming and hooting.

"Don't listen to nonsense, Starlings. Neither the Reghen nor I would allow any such torture here," Chaka said, with a serious tone in his voice.

The Guides had strict rules for everything—what we trained on, when we rode horses, where we went and didn't, when we slept. There was a Truth for everything, and we had to follow it blindly. The children had only one rule among themselves: the strong beats the weak wherever he finds him. This change was the hardest. One moment, I had to be an obedient and brave dog; the next, a devious, quick, ruthless snake.

When the older children left, and we were alone in our hut, Bera the ninestar Guide told us: "Beware of the older boys more than anything else. They will beat you to death just because they can if we are not around."

Anak turned his head around uneasily as if he were already upside down on that tree, a rope tightening around his neck.

Bera continued. "Hey, don't be afraid. They don't often hang someone from the oak's branch. There are countless ways to die in the Uncarved."

"Tell us a few," said Gunna.

"If I do, we'll be here all night. But the Wolf was true about one thing. They always bleed to death."

XVIII.
Archers We Need in the Thousands

Fifteenth spring. Uncarved—Owl.

The Greentooth was always certain that I wouldn't survive even nine nights in the Sieve. I had already passed nine moons Uncarved. The trials grew tougher each day, but I grew stronger and taller every night.

Until the winter, the first truly ruthless trial, came again. The nights fell cold, and everyone stayed near the fire. The mind had time to think and suffer, restless. I could smell it. Only a few thousand paces to the east of us, a new Sieve was seething in its frozen rage. Rain or snow would take my mind back there every night.

The Guides spoke of a ghost with long brown hair and snow-white skin. They said it had been seen on a frosty, moonlit night, riding among the weeping willows that kissed the Blackvein. I wasn't allowed to go to the Blackvein, but I too had seen the ghost, on one of the few nights that the Ouna-Ma brought the gift of crazygrass. She came in my sleep, a pale girl on horseback, and touched my hand. Cold skin. Her dark lips, rosy no more, whispered to me: "I am riding, Da-Ren. War horses. Down by the Blackvein. Come find me."

We managed to become Owls that spring without losing anyone to bleeding or burning in the pyre. No one got a carving either. New Starlings joined from a fresh Sieve.

The one thing we didn't miss was the Stories. The Reghen and the Ouna-Mas came often and had a Legend for every death. We were closed up in the same camp and the surrounding fields. We hadn't been anywhere else in Sirol.

One night, Lebo asked the Reghen: "When will we mount war horses? We've been cooped up here so long."

"You have summers in front of you for everything. You have to master the bow without being on a saddle first," the Reghen said.

"What kind of Leaders will we be? We've forgotten what other boys look like," said Malan.

"Girls too," added Noki.

Noki was too smart to want to become a Khun. Sooner or later, he'd make it a point to carve his arm by himself.

"You are trained better than all the others."

"How? Everyone trains with bows everywhere. We just do the same," Malan said.

Chaka stepped in and raised his voice in anger. "Do you want me to send you all through another Sieve? That should straighten you out! Do you know how many tents with Archers are training south of here?"

"A hundred?" asked Malan.

"Five times that many. Countless. Six Archer boys to every tent. Do you think that you are the best Archers? Thirty of those tents are just girl Archers."

"What did he say? Girls with bows? Ha!" said Gunna.

Noki came closer to the fire with unexpected interest. The only other time he had had a spark was when an Ouna-Ma had come into our hut.

"And some of the girls shoot better than you," said Chaka.

"So, what makes our training the best?" I asked the Reghen.

The Guides gathered around, and each one said a different thing.

"You listen to more Stories. Many more."

"Every morning, you face only the best, the other Uncarved."

"You train with the next Khun, whoever that will be."

"It's the best training because we tell you so," said Bera.

"You are fewer and can train more. You don't wait in lines behind hundreds of others."

"And, most importantly, Darhul is at your heels all day long because you know that we seek only One. Archers we need in the thousands," said Chaka.

Bera was right.

The one I felt sorry for that second spring was Redin. Whether or not he was the son of Druug, the Leader of ten thousand Archers and three thousand more Archers in training, made no difference. Everyone treated him as if he didn't deserve to be; because he didn't. He was slower and weaker, and he had to sweat a lot more just to keep up with the rest of us. He was good only at sweating.

The older Uncarved knew right away.

"If that boy is Druug's son, then his mother was not a She Wolf."

"Maybe a kitten."

"The Legend of the Kitten. That's a good Story."

"Son of Druug, meow, meow." Everyone laughed and clawed their fingers like little paws.

The Uncarved boys had little to do after sunset, so everyone kept adding to Redin's misery. It was the best pastime for those few moons until he left for good. The strong ones found a weakling and tore him to shreds like the eagles do to the pigeon. The worse the humiliation, the funnier it was.

"I can't go back if I don't become Khun," he would say to Noki and me, the only ones who still cared to listen to him.

I shook my head without answering. I believed that he would see it in the stars, he would see it in the Blackvein, if he looked long enough. He would see his face mirrored there sooner or later. He would see that he wasn't the next Khun.

Redin finally met his fate on a spring day of clear sky and bright light when we had a bow contest. He struggled hard from the first round, always last, to gather his arrows that had fallen over the field and the shallow stream. The one who had the quiver with the fewest arrows at the end of the day got jeers from the boys and slaps from the Guides. Chaka called three times for him to come back, but Redin either didn't hear or pretended he didn't to win time. This had happened so many times before.

Chaka looked at the ninestar Guide, and Bera gave the command without hesitation: "Owls, aim your arrows. Rain from the sky!"

In the beginning, no one obeyed. We all just looked at one another.

"Last time. Come back, you fool, now!" Chaka shouted to Redin.

Redin didn't even turn to look at us; he was knee-deep in the stream. He wasn't even searching for arrows. His fists punched the water again and again, and he was swirling around like a madman. He knew. The spring water was crystal clear that day. He probably saw his face in there. He saw a Fisherman. Not a Khun. It was time. Even Druug, if he was his real father, would have agreed that it was the only honorable thing to do. He, more than anyone else, would have agreed. There is a stream that no man can cross and still keep his dignity.

"Shoot! Or by Enaka, I'll carve each one of you tonight!" Chaka shouted to all of us.

Someone to the right of me—I didn't see who but could guess—let the first arrow go. Others followed. And then all. Many times. When Chaka raised his hand we stopped.

"I didn't aim at him," said Akrani next to me.

"Neither did I," said Gunna.

No one aimed at Redin. At least no one admitted to that. Everyone aimed high at the Goddess's embrace.

"Did you shoot from the hunter's quiver?" I asked Malan. One of the hooked-shoulder head arrows was still on his hand.

Everyone turned to look at Malan.

"I don't remember," said Malan, shrugging his shoulders indifferently.

"Those arrows are man killers," I said.

"Let's go see yours. See what those are," said Malan.

We walked to the stream and pulled Redin out of the crimson water. I had never in my life seen a body pierced so many times. Not even in the bloody campaigns afterward did I see one. For the son of the Leader of the Archers, he was properly dressed for death, the starling half-feathers on the arrow tails a grim golden-green adornment.

We had to get our arrows back. Mine had a brown line, the color of her hair, painted on the shaft before the feather fletches to stand out from the others. I found one of my reeds three fingers above his navel. I took that one out with one pull. Malan's arrow was next to mine. I hadn't aimed high enough; I didn't shoot too many. The other children had a hard time, especially those who had struck the feet and head. If we didn't take out all those reeds, he would flare up in the funeral pyre, even if he wasn't laid on wood.

"Are you scared, Da-Ren?" asked Malan.

No one admitted to being scared or startled.

"Sad day, but it was long coming," said Bera who had joined us by the stream. "You're no longer the greenhorn of the Sieve." He knelt and we followed his example. "A prayer for the first Uncarved," he said. "Death became your brother today. This is your first kill. Bury any guilt you have. Your arrows were aching for this. They danced alive for the first time. For their virgin killing."

This didn't sound like a prayer to me. More like a triumphal celebration of death. No child talked proudly the rest of the day about what had happened. No one could claim or fear that he killed Redin. No one knew who the fateful arrow belonged to. The first, the second, the one that ripped through the heart.

When darkness fell, the Reghen gathered all twelve of us around the fire with the silent Ouna-Ma. This one was younger and darker, and her head was shaved clean.

The fire had just started to flare, and my breath was still the only thing that warmed my hands. There was a bit more space for everyone around the warmth from that night on. I had taken a firm hold of my short blade, and with its tip, I was carving the wet dirt. I wondered if it was my arrow that had found Redin first. I wasn't the first one to shoot.

I stared, bewitched, at the eyes and lips of the Ouna-Ma, and a flame grew between my legs. The Reghen began another Story. We heard many of them at the camp of the Uncarved.

The Legend of the First Leader, Khun-Nan
The Fifth Season of the World: The Second Chapter

Know this, you Uncarved Owls of the Tribe.

When the Fourth Season, that of the Annihilation, ended and the Fifth, that of the Leaders, began, a fierce warlord, but not yet Leader of the entire Tribe, was Khun-Nan. He had fathered three daughters and three sons, but all save one died during the march to the West. The survivor was his youngest daughter, the one who had been given since birth the name Ouna-Ma. She was the First Ouna-Ma the Blind, the one who could see beyond this world. When, during the night, she would look out, eyeless, at the eternal darkness and scream, everyone's heart froze with fear. Because they knew it was the Voice of Enaka she let out, the Voice that should not be heard by mortal men.

But in the solace of her darkness, the Ouna-Ma had found the Sight and could even look into the eye of the Demon Darhul. That is how, they say, she had first lost her sight as a small child. She had slipped one night out of her tent and gone down to the shore of the Black Sea, and there she had spotted, first and alone, Darhul himself rising from the night's waves. Enaka descended, riding on her chariot, pulled by Pelor, her brave horse, and sent lightning bolts to save Ouna-Ma from the jaws of the Demon. Her life was saved, but her sight taken by the lightning. From that day on, she could see only Enaka and Darhul, the otherworlds, and nothing else.

In her sixteenth winter, on the first full moon of spring, Ouna-Ma stopped talking. She even stopped screaming, and she silently kept pointing north. For one whole moon, Khun-Nan tried to persuade the Tribe to follow the Ouna-Ma's prophecy and head north, but the other warlords mocked him. The Tribe then was a lawless horde, and warlords over struggled against the future Khun.

On the second full moon of spring, Ouna-Ma's screams were echoed across the camp for the first time in a long while. A brutal northerly chill descended fast and embraced everyone that night. The men looked to the sky, and they saw a black shadow starting to slowly hide a full Selene. At once, they started crying and screaming, tearing the flesh from their cheeks in despair, because they knew. This had been long foretold to be the second sign of the Annihilation.

"Ravenfeather, the vilest of Darhul's nine heads, flew out of the sea and swallowed Selene whole." That was what they said about that fateful night. Selene, the heart of Enaka, was in the belly of the Beast, though they could still see her bleeding and shining ever so faintly.

Many warlords fell to their knees and begged Ouna-Ma to bring back Selene and ask forgiveness from Enaka.

"Follow my father," she said, the first time she spoke men's words. And only when they swore to do that much, before dawn, Selene lost her red color, and a thin, golden peel of moon appeared. Slowly, the round heart of the Goddess burst out of the belly of Darhul, glorious and full again. And that was how Selene stayed for the remainder of the night, and never again did the Ravenfeather dare swallow her.

"So will Selene disappear and return, just as your faith in the Goddess," said the Ouna-Ma.

Before dawn, the men separated into two camps. Most wanted to follow

Khun-Nan and Ouna-Ma, but a few remained faithless. Khun-Nan then raised his bow and told his supporters that whoever would follow him should follow his aim, and that all who refused him would fall.

With the first arrow, he aimed to the north, and at least forty arrows from brave warriors cut through the sky in the same direction.

With the second arrow, he aimed at his most ardent adversary, and forty more arrows followed to rip the chests of anyone who still stood in opposition.

And with the third arrow, Khun-Nan aimed at his own woman, the wretch who had borne his six children, the five who had died and Ouna-Ma.

After a while, the women, more than four times the fingers of two hands, fell dead from the arrows of their warrior mates.

With that bow, Khun-Nan ended forever the customs of family, that abomination of same man and woman under the same hut forever, from the Tribe.

"From this day forth, every warrior can mount any unfilled woman he desires. Except for Ouna-Ma, who will lie naked with whomever she chooses," said the First Leader of the Tribe.

The few men of the Tribe swore never again to raise children as their own, nor ever to learn which ones were theirs. They were to leave all the newborn together to be raised by the women of the Tribe. All swore that none would ever again live with a woman in a tent as a family; all would be warriors in Packs. They swore that any woman one brought, slave or of the Tribe, would also belong to all others.

Those who did not obey were massacred, in the last family ritual of the Tribe, and the many marched for the North, with Khun-Nan, on the route toward salvation and glory.

As long as the Tribe obeyed the First Ouna-Ma, the golden disc of Selene never bled again and was never swallowed again by any demon in a cloudless sky. The One Leader was Khun-Nan.

Our Father is a Legend,

Our Son is every Archer,
Our only Mother is Enaka,
Our one Daughter is Revenge.
This is the Tribe.

Thus declared the Ouna-Mas, the Voices of the Unending Sky.

The Reghen stopped and covered himself beneath his gray hood. Redin, the first Uncarved we had lost, did not hear this Story. His ashes had already risen to the Unending Sky. The Sky where we had aimed our arrows as Chaka had ordered. But Redin's father, Druug, would understand. He would have shot the first arrow.

XIX.
Now I Am Ready

Island of the Holy Monastery, Thirty-third Year.
According to the Monk Eusebius.

It took Baagh forty long days to persuade the First Elder and the rest of the monks to remove Da-Ren's chains.

It was just three and ten days after the barbarian's arrival when Baagh requested to speak during the morning meal in the refectory. The monks did not object. It was the only suitable communal congregation for such conversations—a brief recess from prayer. He stood so he could be seen by all to the left and the right of the long cedar table and said, "It will be a pious act to free this man of his chains and record his story."

The monks stopped moving their spoons and looked up at Baagh. They had heard all stories of Heaven and Hell, God and Devil, the eternal truths. The story of a sword-bearing barbarian was not of any interest to them. They preferred that the barbarian remain chained. It is rare to find a story that deeply stings the minds and hearts of the wise followers of the Faith. But as fate had it, that was the kind of story I ended up writing.

"A few days ago, you ordered for him to be chained," said the First Elder.

"He has no evil intention."

"I cannot endanger everyone based on your words, especially if they change so often."

"On the contrary, that is exactly what you must do, old and wise comrade. That is why a trireme of the Imperial fleet brought me to your island, and that is what the gold-seal edict commands," Baagh replied.

"Did you know all along that the barbarian would come here?" asked the First Elder.

"I expected it. I wasn't sure."

The wooden shutters of the big hall were banging fast and angry against the wall to announce a sudden summer storm. The First Elder looked at me silently, and I ran to shut them.

Baagh and the First Elder were about the same age. Baagh was probably older, but he didn't have the short snow-white hair or the First Elder's soft hands. Baagh's silvery-gray hair fell back and sometimes stood on the air in separate clumps. Looking at his hands, you might guess that he had once been a warrior or a farmer.

Baagh continued with a calm and patient tone of voice, certain that his wish would prevail in the end.

"The Emperor and his generals will want to read this man's story. Protospathos, the First Eunuch himself, asked it of me. He has met this man."

"The First Eunuch of the Palace met this barbarian?" interrupted the First Elder.

"Yes...and he too believes, as I do, that his story is of vital strategic and military importance. Especially if it is detailed. A matter of life and death. Thousands of lives of the faithful will be saved. Believe me; they will be indebted to every written word."

"I thought the only thing that mattered to you was to save this barbarian's soul," said the First Elder.

"If that is God's will, so much the better. But the important thing is to save other lives. Of the faithful. The many."

"We are ascetics, neither warriors nor eunuch advisors of the palace, Evagus."

"But, just as our Emperor, we too serve the One God. We have a sacred duty."

"Won't he leave to go to find his wife and daughter if you free him?"

"No, elders, he knows that his only hope for salvation is to do as I say."

"Are you certain?"

"Yes. And you will be too when you read his story. There is nowhere left for him to go."

"My heart fears for the innocent," the First Elder said, after moments of silence. "Here is what I will agree to do: We will keep him chained for one more month, and we will pray for him. We may release him after the celebration of Pentecost."

"Why wait until the birthdate of the Faith?"

"All of us should pray till then for the fire of the cloven tongues of the Holy Spirit to enlighten us before we make our final decision. The clouds of this man's sins and my fears obscure my judgment. If God wants him to live till then and you are still sure, then I might allow it," said the First Elder.

He continued the conversation with Baagh in a low whisper as they left the refectory, away from all other ears.

It was the beginning of the honeyed season of summer when we freed him, exactly forty days after he first set foot on the island. Da-Ren's legs were weak after being chained for so long. For the first few days, he had trouble walking, so I had to help him climb the steps. The pain in my shoulders every night felt as if they had been split in two, and I could find no comfort even in sleep.

It took him weeks before he resembled the man who had charged up the thirty-eight and thousand steps like a demon wind that first day.

Baagh ordered me to accompany Da-Ren on his walks, and we went out of the monastery together, always in the late evening before hesperia, at the most graceful moment of the sky. We would exit from the villagers' entrance of the castle wall and walk on the footpaths that led away from the monastery to the north and west.

The worried villagers stole glances. They weren't looking at me. None of them had ever seen anyone like Da-Ren before, his face and body chiseled like a living statue of the barbarians of the North. He was a young man, older than I but hardly over the age of thirty.

"Was Da-Ren handsome?" I asked myself many times.

How could I, man and monk, appraise male beauty?

As terror I came to know him; in terror I lived with him from the first day. But the women of the village, young or old, married or widowed, innocent or wicked, would have many tales to tell in the years to come.

"This dark two-legged beast came one night in my sleep and forced me on all fours. He buried his fiery sword in my belly." That is what the farmer's daughter, five and ten years old, said when she bore, unwedded, a boy child. The baby had one brown eye and one green. The priest who heard her confession of the barbarian's vicious acts absolved her of all sin. The priest also had a green eye. The other had been taken out by a pirate's dirk when he was a boy. Both of her father's eyes were brown. The peasants and the priest asked for Da-Ren to be put to death by the monks, but Baagh rejected their plea.

"The infidel comes in through my window every starless night. In the unholy darkness, he grabbed my head with his hand and made me lick the gates of Hell. I lost my mind after that and can't remember any more," the miller's widow said when she was unexpectedly found with a seed growing in her belly.

Even the married women had some stories to tell, but they were less eager to repeat them. He was as handsome as unspeakable sin, they all wanted to whisper, no matter what words they used. Quite a few monks believed most of the stories in the beginning and commanded me to find him some kind of work away from the villagers' settlement.

"He has to labor for the common good. That is a mandate. He must be of service to the monastery. Solitary work," the First Elder told me.

I took him around to show him the various jobs he could do. He could weave baskets of the kind we traded with merchant sailors or help with the crops and the olive trees. I didn't dare think of the food preparation or laundry. But when I urged him to begin such work, he refused, bringing his eyebrows together in bewilderment.

"I can't labor in such tasks," he told me and showed me a scar on his left arm as if that was supposed to explain something to me. I had not heard his story yet and didn't know if he was a warlord or just lazy.

"They won't let you stay at the monastery if you don't work," I told him.

My anxiety ended a few days later when we had to carry rocks to rebuild the church. Men were laboring in heat to carry the rocks from the eastern cliff to the cove and from there up the thirty-eight and a thousand steps. Work for the devil.

"I can do that," he said pointing at the man who was carrying a basket on his back filled with rocks. When Da-Ren began to work, faster than anyone else, all the monks and men from the village rejoiced, even though the women's sordid stories continued unabated. He carried the rough stones that we needed for building and anything else that was heavy up to the Castlemonastery. When there was work, he did the work of twenty monks, but most days he didn't have anything to do, so it was a blessing when we began the morning scribing of his story.

For months, I read him tales and waited for the day when he would begin to recite his. All of our meetings took place in his unsanctified quarters, not in the monks' building. Guests did not stay in the two-story building with us, but in cells attached to the walls, like sand-colored wasp hives. Their few windows had the most beautiful view as if one were sailing eternally on the sea. They also suffered the worst cold in winter and scorching heat in summer.

From these cells, visitors could gaze at similar barren islands with steep cliffs rising from the middle of the blue-black waters. This was the only picture of the rest of the world. Spring is a God's gift in my land. Even those barren islands blossom like carefree painted pictures of Paradise then. But they are nothing more than gray stone lands of exile in winter. Not even the rats survive.

"The visitors are not members of the commune. They only have their one foot in. That is why they stay in the cells along the walls that border the monastery," said the First Elder, explaining the symbolism of this practice. It would have been more virtuous of him to simply tell me that he was afraid of the thieves who came supposedly for worship and pilgrimage.

Da-Ren did not pray with us. He never ate at the long table and did not enter the holy shrine with the cross-shaped wooden roof. But through the work of his arms and legs, he earned his bread honorably. The same couldn't be said for his soul.

One night during Da-Ren's first winter in Hieros, the sky clouds swirled like black tentacles and the sea's dark belly boiled angrily. Sky and sea embraced and set out to drown anyone caught in the middle. The monk awakened me by pounding on my door. His face had the color of a rotten fish.

"Come at once," he said.

I ran past the row of slow-moving monks who had come out of their cells nervously crossing themselves. One of them called out to me: "You brought the cursed demon to the house of the Lord. May God protect us."

I crossed the courtyard and, soaked to the bone, climbed the steps to the cells in the wall. As I was approaching his cell, I could hear Da-Ren's screams whenever the thunder stopped. Baagh was already there, wiping

Da-Ren's brow with a wet cloth. The gaze of the barbarian was traveling far away, as if the storm had awakened the wolves within him. He was mumbling in his native tongue, but I caught only a few words, which Baagh translated.

"Remember what I say to you, Eusebius. If you repeat these words to him when he recovers, he might start talking to you."

Baagh was saying things I was hearing for the first time.

"Ouna-Ma... she rides me naked... black clouds I fly... mud... under my body ... bound... poles... leeches... suck... scorpions... warm in armpits... hot... they suck poison... Zeria... eyes... Ouna-Ma."

I remembered the words, but I wasn't about to repeat most of them.

"What did you give him to drink today? Wine?" asked Baagh.

"No, only water."

"What did he eat?"

"He had a feast. Ate a whole fish. We were all fasting and would have thrown it out. The fisherman—"

"What do you mean whole?" asked Baagh. "The head too?"

He searched the cell and smelled the leftovers in the wooden bowl thrown into the corner.

"Snapper. Damn, Eusebius, the head of this devilfish brings hell's nightmares. This man will suffer for days and nights. Water, much water only. And chamomile."

"What does *Ouna-Ma* mean, elder? He whispers it often when we are out walking and in the courtyard when he sees monks in their robes. What does he mean?"

"They are witches. Of his tribe."

"You mean, women?"

"Yes, women. Priestesses of a false and hemovorous faith. You will learn of them soon when he starts telling you his story. Remember to repeat these words to him when he recovers. That is how you will find the path to his mind."

"I remember all that he has said so far. Once he mentioned the accursed city of Varazam, elder."

"Yes."

"But Varazam is deep in the eastern deserts. That's the other end of the world from the northern river where these barbarians dwell."

"That is where Varazam was. You're correct."

Baagh's lower jaw began to tremble when he uttered these words, and the weak flame of the candle sparkled the tears in his eyes. He quickly made to leave in an effort to hide his emotions.

The massacre of Varazam. The most tragic chapter of the Apocalypse. Had either of them been there? Both?

"Zeria…Zeria…Aneria…" Da-Ren continued mumbling with his eyes closed and his face sweating cold.

So passed the first winter and spring. I did nothing else but read stories to him in our tongue, the one of God. Summer came again, marking a whole year from Da-Ren's arrival.

Baagh still hadn't left to seek the powerful monks in the south and the east who would help Da-Ren save his wife and daughter. How they were supposed to accomplish that, I had no idea. Baagh had declared quite clearly that he would set out to find them only when Da-Ren had begun to tell his story. It seemed impossible to me that something like that would ever happen. He refused to say anything—still negotiating with Baagh.

"Why do we continue to lie to him, Baagh? The Sorcerers he expects are not going to come, and there is no help that they can offer him," I said one Sabbath. I had wasted time away from the Holy Liturgy while pleading with Da-Ren to start talking to me.

"Because I need his story with every detail intact. And because revealing the truth to him will only bring death now, Eusebius. To us and to him. Time is our guardian angel. I adjure you to continue the lie for the safety of all of us. God will forgive you."

Days later, I deliberately fed him snapper that had gone bad, but nothing happened.

"Do you have enough papyrus?" Da-Ren asked me.

"Yes, whenever you want we can start."

"I am not ready to talk yet. Did Baagh invite the almighty Sorcerers? We are losing time, Eusebius. Zeria. Aneria. Death."

He was mumbling names that didn't mean anything to me. One day, he talked as if he had to leave that afternoon to find his wife and daughter, and then he forgot them for a moon or more as if they had never even existed.

I had plenty of papyrus to last until the next merchant ships came in the spring. I had new reed pens tied with linen cord just waiting for the task. I had ordered from the sailors of the merchant ships better pens, those that were soft and hollow, which I could fill with ink and squeeze to bring the ink to the nose of the pen. I had even found a seashell to use as a big bowl and had fivecleaned and shined it till it sparkled. It was filled with ink, made from iron salts and oak gall. The ink was waiting, and so was I.

When almost a year of hospitality had passed without even one written word, I began thinking of using those supplies to copy once more the great Holy Book of God. More copies would always be needed. Otherwise, all the papyrus and the ink would go to waste.

During one of my afternoon summer walks with Da-Ren, it started to drizzle. It brought an unexpected, welcome coolness as we were descending the northwestern slope. I suggested that we turn back, but Da-Ren pointed toward the southwestern side of the island that lay ahead of us, toward the settlement. There were about thirty huts, made of mud, clinging to rocks of the same color. In the summer, the villagers whitewashed their mud huts to relieve them of the relentless sun. A handful of refugees, poor and helpless, lived there with their families.

They were protected by the Castlemonastery, and they worked hard for that protection.

"First, we will go there," Da-Ren said.

"They have explicitly forbidden me from taking you there. The women—"

"I have never touched any of their women."

"They have seen you, though. And what they have to say about it can cost you your life. Don't ask for this. Not even the monks go there often. And I don't know what the villagers will do if they see one like you in their homes."

"One like me—a barbarian, you mean. I am unarmed, Eusebius. And I am going, no matter what you say. Follow."

The first two mud huts we reached looked and sounded empty of peasants. Chickens were squawking, and a gray dog began to rub against Da-Ren's legs as if it smelled its wolfen brother on him. Da-Ren stiffened for an instant. Even though the dog wagged its tail happily, Da-Ren sent it away.

A horse whinnied, and Da-Ren jumped at the sound as if he had been resurrected from eternal death. He found the stable and ran toward it. I ran behind him. Tied in there was a flea-infested brown mare. It was one of the island's few horses, used mostly as a pack animal and to occasionally carry a new bride to the church.

Da-Ren embraced the horse at the neck with his arms and pressed his face to the side of the animal. He remained that way for a long time. He whispered words into the animal's ear and stayed with it, neck to neck. I had never seen such peace on him before. The rain grew heavier, and it made me even more impatient to return to the monastery, away from the world of men.

I asked Da-Ren to leave before the villagers saw us, but he looked at me with a wandering gaze. He was embracing the animal, the two as one.

After the rain had stopped, he let go of the horse and said, "Now, I am ready."

"What do you mean?" I asked him.

"We'll start my Story. Tomorrow. Rest well today. Pray."

"What happened?"

"The horse. Its smell. It takes my mind back. We have to come here again, and often."

The sun was setting dark red, the color of the ink that had arrived for me days earlier. The next morning, I installed a sand-rubbed wooden table in his cell and prepared to write, as faithfully as my mind and conscience allowed, whatever he recited. He used simple words, those that he knew and a few more that he had learned with me. I would ask Baagh for help at the beginning of each afternoon, in an attempt to add some richness to his language. Each time his memories and strength ran out, Da-Ren would go to find the scent of the horse. After a while, he bought it from its fortunate owner. He paid a lot more than that horse was worth.

From dawn till dusk each day for a year, I had to listen, understand, find the words, and write them casually and simply. I repeated this ritual the second year, with some improvement, and more carefully the third, by rewriting every chapter. Three times, three years, we wrote his story, starting every year from the very first night of the Sieve. At night, he recounted his life. In the morning, we welcomed the sun's light to capture his memories on papyrus.

In the beginning, I had enough spare time to pray for both of us. As his story boiled, there was less time. I still tried to pray. I had to. My prayers fought with the waves, the ink, and the blood. Until they drowned, brave.

XX.
Born Only to Die

Sixteenth spring. Uncarved—Mauler.

"Thirty? Did he really say thirty?" asked Noki.

"Yes, he did."

Thirty tents with Archer girls our age were training a few thousand paces to the south of us. Noki would not shut up about that and tried to persuade me to go with him to have a look. We hadn't seen a female with two legs that wasn't an Ouna-Ma for twenty-four moons. Even if the Ouna-Ma showed up one night with dog fangs and thick black hair on her back, no one would care. She was the only woman, a goddess and mother, the one full-moon night she'd come to us.

I too was curious, but didn't have Noki's desire. Not yet.

I remember little from that third spring. Maybe because I hated the name we would carry from that point on: "Third of five times spring in training: You are not Starlings or Owls. You will be called Maulers."

Wretched animals, vomit of Darhul.

We were twelve young maulers.

We had started to ride the previous spring. Unlike the maulers, the horses were animals truly favored by the Goddess. That sixteenth spring, I became one with the horse, though it would be a while before I had my own. The Guides wanted us to learn to ride different horses.

"Our Tribe, we are riders, right?" I asked Chaka, after the first moon I spent on horseback all day.

"Yes, so it is," he said.

"But we don't have many Stories about horses, almost none."

He squinted his eyes, as if my observation had taken him by surprise. He thought for a while and then told me: "What you said is true, Da-Ren. I have many Stories in my old age, but none about my horse. None about my legs, my balls, or my hair either. The horse is part of me. It has no Stories because it is in all of them. Never betrayed me. Never led me down the wrong path or harmed me. I have become one with the horse, its skin is my skin, its blood is my blood."

"I heard Stories about starving men who drank the blood of their horse to survive," I said.

"Even then, it is an honor for both. I just told you, the horse has no blood of its own. Its blood, your blood, it is one. Your horse is your life; even its death is your life."

Our boots and the skin on the saddle were made from horse hide. Craftsmen had glued my bow together by boiling horse bones and tendons. I usually had a piece of horsemeat that had dried for half a day underneath my saddle to eat at dusk. When we were thirsty, we would drink the stingy spirit we made from mare's milk, and our heads would feel lighter. Before our first campaign, each of us had to be three as one: horse, bow, and man.

The horse was life.

Except if one proved a clumsy rider; then it was death.

We lost three more children, whose names are not worth mentioning, leaving nine Uncarved Maulers. One busted his head falling from a fresh gelding. That was the boy's solemn Story for the stars. The second one had just broken his arm in a fall, but that was a grim destiny in a tribe of warriors. Broken arms rarely healed. They carved him alive, but I never saw him again. The third was a strong boy until winter came and he started to spit blood from his lungs. They ordered him to a small tent near our hut, and he died there alone. We didn't move him or lie him on a funeral pyre. The Guides burned the whole tent and sent him to the Unending Sky.

For a ninestar, I continued invincible and grew taller each spring.

When we were not riding, we fought with unsharpened blades, with sticks and by hands, man-to-man, until the afternoon. On the rare occasion when we finished with these fighting exercises early, we listened to Stories.

We were never sent to pile horse dung for the fires. Such petty and dishonorable tasks were handled by the other children, the ragged and the stupid, four times carved. But they were necessary too. They sat from morning till night stirring horn, glue, and wood to make the snake-curved bows of the warriors. We were the Uncarved, with all the glory, fear, and ill fate that would bring.

The beatings in the camp of the Uncarved had lessened. Younger and smaller recruits had come, and, like any fresh meat, they needed a good pounding. We would make fun of them during their Starling spring.

"Go to the Reghen's tents and bring the pails of horse piss."

"Go to the Guides and help them boil the glue."

I couldn't see it back then but that spring would be the last carefree time of my whole life. As if afraid we would turn soft, the Guides started taking us out for trials with all the other youths, the thousands of Archers in training, the hundreds of same-aged Blades. The carved warriors-to-be. The beatings became worse. When the other boys would get close, all they wanted was to see if they could take one of us. I made up for the carving that I was missing with bruises everywhere. I could take on two or maybe even three of them, but there were always more. And there were only nine of us left. They were five times a hundred times a dozen. They were uncountable. Someday, by Enaka's will, one of us would command all of them and they'd bow. But not yet.

Their carvings—usually three, rarely two or one—had swelled with the winters and had become wavy scars, deep and hairless. They crossed the entire arm, parallel to one another. No one confused them with anything else. They weren't elaborate carvings or the result of accidents. They were straight blade cuts, as if the poisoned talons of Darhul had dug deep into the skin. With time, the scars on their arms took on a rosy color, shameful, and visible from a distance. The boys' eyes would bulge wide and red and then gleam yellow when they pointlessly searched our left arms.

"What are you looking at, Rabbit? No scar here."

We always called them Rabbits, to remind them of the fateful last day of the Sieve. They would stare silently. We exposed our left arms naked no matter the cold when we were riding around Sirol.

One very hot day of summer, we had a grueling competition with the bows. Three thousand Archers in training, but none who could compete with us in all the arts of combat. But, from the thousands, they managed to pick out a handful of shooters who were better than we were. And they beat us. Barely.

Noki had seen the long-haired Archer girls for the first time, and he pointed them to us. They were more than fifty of them, tall and strong on horseback, screaming, aiming, and laughing wildly. Despite all the noise, their moves had grim seriousness and discipline. Their hair was tied back with red ribbons and so were their horses' tails. Their wild battle cries dripped like liquid fire into my ears and down my heart and to my groin.

Noki tried to get closer to the girls, but the young Archer men cut him off.

"If I see you looking at them again, I will chop you to bits," said one of them. He had another thirty with him, and there were only five of us.

That same night, Malan and I followed Noki in his exploration. To wash off the defeat, we said. But ever since I had seen the girls, my mind

ached for nothing else but to see them again. We took our horses at
twilight and left our camp unnoticed. We kept the horses at a slow pace
and left them to graze far from the Archers' camp. We tiptoed carefully
along an endless expanse of tents after darkness fell. They didn't have
wooden huts like ours, all their tents looked the same. "Archers we need
in the thousands," said the Stories. Noki tried to sniff out where the
female Archers could be.

"They're probably stashed away in a corner of the camp," I told him.

"Nah, I'm sure they have them right in the center," he answered.

He had better instinct on all things woman.

It made sense. Everyone could admire them, watch them in the
middle of the hundreds of tents. Nobody would be farther or closer.

We reached deep into the belly of the camp and heard a woman's
screams. The three of us crept closer to the tents from where the sound
had come and hid behind some hay bushels. In the middle of a fenced
ring, bathed by the early moonlight, stood many girls, three times the
fingers of my hand, sitting around the fire. Not an ugly one among
them. Not a beautiful one either.

One of the girls, close to my age, stood up and sang some words that I
couldn't make out. She then slipped off the short, sleeveless tunic that she
wore over her trousers. She was half-naked, fresh, and strong. An older
woman approached her, not an Ouna-Ma. From the clothes she wore, she
must have been an Archer or their Guide. Her blade was warming
unsheathed near the fire.

The girl put a cup to her lips and emptied the contents into her
mouth. She closed her eyes, and another one blindfolded her. Two other
girls laid her on a large wooden board. They held her down with four
hands and put a piece of wood in her mouth for her to bite.

The female Guide took out the blade and stuck it to the bottom of
the girl's breast. With one excruciatingly slow movement, she cut off the
girl's right breast from one end to the other. My mind was cut in half as

she bit down on the wood and let out a drawn-out moan.

The older woman kissed the girl's freshly cut breast and left it beside her. Noki threw up next to me, making a lot of noise. I hadn't eaten much that night. A second woman took out a wide iron slab from the fire and left it for two breaths on the girl's open wound. The girl's scream ripped through the air just before she fell unconscious. Or worse.

"What in the Demon's name are they doing?" Noki said. Some heads turned in our direction, and we hid.

The girl came back to her senses after a great effort from the rest. She was trembling in a warm midsummer night. The others gathered around her and embraced her one by one. The older one warmed her with a hide, and they all sang solemn words together. "Revenge…honor… Enaka…stars. Our One Story," these are a few of their words that I heard.

A second girl took off her tunic. Noki was ready to rush in and stop the bloody spectacle when Malan grabbed him by the hand and whispered, "I've heard of this. They cut the right breast. For the battle. Have you ever tried loading from your Skyrain quiver, pulling the bowstring and shooting six arrows as fast as you can?"

"Oh, yes, I—"

"In full gallop with a big apple underneath your jerkin, jiggling left and right? If they don't lose a breast, they'll die in the first battle. If they're lucky and are not caught alive," Malan repeated.

"Bitches of Darhul!" Noki said again.

It was not the sight he had come to see.

"Lower your voice," whispered Malan. "Why am I even talking to him? Stupid," he mumbled and crawled away from Noki.

We saw the awful scene a second time when another girl's turn came. I didn't look so carefully. I turned my head to gaze at the stars above. For the first and only time, when I heard the second girl's screams, I was glad that Elbia was looking down upon me from up high.

We did not manage to see a third brutal amputation. We heard footsteps approaching in the moonless night. Small flashes of torchlight accompanied them.

"We leave now!" Malan shouted at me.

I grabbed Noki's arm to make him follow.

"Lay off!" Noki said, his eyes fixed on the girls.

"Now! Leave the fool! Run!" Malan shouted, louder this time.

It was too late. Instead of me pulling Noki, other hands, many of them, were pulling me. Boys' hands.

There was nothing more amusing for all those shithead carved Archers than to find a good reason to beat up an Uncarved. One so much better than they were. A few of them would sneak into our camp from time to time to witness the best of the Tribe. They had seen our wooden huts, our gray-white horses, and they had smelled the crispy skin of the young lamb we had roasted.

They had their fun with us till daybreak. The blood from my mouth mingled in the night with the first green leaves and red poppies of the earth. For many days, my whole face was red and purple. As the blood traveled downward, the bruises on my chest became a yellow-green color. Malan didn't walk for an entire moon. I got a few broken ribs and couldn't ride for two moons. The three of us could drink only milk for the rest of the summer. No meat. I shriveled to half my size, like the girls.

The Guides did not punish us. They nearly died laughing when they dragged us back to the Uncarved.

"You're lucky that the boys caught you. If the young Archer girls had gotten their hands on you, they would have roasted your cocks on a spit."

My luck hurt a lot, especially when I tried to lie down. My body had swollen, painted like a rainbow all over, and felt as if I were being pierced by frozen spears every time I moved. I learned to gather the yellow arnica flowers which grew in Sirol, ground them to a paste, and place it on my bruises.

At first glance, the three of us had become laughingstocks, but in truth, everyone looked enviously at our deed as an act of bravery. Even the Guides. The other boys were so jealous that they asked us every night about what we had seen. Again and again. Noki had to recount everything through his teeth—those that were still with him.

The Ouna-Ma who came to tell a Story that moon looked at me with eyes different from any other time. As if there was a slyness in them, like the spark I had in my eyes when I was devouring juicy meat. I didn't understand then. I had felt the heat in my sixteen summers but didn't know what to do with it.

I learned to adore milk during those moons. When at last I ate meat again, I didn't enjoy it, at least not in the beginning. I was just proud that I could even chew again.

Malan held on to a stick for support. He limped badly and was still waiting for his leg to heal. He approached me one night and talked to me for the first time about that day.

"I told you to run. You should have left the fool behind."

"We go together, we come back together," I answered.

His hand was trembling as he was holding the stick. He still couldn't walk well. He came close enough for me to smell his mouth rotting from the hunger and spoke very slowly. "Do you know why you will never be the Leader of the Tribe, Da-Ren? Yes, never. I will tell you, so you have time to swallow it. You care too much about those who were born only to die."

There were only nine of us Uncarved Maulers left. If the Great Khun-Taa, the glorious Fifth Leader of the Tribe, did us the favor of falling dead in two winters from that moment, not before and not after, one of the nine would become Khun in his place.

And soon we were eight.

One cold autumn morning, we found Anak hanging upside down

from a tree, as the older Wolves had told us we would find him someday. They had always had it in for him. He was the ugliest, stockiest, and the first the older kids would tease and beat. He wasn't dead, and hadn't been torn apart. The dogs hadn't gotten to him yet, though they were jumping all around him. If somebody could shit upside down, he would have. He was very much alive, maybe even better looking, with his long hair falling back toward the ground.

The ninestar Guide, Bera, approached and took out his blade. He didn't go for his neck. Anak's wailing was the same hanging upside down. Bera sliced two deep carvings on Anak's left arm. With one more movement, he cut the ropes and took him down.

"Don't take anything with you from your hut, Anak. Not even your bow. Just get lost! You will go on foot to the end of the camp until you find the tents where the Archers are trained, and you will tell them that you have come from the Uncarved."

Anak started to say something but got his answer from Bera before he even had a chance to speak.

"If you make a sound, I will carve you two more times until you stink of fish guts every night. Now get out of here."

Anak left running, with jeers and flying stones following him.

"Anak was the best archer," I said to Bera that night.

"Well, at least they won't throw him out of there, too, and send him to gut the fish," he answered.

Anak hadn't done anything wrong. His legs stuck around the saddle better than any of the others. He could gallop without a saddle, lying down on one arm. He could turn his body and send his arrow two hundred feet as he galloped away from the targets. I didn't expect him to be carved so easily.

"We were too late with that half-wit," Chaka told Bera as if he could read my thoughts. "I told you to carve him on the second day he was here."

The Ninestar turned to me and said, "Chaka is right. Every Uncarved can master the bow. One might become Khun even if he is second at the bow. But when one becomes the fool we laugh at…then we better carve him early and many times. Each pack of men has its fool, and that much is true, he will never be a Leader."

The Reghen had another Story about how the light of Enaka blinded the enemies of the Khun. The Khun had to have light, to draw it and to command it. The light had to serve him. It just happened. One was born with it. You couldn't learn it or master it through any trial.

"The Sun dawns and etches in glorious light the path for the next Leader of the Tribe every morning. The son of Enaka knows. He blinds the enemies of the Leader." They reminded us at every dawn.

"All of you, remember this one thing," said the Reghen. "The Guides think they know who the next Khun is. But, in truth, they do not. Only Sah-Ouna knows. But you, the Uncarved, know something else equally important. You know who will never become the One Khun. You know it better than Sah-Ouna."

On the other side of the fire, Noki was slowly scratching his groin. Malan nailed me with one eye like a searing iron for a girl's breasts—as if he wanted to remind me that he knew something important.

That I would never become Khun.

XXI.
A Woman

Seventeenth spring. Uncarved—Eagle.

"Noki kissed the Ouna-Ma on the mouth."

That day I heard this Story, word for word, so many times that my ears started to grow wolf hair. The night before, I was unlucky enough to be sent away on an uncommon chore. It was something the Guides had come up with so that we wouldn't forget the winter cold. My turn had come.

The trial frightened the Guide more than it did me. We were patrolling on horseback on the borders of the Endless Forest, near the lair of the blood-eating Reekaal. The Guide's face was white as snow and held a full moon talisman in his hand while whispering continuously to himself. Nothing happened to us, just as nothing had ever happened to anyone else I knew who was afraid of the abominable Reekaal. For demons, Firstborn of Darhul and close neighbors, these Reekaal were a quiet lot.

The only misfortune of that night was that I missed the Story that the Reghen and the Ouna-Ma brought. And even worse, I missed the moment when that hot-blooded Noki got up in the middle of it and took the Ouna-Ma into his arms. With one hand, he took off her crimson veil and kissed her on the mouth—as the others cheered. Even the Guides laughed before they started on him with the whip.

I had seen this rare scene before, man and woman kissing, but had never cared to ask. It just seemed so strange, funny, and disgusting—two people kissing in the mouth. When Balam and Akrani tried to show me what Noki did, I looked at them as if they were stupid. Truth be told, they were stupid—the stupidest of the eight of us left.

And after that night, we were seven.

We waited till dawn for Sah-Ouna's verdict.

"What will the First Witch order? Do we carve him or nail him to the cross?" wondered the Guides.

He was lucky. They carved Noki three times, each carving deeper than the other. He was smiling.

"What did you do? What Reekaal got into your head, Noki?" I asked as he was taking off the wolf hide of the Uncarved and packed his quivers and blades.

"I was raised with the Blades, the warriors who work only with knives and are the first to raid the villages. And the ones who fuck the most."

"The ones who what?"

"You still don't know what is in between your legs, do you? I was raised differently. I am different. When I was a boy, the Blades used to ride slave girls all day, outside, in front of all of us. They rode them until they couldn't walk on two feet. I know. We're all still virgins here, and I am in my sixteenth spring. Do you know that the Archers of our age have been riding women on all fours since last spring?"

"Why do they ride women?"

"I don't have time to pull your pants down and give you a lesson in the ass. Next time I see you, maybe. But now I'm in a hurry. I'm leaving for the Blades."

He was already covered with the dog hide of the Blades—*Darhul's damnation; a dog hide*—but he was smiling and standing tall, not looking down in shame.

I wouldn't see him again for a long time.

"Noki left because he wanted to ride slave girls with the Blades," said Bera. "For a woman." He spat down at the dirt and slowly shook his head in disbelief.

"He said that you keep us like virgins for the Ouna-Mas. We can only jump over them and not the slaves," I said.

I couldn't even understand my own words. The words just jumped out of my mouth without any meaning. I had to go back to the first night of the Sieve. That was the last time that I had had so many questions at once. Bera explained a few things, but without having seen what in the Demon's name he was talking about, it only created more questions for me.

That night, I dreamed of horses jumping over fences.

And before Selene shone full again, we were down to six. The most useless of the seven, Urdan, couldn't even shoot an ox when he galloped away from the animal. It was what we called "Enaka's shot." All the rest of us could turn our bows and aim backward in full gallop, have only our feet in the stirrups holding us on the horse, shoot our arrows, and pierce a standing target, a pumpkin head usually, up to a hundred feet away.

Urdan got not one, not two, but four carvings. They kept him in our camp as a miserable Carrier, hunting rabbits with the Guides. He was good at opening up rabbits—seems that was the only reason he had made it to the Uncarved. He cooked them too. Urdan would come back from the hunt, never raising his eyes to meet ours, with his rabbits and squirrels hanging over his back. One evening, he brought a deer but even then he seemed sad as the rain, lifeless as his prey. The Uncarved boys didn't leave any meat for him. He slept with the Carriers and the slave cooks, and we never spoke to him again.

Nobody made fun of Urdan. We were already on our Eagle spring. Come next winter we would be the oldest Uncarved; Wolves. Urdan had endured so much for so long, and his misery was not a laughing matter. It was a nightmare to think that an Uncarved could end up so low after a single night.

"I can't imagine that. A fate of squirrels," said Gunna.

"Well, it can be much worse," said Malan.

Urdan's Story of skinning rabbits and squirrels didn't last long. One day, they brought him back—or whatever remained of him. A pack of ravenous wolves had come out of the Forest, searching for warm meat in the frozen mud. The animals chased Urdan, but I don't think he managed to shoot any arrows behind his back as he ran from them. The wolves kill, but they do leave an honorable sight. They tear, rip, and eat, but the body still looks brave. Like one of a warrior who fought but was defeated. The flesh-eating birds are the worst. They come afterward and clean the carcass to the bone. The cheeks, the lips, the eyes. Urdan left us with a Story and a sight unworthy of Enaka.

"Another one bleeds away. He disgraces me and you," said Chaka. "I hope the rest of you fare better."

But it was no surprise. No matter how much crazygrass we could drink, we could never believe that Urdan might rule the Tribe one day. Same for Mad Noki. The truth is that except for me, I could see only Malan and Gunna as Leaders. And most of the time, none of us.

We were gathered around the fire, gulping down snow-watered millet gruel, when Akrani said to Chaka, "Why are we even trying to become Leaders? Gunna will always be first in all of the combat trials."

Gunna was not first with the blade. He was slow, and I had worn him down in every duel, except for the times he had grabbed me with his hands, which were about as big as my legs. Though I, too, was quite tall and strong for our Tribe.

It was the night Gunna had gone patrolling the Forest border with a Guide, so we talked about him freely.

Chaka answered right away with a roaring voice: "What are you talking about, Akrani, you fool? What is Gunna's strength next to that of the One

Leader? The Khun has hundreds of hands and legs, thousands of horses and eyes, his power spreads over rivers, from the steppe of the east to anywhere we have warriors guarding. At his signal, the Khun lifts all his hands and horses, and they follow him blindly. Sah-Ouna will not choose a Leader for the size of his arms."

"But then, why did you send Urdan away for failing at the bow?" I asked.

"There is a line. If he can't even shoot a bow straight, no matter what the Khun commands, no warrior and no horse will follow. Only some sheep, maybe," said Chaka.

Night fell cold, and we went to sleep close to the fire. I awoke not much later. Gunna was shaking me and yelling, "Help me! Wake up, Da-Ren."

I held his hand to get up, but my hand slipped. He had blood all over his arm and was dripping on me. We were both shouting now, and everyone got up at once.

"What's wrong with you? Where is Tzeba, your Guide?" asked Chaka, who came into the hut after Gunna.

For our age, Gunna was the largest beast I had ever seen in all the camp and already as big as a Rod, a Khun's fearsome guard. He was shivering from cold and mumbling to himself.

"I don't know…the Reekaal got him."

At dawn, we followed the trail in the snow and found Tzeba's body, his guts spilling out of it, at the Forest's border. Both of his legs were missing, cut high above the knees, as if they had been chopped with a heavy blade.

"Those were not wolves," said Bera.

Gunna spoke of two giant shadows that moved with the hound's speed through the branches.

"They were not men, but they were on two legs. They each had a head—"

"Yes?"

"…like Ouna-Mas. One shadow fell on Tzeba. The other ripped me with its claws but couldn't throw me off my horse. I galloped away."

"What do you mean? A woman with claws cut him in pieces?"

"It was a giant naked shadow. Tall as me. Man, woman, I don't know," mumbled Gunna, shuddering at the sound of his own words. "I looked back. It lifted him up in the air like a baby and threw him to the ground like a puppy."

"That's nonsense. Don't listen to him. A bear, that's all it was," said Chaka.

"A bear? This early?"

If it were anyone else, I might have believed that it was nonsense. Gunna was no coward. And he had four large scratches, carvings almost, on his huge arm.

The horrible death of Tzeba was one of fate's few unexpected gifts for me. In his place came Rouba, the old Guide, the one who had taken me under his wing during the Sieve four winters ago. The first time I saw him at the crack of dawn, I ran to him, cheering and jumping. When I saw him again that first night, my thoughts darkened as the other faces of the Sieve came back with him.

There were fewer of us Uncarved, and Rouba took an interest from the beginning to practice more with me. Chaka didn't seem to care, and he allowed that.

"You've grown strong," Rouba said after a few days when I showed him my skills with great vigor.

"Chaka seeks only One," I said.

"You're strong enough to make a thrice-carved warrior instead of a fisherman or a boot maker. One of these Uncarved boys is going to be the next Khun. Khun-Taa's time is coming."

"There is no way I'm letting these fuckers—"

If any one of the other boys was Khun tomorrow, I would find a quick and disgraceful death. That much was certain.

Rouba was not impressed with my fat mouth.

"I spoke to Chaka. He doesn't think of you as First. Maybe second or third. He said you need practice with the bow," Rouba said as we were parrying each other's long blades.

I kept hearing Chaka and Bera and the rest, as they had spoken every day for the past three winters:

"This snake-curved bow is the life of the Tribe."

"Without Enaka's gift of victory, we are dead."

I had never loved the bow. I wanted to see the eyes of my opponent in a blade fight. When they were glimmering with fear, I'd strike fast. When they were shining strong, I'd wait patiently to rip that confidence out of him until he was swinging, desperate. The bow had none of that. An arrow could sneak through from half a thousand feet away and open up a man like a sack.

I did all right with the bow, but I just wasn't the best. I had become taller, and the shorter, stouter boys were better on the horse. I was quick and better with blades for the same reason. I hit them from above before they even had a chance to touch me. Even Malan. All except Gunna.

"You will grow up to be a Blade," Rouba said as our irons were clanging against each other.

The Blades were warriors, not helpers, but their Story was not one for the stars. There was no Legend of the Ouna-Mas that ever spoke of brave Blades. Only about Archers. The Blades fought man-to-man with iron and almost never with bows. They usually came in when the battle was dying out. Like the flesh-eating birds.

"The Archers are hawks; the Blades are vultures," Rouba would say.

"I will be Khun," I answered him.

At that point, he hit my blade hard. As I took a clumsy step backward, he tripped me with his leg. I fell ass down. It was the last time he managed to do that. I was getting stronger, and he was growing older every dawn.

"You are a ninestar, Da-Ren, and you're not even First among the Uncarved yet," Rouba repeated.

Once on every Eagle moon, Chaka spoke with the Reghen and announced the order. He would tell us who was First in rank among our equals in age. The joking around was coming to an end. If our turn was to come that winter, the eighteenth for me, he wanted us to be prepared. The battle among us had simmered for four winters, but it now started to boil. Sah-Ouna was often at our little ceremony. One red ribbon was tied around the arm of the one who stood out as First.

But Khun-Taa proved immortal, like Darhul. Soon we would be named Wolves and enter our last spring Uncarved. Gunna was First most of the time, Malan quite a few times, and I fewer. The others, never.

Since we had become Eagles, our training changed, and we began to go out all over Sirol. We saw men, animals, slaves, women, even the orphans' tents. We had to learn everything fast—about siege machines, battle tactics in the open plain, and techniques of enemy encirclement. We went to the tanneries, the Blacksmiths, and the slaughter yard. We should have stayed at the slaughter yard for a whole moon for training. It would prove useful in our later lives. In mine, for sure.

The one most useful thing we learned was how to count. Up until then, I didn't know hundreds or thousands. I could count up to a few tens—until forty, a single Pack of warriors—with great effort. Most of the time, I wouldn't count. I knew by instinct if someone was missing or if something was spare.

"A Khun must know how to count Packs. He must know how many warriors there are in fifty Packs. And distance, feet and paces, thousands of them, or else he cannot ever lead a campaign," the Reghen told us.

My mind opened quickly when we were let loose to see and to learn in Sirol. I started to wonder. And so did my dick. I was still a virgin, but by now I had seen many warriors and slave girls fucking in the camp outside of the tents in the summer. I even saw Noki once. He was carved, but his calm smile was exactly the same, as if he didn't care. The rest of them did care. Women looked at us as if they wanted to ride us, men as if they wanted to beat the shit out of us.

So passed our Eagle spring, summer, and fall in training, the last careless, colorless ones. And then came the winter of the Forest.

It was that time before the three-day full-moon Great Feast of my eighteenth spring and the most important day for the Tribe.

Chaka was dead serious and grim when he delivered the news. "Listen, you are the last six Eagles. We are a few days from the Great Feast. After this ceremony, you will become Wolves and enter your final training. Now your turn has come. I'll carve the four older boys during the Feast in the Wolfhowl. You'll be there."

"Wolfhowl," mumbled Gunna. Balam, Akrani, and Lebo did the same.

The sound of the word took me back to the arena, with naked, barefoot, twelve-wintered ghosts around me. "You will join the Goddess's Feast, along with thousands of other warriors, Ouna-Mas, Sah-Ouna, and Khun-Taa. Together with the men and the Witches," added Chaka.

The next morning, Rouba said to me, "Things are not good. I fear for my Tribe, boy."

I knew his fears. They were spread around Sirol, slithering like Darhul's snake heads, poisoning every man's words.

"We have to leave this place. Everyone talks about it," I answered.

"Yes! By Enaka, yes! You, the young ones, don't feel it but we the old have known it for long. We always traveled, since the age of the first Khun. But you have been trapped since birth. In this iron valley," said Rouba.

Sirol itself meant "iron valley," a name to honor the red, iron-rich soil which gave birth to our blades.

"Where will we go, Rouba?" I asked.

"That I don't know," he said. Rouba went on his right knee and started drawing with an arrowhead on the dirt. He took all the time to explain. "West and northwest is the Endless Forest. South, the Blackvein. And farther south the cities of the Empire."

"Can't we go there?" I said.

"We have; many times, we went as far as we could. We reached Sapul, the untrodden city. To the northeast; the vast meadows. They lead back to the steppe, the sacred soil we came from."

"Why don't we go back to the steppe?"

"Sacred soil, but barren now. What's left? Nothing. Oh, here, to the southeast, the Black Sea."

I had heard all this from the Reghen many times, but I liked to listen to Rouba explain it in his own way. The Black Sea, the slimy lair of Darhul and his nine heads.

"The curse is, we are too many. It would take a moon to cross even the Blackvein; all fast horses and oxen carts."

"It is the Forest then," I said. "That's what the Ouna-Mas say. The West is our destiny."

"Is that so? The Ouna-Mas haven't spent a night in the Forest. Ride for two moons north; keep the wood to your left. The wall of trees will not end. It goes on forever. And if I am right, it is that way to the west, once you are in there."

"Have you been...in there?" I asked.

He lifted his eyes, and looked to the west while he kept talking.

"One whole moon on foot into the wood. I kept going west. I found just rocks and trees. And more of them."

"Did you see the Reekaal?" I asked.

"Huh, no, none of those bloodeaters. But I saw the Dasal. Many times."

I had never heard much about the Dasal.

"They are savages, they live in the Forest in small settlements," Rouba said.

"Are they a big Tribe?"

"No big Tribe can survive in the Forest. They are scavengers, only a handful, and useless as warriors. I've seen them, unlike the Reekaal. The Forest hunters, the Dasal, are real," Rouba told me. He was the first one ever to speak to me about the Forest without repeating Legends.

We had settled in Sirol, where grass and water were abundant for the horses and there was enough iron in the earth for making weapons and tools. The warriors kept raiding the surrounding areas, in the fall, always away from the Forest, but things became more difficult with each passing winter.

That same night we had all gathered to listen to Chaka about the Feast of Wolfhowl.

"This is unheard of," said Bera, looking around for others to agree. "How long have we been stuck in the same valley?"

"Summers and winters come and go," said another.

"Without a campaign, we'll crawl starving and naked of glory to our deaths," added Chaka.

All agreed. They were cursing because the meat slices were carved thinner and there were no fresh horses to replace the dying. They kept looking at the hut's entrance to make sure that none of the Reghen's two hundred ears and eyes were close and continued.

"Khun-Taa is too old for new campaigns," mumbled the venomous tongues, especially those of the fivecarved Guides who were the same age as the aging One Leader of the Tribe.

"We have waited long enough for Khun-Taa to die. The time has come for Sah-Ouna to bless a new beginning. Now, at the Feast of the First Moon of Spring," said Chaka. "But first, you will join the Blades tomorrow. They leave for the Forest."

"To the West?" I asked.

Rouba, who until then had been listening silently to the others, spoke: "Don't send them in the Forest; they cannot fight there. Archers are useless there; even horses are not much good."

"They are not going deep. One day, in and out. I've got my orders and that's how it's gonna be. The Reghen ordered a manhunt. They want the Uncarved to join," said Chaka. "The Great Feast is upon us."

"And Sah-Ouna needs fresh lives to sacrifice," added Bera. "I'll go with them and the warriors to guide them." He didn't look excited about the hunt.

At dawn, the childhood Stories of the most carefree era of my life and my training with the Uncarved came to an end. There was no ceremony. I swallowed the cold gruel, strapped the scabbards and the bow onto my back, and jumped onto my horse. By nightfall, I had fallen into the black-and-blue waters of life where only grown men swam.

I was to find out at last.

The one thing that turns a boy into a man in just one day.

It was so simple.

The one thing that lifts him up in the air like a baby and throws him to the ground like a puppy.

No one had told me till then.

XXII.
Blue

Eighteenth spring. Uncarved—
A few days before I became a Wolf.

"A woman. Othertriber, young, soft, the one with eyes of color. We fetch her; we bring her back for the Great Feast of Spring. Then we come back," said the Chief of the Blades. These were his only words before he put boot on stirrup to lead our pack forward.

The one with eyes of color? He was on horseback and had no time for my questions.

Cloudy but windless dawned the day of my first manhunt. The kindred spirits of the wolf, the mauler, the eagle, and the owl were on our side as we marched out of the camp. We would hunt together. A dozen Blades led and paid little attention to us. Two Guides and whatever was left of my pack, the six Uncarved, were riding farther back, next to the oxen-pulled cages.

The Blades were chewing on dried meat, and most of them were talking and joking around while their Chief rode first, sulky and quiet. Everyone would steal glances toward the Forest, which rose to the left of us. A lifeless brown-and-gray wall.

"We're not going to fight pumpkins today," said the ninestar Bera.

"Where are we going?"

"Half a day's ride, toward the north. We will enter the Endless Forest by afternoon. The Blades will hunt the Dasal. It's where the Trackers saw them a few days ago. They've come south for the winter."

"The Dasal are evil spirits. Shouldn't we bring more men?" asked Lebo.

"They're flesh and blood. All you have to do is put them in the cages after the Blades capture them. And watch that they don't escape."

"But the Legends—"

"We all know the Legends, kid. Any othertriber who lives in the Forest is a demon. The Dasal are not Reekaal, but they dwell in there too."

The horses continued their course on the outskirts of the Forest, without entering. The Blades told us that the oxen and the heavy carts couldn't move through the dense tree branches and the rough paths and we should stay out of the Forest as long as possible. Maybe it really was that way. The Blades were not the greatest warriors of the Tribe, and the horses were useless in the deep wood.

All my fellow Uncarved had come: Gunna, Lebo, Malan, Akrani, and Balam. Chaka had tied the red ribbon on Malan's arm, and the pale-faced boy was First among us.

Gunna was repeating the Stories we had all heard from the Reghen about the Reekaal. He hadn't stopped doing that since the night he had seen them. Or whatever it was that he had seen. The Stories sounded even more frightening because the giant recited them.

"Lidless, red eyes, never close. They skin alive any who enters the wood. Their nails, long as blades." He pointed at the scars on his arm. "They hang their prey from the branches and rip open at the neck. Suck out the blood and marrow while life still twitches… The Reekaal bewitch the trees and can enter the bodies of the Dasal. Every living thing in there, tree or man is their servant."

"Nonsense for seven-wintered children," mumbled the arrogant Balam, riding next to me with his head high. "I'll kill the first one I see."

"Have you ever been inside the Forest, you featherbrain?" Gunna asked him.

"Don't talk to me that way. Soon I will be the Khun."

"Like shit you will be! Just step in there first. Come on, go fetch us a kill."

"We won't see Reekaal; they only come out at night," said the Ninestar.

"Tell them about the Dasal, Ninestar," said Lebo.

Balam let the reins and pretended to jump on him with his two arms stretched out. "Boooooh Dasal!" he yelled.

Drops of sweat were shining above Lebo's lip and his first young beard. The veins of his neck were pulsating, pumping the blood to feed his first warrior Story.

Midday came, but the sun was still hiding behind a patch of faint clouds. We were late, but the Blades continued at a trot. Night was going to catch up with us.

"I've seen the Dasal many times. They live in small settlements, huts, in the deep of the wood. They don't have horses or strong bows like ours," said Bera.

"How do they fight?"

"They don't. Not us, they can't. They hunt, gather mushrooms, and dig for roots. We'll catch a few for Sah-Ouna's sacrifices and go back."

"But do they have eyes of fire, red and yellow? Like Gunna claims?" asked Akrani.

A loud raspy sound, like the sharpening of long knives, flew out of the thick bushes. Everyone froze.

"What…what was that?" cried Lebo.

"Shhhh, demon's howl," said Gunna.

"Pheasant," said Malan, calm as an old Guide who had been there many times.

Not much later, two of the Blades came out of the bushes holding the pheasants pierced by their arrow shafts.

Bera turned to us and continued. "Eyes of fire? The Dasal? No, they aren't owls."

Lebo jumped in. "The Dasal have green eyes. I was raised in the Trackers' tents before the Sieve, and I heard all the tales. One thing they all said, is that the trees themselves were the Dasal. Man is tree and tree is man."

There was a grin on Malan's face as he turned and whispered to the rest: "Pheasant is demon and demon is pheasant." Balam tried to muffle his laughter.

"Keep speaking, Lebo," I encouraged him.

"The branches come alive and grab you; their tips get under your nails and into your nostrils. The Dasal don't kill with an ax. The tree holds on the living for entire moons, melting their bodies, emptying the blood. It takes many winters for a man to die this death until all warm life is sucked out and he wrinkles like a one-hundred-wintered, rotten corpse. The Trackers used to say that they saw warriors, still trapped within trunks, after tens of winters, living dead."

"That is stupid talk, Lebo," Balam said.

"Those Trackers have some crazygrass Stories," said Malan.

"Yeah? Ask the Blades who have come here before. They will tell you what they've seen. Dasal with blue eyes, the color of the sky. That is why we are here. Sah-Ouna has ordered them to find a blue-eyed or a green-eyed one for the sacrifice. She craves for the eye that has the gift of the Sky and can see into the future, even after she rips it out of the head."

"There are no people with blue eyes, stupid."

The Chief of the Blades heard our senseless words and joined in. I expected him to say there were no such creatures.

"The Dasal are just men, but when you catch them with the neckrope, they know they're going to die and will fight like wolves. If you're not quick enough, they'll bring their ax down on your head or stab your chest with a hunting knife. They are strong men. They hunt in the Forest all day, living next to the Reekaal, and are not afraid. You strike to kill. No fear or hesitation if you are in danger."

We had come far north, and the wood in front of us thickened and darkened a bit more every time I looked at it. Milk-colored fumes were rising above the treetops, and it wasn't fog.

"Campfire," whispered the Chief. He motioned silently for us to dismount and wait. "Grab your cudgels—no blades or bows. I don't want holes in them. Open the cages, and wait here."

At once we were all on foot, except from Balam, the featherbrain who dreamed of being the next Khun. He waited frozen still on his horse.

"Are you afraid, Balam?" the Ninestar asked.

"No, but—"

"The Blades are not our best warriors, and they aren't afraid. You are an Uncarved. Get off your horse now!"

It was the beginning of spring, before the first moon, and the land had not blossomed. The trunks of the first oaks stood out dark and motionless in front of me, but farther back the naked branches and the dead leaves mixed into one dense gray cloud. That was where the Blades and the Guides disappeared, on foot, with knives and neckropes in hand.

We alone, the Uncarved, stayed behind, guarding the cages and trying to make no noise. The Blades had been away for some time, and there was no sign of them. There at the Forest's edge, I hung from the fangs of the gray monster, just outside its mouth, but still, it made no move to devour me. A sun I couldn't see was setting behind the wood when a medley of cries and moving shadows came through the trees. The second Guide appeared and called us to get deeper into the trees.

"Move. The Forest won't eat you."

Everyone moved slowly, cursing the boots and the cracking leaves.

"Don't wake anything up," said Gunna.

The branches started to come alive, moving, dancing, embracing, whispering. I tried to listen to their calling. This was where I had last seen her, Elbia, the girl with the brown hair, her ghost among the oaks. She was hiding from me, for a long time now. I missed her.

"What comes out?" Gunna asked when he heard the leaves crackling.

"Kill it first, ask later," answered Malan.

Cries and other sounds grew louder. Shadows first, then figures of men were emerging from the wood.

Balam, shaking, held Malan's hand. Malan pushed him hard.

"Are you fucking stupid?"

A handful of Blades were yelling and running toward us, one of them pulling a rope. Behind him followed the first Dasal, with the rope wrapped around his neck, trying not to choke to death. He tripped twice over fallen branches, and the grip tightened even more. The prey was tied up and thrown at our feet. Gunna tried to grab him, but the Dasal started kicking hard.

"Use your cudgel, kid. Don't kill him," shouted Bera.

We hit the bearded rag-covered man a few times to weaken his legs and threw him into a cage. Another followed, and another, until we filled two cages with Dasal. They were covered in mud and growled like wounded bears. Some were still kicking to break the cage. Lebo, Gunna, and Akrani were sticking their blades into any arm or leg that moved. Lebo had wounded a man deeply, and his leg was bleeding badly all over the others in the small cage.

"Let's get out of here," one of the Blades said as they brought in the last one.

"It will get pitch-dark soon," Bera said.

"A woman; I saw one of color. She was with them. Bring her to me," the Chief replied.

Looking at the Dasal made me want to kill a man for the first time.

They boiled my blood with just their mad stares of despair as they tried to escape.

"Is this man or animal?" I wondered aloud.

I hated them with a passion from the first moment. So weak; they disgusted me. No brave warrior would allow himself to be caught by a neckrope like a foal.

"Wake up!" I heard the voice, and a loud blow woke me.

I was still staring trancelike at the Dasal's cage. The Blade who had hit me threw a body at my feet.

"Wake up! Put her inside. I'm bringing the rest, and we leave," he said. "In the third cage, by herself. That one goes to Sah-Ouna!" he yelled, already running to gather the others.

A savage creature stirred at my feet, hair black as starless night, coiled with mud and dried leaves, fresh cuts and scratches bleeding on her elbow and knee. This wasn't a man. The body was thin and delicate. I lifted the cudgel, ready to hit its back before it tried to get away. She lifted her head and I saw her eyes.

My right hand froze in midair, and my left gripped her arm tightly. Her blue stare of agony flowed ice-cold up to my head and down my knees. My hand wouldn't come down to strike her. My heart beat like a hundred hooves. My eyes watered warm.

There she was, Enaka herself, the Great Mother, she who bore the bright stars, appearing before me for the very first time.

The one of color.

The Goddess was unjust with me. From that day and beyond, I would encounter many women with eyes the color of the sky. But when I saw her that evening, First, otherworldly, she was the Only woman in the world. And the Last.

There I saw for the first time the black star, the one that had fallen from the Unending Sky and frozen the steppe. In the black of her hair.

There I saw the Blue Drakon, the Crystaleyed who guarded the rivers of the North. I saw him unleashing the waters and flooding the Iron Valley. In the blue of her eyes.

There I saw my Legends, those that would haunt me forevermore.

She was slim, with skin as smooth as my blade. She struggled and screamed, kicking me in vain. Another scream to my right, a different one. A boy slaughtered, boots crushing wooden planks. I turned my head; men running. Blood was gushing out of Lebo's neck; his own blade stuck there. The Dasal had broken open one of the cages and were running away. The fastest were already lost behind the trees. Gunna, Malan, and the other two were chasing them.

"Stay here! Guard them!" shouted Malan, showing me the other cage. "Don't let her go!"

Never let her go.

I was all alone with her at my knees and the Dasal in the second cage. She bit my hand. But it didn't do anything. *Never let her go.* The fear in her eyes, the only blue shining in a dusky forest. I could hear the Blades shouting; they'd be back soon.

I saw myself at the Great Feast of Spring, only three nights hence, watching the blood running from her long neck on Sah-Ouna's tree trunk. The eyes of color frozen—torn out. Another sacrifice. The Goddess had quenched her thirst.

Lebo's throat had emptied on the dry leaves, through the first and only carving he would ever get. I was the only one guarding the cage with the Dasal, and they were repeatedly kicking it to break free.

A few steps ahead, I saw the oak's hollow.

And I knew.

I held her by the forearms and stared straight into her eyes. O, my long-lost ghost! "Oaks," I whispered. To her. To myself. "Oaks!" *Elbia knew.* "Children are oaks, not firs. They live. In spring."

I finally knew.

I was dragging her by the forearms, and her wailing was becoming more desperate.

I was forever defeated at that moment and chose my own poison. I turned my back that day on the world that had born me, to embrace a new one. I had been born only to die, Malan would say.

I pushed her into the hollow of the oak; she tried to run the moment I let her but I threw her back in. The shouts of the Blades were closer.

"Shhh, shhh!" My finger on my lips, my other palm shutting her mouth. She understood. She stopped screaming. I threw leaves and branches over the hollow, hiding it completely. The Dasal were kicking hard to break the cage. I turned with demon's speed, took my blade out, and poked them.

"Help us!" yelled one of them in our tongue. My betrayal. They had seen. Rage and surprise, shame and dishonor, weakness and terror. The branches of my mind were strangling me. I pushed my blade, not deep, but enough to make him bleed and shut up.

The Blades returned, and with them were Gunna and Malan, with two of the Dasal who had escaped. Darkness was fast swallowing the hollow oaks. What screamed near us was no pheasant. *A wolf? A Reekaal?*

"Da-Ren. Da-Ren. Where is the girl?"

"She got away in the wood, there," I pointed in the opposite direction.

The Ninestar punched me in the face.

I supported myself on one knee, dizzy from the blow.

"They would have gotten away," I said pointing to the Dasal in the other cage. "I was alone."

"You all did shit today, useless turds! Load your dead one on his horse, and let's get out of here."

"We have to find the girl," said the Chief of the Blades.

"The night is here. Listen around you. Reekaal. We are not staying here for one more breath. Out, there, away from the trees, all of you, now."

"Sah-Ouna said—"

"To the snakes with Sah-Ouna! Have you ever seen an Ouna-Ma in the Forest at night? We leave now!" yelled the Ninestar.

"She had blue eyes. Did you see her?" insisted the Chief.

"I don't care if they're gold. We leave now! Before we lose all Uncarved Wolves." Bera was screaming his lungs out. Whatever fear he had in him, he used it to appear angry and determined.

"We have orders," the Blade said.

"What orders, aye? Kill us all? To leave the Tribe without a single Uncarved? Move out of the dark, in the moonlight. Now!"

I cast a final glance at the hollow oak. I couldn't see two blue eyes looking back at me. I would see them constantly—whether I wanted to or not—whenever I closed mine. And I shall until the end of my life.

I had betrayed Enaka, Khun-Taa, Rouba, Bera, Chaka, Lebo, Sah-Ouna, the Reghen, Malan, the Uncarved, the Sieve, Khun-Nan, the First Ouna-Ma, the Sun, Selene, the stars, and all but one of the ghosts of my entire Tribe.

"Sah-Ouna will hear of this," the Chief shouted to Bera.

"So she shall! I am a ninestar Guide. You don't scare me."

I spat a glob of blood on the dirt. A warm smile, the joy of guilt, the only things to fill my empty stomach. I whispered of my brave and disgraceful deed to my horse, the only one who would always take my side, no matter what I had done, and trotted into the night. I wanted to gallop and scream with pride but had to stay in pace with the carts and the rest.

We were back in the wide-open valley. My horse knew. The Forest knew. I finally knew. The clouds parted. Selene would be full in three nights. Her light was falling silver on my ninestar destiny.

What did you do, Da-Ren? Enaka knew. She saw.

XXIII.
I Dreamed of Redbreast Robins

Eighteenth spring. Uncarved—Wolf.

I killed a man for the first time a couple of nights later, on the second of the trinight Great Feast of Spring. It was the time when the Tribe, hungry in belly and in spirit, waited to hear Sah-Ouna's prophecies. An old woman would carve a new fate for thousands of warriors. For many winters now, the arrows had been ready, searching for the next prey like starving hawks. One single command from Sah-Ouna would be enough to set us on a march toward the West to fight the Final Battle.

Sah-Ouna wouldn't speak until the third night and the first two nights were reserved to honor Enaka who had awoken weak and thirsty. The sacrificial blood was the sacred elixir that would lift her from a deep winter's sleep to welcome us into her bosom. Many animals were slaughtered on the first night: the heads of horses, goats, rams, and sheep stood dripping from the stakes around the Wolfhowl. Their dead eyes kept away the evil spirits of the Forest. More than ten thousand warriors sat around the Wolfhowl on the surrounding mound that was encircling the arena. It had been raised high and inclined steeply to seat many rows of men so that all could be there for the Great Feast.

The virgins who were of age to become Ouna-Mas approached Khun-Taa naked and proud, and received their first red veils from Sah-Ouna, plunging the men into dark dreams. Othertribers fought with shield and sword against Archers on horseback in mock battles. They fought bravely but fell pierced. Captured Sorcerers of the Cross from the South were thrown as live prey to the maulers. There was no fight there.

The flasks were always full of mare's milk-spirit and passed around to keep the warriors light-headed. There was meat for all, but in meager amounts. Food had become scarce. The dogs and the vultures found plenty to feast upon; the warriors, not so much. On the last night, cups of crazygrass would replace the milk-spirit and men would swallow them happily along with Sah-Ouna's prophecies.

The four Uncarved who were older than I had left our camp forever a few days earlier. They had entered their eighteenth spring, losing any claim to become the next Khun of the Tribe. Chaka held a brief and gloomy ceremony. One of the four received one carving and became Chief of an Archers Pack. He was given forty men to command. The other three received three carvings and followed the fates of thousands of other warriors. Khun-Taa had managed to devour four more of his children and was not planning to ascend to the Sky anytime soon.

My time had come after five times spring.

We were Wolves, the five who remained: myself, Malan, Gunna, Balam, and Akrani. If the Goddess finally called Khun-Taa to join her, then Malan, who had been named First on the previous moon, would become the Tribe's sixth Khun. Over ten thousand warriors would be waiting for him in the Wolfhowl with hungry eyes and bellies.

"If they ever let someone so young become Khun," said Rouba.

"But it is the Truth, the rule of the Reghen. He is an Uncarved. They all have to kneel in front to him," I answered, surprised at his words.

"It is the Truth, so we are told, but Khun-Taa has been the One Leader for thirty winters now. Most have forgotten the Truth. You don't know how they'll take it. What will the Leader of the Archers or the Blades do?"

"What can they do?"

"If it were me, I wouldn't let you. Any of you," Rouba said again.

Useful things, the rules and the Truths. For games and silly trials. Useful for children.

But the end had not come for Khun-Taa. And we were brought to his tent to be reminded of that. The morning of the second day of the Feast, our small camp filled with Rods on horseback. Not one of them dismounted. They came in haste and delivered an order: "Chaka and the five Uncarved Wolves, follow us now, to the tent of our Khun."

Only two nights earlier, we had returned from our first manhunt, diminished and humiliated.

Khun-Taa accepted us into his tent. It was even bigger than our hut, but it didn't make a great impression on me. The torchlight was flickering weakly, as if someone were getting ready to sleep forever in there. As if the Khun didn't want to show how old he had become. He drank from a wooden cup and not from the loot. He looked much older than Chaka or Rouba.

The bear hides of the Rods surrounding him and his thunderous voice were the only things that made him seem formidable in our eyes.

"Who are you?" Khun-Taa asked without getting up from his unremarkable wooden throne.

"I am Chaka, my Khun. In charge of the training of the Uncarved."

"And what kind of training is this? Unarmed Dasal weasels kill them, and they can't even capture a girl? You found one of color they say? And let her go?" Sah-Ouna was beside him but kept silent. "You have been ridiculed far and wide. You call these cowards *Uncarved*? The warrior Packs fear for our future," Khun-Taa continued.

The countless days I'd spent with the bow, the blade, and the horse meant nothing at that moment in the Khun's tent. Now that the dawn of the biggest trial had come once again, I knew our training was flawed; and so did Chaka and Khun-Taa.

"It was their first time. It will never happen again," said Chaka, lowering his head in shame.

"I should have sent Fishermen. They would have done better. Your shame must be washed clean, tonight even, before tomorrow's moonrise. The five boys will fight in the Wolfhowl against the Dasal you captured. Now get out of my sight!" ordered Khun-Taa.

"Yes."

"And be thankful to the Goddess, all of you here and out there, that I will not die soon."

That was the dreaded Khun-Taa. He had survived as Leader of the Tribe for thirty winters, and all said that in his old age he had become wise and just. As a youth, he had been a mad beast. He had wiped out every living creature south of the Blackvein and left the fields barren. Fire and salt were all he had sown. And now our people were starving. When he had grown old, he had drawn the Tribe back north of the river and had spent his nights with the younger Ouna-Mas. He had waited for their tongues to whisper him his destiny, but the faster their tongues kept working, the more confused he would become, and so he remained appeased in his tent. Just and wise.

There was only one thing he didn't know despite his newfound wisdom and the destiny tellers.

When he would die.

We left the tent like beaten pups.

"Tonight, you will fight to the death. Prepare, or else the demons will take us all and feed us to the dogs!" Chaka screamed at us, and his face turned red.

"Will we fight in front of all of the warriors?" asked Malan.

"That's what the Khun ordered. In front of him and the thirty thousand warriors. The Truthsayers and the Redveils."

Back at the camp, no one rested. We all left with bow and blade to practice and to forget our anguish for a while. I found Gunna piercing pumpkins in the open field. My ears caught a flapping sound and I looked high. Gunna raised his eyes and his bow, aimed twice and shot two small birds in flight. We all knew that he would have easy work that night. He looked at me, free of fear or worry, and said, "Fucking redbreasts. These robins started singing before dawn again today."

"Those aren't redbreasts that you hit. They were starlings," I told him.

"I don't know what they were, but now they are redbreasts," Gunna said with a loud, broken laugh as if he had just swallowed the robins, feathers and all.

His eyes had begun to blur from a young age, and that could be an ill fate for a warrior rider. A deep, blind puddle, a false step of the horse. Maybe he really had seen the Reekaal that night in the Forest. Like the cloudy-eyed Guide in the Sieve.

Before dusk, Chaka, Rouba, and the Reghen led us to the Wolfhowl. It was already full of thousands of warriors. They were seated higher and surrounded us, their deafening shouts rising from above our heads. I felt something dancing on my leg, but it was only Malan's fingers trembling uncontrollably. Impatience, fear, death or victory. If I had to use a bow, I wouldn't be able to shoot even a bear at twenty feet. The Dasal were locked up in five cages in the middle of the field, the maulers and the Rods guarding them. Hundreds of torches were lit around the Wolfhowl, engulfing us in fire and leaving the sky dim in comparison. The stars were weak, but my legs had to be strong.

The rules, as announced by the Reghen, were simple. Each one of us and each Dasal could choose only one weapon. The fight was to the death. If a Dasal won, he won his life. That was the inviolable Truth of the Wolfhowl.

"All these thousands of warriors! Did they come just to see us?" asked Akrani.

"They were itching and asking me about each of you all day.

Everyone is on edge," said Rouba.

"For us? We're not even warriors yet."

"Khun-Taa reeks of rotting flesh and old age. They are starving. They smell that one of you will be the next Khun before the following spring, but they don't know who. And then…the Dasal are strong men and everyone says that some of you won't make it through the night."

That was my future, and no Ouna-Ma was needed to foresee it. The One Khun. Or a corpse for the pyre. Nothing in between.

I looked at the Dasal. They had taken them out of the cage.

"Do they know that if they kill one of us they will be free?" I asked Rouba.

"Yes, one of them I know well. He speaks our tongue."

"You know him well?"

Would he know if the girls among them had blue eyes? It wasn't the right time to ask him.

"Yes, they trade with everyone. Don't listen to the nonsense stories. For a long time, the Dasal have been supplying us with belladonna, crazygrass, and herbs from the Forest. We give them barley and wheat."

They untied the Dasal and let them choose their weapons. A couple of them ran first to grab the heavy single-bladed axes.

"They think we're trees," laughed Gunna.

None of them chose the bow. They would never have managed the double-curved bow without practicing for many summers.

Gunna went in first and chose to fight a strong Dasal. The Dasal wasted no breath and started running and screaming toward the giant with his ax. Gunna's first arrow found him in the stomach. As the green-eyed man lay fallen and writhing in pain, Gunna walked toward him and pushed the second arrow into his neck. A river of blood crimsoned the Dasal's torso, and then his knees and Gunna's boots.

Gunna walked back toward the rest of us amid loud cheers.

"Redbreast, he is a redbreast now," he said, the gagging, broken laugh again roaring out of his mouth.

Balam went second, brave in stature but a coward when it came to death. He chose for himself the oldest opponent and a bow. He was never even a stone's throw from the Dasal. The old man, trembling and panicked, tried at once to run away, but the arrow found him in the back.

The games proved too easy and boring for the bloodthirsty audience. I could see men all around me getting up and leaving. They were raising their hands impatiently and booing in disgust. It was my turn now, and thousands of warriors around me were already jeering.

"Give them a rabbit to chase. It would be more difficult!" someone behind me yelled.

A rabbit. I had lost to Malan. In the Sieve.

His words brought me to my senses. The moment had come for me to stand out and become worthy of the honor of the First Leader, the next Khun. Enough about the rabbits; it was time to lift the curse of defeat which had haunted me for five times spring.

I was the third out of five. I chose the largest, strongest-looking Dasal who was left. I then approached the pile with the weapons and chose a long blade instead of a bow. That woke up the crowd. Many, Blades probably, were cheering, but most, Archers probably, were booing even louder. But all of them were now enjoying themselves as they should.

The Dasal across from me was tall, as tall as I, and much older. The deep grooves on his face reminded me of the trunks of dry old trees. I now believed Lebo, who said before he died that at night they become one with the hollows of the trees and that they were born from them. He snarled and swore in a mysterious dark tongue. He lifted and swirled the heavy, one-bladed ax in a menacing manner as if it were made of straw. I moved toward him. He was not a man, not with those lizard-green eyes. Or a warrior, either.

He raised the ax and tore the wind, but it found only dirt. Before he raised it a second time, I plunged in to put a hole in his chest and get it over with, but he was quicker than I thought. His ax found my long blade and threw it out of my grip. It took a few breaths before I felt the tingling and realized I had lost the tip of my little finger. In my first fight. I heard the sighs of our warriors. Scattered boos. Khun-Taa was whispering to the ear of the first-veiled Ouna-Mas next to him. He was probably asking if she foresaw my death.

The Dasal chased me, and I retreated a step. I let him get close, but I was fast, too. When he missed me, I got behind him and picked up my blade off the ground. I let him rip the air many times aimlessly until he lost his strength.

I waited for him to lower his ax one more time. Before it was up again, my blade struck his left arm above the elbow. He fell to his knees with a howl which was drowned immediately by screams that would crush a defeated man to the ground. He raised his right hand, the one with the ax, but it just hung there. I hit him again on the left arm to be sure. His ax fell to the dirt. I fed on the warriors' cheers of victory, and I hit his half-cut arm a third time to finish the job. His arm fell to the ground along with its rags. Blood spurting out, covering my body and his. He was squealing, but I could barely hear that either, even from two feet away. Ten thousand maddening bellows flowing from my ears to my hands. I grabbed his ax and brought it down to his neck. Blood of the othertribers! So beautiful and crimson it was. To kill for the Tribe. *I am worthy, father.* All those men watching me, they were all my father. Any one of them could be. I would wash myself off with the bitter mare's milk-spirit which my fathers drank.

Khun-Taa himself was standing up, and the crowd was still going wild. As if it were his own feat, Gunna took the cut arm and walked around the field waving it at the warriors.

"Look at us now! Are we Uncarved or not?"

I was so thirsty. Rouba gave me a waterskin and I emptied it on my face; Blackvein's water and the splattered blood of the green-eyed became one on my tongue. Malan was First among us and would fight last. It was Akrani's turn.

We threw Akrani the Uncarved into the funeral pyre the next morning at daybreak.

"Unlike you, I choose the bow. It is fast and clean," he said to me before he walked to the center of the arena. "I don't want to lose a finger."

I shrugged my shoulders. My little finger started stinging the moment he brought it up. Rouba shred a stripe of his own tunic and tied it.

"More water," I said to him. I was still thirsty.

The Dasal across from Akrani was a wiry man, almost forty-wintered. I would not have chosen him. All this time he had waited calm, with eyes closed in his cage; his arms over his knees. The Dasal chose neither ax nor blade. He picked a shield, the only one there. He fended off the first arrow and ran toward Akrani. The second arrow didn't pierce the shield either, but the third one flew very close to his ear and got tangled in his ragged hair. But he kept running toward the Uncarved. There was no fourth arrow.

When the Dasal closed on Akrani the sharp round shield became a hammering ax and a vengeful blade. Akrani's light bow was a useless weapon in a melee. He fell dazed on the first blow of the heavy shield. The Dasal, holding the two ends of the shield, brought it down with rage onto Akrani, snapping his neck, smashing his head, and shattering his teeth. I could hear around me the sighs and the "aaahs" of shock and dismay after each blow, as if the Dasal were crushing thousands of warrior skulls, the skulls of our fathers. The Rods finally burst onto the field, with their long spears, and forced the screaming Dasal to stop.

Our stupid smiles and cheers disappeared. A deathly silence fell across the Wolfhowl. Chaka shouted for us to take away the body and the red-brown pulp that used to be Akrani's head. I chose the shield. It was the only fast and clean way to scoop Akrani's brains up from the dirt. The hungry mauler, his eyes glowing chestnuts, growled and walked around us impatiently as we carried the body away.

Thirteen of us had come Uncarved from the Sieve; four were still standing.

In the Stories of the Reghen, we were always victorious, but in three nights we had lost Lebo and then Akrani. The Tribe's Legend claimed that the Uncarved were the best warriors, picked out from the thousands of youths who'd endured the Sieve. But the Legend had forgotten to tell us one thing: that the othertribers could kill us with equally great ease and greater hate. Even in the midst of the Great Feast.

At the peak of youth, when the soul is quicker than the feet, any Uncarved boy was certain that, up there, Enaka had eyes only for him, the One destined to be Khun. But all it took was a three-finger-deep blade in his first fight and the proud boy was nothing but ashes ascending to the Unending Sky.

With the Wolfhowl still silent after Akrani's defeat, it was Malan's turn to deal with the last of the green-eyed. The Dasal had chosen the shield as well and looked almost as strong as the one I had fought. That was when I began to fear that Malan, too, might fall. He was the closest thing I had to a brother. I wanted one day to beat Malan. I wanted to beat Malan every day, but I didn't want to see him dead.

He wasn't the surefooted Malan of the Sieve. He was staring left and right. I could smell his fear. He was the rabbit in this fight. I could see ahead, and I saw his death. Malan lifted a blade, a smart choice against the shield, but I knew he wasn't as good with iron. It was his first time fighting in front of everyone, the first time he had to kill with his own hands. The first and the last.

The time had come where I would finally beat Malan in front of everyone. The wind was rising stronger, cooler in the Wolfhowl. I was so thirsty. Victory was mine. The Goddess would grace me with… Raindrops? Raindrops were falling on my face. Thicker; more and more of them.

I should have known then. Enaka and Sah-Ouna had forever thrown their guarding veils over Malan. The exact same moment that the fight was about to begin, the Sky obediently unlocked the rivers of the Goddess and dropped them over our heads with thunder and lightning.

The Reghen looked at Sah-Ouna.

"Darhul is strong tonight!" the Reghen turned and shouted to Chaka.

The Reghen looked at Khun-Taa.

"Tomorrow!" he shouted again and for the last time.

Three breaths later, the rain was coming down, a pitiless, heavy gray veil. The thousands of warriors emptied the Wolfhowl in a stampede. We were soaked and alone in the middle of the arena. Rouba and Chaka set free the Dasal who had smashed Akrani's head, and he disappeared in the storm. It was what the Truth of the Wolfhowl had decreed. A victorious man lives again. We dragged the last Dasal, the one who hadn't fought with Malan, back to our camp and I put him in a cage across from our hut.

"I'm Veker," he told me as I was locking the cage. "Let me go. I have always been a friend of the Tribe. I bring you the crazygrass."

I spat in the dirt with disgust.

"You will fall in the Wolfhowl tomorrow," I told him, wondering how he could speak our tongue so well.

He lowered his head, and he knelt as if to worship me.

"You saved my daughter," he whispered.

He wouldn't be able to find a word to thank me in my tongue. I pretended not to hear.

"Zeria, in the oak," he said.

Zeria. The one of color.

I turned my back on him and ran away before anyone else came close enough to hear. I was unlucky that Malan had not opened him up.

I slept on a full stomach, hurrahs from jubilant Gunna and Balam, the two of three remaining older Uncarved, and from the younger ones.

"Da-Ren's Story is in every tent, in every fire tonight," Rouba said loud enough for all to hear.

Right there, he was the one father I had. The one true Guide, to lift my spirit high. The one I wanted to make proud.

Malan had disappeared into a corner of the hut, and none of us bothered him. The next dawn would bring his greatest day.

I dreamed of redbreast robins.

I opened my eyes in the heavy darkness of the night and awoke to Malan shaking me out of a deep sleep.

"Da-Ren, wake-up. He got away," he whispered.

"Who?"

"The Dasal escaped from the cage. You have to help me find him. I saw him running. To the Forest."

"Wake them all up. The Guides."

"No, we two must find him. He's mine, Da-Ren. Come on." He pleaded like a child.

"We will not go alone."

"You didn't lock the cage, Da-Ren. It's your fault. Help me now!"

Malan grabbed me by the hand. He had never done that before. I was fully awake and putting on my horsehide boots. We were tiptoeing out of the hut. It didn't even cross my mind that it was better for me if Veker escaped. He was the only one alive who had seen me hide the girl inside the hollow oak.

Zeria, he had called her.

Malan had taken bow and quiver with him, but in my confusion, I had grabbed only a short blade. The rain was still falling heavily.

Malan shouted, "He went in there, I saw him!" We pointed into the dark, where no one from our Tribe ever went. We had no torches—

they'd be useless under the Sky's fury. I did what every stupid, invincible seventeen-winter-old would do—I charged toward death.

Malan signaled for us to separate, and slipped out of sight. I ran through the tangled black trees with all my heart and strength. Selene was lost behind the clouds and the wooden skeletons that got in my way. A tall hideous shadow moved to my right, and then an arrow shaft broke on the tree next to me. I hid behind the trunk and stopped to catch my breath. It was the worst thing to do. My mind betrayed me. My shaking legs slipped in the mud. I wasn't even a thousand feet into the Forest, but, there, for the first time, I succumbed to an untold horror. The cold yellow sweat paralyzed every joint in my body. The shadow again. Some creature fast, menacing. Hunting. I was not new to the embrace of death. I had felt it every moon since the Sieve, but that moment, the black drooling tongues of the demons were touching my feet, my head and my hands. I was inside of the monster. It had swallowed me. I cut the air again and again with my whistling blade, defending myself against the branches. Its talons were coming down to rip me apart. But I hit only air, raindrops, and dead wood.

Only a short time prior, I had slain the strongest of the Dasal in the Wolfhowl. But here, his ghost roamed free. I was inside the Forest's green-and-black belly, and it was grinding me into a pulp of sweat, rain, and mud. I couldn't find my way out. For one instant, I asked myself if Malan had really woken me up, if I really had run like a fool to go in there, or if it was a nightmare. I fell to my knees and put my hands over my head; I didn't want to open my eyes ever again. I screamed from the deepest part within me. "Maaaaaaaaaaaaa!"

Malan? Mother? Was I calling her for the very first time? The word did not come out. I called her again.

I heard the shouts of our men—the only mother I'd ever had— and as I looked toward my right, I saw torches appearing and disappearing. The horns of distress were blowing throughout the camp of the

Uncarved. I followed their cries, crawling fast on all fours until I found the Guides who had come for us. I came out of the Forest as if I had come out of a woman's belly into the light. The rain had eased.

That was my first night alone in the Forest.

The same night I killed my first othertriber.

The same night I learned her name.

The same night I discovered the green fear.

I had become a warrior.

The thought never crossed my mind, that Malan himself had let the Dasal free.

Who thought like that?

Enaka had pitied him.

I didn't think for a single breath that Malan had tried to kill me with an arrow in the Forest.

Who thought like that?

I was seventeen winters, eighteen springs young.

When I first saw Zeria.

I would again descend into the womb of the Forest.

It had conquered me.

I had already fallen in love with it.

That which I feared. That which was forbidden.

Before I even knew what love was.

I would find it there.

XXIV.
Skeleton

Island of the Holy Monastery, Thirty-third summer.
According to the Monk Eusebius.

In the damp of the night and the scorching heat of the day, Da-Ren and I wove the words of his story into bloodstained flower wreaths. My hand, already tired, dropped the reed pen when Da-Ren said his story hadn't even started. Baagh warned me sternly before he left that these words would one day be read by the Emperor of Thalassopolis himself.

"The written codices will go to the Polis of the Kings. You write for the power-wielding Emperors, but also for the many," he told me. "For those you will never see. Not for the few monks around you."

How was it possible that the thrice-sanctified soul of the blessed Emperor could hear of such malevolent and brutish acts committed by these barbarians? For the first time, I considered that maybe not everything should be put to papyrus. And what kind of prayer or repentance could befit this savage man who lined up corpses as fast as I lined up the words?

"You killed a man. An innocent. You enjoyed it. I can't write that. I will not. Do you repent, Da-Ren?"

I had set a rule that now proved foolish—whenever he referred to the death of another human being, we would fast for one full day, without even water.

"If you don't change that rule very soon, you will die of thirst in the sunless cell, Eusebius," he told me with a sorrowful chuckle.

And it was the truth. Even if I had all the strength of the saints, my emaciated body would never be able to finish this story. I changed the rule to require our isolation in the cell for one whole day, but that hurt Da-Ren even more. Especially when death rained down onto our papyrus, and we had to remain within the four stone walls of the cell for many days.

"Let's get outside of this tomb that you have stuck me in, Eusebius. Did you find an innocent victim and go green with fear? You have only just brushed against the first branch of the forest. Prepare to swim in the red sea of guiltless blood. You will be searching for air in vain, as I do in this hole. If you cannot endure it, then leave. I have no pleasant stories to tell you."

Da-Ren could have killed men without remorse in his previous life, but for me everything had to be deciphered as an ancient symbol on papyrus: symbols that I had to read, to find the way toward God and forgiveness somewhere within all this barbarism.

"What did you feel? How did you sleep at night?"

"What are you asking me?"

"Do you repent?"

"Oh yes, every night, but not for that night."

"Did you hear them at night, the screams of the innocent Dasal? That was not your enemy that came to harm you. You killed him for fun. That other boy with the rain of arrows before. How many unspeakable horrors?"

"Too many to count. That was only the first day. Then every day. Can we go outside, Eusebius? I can't breathe in here with all this candle smoke. Let's go fishing today."

When he began to talk that way, we had to get out into the light and go to the sea. He had undertaken the task of fishing for the needs of the monastery. For many days, there were no supplies or stones for him to carry up the endless steps. He desperately searched for something to do during the times I was away at my prayers. Something other than punching his fists into his cell wall waiting for the Sorcerers of the Cross who would come to save his wife and daughter. After a while, I realized that what he really wanted was to slice the sea with the oars and to rest his eyes into the blue.

I did him the favor and climbed down the steps to reach the rocks next to the harbor where Da-Ren liked to fish. We stayed in the small boat for a long time, and he would dive into the sea and come up for air. He managed to catch a few small fish with his spear. Nothing like the experienced fishermen of the island, who dove deep and disappeared for a long time beneath the water.

When the day grew hotter, he lay down in the boat with his eyes closed, as if waiting for the sun to devour his whole body and leave only his bones. The heat brought to my mind the funeral pyres at Sirol. The story of his tribe was written all over his body, with knife wounds, lashing scars that still whispered the name "Elbia," from the right side of his forehead to the soft part of his neck on the left. His body was criss-crossed with large scars, one under the lowest rib on his right and one on his left arm, but he hadn't told me the stories of those two yet. He touched the scar under his right rib with his fingers.

"What do you ask of me, Eusebius? To tell you what I felt? What do you want to hear?"

I had to find the Demon. If I knew the name of the Evil one and removed it from inside of him, then my mission would end in victory. Only the humility and patience of a monk could uproot the beast.

"Yes, what happened inside of you? Did you feel guilt, fear? Joy, perhaps? That is what I must know, Da-Ren, or else how can I bring your story in front of the elder monks?"

A ship appeared on the horizon. It was too far away for us to distinguish what trade it was. Da-Ren locked my head in his arm with one hand, grabbed my jaw with the other, and forced me to look in the ship's direction.

"It's coming. You see it. At dawn, it will be here. What do you feel, Eusebius?"

"Let me be!" He had almost taken off my head.

"What do you feel? The pirate's knife on your throat? Is the blade cold? The wheat that the merchant brings us? Is the wood-baked bread tasty? The princess of Thalassopolis who sailed to come and burn only you with her lips. Is her skin warm? Is her tongue wet? Now. Now tell me. What do you feel? Or does the sun blind you so you cannot see?"

What did I feel? *Her tongue.*

"Twenty years later, Eusebius? If I ask you after twenty years, what will you tell me about what you felt just now?"

Da-Ren rowed the boat closer to shore and jumped back into the water. It was only up to his waist. After a while, he saw some movement around the rocks on the seabed and started poking around with his spear. He put his left arm deep into the water as if to grab something. I laughed afterward. A reddish-colored octopus was wrapped around his arm, leaving a trail of dark ink in the water behind it. Da-Ren jumped back, startled by the creature. It was perhaps the only time I saw him frightened by something so funny when the slimy tentacles wouldn't release his arm. The beast was no bigger than the palms of two hands. Its eyes opened wide to meet Da-Ren in the final battle.

"You have to bite it behind the eyes, and then it will die," I told him.

The octopus refused to let go.

He didn't believe me. I shook my head back and forth with mocking eyes and raised brows as if explaining to him that he already had the answer. After some more hesitation, he did bite it, and the slimy thing lost its strength. It would die before I counted to eight.

"Haaaa! Do you believe this?" he shouted, looking at the tentacles and the head of the octopus, which had opened wide for its last dance under the sun.

Fishing was over for the day.

In the one thousand and more days that he remained with me, that was perhaps the only real smile and the only cry of enthusiasm that left his lips.

"You have to beat it forty times against the rock to soften the meat," I told him. "Otherwise, you can't eat it."

"I would never eat that, Eusebius. I am no barbarian."

We both laughed. This time, he believed me. He grabbed the octopus, raised it high above his head, and slammed it down on a rock over and over again. In between each hit, he would stop for a breath and give me an answer, a different one each time.

"I'll tell you what I felt, Eusebius."

The octopus crashed onto the slippery rock.

"I felt satisfaction. I had killed an othertriber with ease.

"Pride. Ten thousand warriors cheered for me.

"Joy. I wouldn't die like the others.

"Fear. The black forest had frozen me dead."

The tentacles slowly started to soften. Cut into square pieces, boiled, and served with olive oil and wild greens. And a cup of watered wine. That was my desire. If only that could be our greatest sin.

"Love. Zeria.

"Compassion. Akrani had helped me very much with the bow that first spring.

"Guilt. I had betrayed my Tribe.

"Is that correct, Eusebius? Have I learned your words? These feelings that you have?"

"These words are the powerful shields of God and Satan in their never-ending battle, Da-Ren. Choose them wisely."

"Sorrow. Lebo rode better than any of us. I did not expect him to fall so young."

That was a very ill-fated octopus indeed.

"I felt merciful. That word I learned much later.

"I felt unstoppable. Uncarved. Immortal. Wolf. Shit. Snake. Cursed. In love. Frightened. Fearless. Brave. Rabbit. All in one day."

"Tell me."

We were getting close to the truth.

"Do you understand?"

I think I did understand.

"There was a storm of confusion in your head."

"You understood shit, Eusebius. Don't ask me again what I felt. No matter what I tell you from now on, don't ask me again. I felt everything in one day, and now that time has melted all of it away, I feel the same things differently."

"You talk like a madman."

"I will tell you what I sensed with the eyes, the hands, and the nose. The blood of the Dasal was red like ours; her eyes, blue. The meat that night was tender and juicy; it rained iron needles, and water seeped into the tent. I felt the rain, the knife, the smooth skin of my horse, Bera's slap. That's what I felt."

I picked up the basket with the few small fish. Da-Ren was still clutching the badly beaten octopus, as if he didn't know what to do with it anymore.

I had to explain to him. For his own salvation.

"For your own good, Da-Ren. God will not understand. We are not animals." I moved away from him as soon as I said the words, afraid that he might hit me. "People have two paths to follow: that of God or that of the Devil. And throughout every moment, they are being judged by God and tempted by Satan. None of our Sorcerers of the Cross, as you call them, will ever sit to hear this story if you do not repent first. If they ask me how you served your penance, what can I tell them?"

An old fisherman with a child tied their boat in the hidden harbor.

Da-Ren answered me before we began climbing the thirty-eight and a thousand steps for yet another time. He turned and looked at the sea. It expanded endless like the steppe, bottomless and untrodden, and diminished every hope of escape.

"I hate this island, Eusebius. I know the games gods play. I know I already died years ago and Enaka abandoned me here. I feel it, since you want to know what I feel now. My slow persecution after death. I feel it deeply. I know."

"Don't lose hope, Da-Ren. Believe in God, and he will redeem and cleanse your soul, leaving it white as snow and carded wool."

It was from one of the psalms of Matins, the ones we sang to raise the soul to the heavens step by step. He softly snorted a short, ironic laugh.

"I hate this dry sun and the salt waves, the northwest *skiron* wind that shaves the black stones and bleaches them, the warm *livas* wind that has razed all the slopes. What do you feel, Eusebius? You tell me."

I had come to this arid island from the mainland many years before along with other refugees in a wave-ravaged boat. I was not even eight years old. There was no tent for the orphans here as in Da-Ren's Sirol. The refugees sent me to the monastery as an inexpensive offering to God so that He would help them on this parched land.

I hadn't lived even for a moment as a common man. I didn't know what I could feel.

"We have died, Eusebius. That is what I feel inside of me every night when you leave me in my cell, away from Sirol. They have brought our bones here. You are the skeleton of my life, and I am its demon. Both orphaned of flesh. You stand there in your cell across from me, motionless, speechless, expressionless, fleshless, white as old bones. You bring me closer to death with every slight move you make."

Indeed, we may well have been dead. Perhaps the punishment of Hell was to believe that we were still alive, could still hope for salvation—and never achieve it. That would be the worst persecution. I had not lived joy, sin, love of the flesh, but neither had I experienced any great sadness since I was eight. Was this the life of a man or of a wingless Cherubim?

"In the Blackvein where I grew up next to the Forest, the land whispered, sang, and bellowed. You could hear the horses, the women, the wolves, the wild boars. The swallows and the robins chirped; the birches, the willows, and the oaks grew leaves, hard like papyrus, brown like leather. The wood awoke, bled, and died. The men, the wolves, the eagles hunted. We drank water, snow, we hid in the fog; I could hear the frogs and the lightning bolts. Here, there is nothing. Only this sun, its blinding light eating the papyrus and my skin, and questions—how did you say it—for madmen."

He was going to break; I could smell it. I had to keep quiet now instead of persisting with my own preaching. I did the opposite.

"You killed an innocent man, Da-Ren."

"I never managed to kill the guilty ones, Eusebius. Never!"

Unlike the two of us, who were still very much alive, the tentacles of the octopus were dead for sure after the beating. Before we began our ascent for the cells, Da-Ren threw the mashed sea creature to the barefoot boy who was helping the fisherman next to us. We were fasting anyway before the summer feast of the Blessed Virgin Mother.

"Never. For that alone, I regret and I repent."

XXV.
The Final Battle

Eighteenth spring. Uncarved—Wolf.

O Goddess, sweet and beautiful,
come listen to your children.
The Sun has hidden from the Sky,
the black star shocks the darkland.
The red-eyed eagle flies blind,
his blood rains on the gold steppe.
The man bewails for his horse,
the woman mourns her offspring.

O Goddess, bright and powerful,
now stay with us this night.
The darkness cries the sorrow's song,
the fear rips our loins.
Bring back Selene's gift to us,
we beg you to reveal her.
And I will bring as sacrifice,
a young heart of my own blood.

The Song of Sah-Ouna at the Feast of Spring

The world was full of signs of the Demon's darkness and the Goddess's light, but only those longskull Witches could read them. We had visited most of the small camps of each Banner by that time. Even the Khun himself had summoned us to his tent, though it was only to shout his fury at us. But when it came to the tents of the Ouna-Mas and the Reghen, we had taken a peek only from far away. Some signs should remain hidden from the common folk.

But there were other signs that everyone knew about. The most horrible of all was the Springdarken, the hiding of Selene by the clouds on the night of her full glorious brightness. And if that occurred on the full moon of the Great Feast of Spring, then sorrow and fear fell like heavy sheets of gray rain across Sirol. The Springdarken had happened only once before as far as Rouba could recall.

"It was during the last spring of Khun-Mervak's reign, our Leader before Khun-Taa. And Enaka sent him to his death soon after that."

The Feast was cut short on the second night when the Sky unleashed waterfalls, crying for my great victory, Zeria's mourning, her father Veker who had escaped death, Lebo's blood, Akrani's death, my terror in the Forest, and Malan's shame. The prisoner he was responsible for had escaped, and Malan had become the laughingstock of the Uncarved in the camp, all in one morning. No one blamed me. I had won my fight, killed the man.

The day of the third and most important night of the Feast, that of the full moon, dawned. It would be the night when the Voice of the Goddess came through Sah-Ouna down to Sirol. The Unending Sky was angry and black as a raven's eye. It didn't shed a single tear of rain. It didn't clear blue for even a breath. Men, women, and Witches stopped every few steps to see if the Sky would open up. But the whole day passed under a Springdarken cloak of clouds.

It was only after the setting of the sun that the Goddess finally triumphed, and her beloved daughter Selene came out upon her chariot in all her brilliance, fighting Darhul's cloudbreaths. As she was riding glorious in the Sky, the clouds changed to white and then to black again and finally became a copper mist until they ran away frightened.

It would be a Great Feast again, and everyone walked lighthearted once more. Everyone except me. I would have preferred a Springdarken like the one long ago, the omen that had brought the death of the Khun.

Malan had been shamed. Soon, I would be First. If Khun-Taa died. If Enaka willed it. I was so close.

The First Witch had offered our sacrifices on the first day, and the fights in the battle ring of Wolfhowl had finished on the second. The third night was going to be brief. We all waited for one thing: to hear Enaka's commandments.

Sah-Ouna filled her chest, and sixteen Ouna-Mas circled close around her, repeating her words so all could hear. Few things were more beautiful than the voices of the Ouna-Mas.

Listen, men, to the truth Enaka sends us.
Weak is the Sun of this spring!
The firstborn demons of the Forest, the Reekaal, have achieved great power.
Their souls have entered and now command the will of every tree. They have possessed the bodies of the Dasal and have covered the Forest with blood and terror, where Selene cannot see. Stay away from there. Stay away from the West. This spring is green and black and does not favor battle against the Reekaal.

The heads turned and twenty thousand warrior eyes fell upon the four of us Uncarved Wolves.

"They are looking at you, kid," said Rouba.

"Me?"

"You killed a Dasal just last night."

"Gunna and Balam killed one too."

"Nobody remembers that. Not bloody enough."

And the Dasal was possessed by a Reekaal she said.

"You are a hero now." Half of the old man's face was smiling.

The hairs on my arms had become iron needles, my balls heavy as battle hammers. "Da-Ren, the one who killed a Reekaal," that would be the Story around the fires.

Chaka needed no ceremony. Sah-Ouna was still singing when he unwrapped the red cloth from Malan's right arm and tied it on mine. And there it was. I had reached the fifth spring of training without bleeding to death, and I was the First in the Uncarved. Five winters after the Sieve, I had finally beaten Malan. If Khun-Taa died within the next thirteen moons, before the next Great Feast of Spring, I would become the Khun of the entire Tribe.

Khun-Da-Ren. Somehow it didn't sound right.

I turned to Rouba and asked him, pointing to the mounds with the countless warriors all around me.

"How can one command so many men? Will they obey?"

"If you believe it, you can."

"How do I believe it, Rouba?"

About two hundred feet away from us, Sah-Ouna sang to Selene, "O Goddess, sweet and beautiful, come listen to your children…" before she would announce another Truth of the Goddess.

"How do you believe?" he repeated my words and paused for a while. "Look at him there to the right." He pointed to the ugliest and shortest man with a mauled nose disfiguring his face and two dull eyes in the center of it. "Do you believe that he is the One Leader? Is he better than you?"

"Him? No."

"The one next to him? Is he better than you?"

This one looked like a strong warrior but only that. He was holding his meat with one hand, munching like a rabid dog and scratching his ass with the other. He was no Leader.

"No."

"Look at all of those around you one by one. When you recognize one as your Leader, kneel before him and accept him. Swear to die at his command. If you do not find one better than you, go to the crystal waters of the river and look at your own face. Now, be silent. Sah-Ouna will speak."

Sah-Ouna had finished her invocations to Selene, and she turned to face in our direction. I thought she was looking directly at me as she opened her mouth.

Now listen, all warriors of the Tribe.

Enaka commands this: These moons bring dark omens, but the seasons will change again. The Final Battle is coming for all the powers of the Unending Sky, the Earth, and the Darkness. Enaka will stand by our side; she will redeem the victors and accept them up there next to her. Fire and rain, our arrows, will annihilate the othertribers who have lost their souls to the demons.

The battle will be in the West, but not now. The next Khun is the one who will first pass through the Endless Forest.

So Enaka decrees.

"I am," I answered to Rouba, my eyes wide open, a smile at my lips.

"The One," he completed.

How wrong we both were.

Sah-Ouna's words ended any dream of campaigning toward the West anytime soon. Definitely not that summer. Our ninestar Guide, Bera, who listened sitting down in the last rows of the mound, yelled the loudest, as if he wanted to start a rally: "The Witch defies the Leader."

For some reason, Witches and ninestars had a dislike of each other.

"Shut up! She frees him. Khun-Taa is too old now to conquer the West," answered Chaka behind me.

"*I seek only One.*" I heard the words in my head again.

Under the bright light of Selene the Great Feast of Spring ended, and we started to make our way back to our camp. As I was moving through the thousands of drunken roaring men, I saw Noki, my old comrade. I embraced him tightly.

"Ha, Da-Ren! My friend."

"Noki, how—"

He had no time to waste with me in my night of glory.

"I am going to get myself a slave girl for tonight," he said, his face glowing, drunk and happy, never slowing his stride. He didn't even notice the ribbon of the First around my arm. "That's what the Great Feasts are for," he said as he disappeared.

Noki went where the Uncarved had yet to go, and I returned to the fire of our hut that was now warmer than ever. Only four young Wolves were left to share it. Four springs earlier, we were thirteen Starlings.

We sat in silence around the fire. We had gone through some hard days and even harder nights together, especially the past three. But still, we had no friends around this fire to give one another courage.

Balam had a stupid smile on his face because he didn't know what awaited him. Gunna roared with the deep laughter of certainty because he was half-drunk and still so sure that he would be the next Khun. Or was it the other way around with those two?

I wore a silent grin because I had the red ribbon around my arm, and I knew I was the best.

We fell asleep with those smiles on our faces.

As if we were still children in the Sieve, the Reghen and the Ouna-Ma woke us in the middle of the night for a Story. Their Story. And ours.

The Legend of the Reghen
The Fifth Season of the World: Part Four

Tiny red stars dotted the body of the First Ouna-Ma the Blind. Her bowels grew rock hard and wouldn't turn. Enaka wanted her close in the Unending Sky, to shine, to become the largest star next to Selene. Her time had come. After a while, the sorrow of her death consumed Khun-Nan, the first Leader. His last child had left. He had disunited all the families of the Tribe, and everyone had forgotten their wives. He had no male heirs, and even if he did, he had never learned of them.

"Who will be our next Khun?" the warriors asked over his dying body.

"Call the Reghen," he said.

The three Reghen selfsame brothers, the ones who had killed the Ice Drakon of the North and the most famous warriors of the Tribe, heeded the call. The Third had died but was always with his brothers on their robes, marked with a red circle.

When they arrived, Khun-Nan said to them, "You will become Leaders of the Tribe now that I go to the morning star next to my daughter."

The Reghen remained silent, their faces frowning until the Second spoke. "Honored Khun, the Ouna-Ma, your daughter, the Daughter of Enaka, gave us the last Truth before she ascended."

The Second continued, repeating her words:

"Listen to me, Reghen. Do not become Khuns. You are elders, wise men, but your days are numbered. The One Leader must have the gift of youth, be brave and strong; make the earth tremble beneath his feet. His blood must be fresh and crimson, untarnished from fear, envy, and defeat, and only that blood must flow in his veins. He must be free of failure, without even the slightest scratch from battle on his body.

"You, Reghen, must find this new Khun and counsel him. That is what Enaka commands of you. Throw down your weapons forever. You killed the Crystaleyed Drakon; your brother sacrificed himself. You owe no more

arrows or blood to the Tribe. Wear the robes of wisdom, and paint the circle of red upon them so that they all remember your sacrifice."

And so the Reghen explained to Khun-Nan why they could not be Leaders.

And Khun-Nan turned to the rest and said, "These three wise Reghen will bring the Truths of my beloved Ouna-Ma and will tell you how to choose a Khun, but none of them can ever become one."

Khun-Nan closed his eyes. Six sorrowful eyes wept for him, four loving hands covered him.

"There will be a slaughter. The inept and the envious always believe that they are better than the true Leaders," said the First.

"Khun-Nan did not leave an heir, but Ouna-Ma left a Truth," said the Second.

"The One Leader must remain standing through an arduous trial, unscathed and Uncarved!" roared the Third from stars on high.

This is how the Sieve came to be. The first Sieve had only youths twenty-winters strong because the Reghen had to choose a new Leader immediately. Khun-Ark was proclaimed the winner.

Bloodshed was avoided.

During his reign, Khun-Ark, the Second Leader of the Tribe, created under counsel of the Reghen, the traditions of the Sieve of the twelve-wintered and the Uncarved. And from that time on, we have followed this path.

The three brothers, the wise Reghen, always served beside the Leader. They chose the new Reghen, who would replace them once they had gone. And they chose new Ouna-Mas, who in turn chose new ones. They let them suckle as babies from the She-Wolves by the river to find the voice of Enaka.

Their previous names were hidden in a talisman around their necks. They wouldn't even use them among themselves, and they agreed to all be called Reghen.

As the Tribe grew, so grew the Reghen.

There are now one hundred of them, and all share one name. They have two hundred eyes and one hundred tongues, but only one Truth, and they watch everyone, everywhere. For the Tribe.

Thus declared the Ouna-Mas, the Voices of the Unending Sky.

Another day, one of bright spring, dawned.

"Don't do anything stupid now," Rouba told me as soon as I pressed the stirrup with my boot that morning.

But I had no idea what could be stupid. Anything could be a hidden trial that would make me second to Malan again.

"You are the next Khun," Rouba said to me. "As long as you believe it."

How wrong he was.

I enjoyed a few days of false triumph, waiting for something to happen immediately, waking up every morning expecting to hear about the death of Khun-Taa. But the only thing changing around me was the blossoming meadows.

And then came the fateful afternoon when the rumor reached my ears as well: "Sah-Ouna has called Malan to her tent."

"What? To tell him what?"

"No one knows. The Rods said she might invite the others also. Maybe even you."

"Shit."

I hadn't done anything wrong. But I was not her chosen one. I stopped speaking to Malan. I hung on the words of the Guides to learn more.

"Fear not. You are the First," Rouba kept telling me.

"It is not that simple," Chaka objected when he heard him.

We had gone out that morning to shoot arrows again, as the bow was still my biggest weakness. The contest was coming up, and I didn't want to lose the red ribbon.

"Sah-Ouna already knows who will be Khun. Has known for a while now. She sees. I made you First, Da-Ren, because you deserve it, but if you do not have her favor…" added Chaka.

Balam, the fourth one, would never be Khun, and that was settled quickly. Only a few days after the Great Feast, he got into a fight over a piece of meat with an Uncarved two winters younger. He lost the fight and three teeth and won three carvings. Gunna had fallen down, coiling in laughter when the young Uncarved Mauler had started kicking Balam in the ass again and again.

"The little guy is possessed by a Reekaal spirit. That's why he kicks you around like a puppy," Gunna said as he bade Balam farewell. Balam left with only his shame and his bow. There were three of us left now. Or, really, only two, since Gunna was not born to be Khun and command the destiny of thousands. He was a kid in the head, the biggest kid I had ever met. As in the Sieve, it was down to Malan and me to fight it out.

Rouba was always looking out for me, now more than ever, and he gave me a chance and the challenge to change my fate.

"You carry a heavy burden, young man. The Ouna-Mas fear your ninestar mark. You have to come closer to them if you want to become Khun."

"How?"

"I mean to really come close to them. I don't speak in riddles like the Reghen. Do something they need done."

"Like what?"

"Paran. The youth who was carved three times last spring. Do you remember? He would come with me to the Forest and gather herbs from the Dasal to take to the Witches. He is now a Rod, guard at the tent of Khun-Taa. And he sleeps with two or three Ouna-Mas every night.

Come with me, Da-Ren. Tomorrow I will go to the Forest."

"But we can't go to the Dasal. Sah-Ouna forbids it."

"That shit is for the men, not for the Leaders. The Witches need belladonna and crazygrass. I never told you this, but they send me to the Forest almost once every moon. I am one of the few who speak to the Dasal."

That night, I dreamed of two blue eyes looking at me, sparkling through green oaks.

The next Leader would be the first man to pass through the Forest, the prophecy had said. Rouba was the best possible company for me. He would help me beat Malan. To beat Sah-Ouna. To beat the Forest that had swallowed me alive the last time.

Rouba and I started out for the Forest in the middle of the day after our morning trials. The dark embrace that had encircled me that rainy night was no more. It was now another world—alive, enchanted, and magical. The sun's arrows were streaming through the leaves and painting everything green and fire white. It was swallowing me alive again. But this time, it was my choice.

"Asphodels," Rouba said to me. The white flower of death had bloomed early in the Forest of souls.

"Snake! Don't be afraid. A mice eater! Look at his skin; it has four colors like different arrows next to each other," he called out to me when I screamed as if Darhul's offspring were slithering at my feet.

"Hellebore, the evergreen flower. Pick that one. The Ouna-Mas need them."

The gnarled branches of the eternal oaks had reached back to the dirt and sprouted their own roots. Even those gloomy-looking winter skeletons were now green and had become hospitable tents. Their leaves filtered the sun, making its light soft and its heat bearable, not fierce and scorching as it was in the valley. I hadn't seen any Reekaal or wolves, although we did find some wolf prints.

"Aren't you afraid of the Reekaal, Rouba?"

"Reekaal? Never seen them. But to be safe, I come only during the day to meet the Dasal. At night, this Forest sleeps and its other half awakens."

On our first visits, we never made it to a Dasal settlement. One of them had come south to meet us with a small sack of herbs and roots, taking in exchange a bigger sack of barley. He appeared and disappeared among the shadows of the trees. His clothes were rags that had been dragged through the leaves, his colors were a tree in bloom, and he smelled of wood. His forehead was cracked bark, and his stare was a sharpened ax. He didn't have blue eyes. Not for an instant did he seem to me possessed, although he did stick his neck out to look around like a hunted animal.

"If you ask them, they will tell you that *we* are the bloodeaters, the Reekaal," Rouba said.

I went with Rouba into the Forest almost every seventh day. I went so that I could become Khun. I would then go to the Ouna-Mas' camp with my sack on my back, which I never opened. There were herbs in there whose scent alone could kill me, Rouba had said, maybe just to scare me. I had never been allowed to the camp, though, and had never seen Sah-Ouna. The Reghen and the young, silent Ouna-Mas would take the herbs at their camp's entrance.

All I could do was listen carefully to their Stories. The day of my destiny was near. If I did not become Leader before next spring, I would forever lose my chance. Rumors traveled like the plague from fire to fire in the nights and reached everyone fast. Khun-Taa, the Fifth Leader of the Tribe, was ill and coughing blood.

"The End is near," Sah-Ouna had said at the Feast. It was certain and unavoidable, and only fools and the faithless couldn't see it. Whoever was unprepared would perish. The camp of the Uncarved was boiling.

I worried more with each passing day, as I still had no sign from Sah-

Ouna. But I still had the red ribbon of the First around my arm. Gunna and Malan weren't the kinds of friends to help me. I had only old Rouba.

"We are whatever the others remember from our last Story, Da-Ren. If it is one of wonder, no one remembers the one before," Rouba told me.

Everyone knew the Story of when my mother bore me. I had to find the Story of my father—to make one up, just as every man did when he became a warrior. A memorable Legend about my mythical father. Khun-Taa's father had reached the Black Sea and had shot one arrow for each of Darhul's eighteen eyes, the Legend said. When my name was mentioned around the evening fires, there had to be a Legend to go with it. And not the one about the triangle on my neck.

I had proved that I was the bravest during the Wolfhowl. I was the best with the blade, and that was something everyone knew. It was the third moon of spring, and we had bow competitions. I wasn't good at that. Danaka with the female Archers and Matsa, long-forgotten names of the Sieve, were there.

We competed into a huge field, a thousand feet away, in circles. On the second round, we galloped to the center of the field and had to shoot as many arrows as possible at water pumpkins that were placed on stakes. There were twenty in a row, exactly in the center of the field, painted black on one side, so they looked like real heads with hair. Half of them faced one side, and half the opposite side, all mixed up.

We had to hit them on the front side and only that one, every time. Some we aimed at while galloping as our horses approached the target, and for others, we had to shoot backward after we passed the target on horseback. Whoever was second with the horse ran the danger of not finding a target to hit or even being hit by the arrows of the first.

My feet were on the stirrups and my hands free to aim and shoot holding only the bow and the arrows between my fingers, five by five. I hit eleven to fourteen each time. No one hit more than I did. In the last round, only I, Gunna, and one Archer boy remained. I hit nine, the Archer six, and Gunna only five out of twenty. I beat not only the other Uncarved but also the best of the trained Archers as well.

What else did I have to do to prove that I was the next Khun? My two fists rising high, one holding the bow, the other the red ribbon for all to see. Malan was dishonored after the fight with the Dasal that never happened, and Khun-Taa was half-dead. But I was still fighting, not with water pumpkins, but with curses, prophecies, and invisible ghosts.

"It is unfair," I said to Chaka when the bow trial was over. "What does it matter what night I was born?"

I was dripping with sweat, and so was my horse. I could hardly stand on my legs when I dismounted to drink some water.

"We go now! Mount another horse and follow me," he said.

"Right now? I rode all day."

"If you care about being Khun, you follow me now," he said.

I jumped on a fresh mare and we galloped the horses until we reached a bare hill that was the northeastern border of Sirol. It was close to the Craftsmen tents and the catapult firing ranges, a corner I had rarely visited. We climbed the hill as the sun was cutting Sirol's ponds in half with a blade of fire. Smaller fires outside the tents looked like tiny sparkles on the earth, reflecting the stars in the sky. More than ten thousand tents once I learned how to count. The Tribe was cooking, singing, dying, and fucking beneath our feet.

"Do you want to rule over all of them, Da-Ren? Or just beat Malan?"

"What's the difference?"

"There is a huge difference!"

"Yes, I want to rule over all of them."

"Yes?"

"Yes, Chaka."

"And do what, my Khun? Where will you lead us? Do you know

what's out there?"

My stare followed his hand as it made a full circle over the purple darkness beyond the river to the south, the black darkness in the east, the hazy nothing to the north, the bronze sunset over the Forest.

"Everyone is coming at us, Da-Ren."

"Who?"

"Everyone. And from everywhere. The Final Battle. Sah-Ouna said so."

"You believe that?" I asked.

My horse snorted in fear as if it had smelled a jackal.

"Can't you see? This world is ending. When I was young like you, everything was so much simpler. We did not have siege machines or all-powerful enemies. We had weaker bows. You wouldn't even hit five water pumpkins with them today. Now we want gold to trade with; we need to find craftsmen from other tribes to build the machines, to trade wheat, barley, and flax for clothes from the South. Everything has become gold, machines, craftsmen. This is another world. There is no bravery anymore. Three thousand arrows leave our bows and annihilate everyone within a four-hundred-foot distance. Only machines. The world runs like a mad bull to fall off the cliff."

I had heard about gold but didn't know what it was good for.

"That was always the Story of our Tribe," I said.

"No, there is not enough for all of us anymore. We are going to eat each other alive. Our enemies are descending, the Trackers have seen them," he mumbled to himself.

"We will find meat and horse on the way to the West."

"We will find shit and death! Who will lead all of them to the West? Who can cross the Forest? You? Are you the One of Enaka who will ride First among all in the Final Battle? Or just a common mortal? Just like the rest of us? Or…or a cursed ninestar?"

My eyes had filled with tears in the night—from rage if it had to be from something.

"You gave me the red ribbon of the First Uncarved, Chaka." It was the only thing I said with the voice of a little child.

"And I would give it to you again. Because I have known you for five winters. But those down there? Most of them—"

"What?"

"If they see the mark of the ninestar before the battle, they will run scared like panicked sheep. They have feather and grass for brains. They are stupid. Do you understand?"

"Yes," I said with my head down.

"No, you don't. That is the one curse of the Uncarved. You grew up only with the best for five springs since the Sieve, and you don't know. The ones down there are in pain. They are hungry. They don't have many nights. You will not have five winters to win them over. They will see your mark, and they will know."

"It's not like that."

"It's exactly like that! That is why we have marks, banners, sevenstars and ninestars and longskull Witches—so the many and desperate don't lose time thinking."

"What can I do?"

"Nothing. You can't. I seek only One. Not the best or the bravest. I seek the one they'll fear. The one they will believe in," he said as he pointed down the hill.

My mare lifted her head; she had smelled something. The moonlight shimmered on the silver-gray back of a jackal crouching ten paces away. Two small shiny white holes, his eyes, were watching us.

How right he was.

XXVI.
The Calling

Eighteenth summer. Uncarved—Wolf.

It was the calling of summer. The hot easterly wind blew softly and blended with the chamomile and the fragrant yellow-white mums. The mosquitoes fell on us like a raging storm and Sirol filled with bloated corpses that rotted faster than we could burn them. They gave off a sickly-sweet scent from their blackened, rotten livers. In the summertime, I always confused those two scents, of chamomile and corpses, as they became one very fast.

That was when her calling came as well.

"Sah-Ouna summons you in her tent," the Reghen told me on the first day of the third moon of summer. The moment I had been waiting for had come, my only chance to make amends for being born on a cursed day. I wore only a white linen tunic above my trousers. I went to strap my blades and quiver around me, but Chaka didn't let me.

"You don't go to the First with iron."

Alone, naked of weapons, I rode to meet my destiny.

"Cover your face with this veil," Rouba advised me.

It was a rare gossamer cloth, made by the othertribers of the south or the east, but certainly not from anyone in Sirol. Suitable for women. And for mosquitoes. I took it.

I followed the central path of Sirol, that of the packhorses and the supply carts. I crossed half the camp, arriving at the tents of Khun-Taa, and in the distance, I saw and passed the Reghen's tents. Khun-Taa's guards, the Rods, stopped me soon after that, at the entrance of the settlement of the Ouna-Mas, close to the Blackvein.

"Get off your horse, Uncarved," said one of them.

I was nameless to them. I just had a title that tomorrow could mean everything, or nothing.

Square tents—some with black and others with red painted stripes—were in front of me. The settlement of the Ouna-Mas did not have the traffic and noise of the rest of Sirol. It was a camp of shadows, fire, and smoke, of skinny cats and eagle owls that mostly stayed asleep until dusk. In the middle of the day it looked deserted.

Few Redveils walked around the tents; none of them alone. Their dresses were long but airy with a tied cord defining their slender waist. Below the waist the fabric was slit many times vertically, and the dress was reduced to black dancing snake ribbons. The skin of their legs was visible in their summer step. Their sleeves were short, above the elbow, to show the painted red designs on their arms. This was their summer garb that made the blood rise hot in a warrior's head. Unlike the Reghen, the Ouna-Mas were unique in ways that were unknown to us. One had to look up close at the henna designs and to the different shapes of the half-shaved heads to see that they were all different from each other.

The Rods led me outside of a tent that was twice as big as the others, with wolfskins hanging from tall poles to the left and right of its entrance. That was all I had a chance to see. Their Chief tied a cloth around my eyes.

"Sah-Ouna is not ready for you. You will wait here," he said.

"Yes."

"Listen to me. Do not take that cloth off. Whatever happens, whatever you hear."

I didn't answer. He pushed me to my knees. The dark cloth was tied tightly behind my head, and light turned to utter darkness. My arms just hung down, my hands empty.

"Sah-Ouna will come at dusk. But if you take off the cloth, even for one breath, I will throw you out of here, and you'll never see her," the Rod said.

I didn't hear his voice again. Silence fell for a few moments until I heard growling next to me and then that familiar and panting sound from the Sieve. My hands were not tied, so I could raise them to feel around. But I didn't. The mauler licked my arm, and the hairs on the back of my neck stood up, frozen in the heavy heat. His piss, burning hot, flooded the dirt in front of my knees. Its smell brought back to my mind Greentooth, and the pails that she used to load me with. I held my breath and waited for him to stop. He left as he came, but I could still hear him. I didn't open my eyes. The blindfold was drinking the sweat of my brow, the heat was scorching my skin, and the smell was deep in my nostrils.

It was much later that I heard the voices of the Ouna-Mas, rising crystalline and lustful in front of me. I couldn't see their faces. I had heard this song many times. It was the easiest, the simplest, and the strangest at the same time. It spoke of brothers and dreams. They hit some long wooden tubes that made a rippling sound, the kettle drums came in strong, and the cymbals broke the rhythm from time to time. In the beginning, the Ouna-Mas were silent, and only the sounds could be heard. Then the words started coming out.

One word for Selene.

One for the wolf.

One for the horse.

For the Ouna-Ma.

One for the Sun.

One for the bow.

Their voices stretched each word for a long time, and with eyes closed I envisioned the Witches dancing, each word of theirs becoming a serpentine ribbon from their dresses and wrapping around me. In the middle of the song, their voices became a plea, a prayer, and then they started again from the beginning. I could feel them closer every time. Their words were now licking me everywhere.

An Ouna-Ma came so close that I could smell her skin. I didn't see her, but her whisper burned next to my head. Her mouth was right there, and her lips brushed against my ear.

"Da-Ren. Crystal-cold water," she said, putting a cup to my mouth. I was melting like a candle in the fire. I drank it as a newborn life.

I had come to their camp in midmorning to see Sah-Ouna. I remembered that, but I didn't know why anymore. To ask for what? What would my first words be?

Their song began yet again, the prayer more melodious than before.

Another Ouna-Ma approached. Her voice was different. Burning hotter than the first.

"Da-Ren. Ninestar fire," she whispered.

I felt her breath traveling over my neck, and it sent shudders down my spine as she put her tongue in my ear. I tried to raise my hands to touch her, to feel her, but she had already left. Another hand, a woman's, cool to the touch, grabbed mine above the wrist. "Don't, Da-Ren! Don't open your eyes; obey Sah-Ouna." A second hand touched me. And a third. They didn't hurt me or pull me; they just gently caressed my skin. Countless hands were all over my body. It was late afternoon by now—I could feel it in the sun that didn't burn anymore. But still, I trembled as if a freezing wind had embraced me. As unexpectedly as they had come, the hands disappeared. I wanted to find them again, but I didn't open my eyes.

"Close your eyes. Or else you will lose them forever."

I heard a low and deep voice behind me, and I guessed it was Sah-

Ouna. Her words were warm, not threatening. I kept my eyes closed
against my will. The words of the Witches' song began again
rhythmically, now far from me. Two strong men's hands raised me and
dragged me until we entered through hides in a space where the heat
was even stronger.

"Now you can open your eyes," said the Rod.

My eyes stung from tears of weariness and the smoking fire. I was in
her tent. Weak torch flames lit the space, and Sah-Ouna sat across from
me, sitting on her knees on a hide. Deep inside the tent I saw two huge
hooded creatures. They were dressed like Ouna-Mas, but they were tall
and broad-shouldered, bigger than I even. They stood completely
motionless; I didn't know if I was looking at carved, painted statues or
monstrous Witches. Their arms were crossed, and I couldn't see their
faces under the hoods. As the light danced on their bodies I thought I
saw blue ornaments on their strong forearms but I didn't trust my eyes.

"Why are you here, Da-Ren?" asked the Witch.

"What are they?" I pointed at the creatures.

"A dream. A nightmare. Are you afraid? Why are you here, Da-Ren?"

Why should she have the most beautiful voice? She didn't look like
an old woman to me anymore. When I was a twelve-wintered I
remembered her as a vile, scrawny bitch. But now I saw a figure slender
as a fallow deer, and her eyes shone with the black fire of the forest
animal. Her skin was unwrinkled, and though I remembered it pale, it
was now dark. I was starving. She did not have the long head of the
Ouna-Mas. Neither veil nor hair bun could hide that. I wanted to touch
her, to feel the power emanating from the Goddess herself. For a
moment, I thought the hooded creatures moved under the half-light and
were looking at me.

I hadn't answered her.

"Why are you here?" she asked me again.

"You called for me," I told her.

"Did you open your eyes out there?"

"No."

"Everyone does. When they touch."

"I speak the truth; I didn't open them."

She nailed me with her stare, trying to suck out the lie from inside me. But she couldn't find it.

"You speak the truth," she said.

I hadn't opened them, not even for one breath.

"I want to become—" I went to say.

"You know what you want to become?"

"Yes."

"But you don't know what you are. Why didn't you open your eyes? Maybe a demon's daughter stole them from you, Da-Ren?"

"No."

"In the Forest. Blue?"

How could she know? Even I had forgotten the blue eyes for a day. This camp of shadows, the tongues of the Ouna-Mas touching and singing to me had erased them.

"No."

"You didn't open your eyes. But you did see the blue. Your mother, Da-Ren."

How did she know? She caressed my arm, moving from the elbow upward while thrusting the words inside of me like a knife. What did the demon want inside my head?

"I was raised an orphan."

"Yes, yes, you were sent to the Greentooth as a baby, your mother screaming and cursing when they took you from her. I remember as if it were only yesterday when they first brought her from up north."

I didn't care about my mother.

"She bore you a ninestar. On purpose. It was what she wanted."

"I am not—"

"You are. Her blood. Her darkness. Her curse on us. Even the Goddess can't see inside of you. I do."

"I am First of the Uncarved," I said.

She did not answer to that. She filled two cups with steaming black water.

"A great trial awaits you, Da-Ren. If you pass it, the Goddess will accept you."

"I am not afraid."

"You have to learn fear, desire, and terror. You did not open your eyes. You endured in the darkness. No one is that strong unless he is a son of the darkness."

I had to find the words, the pleas, the wishes. This was my one chance. Sah-Ouna extended her arms to give me the cup. Her arms so close to my chest. A memory, an image of the past. *Elbia.* Elbia, the sacrifice of the Sieve returned to my mind.

"Drink now, but once you are back outside, you must not open your eyes. Promise the Goddess."

"I promise."

Someone was walking to my left in the darkness of the tent. I couldn't see. Sah-Ouna offered me the cup to drink again. I smelled the crazygrass. I didn't want to swallow the black water that steals the mind. I kept it in my mouth. Sah-Ouna, smiling calmly, pressed her fingers on my cheek as she had done on the first day of the Sieve. I kissed her hand spontaneously with desire.

Darkness consumed me and I was embracing it silently.

"Spit it out my love," I heard two lips whispering behind Sah-Ouna. It was there behind the Witch, Elbia's ghost-white face. Her empty eyes were no longer brown; her mulberry lips, no longer the color of rose petals.

Sah-Ouna turned to look back and then turned to me again.

"How? You see her, Da-Ren?" As if she could see Elbia too. She blew the dust toward the girl with a hissing sound. Elbia's ghost vanished. "Do you see in the darkness of the caves, Da-Ren? So many surprises you bring, young one! You desire her? Now you can have her," she told me. "Just close your eyes," were Sah-Ouna's last words to me.

I had swallowed the black water. I was lost.

She was beautiful and young, like an untouched Ouna-Ma before her virgin veiling.

I closed my eyes. I dreamed of her naked.

She took on the face and body of a grown-up Elbia.

The breasts of the Witch, small and upright, chirped dark songs.

Maybe she was naked. The crazygrass.

Even now I don't want to admit it.

I felt her hands gently embracing me, fire burning inside. Elbia's body. My eyes shut, my body riding a dark horse.

I awoke from a heavy slumber. Only a few embers around me; neither Sah-Ouna nor the hooded creatures were there. Those were not statues. I remembered Gunna describing the monstrous Reekaal who had attacked him one night in the Forest.

The Rods came in, blindfolded me again and took me outside of the tent where they left me alone. I heard the song of the Ouna-Mas from a distance. "Don't open your eyes. The Goddess is watching," Sah-Ouna had commanded me.

"Everyone opens their eyes," she had said.

Was it fear or desire? Shame or unsatisfied lust? Had she defeated me? I could still defy her. I raised my hand, tore off the cloth, and threw it away.

I wanted to see. Twenty paces from me a group of Redveils had gathered around a tall fire. One of the hooded shadows stood much taller than the rest next to the angry flames, while the serpents of their dresses were moving around it. The tall shadow removed its hood, and I looked at it, him, whatever it was, for the first time. In the distance, I saw a longskull, I saw a man, I saw a seven-foot tall monster, his enormous arms opening wide under his robe like wings, fingers like talons emerging, eyes glowing in the reflection of the fire. Potent crazygrass that was. It had made the Witch beautiful and conjured Elbia and the Reekaal. My body was freezing as the day's sweat met with the first chill of the night. The Ouna-Mas stopped their song and turned to face me with eyes like smoldering coals. The huge monster was burning silent, his body and arms painted blue like the heart of the fire. *The Cyanus Reekaal* of the Legends.

The one of color. I had to get out of there.

"Run away, Da-Ren. Run, now," whispered the white-eyed ghost girl again.

I ran without looking back, found my horse still there at the gate of the settlement, and disappeared into the night.

Enaka was the only one still watching me from above. Her First Witch had made me promise to keep my eyes closed. I had betrayed her yet again. Sah-Ouna, Elbia, the Ouna-Mas, Enaka, the Greentooth, even my own mother. This one and only night, all the Witches of my life—alive, dead, and eternal—had called me to them and fought for the right to nest in my heart forever. They were all defeated. The night didn't scare me. It came, licked me, and passed over me like a summer breeze.

And the day dawned blue.

XXVII.
The Legend of Er-Ren

Eighteenth summer. Uncarved—Wolf.

Rouba and Chaka were waiting up for me when I returned to the Uncarved in the middle of the night. A Reghen was with them.

"It is the command of Sah-Ouna that you leave for the campaign to the North. The Archers will go after the Garol, who have risen up," the Reghen told me. "We have to see if you are worthy and ready to lead the Tribe," said the Reghen.

The trap is always baited with a great promise.

"Did you see her? What did she say?" asked Chaka.

"Who?"

"Sah-Ouna, Da-Ren. Who else? Where there any others to see?"

"Yes. No. She told me that a great trial awaits me. If I pass it, she will…accept me." I struggled to remember her words.

Chaka and Rouba exchanged glances as if all of this meant something.

"That's it," said Chaka. "Your final trial. The Reghen's words make sense now. You leave at dawn."

"This is a great honor," Rouba told me. "No Uncarved has ever gone on a campaign before finishing his training. You will be riding among the warriors."

"You will go with him too, Rouba." Chaka nodded. "He will need a Guide."

Rouba stuck his blade into the ground to support himself and knelt. "I never dreamed of being in a battle again," he said. He turned toward me. "And you, you Da-Ren..." He had no more words; he was shaking. An old man's love and admiration are hard to conceal.

We shut our eyes, though not for long, and woke up before dawn to pack our weapons and ready the horses. There were few of us, just ten Packs. It wouldn't be a long campaign, but not a one-day raid either. Rouba told me it would be a full moon at least before we were back. The horse that Chaka had given me was strongly built, and I rode taller and braver with each step it took. We moved north, alongside the Forest but never inside it. Almost four hundred warriors in all. The Garol peasants in the north had revolted and slaughtered the guards we had left there. We were to bring the vengeance of Enaka.

"It is a long ride to the Garol settlements, but it will be a quick battle," said the man who was leading us.

"Is that Druug, the Leader of all the thousands of Archers?" I asked Rouba.

"Yes. Is he better than you?"

"His son wasn't, for sure. We were in the same hut, Uncarved Starlings, long time ago. He died an Owl the second spring."

Only one of my arrows had found Redin, the first Uncarved to fall. Above the navel. Any other memory of Redin was fading away.

"Better not remind him of that," Rouba said.

Rouba kept me next to Druug, so I could learn from him. He told Druug that I was there because Sah-Ouna had demanded it. But everyone knew already who I was. The First among the Uncarved. The Goddess had marked me as the next Khun, their future Leader. If only I managed to complete the final trial unscathed.

After a half-moon's ride, we made it to the largest of the villages, the only one that was barely fortified, before nightfall. I had thought the breeze would be stronger up north, yet that was one of the hottest evenings of my life. I was dripping with sweat, and my mind started to stray from the heat on the saddle all day, from lack of sleep, and from being stuck to the animal. Druug sent out a Tracker, and he returned a little before sunset. He had seen from up close the Garol and he was certain that they had seen us also.

"They're waiting for us, barricaded. I count more than six hundred," the Tracker reported.

I turned to Rouba and said, "The Garol outnumber us. And he says they are well protected behind the sacks and the carts."

"They are farmers."

Druug looked at me as if I were a small rat at his feet.

"Why are we riding slowly for so long, boy?"

"The oxen, the carts," I mumbled.

"Yes, the carts what? Do you know how many arrows those carts carry? More than two thousand shafts for each one of the Archers. If I shoot a thousand times, don't you think I'd find a neck or an eye? How did you count them as more?"

He was right. They were very few.

"They don't know how to fight on horseback. They can't ride and shoot a bow at the same time. They don't have our bows. They will be dead before the sun reaches mid-sky. Most of their fathers died in the previous uprising. I was at that battle too," Rouba said.

"Then, why do they?"

"Who knows? Maybe we took all the wheat, and they can't get through the winter. They choose to die this way, fast."

"When do we charge?" I asked Rouba.

He gave me a serious look.

"You and me? Never! We will sleep until dawn is upon us. Then the nine Archer Packs will attack, and when it is over, the last Pack of the

Blades will move in to clean up whatever is left."

"What am I going to do?"

"You will watch. Next to me. We will fill quivers with arrows so that they're ready when the Archers return to refill."

"That's all?"

"What do you mean, 'That's all'? If we don't do that, the othertribers will be skinning you alive slowly by nightfall. Your pelt will make a fitting saddle for your horse. All this shit is important. Go and fill the resin and oil pails for the arrows, if you want more work."

"But you longed to go to battle, Rouba."

"Only to smell it. I can't ride like the threecarved anymore."

At dawn, the Garol saw two whirlwinds rising to the left and the right of the red sun. The Archers got close to the barricades but never too close. They shot their flaming arrows, the rain of death, and then returned to us to refill. In the heat of the day, one spark would be enough to turn the Garol's shacks into ashes.

This went on for quite a while, and the othertribers began to thin out slowly as some of the thousands of arrows found their targets. The dense smoke started rising from the burning carts and huts. They were waiting there, shooting arrows that wouldn't reach or hit our riders, throwing spears not far enough.

I stayed at the back with the supplies. A dozen carts full of countless arrows—shafts made of reed and spruce wood, with iron heads. It took two of the strongest oxen to pull each cart. Each Archer emptied two full quivers onto every charge and then rode back and took two full ones. We had to be ahead of them. They didn't stop coming until they'd shot hundreds of quivers.

The Blades rushed in last, when the sun had risen mid-sky. That was when I started to hear the cries from the slaughter through the black smoke. I couldn't resist.

"I have to go there, Rouba. Sah-Ouna sent me. It's my trial," I said.

"Let's go, but be careful. Hold the blade in your right hand," Rouba told me.

We moved in on horseback so that we, too, could see the battle from up close among the Garol's burning huts.

I remember the screams more, the scenes less. It was now time for the Blades to tear the heads of men from their bodies and babies from the arms of their mothers. Two of them threw down a girl, and their Chief mounted her from behind.

"Worse than the maulers, those Blades," Rouba said to me. "They hurry now because they always get the worst share of the spoils after the Archers."

Rouba had been one of the Archers before they had sent him to rot as a Guide. He had never liked the Blades.

I watched from a distance without getting involved. This was no battle. Hunting wild boars was more dangerous. Some othertribers begged for mercy, and a few fought to the very end. There were no enemies left standing to defend myself from, just women running and screaming, and children watching frozen and silent. Was that my trial? Blades, maulers. Become one of them?

We rode farther into the settlement, where the heat of the battle was still on. An old, husky man had been pierced in the arm by a burning arrow. He lunged toward two Blades with a pickax. On foot, he hacked the first, and with his arm burning, he jumped onto the second rider and threw him off his horse. As the flames started covering both, the old man shouted to a Garol boy that was standing there frozen in fear. The boy climbed on the Blade's horse and galloped away.

"I can't believe it!" I shouted.

The old Garol fell when the flames spread to his head. I could swear that for a few moments, there on his knees with his head in flames, he cursed us with all the strength of his soul.

"Not all Garol are chickens. He was brave," I said to Rouba.

"They were all brave to be waiting for us here, Da-Ren. So? His son will crawl like a slave or get slaughtered like a pig," he said, showing me the screaming boy. The Blades had already caught him and were dragging him with their neckropes.

Weary from the day's battle, the warriors ate and drank whatever they could find. Not much.

"Eat something, kid."

"I am not a kid," I said to Rouba who offered me a piece of stale bread he'd found in one of the huts.

There was a brown-haired kid a few paces ahead, face down, resting on a blood puddle. I was not a kid anymore.

"You did good!" said Druug.

"Those quivers were always full," added an Archer next to him; two carvings on his left arm.

"We need to prepare a pyre. We lost eight. All of them Blades," said the Tracker who came to report to Druug.

"No surprise there," said Druug.

I was eating next to him. As the Archers walked by they stopped and stared. It didn't take me long to understand that they weren't staring at Druug. I had taken off my sweat-drenched tunic and my left arm was exposed uncarved.

Envy, fear, awe?

"You are their last hope," said Rouba as if he'd read my mind.

"Those poor fucks here—they were starving," said Druug, pointing to the scattered bodies of the Garol. "This is no good. We need to raid farther away. North, south, west. The Khun should march the Tribe, or come next winter, we starve too."

The Khun should... He was talking to me, already giving me advice.

"But why did we kill so many Garol?" I asked. "Now who will sow wheat for next summer?"

He turned and looked at me, surprised.

"There are plenty left alive. No need for women."

Or children.

Rouba turned to me as well and there I realized that I had said the wrong words. Not what they expected from their future Khun, their last hope. "When you are on a campaign, you never ask your Leader *why*. Why, why, stupid boy. *Why* will freeze your limbs like a poison-tipped arrow!"

I shut my mouth, but my eyes still asked why. A bad habit of mine. When I did not get an answer, I kept asking. Rouba saw that.

"Why? Because they are the scum of Darhul. That's enough. When the campaign ends and you return to your tent, some winter's night when you have nothing better to do, then ask *why*. But in the summer, when you are raiding, never ask *why*."

Before nightfall, the Blades hung the bodies of the Garol leaders high upon the trees to rot unburned so that the young Garol would learn and the old would never forget. They didn't ask me to help them with that.

I dreamed of boys dancing around a campfire.

The next morning, we packed for our return. Druug left behind one Pack to guard and enforce the Truth of the Tribe and harness to work the few we spared. We started the journey back to Sirol, victorious, though I still didn't know what my trial was. To fill the quivers? Under the searing summer light, I looked at one of the hanged offspring of Darhul, a young man with long brown hair.

"These men here, Rouba…"

"Yes, I saw them."

"What? Is it so obvious?"

"They look a lot like you. Maybe your mother."

"But then how…"

"Don't ask and don't search, and the Demon won't find you. Forget it, move forward. You are not like them. Not anymore. Never were."

I didn't know who my mother was, but Rouba from the first night of the Sieve, was the only father I had ever known. I covered my face with a cloth he had given me for the dust and the mosquitoes and galloped far away from the dangling bodies of the brown-haired men.

The battle had lasted half a day, but the return would take another half-moon. That was my first real lesson in the truth of war. We had to ride for one moon so that the Archers would fight for half a day and the Blades would mount women for a few breaths. The campaigns were endless rides on horseback and dull waiting before and after the short battles.

"Khun-Taa may call upon you to tell him what you saw," Druug told me.

But that was not my fate or Khun-Taa's. I was not in any hurry to return to our camp. This trial was far from over, and I could sense that.

On the first afternoon of our return trip, the sky darkened and threatened with a few drops. On the second afternoon, it opened and poured so much that I could hardly see three horses in front of me. The animals slid in the mud and hurt themselves. Some were left for dead, and our supplies were ruined. Even our bows that we covered deep under the hides began to take in water and would warp if we couldn't get them away from the rain. Druug would not allow that. A bow was precious and needed many moons' work to set strong.

"We must hide, away from the open sky," said the Reghen.

The Endless Forest, with its dense green foliage at the end of summer, was close to our right. It was the only shelter that could hide all of us under its live oak branches at the end of the day.

Druug and the Reghen approached me.

"Did he really kill a Reekaal?" the Druug said, talking to the Reghen but pointing at me.

"We were all there; you saw what I saw," the Reghen said.

"What do you think?" Druug asked turning to me.

"What do I think about what?"

"Should we go in there? Into the Forest?"

In the darkness.

He was not trying me. He didn't know what to do.

"Uh, yes," I said.

Yes, I want to sleep the night in the Forest. I didn't give it much thought. The quivers, the Garol, that was not the trial of Sah-Ouna. My final trial was just starting. Three nights in a row, the same thing happened. A raging storm started as soon as the sun went down. Three nights in a row, Druug asked me, and three times I told him: "Yes, we must."

It was there, tucked around our nightly fire at the edge of the Forest, where I first recited the Legend of my father. It was a great Story that I had been forging with Rouba every day for the past moons when we went for herbs in the Forest.

"A Story to make them forget your ninestar mark," Rouba told me.

The fires were large enough to scare away the wolves and the Reekaal, and many men fit around them.

"I thought the wolves were our friends," I said to Rouba.

"Do you want to find out for sure tonight?"

The first night I told the Legend of Er-Ren under the darkened trees, a Pack of forty warriors gathered around. On the second night, there were twice as many, and on the third, everyone. Not everyone, of course, could sit close and hear me, but one told the Legend to the other next to him, slightly changed, adding more blood and lies.

Men love their Stories. That much is true. The Stories they haven't lived and the ones they'll never live.

I remember as a younger boy the Reghen saying, "We have never been and we are not, even now. Only tomorrow, when we rise to the stars, we will truly be. In the Story that we leave behind us."

"Why?" I asked the Reghen one night.

"The flesh lives for a few springs, but then it stinks and rots quickly in one summer moon. The Story endures, strong for countless winters."

I didn't have the voice of an Ouna-Ma, but I told the Legend with all the strength of my heart and lungs.

This is the Story of my father, the one I'd never met, the one who never existed, the one I gave birth to.

The Legend of Er-Ren

It was the heaviest winter that had ever descended from the North. Not ever since the time that the black star had fallen hard on the steppe could anyone remember such piercing cold and relentless snow. It covered everything from the Great River, the Blackvein, to the Endless Forest.

The Pack of Chief Er-Ren, my father, had run out of food in the northernmost outpost of the Tribe, where they were waiting out the winter to protect the frozen pass. Khun-Taa was then a younger Leader and had sent the Pack of Er-Ren to see if the Drakons were moving down from the North. Anything was possible in such a cold winter. My mother had stayed behind in Sirol, heavy with child.

Er-Ren's men, twenty-nine of them, had drunk slowly from the veins of their living stallions for a moon to sustain themselves, and when the horses were nearly dead they were butchered for their meat. But even those supplies were exhausted, and they had meat to last only for five men till spring. They had kept a few horses to ride back in spring, the gray-white ones that the Goddess favored and no one dared to harm.

Fearless, my father strapped himself with his blades, quivers, and bow, and alone disappeared within the rugged Forest to find meat. He moved among the ice shadows for days and nights, and when he was all but sure that he would die of cold and hunger, he came upon a pond. The waters were crystal clear and cool, not frozen, and bluebells covered the grass as if it were spring. Er-Ren realized that he was in an enchanted glade where the Forest spirits ruled the light and the water. But he also knew that at night other demons would roam the same pond.

Then he saw the branches of a bare oak tree changing into antlers and a young deer emerging from within the trunk. The brown-skinned animal stood before him, holding its small head erect, its left dark-liquid eye staring straight at him. Er-Ren chose two arrows that whistled a deadly melody when they flew through the air. He aimed for the heart. The deer froze, enchanted by the arrows' song, and Er-Ren didn't miss. Bluebells drowned in a red puddle. Er-Ren heaved the deer upon his shoulders and started the journey to get back to his Pack.

As soon as he was out of the enchanted glade and stepped again into the snow, a much larger doe, its skin white as milk, appeared before him. Er-Ren let the small deer down and reached for his bow. Just then, the doe opened its mouth and asked with the voice of a woman of the Tribe.

"Why did you kill my beloved child, brave Er-Ren? Don't you know that Enaka protects the young deer?"

Er-Ren was not at all surprised. He was expecting magic.

"And why are you not afraid, White Doe?" asked Er-Ren. "Run and save yourself because I will kill you too." He would have killed the doe already had he not heard it talk.

"I am not here to save myself. I am here to redeem the life of my child," said the doe. "Give me back his body so that I may breathe life into it again."

"I cannot, White Doe; my people are dying without meat. I didn't kill for pleasure but out of need."

"In return, I will offer you my life," said the doe.

Er-Ren looked at the young deer resting lifeless on the snow. Not a spot of blood on the white ground. He could not defend himself against magic. He let the mother approach the deer and she warmed the dried blood of its wound with her snout. The deer sprang to its feet at once and, with quick leaps, disappeared through the wood.

My father took another arrow from his quiver and nocked it. The doe didn't try to run. The snow around it boiled crimson. Er-Ren had fulfilled his mission of death and life and ran to find shelter. But night had fallen, and the Forest had awoken, spiteful and hungry. Er-Ren lost his way wandering among the weeping songs of the night trees, carrying the bleeding doe on his shoulders until his legs and eyes finally betrayed him. He curled himself up inside his hides underneath a tree. It was bare, with thin branches that rose high like a skeleton waving his fleshless hands. They were white with snow on top and black like death underneath.

It was already too late when he realized, in the darkest moment of the night that he was among cursed, enchanted trees. They were the walnut trees. Their fruit was skulls filled with the brains of enslaved children and their trunks hid the Reekaal from the light of day. The smell of the blood of the doe and the skin of Er-Ren roused the demons. In the greatest darkness of the night, they unstuck their naked bodies painfully but quickly from the old trunks of the walnut trees and surrounded him. The only light for Er-Ren was the bright red of their eyes. With that light alone, he fought on the snow for his life and for his kill. He fought bravely, he fought for long, and he fought until he fell. The Cyanus Reekaal, with the flaming, lidless eyes, delivered with his sharp talons a wound that no man could survive.

Er-Ren took out the silver talisman of the wise Ouna-Mas, and that drew the faintest moonlight as his shield. It blinded bright the cursed offspring of Darhul and kept them away, else they would have torn him apart right there.

Dawn came and the Reekaal disappeared inside the trees. My father gathered his last strength to return to his Pack with the dead doe on his back. Paths of red flowers sprouted, melting the snow, wherever Er-Ren's blood fell.

The young deer that he had killed first appeared again in front of him, more alive than ever, and said, "See how this ends, brave warrior. Death brings only death. You should never have come into the Forest, Er-Ren. My mother is the Forest Witch, and you killed her. If you hadn't hunted us, my mother would have come to save you from the monsters."

"I am not here to save myself, but to bring meat and life to my men," said Er-Ren.

"Your death is honorable, Er-Ren."

The young deer lowered its head as if to bow before Er-Ren and disappeared.

My father kept walking with the last strength left in him. As soon as he saw his comrades, he fell dead. But he had already etched the glorious final Story for himself. When the last breath of Er-Ren ascended to the Sky, the doe came back to life and ran away behind the bare trees. A young warrior tried to stop it by throwing a dagger before it was lost, thankfully in vain. A great curse would have been lowered upon all their heads. For the people of the Tribe knew that the White Doe, the Forest Witch, was carrying the soul of my father to the Unending Sky. It was what all does did—carry brave souls to the Sky and cursed ones into the bowels of the earth. That is why their legs are quick but their eyes sad.

Next to the body of my father, where the dead doe should have been, appeared two fat oxen. The next day, winter ended, and I came out of my mother's belly, wrapped in the first sun of spring. Er-Ren's Pack slaughtered the two oxen and returned to Sirol with renewed strength. His death had given them life.

Thus declared the Legend of the brave Er-Ren.

It was a Legend that I had made up with the help of Rouba to protect myself from the Ouna-Mas, the snake Witches of the Tribe. It was a Story that adorned the Witches with respect and honor—a Story of deer, Reekaal, a silver talisman, demon trees, and anything else that fed their madness and their strength.

No one would question the folly I created because I dressed it in their sacred robes and superstitions. No one ever claimed to have seen the Cyanus Reekaal, except for a few Ouna-Mas. And even those Witches did so only after they had drunk crazygrass in the dark moments of the night when their eyes rolled white. Never in the light of the sun. Maybe I had seen him too that night in Sah-Ouna's camp. But I dared not say this to anyone.

So we came to the fourth night of pouring rain, the fourth time that the stormy sky forced us into the Forest. Before I started retelling my Legend, shadows moved in the night mist between the tree trunks. The men strapped themselves with their blades and waited for the Reekaal with trembling knees. They were all looking at me. I had brought them here. I had said the Legend of Er-Ren and the Reekaal one too many times, I was Uncarved, I was the first blade of the Wolfhowl. I was not allowed to be scared.

"No fear. Go to sleep. It is only the Dasal, the forest peasants," I said.

For one night, at least that night, I was the Leader of the Tribe.

I fell asleep and dreamed of Sah-Ouna. She was a little girl. Zeria, the Dasal girl, was with her. So was my mother. All three had blue eyes. They walked hand in hand in the Forest, away from me, getting deeper into the wood.

I awoke, not much later to the frightened screams of my comrades.

"Darhul's demons, the Final Battle. Save yourselves," yelled the men next to me. Some were already running to get out of the Forest.

The Reghen came running toward me, with Druug following him. "This is not a night for tales," said the Reghen as he placed his palm on my shoulder to advise me. "You have to lead, Da-Ren. It is the time of the blade."

"They are Dasal. Do not be afraid," I shouted. But my voice couldn't rule over the nightmares of hundreds of men.

I searched until I found Rouba sleeping in the dark, hunched under a walnut tree. I woke him up with difficulty.

"What is it?" he asked.

"I want you to come with me to find the Dasal. Their shadows are moving around us, the wolves howl, and the men are going mad. I want the two us to go deep into the Forest. That is my final trial."

"Says who?"

"Me. Sah-Ouna. The dream."

My other choice was to return and report to Khun-Taa how many brown-haired Garol, same as me, we had hanged. That is what I should have done—take the safe and easy path back.

But I did the opposite.

I fell into Sah-Ouna's trap.

I did what she wanted. What I wanted.

I let the Reghen and Druug know.

"We two," I pointed to Rouba, "will go to find them alone. The rain has stopped. Get the men out of the Forest and into the moonlight, and don't wait for us."

Druug tried to open his mouth, but the Reghen motioned him to stay quiet. I packed my things, letting the Reghen exchange some last words with Rouba.

"Don't wait for us!" Rouba repeated my words to the rest. He was pulling his horse from the reins with one hand, walking forward at a quick pace. I followed. A calling whispered through the branches and invited me deeper into the Forest.

XXVIII.
Children Hand in Hand

Eighteenth summer. Uncarved—Wolf.

"My end is near, young man," said Rouba. We had been walking for a long while, deep into the Forest, before the first ray of sunshine reached through the trees.

I stopped my stride and turned to face him. "What kind of talk is that?"

"I saw it. It wasn't a sign of the Goddess. It was a man's sign."

The Guide was talking, but he wouldn't look at me. He was already looking to the next world.

"What sign?"

"The Reghen have a secret way, their own, of signaling things. But after so many winters in the Tribe, I have learned it."

"I don't understand you, Rouba."

He was fifty winters old, but that morning he looked twice that.

"You see, the Reghen never touch a man or woman. But when they know that someone is going to die, they put a hand softly on the shoulder. Only then. Always the same. A send-off."

"I've never heard of that."

The birds had awoken early that summer day. There were so many of them, with colors I'd never seen in the Iron Valley. Colors without names. They didn't want to sing about death, and their chirping drowned out Rouba's words.

"That Reghen, before we left, he let his palm rest on my shoulder. First time in my fifty winters that a Reghen did that."

I wanted to tell him that he was talking nonsense. It had to be nonsense. I needed Rouba more than ever before. We were together and alone in the woods. I changed the talk to take his mind away from death.

"Last night, before I came to find you, in my sleep, I had a dream: Sah-Ouna, my mother, Zeria."

He didn't ask me about my mother. We had seen the women of Garol. He asked me who Zeria was.

We reached a rough slope and dismounted. The ground was covered with thorny bushes and tall grass, and at some points, the foliage was so dense that I had to clear the way by parting the leafy branches with my hands so we could see our footing. Rouba had brought an ax, and we chopped our way through the woods to help the horses pass. We didn't need the horses in the Forest, but we needed them to return and couldn't leave them to the wolves.

"If you want to find the summer settlement of the Dasal, we will have to go two or three days north, to Kar-Tioo," Rouba told me.

I did want to find the Dasal.

Rouba continued. "The Forest has grown and risen this summer. I don't remember it being this dense."

"It is pushing us out. Like someone is resisting."

"What did you say?"

"Like someone is—"

"Yes, I heard you. Don't talk like that."

I was fighting the green monster with the ax, opening its skin to get further inside. There was only one reason I was in the Forest. I had to find a way to tell him about Zeria.

"Rouba, is there really a Forest Witch?"

"Yes, and we are in her wood now. There is a Dasal myth. A deer that sings. A White Doe. This is how I came up with Er-Ren's Story."

"My father's Story, is…from the Dasal?"

"Your father's? Yes…"

There was a grimace of hesitation on his face, as if the word *father* actually meant something to him, something forbidden and forgotten.

"You never told me the myth."

"I will, someday. Not now. We're too close."

"Have you ever seen her?"

"Maybe. Once. I'm not sure."

"But you're sure that she lives close by. How?"

"Because there are men here. And where there are men, there is a witch too."

"Why?"

"To feed. Young men are the witch's meat."

This didn't make any sense to me.

"Rouba, why don't we kill the witches? We men have the blades, the power." From far back when I had learned I was a ninestar, I had had the same question.

"Ha, 'kill the witch,' the boy says." His eyes were searching around and forward to danger. "Man needs the witch. Else all he has is a cold blade."

The first evening fell dark fast, and the night creatures rose around us. I took the first watch while Rouba slept, and I was alone with the whispering branches that brought the witch's words.

"Why are you here, Da-Ren, ninestar offspring of the raven-haired riders? You don't belong. You are born of dust and blood; this is the wood of the bluebell and the butterfly. Keep your blades away from my green-eyed children. Don't come further inside me."

This was her only warning, and then the whispering stopped. The Forest, the owl, and the wolf turned silent. I could hear only the fire's crackling.

Rouba rose with a sudden move, as if from a nightmare. "My old head is restless," he said. "I cannot sleep."

"What bothers you?" I asked.

"That's not the way of the Tribe. To abandon us here. Why did the Reghen and Druug let us go so easily? They were responsible for you. Strange. And who is Zeria?" he asked me again.

That was the Story I wanted to tell, and to ask him if the Forest Witch had blue eyes.

"Strange, yes. I will tell you a strange Story, Rouba," I said, and I started to recount my betrayal from the last time I was in the Forest. A girl, a tree's hollow, blue. I hid her from death.

Rouba's face turned sour and worried.

"A man bewitched by a woman's eyes will fall," he said when I finished.

Before I had another chance to ask him or to explain we came upon a clearing. It was barren, and the sun was blazing hot above it. There was no grass or fern on its gray soil; nothing grew there. Only a swarm of flies were buzzing high in the middle of it. Rouba was alert again.

"Don't step on that clearing, stay in the wood, we'll go around it."

He didn't say another word that day and we spent it trying to distance ourselves from that cursed place.

We started our second day moving slowly on foot through the dense wood and then he started talking to me again, unveiling a future he didn't want to see.

"It was her fate to go as sacrifice to Sah-Ouna, this girl you found. Why did you do it?"

I didn't answer. I was looking for that answer myself in the Forest's womb.

"You can't just steal someone from Sah-Ouna's black-horned knife. The Goddess does not forgive such trickery. You owe her."

I lowered my head so I wouldn't lose an eye to a branch and kept moving. The Forest was still resisting, pushing me away.

Rouba continued.

"I am telling you this so you can redeem yourself while there's time. Let's turn back now. I will not reveal your secret. Something stinks here. Druug shouldn't have let you go."

"They were scared. They wanted me to protect them from the Dasal," I answered.

"You, to protect them? Who do you think you are, boy? The young and the stupid may have been scared. Not Druug. Tell me again," said Rouba.

"What?"

"What were Sah-Ouna's words the night she called for you?"

"She said that a great trial awaited me. If I pass it, the Goddess will accept me."

"She will accept you as a Leader or accept you up there, next to her?"

The bushes and weeds were tangling around me, like the words of Sah-Ouna.

"I don't remember."

She said she would accept me. I hadn't understood the Witch's forked-tongue speech. I didn't say that to Rouba. A new fear nested inside of me. Maybe I hadn't been sent to the Forest to become the next Leader, the next Khun. Maybe I had left Sirol forever.

"This is like a trap. The Reghen, his touch, the Witch—she is pulling us closer," he said.

"I am not afraid. I am here to find the Forest Witch," I said.

At the sound of my words, the day's light became ample as a piercing rain of sun rays tore through the canopy. The Forest glowed gold and silver and embraced me. She was not resisting anymore.

"Welcome, Da-Ren," was her whisper. "Feed from my body."

We hunted a rabbit and a deer like my legendary father, Er-Ren, and we lived with the meat and water of the wood. Invisible feminine arms wrapped us warmly that night as we slept among the tree spirits. Mine had blue eyes and golden-green garb. Rouba's descended in a flame-covered chariot from the Unending Sky.

We kept traveling north, or so we thought. The oaks were getting bigger and wide-leaved, their trunks so wide that it took the two of us to embrace them. The moss on the north side of the wood was our best guess of where north was whenever we lost the marks in the sky.

"We've come very deep now. These are the first, the ancient trees," Rouba told me. "No ax or knife has wounded them, ever. They were born together with the Earth, from Enaka's first breath, and they are still standing."

On the fourth night, I thought we were desperately lost as we came upon the same barren clearing again. There was a sickly smell of rotting carcass in the air.

"We are back to the same place," I said and shivered with gooseflesh on my arms.

"I am not sure it is the same place," said Rouba.

"It is, it follows us," I said.

"It's your fear. Ignore it. Don't feed it."

We knew we could not find our way back on our own. When the wolves, our ancestors and protectors, surrounded us at nightfall, we lit a fire and remained within its circle, wearing the wooden amulets that the Ouna-Mas had carved for each warrior. The Ouna-Mas had not forged this Legend with the wolves well.

"One of us needs to stay awake. I have seen men, can't even remember how many, torn apart by wolves. None by Reekaal," Rouba told me.

The horses were snorting nervously. I tried to calm them and hold them as close to the fire as they would come. I took the second watch, and when it dawned, I was light-headed and sweaty.

The light of the day rose low among the slender trunks, not high above them, making the trees form long, dark shadows. In the early morning, the Forest was not green. It was covered with nine shadows of black where the sun didn't hit, gold when it found a crevice, and a blue fog in between the trunks. The sickening smell had disappeared and a crisp morning blossom had replaced it.

I didn't see any huts. But I smelled the fires, and after a little while, I saw them flickering. Not a man could be seen. Or woman.

"Kar-Tioo! We are here. This is the Dasal's settlement. Put down your blades now, or they won't come out. They are afraid."

I obeyed Rouba and threw my blades many paces ahead of me. We were now completely defenseless and at the mercy of these invisible othertribers, the ones whose father, brother, or both, I had killed in my first fight at the Wolfhowl.

The light woke the leafy branches, and the scenery started to come alive. What was still became moving and liquid.

Brown came first. Brown trunks, brown hides, and brown hair of men, walking on brown mud.

Green was still the bracken, green eyes of men and children staring at us. Her dress was green and gold, its hemline cut short and uneven. The Dasal were encircling us with careful steps as they came out of the woods.

Two blackbirds flying silently at summer's end. The tree trunks rising like black spears to the east, outlined by the morning sunlight. Her black hair waving strong as she walked toward us.

Pale sunlight, pale white, their faces, hiding in the shadows of the Forest most of the day. Pale and naked laid my blade on the bellflowers.

Bellflowers, campanulas. *Little bells*, Rouba was calling them. Rivers of them. Violet or blue. Only the sun's rays could answer that. She was close enough now that I could see her sky-blue eyes.

She was holding two small children by the hand. She looked older than the first time I saw her. Like a woman. I recognized Veker next to her, her father. The one who had escaped. His stare stayed on me. Not hers. Our previous encounter had lasted for only a few screams. Did she remember?

Look at me. Last time I came as death, but I gave you life.

Another furtive look. Oh, yes, she remembers.

The torture of a witch. She knows that only one look can save a boy. But she refuses it. All so powerful we think she is. Or shy or unsure.

I cannot be refused, girl. I whisper inside me; no one else can hear my words. They are for you alone. I need to look into your eyes. On my virgin journey into the Forest, I will not be refused.

I was inside it now.

Rouba and Veker were talking. Words were fluttering like vibrant butterflies that a child couldn't hope to catch. They gave us pouches of belladonna and crazygrass to bring back. We sat around the fire. She sat with the men of the Dasal and us. The other women stayed back.

"Is that your blue-eyed one over there?" asked Rouba.

I nodded that she was with the slightest movement of my head.

"I would kill her to save you, but…"

"What?"

"She's their witch. I can't."

"Witch?" I asked.

"Can't you see it? Witch."

We had given them our game, half of the deer that we hadn't eaten. They boiled it in a cauldron with greens and filled bowls to give us. They brought a red, sweetly burning water and filled wooden cups. The men talked among themselves, touching our blades, trying to nock arrows to our bows. We were still unarmed; they had kept them. The women examined us with long stares as they were coming and going. I had never drunk wine before. If I were older and wiser, I would wonder what it was, how it was made, where the Dasal found it, but I didn't think about any of that. Questions like that did not bother me that day. It was midday, and the air was muggy again. Sweet red-and-blue breaths boiled down my chest. Sweet bliss of mouth and body.

She was looking at me again and I was diving into the crystal lake of her eyes. She was not resisting anymore. Afternoon came, and we were still resting drunk under the trees. Thirst tortured my tongue.

Rouba said to me, "They say there is a pond near here. Let's go wash off to clear our heads."

If the Forest was alive—and I was certain it was—that pond was its mouth. A mouth to kiss, to listen to, to devour me. Its green water covered me completely, flowed deep inside of me, everywhere, like new blood. Every part of my body was reborn for a third time.

I was diving in bliss but Rouba was already out of the pond.

"We're leaving!" he shouted at me from a distance, cupping his mouth with his hands.

I could hear his words, but my eyes searched for her. Resistance. Penetration. Orgasm. Danger.

A day made out of a dream was coming to an end.

Leave for where? The Sieve? The Uncarved? For Sah-Ouna? Not even a moon had passed since we'd left Sirol, but I was on the other side of the world. So far away.

I didn't want to leave. I hadn't even said a word to her. I wanted the sun to stop there, to burn all the men around me like tallow puppets that a Witch melts into the fire. To make them disappear. For only Zeria to remain and for that day to come again and again, longer and brighter and to become thirty times summer. Nothing else. That is what I wished for, but I had no Goddess to listen to my pleas. Rouba was already out of the water and dressing. I got out and covered my nakedness. Zeria lowered her head, and her raven-black hair was shining the last light of the evening.

"That's what witches do. Their calling finds you in your sleep," Rouba had said to me days earlier. He had been talking about Sah-Ouna.

Rouba was already leaving. I had to stop this. I turned to Veker. "More." I pointed to the small pouch with the belladonna to make them understand.

"No, we don't have any more," Veker said.

Rouba was looking at me, silent and angry. I pointed again toward the sky. I couldn't leave. Not yet.

"Moon. Next."

The Dasal looked at one another and then at Rouba as if they had all silently agreed to ignore me. Zeria stayed farther back away from it all. I couldn't find her eyes anymore.

Rouba started to walk away from the pond and the Dasal. He turned his eyes toward me and with a rough, disapproving voice, he called, "Your blades. Are you going to leave them behind?"

It was almost dusk, and the sunlight suddenly dimmed as if the cloudbreaths of Darhul swallowed it. The Demon had smelled my weakness. The bellflowers bent in the dark. I heard birds fly away, squawking, alarmed—as if something evil was descending. The sound of rustling leaves, twigs breaking. Rouba turned to look at the trees behind us. I spotted Zeria twenty paces to my left, and at the same moment I saw her also turning, searching for the danger. A cold blast of wind reached me as if the Demon was breathing down my spine.

The Dasal was still holding my blades and was walking toward me. If anyone from my Tribe ever saw that, they would nail me to a stake at once. As he offered them back to me, I heard the whistling arrow shafts ripping through the air. The Dasal turned to look in the direction of the sound, and his screams of pain came before his next breath. A heavy arrow had found its way in between his ribs. He fell to the ground and curled into a ball. A second one landed on the ground a foot away from me. I grabbed it. A broad iron head, a hunter's arrow, one of those that brought death from short distance. The hunter was close and we were prey.

"Rouba, watch out!"

Loud screams in the otherworldly tongue of the Dasal filled the Forest. They were running to hide; they were not the hunters. The finches and the hoopoes silenced and flew away. A woman fell behind the shrubs, protecting a child in her embrace.

"Zeria!"

First time I spoke her name, aloud. I called upon death and she listened.

Rouba shouted at me. Only one word. What did he say? "Down," I think. He didn't talk of Er-Ren or the White Doe or Sah-Ouna. He didn't talk of the blue-eyed witch or the Reghen who touched a doomed man on the shoulder. He had said all of that.

What curse, what hoar frost of the soul kept me still standing and naked against death?

"Get down!" Veker shouted in my own tongue.

But I was still standing, looking at Rouba and Zeria. A good archer needs only a breath. I heard again the familiar whistling of the arrow, the arrow of death and first love, but it was too late. The iron ripped through my flesh, burning as a witch's kiss, and angry as a snake bite, beneath my lowest right rib.

Rouba. I can't.

"Reekaal," was his last word. Two shafts deep in his chest, two eyes wide open. Rouba fell on his back and he didn't move again.

The Sky was descending fast to swallow me. Blackbirds everywhere.

The Goddess, Rouba. Her fury. This pain. I can't stand it.

But I couldn't talk. He wouldn't hear; he couldn't protect me. I had so much more to say.

I didn't have the courage to tell you. But you were right, Rouba. Before we left, the Reghen, I remember. His palm, the gray robe. He touched me. Softly. On the shoulder. Like you. I'm burning.

My guts were on fire; my knees trembled and I fell. And so luck had it that the next arrows whistled above my shoulder and missed my heart. Strong men's hands pulled me away, dragging me shivering.

I had never been cut by a blade or pierced by an arrow deeply. Was that it? The pain was slowly going away now. The legs losing all strength, the blurring mind, the shaking as if the icy north wind were blowing deep down my mouth. Was this the end? A red boiling river of warmth was streaming out of me. As red as the ribbon of the First Uncarved that was still tied around my arm. What was I doing in the Forest's womb? On any other day, I would have seen the arrow coming. I would have tried to dodge it, but, this time, my eyes had stayed on Zeria.

"Monsters. There," Veker cried.

I barely managed to see two tall and thin hooded shadows, maybe human, probably not, moving away between the trees. They resembled nothing I knew. They looked like the giant statues that I had seen in Sah-Ouna's tent, maybe. Gunna before and Rouba a moment ago had said it: Reekaal.

I remember little from then on. The Dasal were dragging me away, their shadows screaming in the fog, the foliage of the tall trees and the blue sky, as my eyes slowly darkened. I remember the cold making me numb, Zeria shouting to the others and pointing to my horse. Zeria wrapping a cloth around my ribs. They dragged the horse next to her. Veker raised a knife; men were pulling the animal down from its long mane. A beautiful mane which reached all the way to its knees. Despair blocked my voice but not the horse's screams as the blood gushed from its rigid neck. Three of them, red elbow-high, were pulling the entrails out with hasty moves. The smell, the retching. My last memory was of them resting me shivering inside the body of the dead horse. My last nest was so warm.

I died that evening. A blue chilling death. Even for a short while.

I sank into the darkness where breaths stop. My horse grew ashen wings, dove into the soil and started flying down the bat caves. One moment, I was lying inside its open belly, and the next, I was riding it bareback. Until I grew dizzy and lost my balance. And then I was falling alone, sliding down Darhul's throat for nights on end, without being able to grab ahold of something. My hands reached out, but all they touched was poison that burned through the clothes and my skin. I continued to fall unhindered until I crashed against a sharp branch that tore through my body under the last right rib—the sound of wood breaking—and I landed like a sack of bleeding flesh in the mud. The mud awoke cold and hungry, lapping at me with a thousand tongues, slowly covering me more and more. I stood upright, and I felt light as my last breath.

My body didn't follow me; it was lying face down motionless next to the thin-branched tree. Charred roots had grown out of the slime, rising upward and their dark tendrils were piercing my skin, pulling my body down. I was watching all this from a few feet away. I felt no pain, as my flesh and the tree were becoming one. The tree was feeding, its trunk and branches growing alive with berries, red as my blood. My skin was losing all color. I had descended into the otherworld, that of Darhul and the dead. Enaka had not accepted me among the stars.

I ran to get back into my skin, back to the living. I pushed my palms in the mud to find the strength to get up again. The dark tendrils tried to hold me down, but I managed to grasp the short blade and hacked at them with madness. They answered back with screams, swirling like a storm of venom snakes around my head. I broke free from the tree as its branches begged for a last embrace. The berries were glowing their own light like torches of gold and blood.

Under that new light I saw them in front of me. Many children, some of them othertribers, some from the Sieve, were standing in the mud. It seemed to me that they hadn't come from anywhere; they were there all along. All of them had black pebbles for eyes, without any white. I walked among them, but their overlapping whispers were so desperate and fast that I couldn't make out the words. I was searching for a child, a girl, the one who had granted me the first smile. I couldn't find her and turned to leave.

Seven children, hand in hand, blocked my way.

"Where are you going? Stay with us, Da-Ren," they spoke with one eerie voice. It was the sound of chilling wind, not warm-fleshed children. To this day, I can't remember if the one in the middle, a step ahead of the others, was a girl.

"I am leaving," I said. "I want to get back to the light."

"There is no light where you go. We know, we come from there. Believe us. Stay!"

I looked around me where the darkness was heavier, and not even shadows could be seen.

"Most beautiful Elbia, if you are down here, I will stay with you."

No one responded, but I could sense her. She was hiding back there. She didn't answer, didn't show herself. She didn't want me to stay in the eternal cold. She wanted to send me back to find the girl with the blue eyes.

I called to her once more.

"I can't find you. I'll return...someday."

The mud danced hungrier around my legs and splashed me all the way up to my neck. The mud heard my promise. The mud didn't want to lose me. It wanted to feed me to the tree with the red berries. It whispered into my ear. "You live, Da-Ren. That will be punishment enough, the only offering the dead will demand. You live to feed the dead. And feed us you will by your blade. Ascend to the light. Go, slaughter the whole world."

The tendrils of the tree grabbed me like neckropes and before I could do anything they became a ladder rising high and growing fast. I held on with both hands. Rising. Light. Blue. Bright.

When I opened my eyes, I was in a hut, warm from the hearth and the summer sun. I wasn't shivering anymore. Why wasn't I in Sirol? How did I get there?

Two blue eyes were feeding me life. They sparkled and shattered the darkness. They brought breath to my lungs again. A smile, only one in the hut. Her fingers cooled my face and traveled down the pulsing veins of my neck. She pulled the leeches from my chest and ribs. With a soft cloth, she wiped the blood where the dark worms fed. Her eyebrows had the exact same shape and color as the leeches. So beautiful.

"Poison," she said, "but the leeches got it in time," showing me the arrow she had taken out of my body. I knew that arrow. I had shot thousands of them.

How could she speak my tongue? Was that another dream? *Poison,* was her first word ever to me.

I didn't have the strength to say much. "Rouba?"

Zeria shook her head ever so slightly and remained silent, stealing all hope from me.

A few days before, I was Uncarved and First.

"My horse?" I asked again.

I remembered the blood running from its neck.

"I am Zeria," she answered, ignoring my question.

"Da-Ren. My horse?"

"You were freezing to death. You had to sleep inside an animal."

My stomach turned with sickness, and a sour taste in my mouth choked me. That was the strong smell still in my nostrils. The chewed food of the horse's stomach. I tried to get up to vomit but couldn't. I was so weak.

"The warmth and spirit of the animal are with you," said Zeria. She got up, and as she walked around, I saw her green dress flowing. It was tattered and old but seemed unfitting for a peasant girl. Gold designs were embroidered on the green fabric, as if it were made of the Forest itself. I had seen such dresses only in the spoils of war.

I stretched with my fingers the skin around my eyes, to stay awake, not to sleep. Not to fall into the lapping mud again. Zeria came and went many times, my eyes shutting defeated each time she left. I found my strength again two days later. She told me that I had been delirious for two days after I was wounded. Two days falling down and two more rising from the caves of the dead.

"Sleep now, Da-Ren," she said and covered me with the smooth deer hide.

I slept a sleep naked of dreams.

When I woke up, she was still there.

"Here, I brought some boiled meat. And berries. Red ones!"

I was all alone in the Forest with the Dasal.

With her.

Without my father.

XXIX.
Kar-Tioo

Eighteenth autumn. Uncarved—Wolf.

No shroud, no matter how many times it is wrapped around, can ever stop the earthworms. I dug the dirt with my nails and a branch the length of a blade until my fingers bled. I had to get Rouba out of the rough grave the Dasal had dug for him. I had asked Zeria to take me there once I had regained some strength. It was a shallow mound of dirt protruding from the surrounding grassy field, the first raindrops of autumn already moistening it.

I unwrapped the shroud only to see the old man's rotting flesh, the color of bellflowers on his skin. His eyes had bulged out whole; his tongue had swollen, half out of his mouth. It looked like someone stuck a purple fish down his throat. I was on my knees, mourning, digging, getting the leaves off him. That was where I finally threw up.

Zeria stayed back, along with the other Dasal and away from me, when I started digging.

"Why did you put him here?" I asked her. "I have to burn his body."

She came closer, hesitantly.

"Don't take him from the earth."

"What?"

"Give him to the Forest; it will embrace him."

"That man was a warrior, destined for the Unending Sky, not the Forest. His ashes must rise up high. She waits for him."

I hoped the Goddess would accept him like this. I couldn't get rid of all the rosy worms that had invaded every crevice of his face and studded the swollen violet skin. The roots of the trees were already drinking his flesh. I started to drag him out of there to build a big pyre. Zeria came closer and pulled my arm to stop. I pushed her away hard, knocking her down. Once again, she was at my feet like the first time, when I had saved her. The same look of anguish on her beautiful face.

I tried to find the words to explain: "If his flesh does not burn, the soul cannot ascend to the Sky."

She relaxed at the tone of my voice and raised herself from the ground.

"In the sky? Up there?"

"That is where the brave go."

"There? To nothing? The skies are cold, empty lakes. Why should he go there? Keep him here, in our earth of life."

"No! Stop this talk now."

"To become one with the tree, the soil, the leaves, the animals, the autumn spiders. To live through them again. The earth fed him for his whole life. His body should feed the earth now. To be born again. In here, life never dies."

I had heard all these mad stories of the Demon's servants many times before. The Story of the Deadwalkers, the Buried servants of Darhul, the resurrection of the Cross Worshippers of the South. All those monsters were real, not just Legends of the Ouna-Mas. And Zeria's words were proof of that.

Rouba had not lived that long to become food for worms. I grabbed a torch from a Dasal and lit Rouba's pyre. He left for the stars as he deserved. Zeria came closer when the fire was dying out and threw a flask of red water over the embers while speaking words I did not understand.

"Are you…the Forest Witch?" I asked.

"You had fallen to the ends of the underworld. I had to enter the mouth of the snake, deep in the caves of the dead, to bring your soul back, Da-Ren."

It was her way of telling me she was.

"The forest spirits did not accept this. I owe them," she told me.

I shivered when she spoke of the caves of the dead. My nightmare returned: the days when I fought off the poison, the mud swallowing me, the seven children with black pebble eyes, hand in hand, wanting to keep me down there. If I had died, I should have risen to the Unending Sky, next to Enaka. But Enaka knew. She didn't accept me. I had betrayed her. Again and again. For Zeria.

The following morning, I opened my eyes late, later than any other time, and Zeria walked in and left a handful of wild red berries and a piece of bread.

"For your journey," she said.

I wasn't ready for any journey.

"I want to…" I started to say.

Her father, Veker, came in behind her and wasted no time in questioning me. "Why did you come? Kala is dead. We could not save him. Cursed monsters!"

I figured that Kala was the Dasal who had been hit by the first arrow, a little before Rouba and I had gone down.

"Who killed Kala? Who shot those arrows?" I asked.

"Who else? Your own kind," he said pointing his finger at my face.

"Why? Why would they shoot at me if they are of the Tribe?"

"You ask? You, who hunted us and caged us? Damn you! They hunt because that's what they always do."

"I will stay here until they come again. I have to get to them," I said to Veker and Zeria.

"You have to leave today. Those who came were hunting you, not us. They aimed at you even when they hit Kala. Are you exiled from your Tribe?"

"No."

"Maybe they know you've helped us. If you stay, we are all in danger," Veker said.

Three strong men had come into the hut. I didn't have my blades, and I didn't want to fight the men who had saved my life. I nodded silently, pretending to agree with him.

"I promise, I'll leave at dawn."

That afternoon, I secretly crept into Veker's hut and found my blades. I strapped them around me, and I was strong and free once more. The next morning when we met again, I was armed. I wouldn't take any orders from him.

"I changed my mind. I will stay until I find out what happened. Or I'll return with a thousand warriors. She will help me," I told him, pointing to Zeria.

"Listen, young man. I can kill you now. Even if a couple of us die, you die too. You rot unburied, and the crows eat your eyes tonight."

"Go on!"

"But I took a vow. When you saved Zeria. You don't die, I'll protect you even though I piss on you and your tribe. But I won't let you near Zeria."

"She is the Forest Witch. I need to speak to her. She is not in danger."

"What witch? Are you mad, kid?" shouted Veker.

Zeria stepped forward and came next to me.

"She speaks my tongue," I said.

It was my excuse to keep her with me—in the beginning when I still needed an excuse.

"So am I."

"Father, I owe him, let me help him. You promised," Zeria said.

Veker's silence and angry mumbling signaled my victory. When they finally left us alone, I asked her to follow me away from the huts.

"Help me," I said.

"What do you want, Da-Ren?"

"I want you to teach me what you know. The magic. So that I can take on the Witches. To see what they see."

"Magic? I don't know."

"You have to!" I said.

"You want to come with me to gather fruit? I have to go. Coming?"

"Fruit? Yes."

"Walk with me," she said.

I followed her that first day, and the second and the third, searching for the food of the Forest deeper and farther each day. We would take different paths every dawn. She would talk about the life-givers and the death-seekers around us, but without revealing her magic, the power I sought. The Forest devoured me slowly. I lost count of the days. We must have entered the first moon of autumn, the most pleasant of all. I felt on my skin that the days were still warm whenever the sun pierced through the thick branches of the trees.

One day, we walked farther than any other time, through tough-soiled paths and rivulets, long dried out by summer and soon to be flooded again by winter. I knelt to touch a plant with small berries, shiny, round, and black.

"Don't eat those," she said.

"Belladonna?" I asked.

"Yes, the witches' plant. We call it Atropos. It was the ancient spirit's name that still breathes in this plant. She is the weaver of fate who cuts the thread of men's lives. The arrow that struck you was seeped in this black poison. You know, Da-Ren…"

She stopped her words, not eager to add more.

"What is it?"

"'Atropos' means 'the fate that will not turn' in the ancient tongue. I stole you from the dead, but you cannot escape the fate you seek. You will die exactly like this, iron under the right rib, someday."

"When?"

"I don't know."

That was a welcomed fate. I wouldn't rot from the fever of the mosquitoes or cough the blood of the winter plague. I wouldn't get shot by an arrow in the back.

"I hear running water."

"Where the Atropos grows, there is also water."

More days passed in the autumn's Forest turning. The blades and arrows I carried with me proved useless, as though I couldn't remember what to do with them. The Forest was not a threatening evil. Instead, it was the first peace I had ever known in my life, even if I had died there a few nights ago. Zeria did not tell me anything more than Rouba had. The berries, the nightingales' vanishing summer songs, the acorns, and the bracken changing color. That was all the magic she would show me.

"I want to learn more. About the powerful magic."

"I don't have any magic, Da-Ren."

"My horse, its spirit. How did you bring me to life?"

"You were shaking all over. Writhing in pain. We had to warm your body before your heart stopped. The horse's carcass gave the warmth."

"And its spirit?"

"I do not know, Da-Ren. It is something we say to honor the sacrificed animal."

"I don't understand."

"The warmth of the horse that wrapped your frozen body—that is the magic. I did not see its spirit. The horse died; you lived. One for one is the law of the Forest. Whatever you see, smell, or touch. Whatever you hear. That is the magic. The next month—"

"Month?" I didn't recognize the Dasal word.

"Month, moon, same word. In the next moon, everything around you, this Forest, will begin to die. Its life will grow old and rot. But it will be reborn again in the spring, stronger than before. Everything living around you, connects together, feeds one another."

"I know all of that."

"I am not a witch like your witches. I only help the children. Our elder, Saim, may be able to help you. But he will not tell you anything different. Saim has told me that the only magic is to watch one oak tree all day, every day, for an entire year. To witness life and death moving slower than your breath."

"Year?"

"For twelve moons."

"That is not the magic I seek," I told her as I grabbed her wrist.

She trembled silently.

"You don't understand. I was raised to be the Khun. I have to return. To stop the curse of the ninestar," I said.

"You're leaving?" She got up and ran away to hide her tears.

I caught up with her where the trees ended and the pond began, but she pushed me away.

"I can't help you, Da-Ren. That is the only magic I know."

"I have to get revenge for Rouba. I can't go back like this. Hunted and defeated."

"Rouba is resting peacefully," she said. "There."

She pointed to the small pond which mirrored the trees around us on its smooth surface. It was the pond that Rouba and I had bathed in just before the ambush. I stayed there with her all afternoon. I killed a fat squirrel, skinned it, and lit a fire. We stuffed our mouths with berries till our tongues and teeth turned black. We drank cold water. Night came, but it was singing pleasure, not shrieking fear as Selene dipped into the still waters. That place where I had died from a poisoned arrow became life itself.

"And the Reekaal? Those who attacked us?" I asked.

She didn't understand. I tried to explain to her, but she just lowered her head to take a better look at me, as if I were still hallucinating from the poison. I told her the whole Story of the Dasal and the Reekaal and my Tribe's Legends of the Forest demons. I spoke to her of the Ouna-Mas.

"Your witches are false. They are not blind from the Atropos. You are."

"The Ouna-Mas?"

"You don't understand. The trees, us, me, you, the fallow deer and the gray wolf, the good and evil spirits are all one. When you are an enemy, you are a Reekaal. When you are a friend, you are a Dasal. The entire Forest is one and knows that. It will protect you or kill you."

None of this had any meaning for me. I just liked listening to her. The magic of her eyes had taken hold, even if her words claimed otherwise.

"We are all servants. You and us. Of the Demon or the Goddess," I said.

"There are no witches or demons. Only moments."

"You don't know what you are talking about. You are a girl from the huts of the Forest," I said.

"But I saved your life."

"With magic."

I wanted to take her in my arms and tell her about how much she didn't know. I wanted to take her in my arms and not say anything at all.

"The arrow was dipped in belladonna's blood. The leeches sucked out the poison. That magic is of the earth, not of your gods."

It wasn't enough. I took hold of her hand, as I had done that first afternoon when the Blades hunters had brought her to me.

"You don't believe me. Tell me then: whose servant are you, Da-Ren? The demon's? Or the goddess's?"

If I said the Demon's, all his nine heads would hear me and find me.

If I said the Goddess's, she would ask me why I had saved the girl's life, why I hadn't taken her as sacrifice to Sah-Ouna.

So I asked a question of my own instead. "So what is there for you if you don't have Demon or Goddess?"

"This. Here. You. Me. Now. The one moment, you want to hide me in the oak's hollow. The next, you want to kill all men. Only the moment exists. The moment is a god and a demon, but it is not blind. It has swallowed yesterday and thousands of summers and has seen tomorrow and thousands of winters to come. That is what Saim says, the wise elder."

"Only luck?"

"It isn't luck. The moment is not blind. It has gathered so much. Wisdom has seeped through it. It has taken root and sprouted within you. You can't escape your moment. The moment will decide."

"Those who attacked me—"

I couldn't look into her eyes for long. Her gaze turned my blood into rivers of blue-crystal death.

"They were of your kind, not from the forest. You know, we also have a story for the ones you call Reekaal that I have heard long ago. But it is the other way around."

She was making an effort to talk in my tongue. The words were running slowly out of her mouth like the first autumn water flowing on the small streamlets.

"How do you know our tongue so well?"

"My father, myself, and only a few more of us can speak like you. They learned from your own, I learned from my mother and father. Many times before, men, women, slaves of your tribe, of other tribes, escape. Where do they hide? In here. You are a tribe of hunters, we are a tribe of exiles. My mother was not forest-born; she was captured by your tribe. The Witches had put her on a mule, blindfolded and facing backwards, and sent her into the woods to die. The wolves attacked the mule. My father attacked the wolves.

"My father would have killed you any other day. Not leeches but a stab in the heart is what you'd get. But he thought you were exiled because you had saved my life. That is why you are still alive. He owes you; he swore the moment he returned from his capture and found me alive. He owes my life to you."

"Where is your mother?"

"She died. Many moons ago."

The leaves whispered a sorrowful song to the last nightingales of autumn, and I came close to her. She ran her fingers through my hair. I did the same. I barely touched her lips with mine. They were soft like the Reghen's touch on my shoulder. We remained still for a few breaths.

I didn't know what I was doing. Her lips still tasted bitter from the blackberries.

"You haven't? Ever before?" she asked.

"What?"

"You haven't even begun to live yet, and you are already looking for death."

My legs were melting in the Forest. My heart was on fire, beating more scared than it had in any trial of the Sieve.

"I have to know, Zeria. What is chasing me? The Ouna-Mas are real. I have seen them do terrible magic, demonic rituals. Only this summer."

"All lies. Da-Ren, listen to me. Stay here. Drown your stories in the pond. They are rotten."

"They are real. You saw the Reekaal. Aren't you afraid? Here, now in the night?" I asked.

"I fear many things. But nothing that lives here in the trees and speaks to me. You speak to me. I don't fear you."

She kissed me again.

My whole Tribe was washing away slowly from inside of me.

"There are no Reekaal, Da-Ren. No wolfmen, no undead. We will go tomorrow to see Saim, the elder who speaks with the trees. He will explain."

The next afternoon, Veker found me again, his voice more threatening and desperate. "If you do not leave at once, you will bring death to all of us. I will not let that happen."

"I am going to see Saim," I told him. "Tonight. And then I'll leave."

He gave me a puzzled look.

"Saim won't speak to you after sunset," he said.

At daybreak, we left with Zeria to find Saim, the Forest Wanderer. He did not speak my tongue, and I could not have words with him. He was wrinkled like the bark, with long hair tangled together with leaves. He sat cross-legged under the eternal oaks, with gnarled long fingers around his knees. But I wasn't scared of him. Unlike Sah-Ouna he had the liquid sparkling eyes of a child. A child who sat and looked at the same oak for a hundred and more summers.

Zeria and Saim spoke for a long time. The old man looked at me at first but then kept his eyes closed while Zeria was talking. She turned to me after what seemed like a whole day.

"I told him everything. About the Reekaal, Rouba, and the Ouna-Mas," Zeria said.

Saim opened his eyes. He spoke, and Zeria whispered his words in my tongue. "Monsters, everywhere around us...so many...to fight..."

He stopped and looked up as if he remembered a lost thought. Without another word he turned his back and crawled his way on the rustling leaves to reach a sack where he kept his possessions. He pulled out from the sack the skull of an ox, its horns in his hands. He pretended to wear it over his head, laughed, and put it down again over the leaves.

"And such evil men. Can you fight them, Da-Ren?"

"Yes," I answered while looking at him.

The sun's rays were falling like a rain of gold, dancing on the sleepy grass. They were helping me reveal the mysteries, unravel the magic.

Saim, holding the ox skull, kept saying words I couldn't understand, and Zeria brought them in my own tongue.

"Yes, monsters, demons. Now I can see them."

That was the one thing I wanted to hear. Now Zeria knew too. I was right—the demons were real. Saim closed his eyes and started raving like a man possessed in a dream of crazygrass.

Zeria brought his words whenever he stopped. "I see the bloodthirsty monsters. They've dwelled here since ancient times. They are the first demons whose empty skulls the blind prophets filled with their magic. And then they multiplied and gave birth to the drakons, the wolfmen, the undead, and the bloodeaters."

Saim pulled a waterskin out of his sack and gave it to me.

I brought it cautiously to my lips. It was water. Crystal, cold spring water. Nothing else. He spoke loud and close to me, his words spitting my face through two rows of yellow teeth, and Zeria unraveled them, "You drink the truth; you will not vomit the lies."

I was still thirsty.

"Ask him more. How do I find the lair of the monsters? I must avenge him." I said, shaking her shoulder to make her listen to me.

Zeria's eyes were veiled with worry. She said the words in her tongue, and Saim's answer came again through her beautiful bow-curved lips.

"Go back to Sirol. Find them. The men. They are the only monsters. Ancient and eternal."

The shields of the Forest trees had stopped the arrows of the sun. Her blue eyes grew dark.

The old man stopped. He motioned with a repeating flip of his left hand for me to leave. He then turned his back on me and started crawling on the grass playing with a yellow-black hopper that had jumped from the leaves up to his arm. Zeria rose. I did the same.

But I still hadn't found the truth I sought.

"Ask him. I want to know my destiny. Is there a brave ending to my

Story?"

Zeria didn't want to, but I pushed her into it.

Saim turned to listen to Zeria's words with his head held down as if he were tired and asleep. He answered her, his incomprehensible words coming out angrily for the first time. Still, her voice brought them full of promise and wildflower honey.

"Why does the end concern you, Da-Ren? Find the beginning first. Go back, to the pond."

I didn't know if these were Zeria's words or his, but they were the words that I sought, even for one night. "Back to the pond." That was the one magic I longed for. Zeria led forward and we made for the pond before the evening light died completely. The blue of her eyes, the black of her hair, the veiling night found us there.

Zeria took off her dress and dove into the moonlit water. Our nights together were coming to an end. I dove too, swimming after her, her feet beating and splashing water on my face. I pulled her from the calf, she laughed and screamed playfully and laughed louder. Selene listened and came closer to golden her skin and silver her hair. I pulled her toward me with both arms, our lips separated by a few playful drops of water. Her tongue moved once in and out through smiling, lively lips. I kissed forcefully like someone who had never kissed before. She kissed me back softer than the dying wind. I entered her forcefully like someone who had never kissed before. The damnation of those eyes I could never escape. It was a complete and soulful embrace. I didn't know what I was doing. I just stayed inside of her. It wasn't burning desire yet. I just wanted to be inside of her. As much as I wanted and as much as I knew. The first time. I was still a child inside her wetness, surrounded by her scent of ripe berries and evergreen shrubs. Two children, hand in hand. It didn't last long. It never faded.

She stepped out of the pond and put on her dress. She came and sat close to me again.

"My mother was not a Dasal. She had lived with your tribe, and she taught me your tongue."

"You do not look like the women of the Tribe."

"She wasn't born of your tribe. She was a slave from the North. She had blue eyes. After she was passed to many brave warriors…and her womb remained empty, they threw her to the dogs in your Great Slaughter Feast of the spring full moon. But the dogs did not dare go near her."

This I could not believe. The maulers never hesitated. But I didn't tell her that.

She continued. "Then the Ouna-Mas exiled her to the Forest. But before she died, she spoke to me of those Reekaal." She shook her hair, and the water drops woke up my skin and my senses.

"I have to know."

"My mother said the Ouna-Mas had given birth to male monsters with long heads, just like theirs. They are their sons and their servants, and they raise them secretly. They train them to murder the Khun's enemies. But they are mad and bloodthirsty, so the Ouna-Mas had to rip out their hearts. They tied and locked them with silver chains. And so the sons of the Ouna-Mas cannot leave their mothers' tents for very long. They must return before daybreak. Or else they will die away from the beating of their own hearts. They hunted you all the way here. Veker says so. He has seen them more times than I have."

"I have been eighteen summers with the Tribe and I have never heard of this Legend."

"No legend. My mother told me she had seen them too. I saw them too. You did too. Only a few days ago. Believe your eyes."

"But you kept telling me that you don't believe in monsters."

"I believe my mother. She said they are men, not monsters. Maybe they are hiding. How many times have you entered the tent of a birthing Ouna-Ma?"

"Ouna-Mas don't have children. I have been to their settlement once. I saw no one."

And yet I had seen, even though I never quite believed it. I had seen two giant shadows in Sah-Ouna's tent, standing still like wooden statues. And I had heard from Gunna. Of those huge Reekaal who had attacked him in the Forest.

That was the last thing I needed. Longhead murderers on my trail with orders from Sah-Ouna. And it was the only thing that made sense. Much more sense than the mythical Reekaal and the Legend of Er-Ren. The sons of the Ouna-Mas. Monsters. Men. In the Witch's tent. In Gunna's nightmare. In Zeria's tales.

Zeria's next words pierced me like ice blades between the ribs. "You will leave tomorrow, Da-Ren."

She was right. There was no more magic to find in the Forest.

"I have to find out who came after me. I am the First Uncarved."

The First Uncarved.

I took a long look around me. There was nothing else I wanted from this Forest. Except her. And I have had her, already. As if I had just woken from a deep stupor that had lasted a whole moon and more, I said the words that I had forgotten, the words that had been lost in the wood.

Run away. Gallop free again. Conquer her, conquer fate, conquer Enaka. Rule the Tribe.

I was growing weak next to the invincible Forest Witch.

Wield the Blade. Avenge. Rule. Ride with men again. Leave this forest.

"I don't want you to leave, Da-Ren. I see only death where you go."

The night had still not settled around us. Half the animals sought shelter, and the other half sought their prey. I saw sparkling dark-yellow eyes following me and heard the hoot of an owl very close. The rustling sounds of men's feet were close behind us. Veker was already in front of me. His men had surrounded me with axes and cudgels. There were more than ten of them.

"Your time here is long past. We are going to get you out of the forest. You won't make it on your own," said Veker.

My fingers were around the blade's grip, but I couldn't take all of them. The time had come for me to leave.

I had entered Zeria. She had kissed me. Her magic had rejuvenated me as if she had dipped me whole into a jar of honey. A horse and the open sky. The stars that the canopy had mantled. Any horse. I had to get back to the Tribe's warriors. I was the First Uncarved. I would let no one hunt me like a helpless deer.

Zeria was hitting Veker on the chest with her fists. She wrapped herself around her father's knees.

"No, let him stay."

"If he stays, he will bring death to all of us," said Veker. "Listen to Saim."

Zeria turned to me. "Throw down your blades. Plead on your knees to stay here," she said. "Stay here." Those were her last words for a long time to come.

I dropped my blades, but I did not know how to plead on my knees. It was time. I turned to Veker. "Fear not, Dasal. I will leave tomorrow. But you must first take me to Saim. We will go together, only the two of us."

I didn't want to go with Zeria. I wanted to hear the true prophecy.

The sleep of the last night was cold. The cold of late autumn, the cold away from her skin. I dreamed of the chained hearts of the sons of the Ouna-Mas, beating alone and bleeding in their mothers' tents.

Veker and his men woke me at first light and gave me my blades, my bow, and Rouba's horse. He took me deep into the Forest through untrodden paths. The Forest was bleeding autumn. A bronze leaf tangled in my long hair. I had stayed there too long. His men followed from a distance. I was not afraid. If he wanted to kill me, he wouldn't have given me my blades.

I spotted a shadow appearing and disappearing like a spirit through the trees as we kept walking.

"Don't be afraid," Veker said.

I wasn't.

Two breaths later Saim suddenly appeared in front of us like a wind-ghost emerging from a tree's trunk. He looked at me without saying a word and only made a grimace to Veker. And yet Veker translated to me.

"Saim asks, 'Why have you returned?'" Veker said.

"I want to know. About my future. Am I cursed by my ninestar mark? Will I bring darkness and blood to my Tribe?"

Veker looked at me, but the fear gave his face the color of the yellow-green leaves.

"What madness is this? Is that what you came here to learn? Tribe of mad beasts!" he shouted.

Saim hissed his next words, his palms covering his temples as if he saw the end of all living things and his despair flowed into Veker's words.

"Blood first, then darkness; that is the end of all of us. Cursed or not, Da-Ren."

"The end of my Story, I mean. Is it glorious or bitter?" I asked again.

"Yes!" Saim uttered the word in my tongue.

"Yes, what?" I asked, my hands raised impatiently with clawed fingers, ready to grab his throat.

He didn't say another word.

I looked back at the rest of the Dasal. Zeria had come and was standing among them, her hand raised and unmoving. A last goodbye.

I pointed to the sky.

"I'll come back soon. By the next moon. One moon, Zeria."

There would never be many words between Zeria and me. The first time I saw her, I saved her life. As soon as I found her again, she saved mine. From the first moment, without thinking or deciding, like blind servants of a forbidden faith, we wove our lives and our death into the same wreath. Words were precious.

It was the only way I could leave. They would have to peel me off the trunks with force, like the Reekaal who had been forever trapped within. I held her last gaze and turned my back on her. My legs were walking fast; the Dasal were dragging my soul. They took me out of the Forest in haste. The next nightfall, they left me alone with my horse under the moonlight, at the clearing of the Forest's eastern end. I held onto the horse's mane and started my journey back to Sirol. The stars, the glowing dust of Enaka's body, startled, recognized me and in all their brightness asked me, "Is it you, Da-Ren? Do you live?"

I asked them to slide through the dense branches and find her for me. Only the stars could now see both of us at the same moment. The wind whipped me, like a Guide's forgotten punishment in the Sieve. I had days to gallop and nights to pray to the stars ahead of me. I had to find who had killed Rouba. Who had tried to kill me. If the Ouna-Mas had given birth to male monsters. If these monsters had been sent to kill me. If the Reghen did touch the Tribe's condemned on the shoulder.

If there was still a chance for me to become the next Khun, then all these snakes would be under my boot. I'd crush them all. I had tied the red cloth of the First Uncarved on my arm again. Maybe I could still make it. I had been away from the camp of the Uncarved two whole moons. Not more. Couldn't be sure. Blue was their color. But, if I managed to fool Sah-Ouna, if I could convince her that I had passed the trial, if Chaka believed me, and if Khun-Taa granted me audience, then there was still hope.

Too many *ifs* gathered, one for each dead star up there.

When I arrived at Sirol, it was already too late.

XXX.
Iron End

Eighteenth autumn. Uncarved—Wolf.

I dismounted outside the camp of the Uncarved at midday. The wind was howling, lifting and rolling the hay bushels from the ground. It brought all the curses of the Ouna-Mas, all the questions of the Guides upon me. Young Starlings and Owls, children of our camp, saw me first and ran ahead to spread the word. By the time I had reached the hut I shared with Malan and Gunna, everyone knew. They avoided my eyes as if I were a ghost. My weapons and my clothes were gone.

"Everybody said that you were dead for sure," Chaka said bluntly.

"Everybody who? I was alone."

He had nothing else to say. The red band of the First Uncarved was tied again around Malan's arm. Chaka didn't even bother to untie mine. He just looked at it for a breath, and I knew I had to cut it away. I was given new clothes, but they were old and worn; whatever had been left behind by the dead and the unfit Uncarved who had been sent away.

It was not the clothes or the red band or the second bow I'd left behind and was now gone. No, I didn't miss any of these. Not even her eyes. It was the Guides and the Uncarved whom I couldn't stand to look at anymore—those, staring at me as if I were a man condemned. Any moment I expected them to come in with their knives and carve my terrible end.

What if the questions came? What happened to Rouba? Why I left the Pack? How I survived so long in the Forest? Did I kill him? What happened to my horse? Why had I returned with Rouba's horse? Did I steal it? Some of this was going on in their minds for sure. If I started telling a Story about a girl and a pond, the true Story, it would be even worse.

"You drink the truth; you can't vomit the lies," were Saim's words. He had poisoned me with crystal water. I didn't want to lie or defend myself.

But there were neither lashes nor carvings. I had one bitter end only: their cold indifference. I told them little. Chaka avoided asking anything, and he wanted to hear even less. He was relieved. His search for the One had ended, and at last he was on the same side as Sah-Ouna. He didn't have to bother with me anymore.

The ninestar Bera didn't lose any time; he walked toward me shouting, immediately when he saw me: "You had no reason to leave the Archer Packs and go search for the Dasal. Who asked you to do that?"

"The men."

Lies.

"The Leader tells his men where to go; they don't tell him. But you are a ninestar. You would have found some way to drown in pigshit in the end."

I said nothing. I had become nothing, and they didn't even allow me to demand anything. I was just relieved that they were not asking.

Had Sah-Ouna demanded it, I would have been carved. But the First Witch didn't even bother herself with me. She had sent me on the campaign but never once cared to learn whether I had returned or what I had done there. She would never again call me to her tent. Chaka went to speak to the Reghen about my fate, and the two of them returned with Sah-Ouna's answer.

"The Reghen says not to carve you." That was all Chaka said and then he stood stiff-lipped and shook his head left and right.

The Reghen wanted to erase any hope I still had. "There are only three of you Uncarved Wolves remaining, and so it should be. We must have at least two to choose from till the final night. But the way you are all dying out lately, we are safer with three rather than two."

I was finished. What in the demon's curse was I thinking? How could I still expect to be First after being lost in the Forest for so long? I had thrown it all away to find Kar-Tioo.

On the fourth afternoon of my return, Malan and Gunna were to compete on the bow. Chaka didn't even let me mount my horse. I watched together with the younger Uncarved—my arms crossed and useless.

It was late in the evening. The day's light was fading, and the horses were tired from galloping back and forth in the field all day. Malan and Gunna continued to aim with their bows at the pumpkin heads that stood on stakes, looking like the servants of the Demon. Harmless, unarmed, and motionless servants were those pumpkins.

Malan had kept up all day with Gunna, but now he was losing. His horse had slowed down and was coming in second. As the sun was setting, he stopped completely and approached Chaka and the Reghen who were watching next to me.

"This field is beaten badly, and there is no light. Let's move to that one," said Malan pointing to his right.

Chaka agreed.

"Da-Ren, get the Starlings and go fetch torches. Put them around the stakes on that field," he said.

I did as I was told and as night was falling the trial continued in the new field but without any change. Malan was still losing. He seemed to be holding back sometimes, as if he didn't want to follow. Gunna's arrows always reached first. He made his rounds faster and aimed better, while all the others were beginning to mock Malan the First with long boos and jeers.

"Gunna will take the red band," I heard someone next to me say.

Gunna was unstoppable and continued to crush the pumpkins and all doubts about who was the best warrior. As if that would mean anything.

I could beat them. I had beaten them not long ago when I was First. Just two moons had passed since I had fought in a bloody campaign. Bearded warriors and Archers had shivered listening to me telling Er-Ren's Story in the Forest. Now I was nobody.

Chaka sent me to put new pumpkins on top of each man-tall stake for one final round, and so I did. I was walking backward instead of running as Gunna and Malan were approaching the targets on horseback. I didn't want to miss the spectacle. Gunna was galloping way ahead, already aiming, and I would be in real danger if he were not a great archer. I didn't know if he'd ever be Khun, but I was certain he'd be one of the greatest warriors of the Tribe for many winters to come.

He was balancing on the horse with boots on stirrups, both hands free on the bow, screaming with rage after each arrow shot. He passed next to the stakes, galloping even closer to me, as I was backing away. He was aiming backward for the most difficult shot, showing off. Gunna, the greatest warrior I had seen. That, I was certain. We are all so certain of so many things when we're young.

And then it happened right in front of me. The brown mare's front leg sank in the ground. A blind puddle? The horse's back arched hard, both knees and its head bent forward and hit the dirt. Gunna came flying out of the saddle, landing flat on his back a few feet away from me. A dull thump came out of the ground and a deadly cracking snap out of his bones. The horse rolled to its right side breathing heavily, while Gunna lay on his back next to me, motionless like a fallen tree trunk. I knelt next to him, my torch illuminating a rictus of pain. His back and left leg were at bad angles, and he was still as a corpse. He wasn't screaming in pain. Those who are in the worst kind of pain never cry. They can't. It hurts. He only tried to whisper.

"Red…"

"Stay put. Don't talk," I answered.

He whispered again something like "Red…first."

Red first? Red band? What on the Demon's name are you trying to tell me, Gunna? "Shhh, shut up now, here they're coming, we'll help you. Stay put, Gunna. You'll be fine." *Damn you! No, you won't.*

I had seen that too many times before. Long ago, in the second spring of the Uncarved, another two of our Pack had fallen. One had broken his head, and the other, a wrist. Fiery rage consumed our Guides whenever this shame came upon the Pride of the Sieve. Someone they had raised for so many summers, chosen by the Ouna-Mas and Enaka. Someone they had ripped away from a mother and a father he would never know, without shedding a tear, just to die like that. To be killed or crippled by a bad fall without even seeing the face of an othertriber in battle.

Gunna was still alive. The pain had turned his cheeks into the color of white cloth and he couldn't utter a word despite trying hard. The Guides and the Uncarved had gathered around us now, but no one was trying to move Gunna. They knew.

"Iron End! Iron End!" shouted those around me.

"Give him an Iron End!"

Iron End. Another not-so-ancient custom. Some of the eldest remembered when Khun-Mervak, the fourth Khun, had initiated it not many winters ago. Someone from the same hut had to end the boy's suffering with an iron. A blade, an arrow, a quick end that Enaka would favor. Either Malan or me. Gunna was crying silently in front of us, desperate tears that couldn't even run down his cheeks.

Chaka turned to Malan with a dejected look and made the move I dreaded: his palm facing down flying fast and flat across his throat. And yet I was relieved he hadn't chosen me, though only for a moment.

Malan left the field for a while and came back with a stretcher. He approached Gunna and gave him from a waterskin to drink, but Gunna couldn't. He tried to pull Gunna onto the stretcher.

"Don't touch him! He is in pain…he…" I shouted. I had no words.

Malan was on one knee, trying to pull Gunna onto the stretcher without luck. He raised his head, his angry stare fixed on me.

"'Iron End,' they said, Da-Ren. Are you going to help? Else get out of here, now."

Gunna's moaning hid much greater pain. Malan called a Guide to help him. The Guide obeyed, and they carried the stretcher with Gunna on it away.

"Where are they going?" I asked.

I looked around me. Not a single face I knew. A few Uncarved Starlings were there, but I didn't even remember their names after two moons in the Forest. A Reghen with no other name. I was alone. There were no other Uncarved from my Pack still alive around me. No one answered me. They were looking at Malan, his red band.

Malan stopped close to the hole where Gunna's horse had fallen and put the stretcher down. He filled that hole and another next to it with dirt and knelt to whisper something into Gunna's ear.

The brief Story that would be on everyone's lips around our fires from the following night onward was this: "Malan told Gunna why he had woken in the middle of the night before the trial: to mark all the holes of the fields. That was why he was coming second most of the day because he avoided all the bad spots. He had marked them in his mind, one by one."

Good Stories become immortal, even if they are only a big lie. This Story would live forever if Malan was chosen as the next Khun, the One Leader of the Tribe. A Leader needed his own Stories, and a Tribe without Stories could not survive. Whether they were lies or real or—as usual—something in between the two, mattered not. They just had to be good.

But on the night I heard the Story for the first time, I knew right then why Malan had asked that they change fields and why he had woken up in the middle of the night: to dig out the holes himself.

We all followed Malan and Gunna at a distance. They had reached the Forest's edge. Malan stopped, took out his blade, and carved Gunna twice, in both arms and his chest. The injured boy's white tunic was soaked on his own blood. Malan took off Gunna's boots. Gunna lay in the dirt, only his eyes twitching and darting from side to side. Malan left him there all alone and turned to walk toward us. Gunna's wrists and ankles were bare.

"How do the Uncarved die?"

"They bleed to death," the older ones had told us on our first moon as Starlings.

Not even the Guides stopped Malan. They knew that in three moons he would be the One Leader.

I didn't have to see the fourteen eyes glowing like embers. I heard them. The wolves—not the Uncarved or the Wolfmen, the wolves—the four legged, the hungry, appeared at the edge of the Forest. The blood and the night had called them. If we left Gunna there, they would soon be all over him. They would go first for his ankles and his wrists. The poor boy could not do anything to defend himself. I had no doubts his spine was broken. He was not going to die well.

"We're finished here. Everyone, back to your huts," Malan said.

I bit my lip, my eyes cutting fast from Gunna to Malan as he kept walking away. Everybody obeyed in total silence.

I signaled to the smallest Starling next to me.

"Hey, come here."

I took his torch and pushed him away.

"What are you doing? An Iron End, they said," I yelled at Malan.

He turned and came up to me a few feet in distance.

"His wolf ancestors will take care of him. They'll protect him," he said with a low, but clear, reassuring voice and turned to walk away.

Didn't I know by now? I should have seen it five long winters ago. Darkness and madness reigned in Malan's head. Was it only I who could see this, or was I blind with envy? No one made a move. Malan made for the huts, and everyone followed him. I grabbed from the back the neck of the young Uncarved next to me. I took his bow and its quiver. I was also an Uncarved Wolf. Protector of the Tribe. I could bring an Iron End myself.

I ran toward Gunna and lit with my torch the dried twigs I found around him. The wolves waited at a distance. They were in no hurry. They had all night. I was alone. It would be their feast sooner or later.

At my feet, Gunna lay taller than ever before. The boy was at the seventeenth fall of his life. A fateful fall. His eyes had no peace in them. They were carving his agony in my heart. Silent screams were his plea for help. Live, die. He lifted two fingers signaling me next to him. I knelt, my ear next to his mouth.

"Red…"

Again, the same. *What was he saying?* "What?"

"Redbreast…" he whispered.

"Redbreast? Is this what you're telling me? You're funny, you, big warrior. Close your eyes, rest. I'm here."

The blood all over his tunic. *Redbreast? Making a joke? Fuck you, Gunna, fuck you for dying on me and having me kill you. You are the last one I have left.*

I raised my bow.

His lips were trembling. Begging. Still breathing.

"I can't save you, friend. I don't have such magic."

In the heart. Two demon fangs, the broad iron arrowheads. The only way the giant would die quickly.

A prayer. *Make one up, Da-Ren. Enaka, I beg you to accept him. Don't send him down to the cold fucking caves.* His eyes stopped twitching. *I wipe away your tears, my friend. They are mine. No one will see them. You die brave.* His wrists and ankles would not suffer from the wolves. There was no way for me to carry his body. It was too heavy. The wolves would not let me.

I ran back to join the rest of the boys. Malan, the First, was waiting for me, standing in front of everyone else.

"Again, a stupid mistake, Da-Ren. I told you to get lost."

I was still holding my bow.

The boys were looking at him as if they expected something more. He made some hesitant steps toward my side. I would strangle him if he got closer. He stopped and took two steps back. All he would dare to do was talk.

"It was not for you to do anything, Da-Ren. Gunna was mine. You will do what I—" he started saying.

I nocked the one arrow I had left on my bow and raised it.

We were both trying to look calm and strong. But my head was boiling hard.

I pulled the bowstring, aiming for his chest.

His legs froze. He looked around to see if anyone was there to save him.

A Reghen jumped between us. Unlike us, he was shaking.

Bera, the ninestar, came toward me. "Stand down, Da-Ren," he said, trying to find his calming voice.

My hands were trembling. It was not fear.

"Drop this bow, Da-Ren, or you die here."

I was biting my lip hard to hold myself from releasing the arrow. Bera slowly lowered my left arm to bring my aim downward, away from Malan. I released. The arrow flew low at an angle and hit the ground between Malan's dusty boots.

The four-legged wolves were howling at the Forest's edge as the brave, muscled body of Gunna welcomed them. At dawn, I alone would gather whatever remained and take it to the pyre.

Malan disappeared in the hut that the two of us were left to share.

"He's a mad jackal. Doesn't anyone see that?" I asked Bera.

"You are the weak one. Malan did the right thing," the Reghen blurted out.

He was a young Reghen. About my age.

"You stupid boy! I hope your horse finds that mud puddle someday," I said.

No one had ever called a Reghen "stupid boy" until then. It was like spitting the One Hundred of them in the face. And every one of their Stories and Truths.

But I didn't want any more of the Reghen's Truths.

It was the first time during my five winters' training that I met a challenge I didn't care for.

Gunna's torture brought no enjoyment to me.

I had not planned it for many moons like Malan had.

I had been poisoned in the Forest.

Blue was the poison of Zeria, of the Kar-Tioo pond.

I was not a Reekaal.

Chaka, the Chief Guide, who had been seeking only One for countless summers, came next to me, his face cold as if I had just crossed his path for the first and last time.

"You are not the One."

That was all he said. But I knew that already.

I was not born to be Khun.

I realized it suddenly, harshly, mercilessly, and irreversibly, as I heard from a distance the feasting of the wolves. As unbelievable as it sounded in my own head, I didn't look forward to being Khun. I didn't have it in me. I cared about the brave. A Leader draws his strength from the weak. Maybe I still had the desire to lead the brave to the glory and slaughter of the Final Battle. But I had no desire to put my dick deep into the brains of the weak, which was pretty much everybody, just to mess around with them.

I couldn't bear to accept that someone was better than I. I couldn't bear having to bow my head to any other Uncarved or Guide. Above all, I couldn't bear the moment in a few moons' time when I would have to say the words "Khun-Malan, my Great Leader." But none of this was enough of a reason to become Khun.

The Reghen were right. All the others who had given me slanted looks when I had put Gunna out of his misery were right. They were right for one simple reason: it was what they wanted. It was what they could believe and sing. Malan's Story. You can't go against the Khun, the one the Unending Sky shines upon. He is the Legend of Legends. You bring your blade down on him and find only air instead of his heart. Your arrows fall between his boots, never higher.

And the Khun knows how to lead the many, those who seek the Witches' signs, the Stories.

"They have been riding better since that night," Chaka said to Bera a few days later.

He made sure I was next to them, listening.

"Who?" asked Bera.

"The younger Uncarved. They take care of their horses, they rest them, and they look out for the puddles."

"What are you saying, Chief?"

"Malan did well. He made them better warriors without even opening his mouth. I say that no Uncarved will fall from his horse again while Malan is among us. Or, by Enaka, I'll sit still and you can piss on me."

Gunna's flesh and Malan's madness fed the Tribe and gave it strength.

That Legend lived for many winters to come. From the night Malan left Gunna at the edge of the Forest, they said that no Uncarved was ever again mortally wounded falling from his horse in training. Many summers passed without losing another boy. Only the Story of Gunna and Malan was spoken. Nothing about Gunna's Iron End. And that was the only Truth the Reghen would sing.

They didn't carve me that same night, though many of them wanted to. Even I wanted to be carved, but there had to be a second Uncarved. But they did exile me for good to the hut of the Uncarved Eagles, together with six younger ones who would never become Leaders. Malan would be alone in our old hut. "To protect you from killing each other," they said, but, at night, Reghen and Ouna-Mas came and went from Malan's hut. I also saw Sah-Ouna slipping in one night. And a second.

I now counted the moons we had left on the fingers of my one hand. If Khun-Taa did not die soon, then the Truth declared that both Malan and I had to be carved. But something told me that Khun-Taa's death was coming fast.

During the next few nights, funny stories popped around the dung fires about Reekaal who shat themselves when Malan went near the Forest. Even if he had never actually been in the Forest himself. Everyone had forgotten what had happened during the last Great Feast of Spring at Wolfhowl. The Goddess had shadowed their minds. Enaka sheds light on the True Leader and darkens all the foes around him.

I had been gone for a long time, longer than even Sah-Ouna would have wished. The Story of my brave legendary father had been forgotten in the Forest, and Rouba, my only real father, had died there also. Zeria had rescued my soul and hid it in an oak's hollow. She had reached the caves of the dead to claim it back.

There would be more sacred ceremonies and other bloody rituals, but the next Leader of the Tribe, the sixth Khun, had been chosen ahead of all this. Everyone knew that.

"If Khun-Taa dies, then Malan will be the first Khun whom I ever trained. He is the One. And that is the way it has always been," said Chaka. "The Reghen say that back in the beginning, every night when we had to choose the new Khun among the surviving Uncarved—" He stopped for a few breaths as the young Uncarved were hanging from his mouth to hear his words. "—there was never any question. When that night comes, everyone knows already who he is."

Why should he whip me when he could utter such words with a broad smile?

My quest ended and my shame became complete on that first night when I slept in the hut of the younger Uncarved. At dawn, I would wake up in a peace I had never known. I would not be Khun; no more would I chase, like a stupid dog, some bone they had thrown in front of me. I had become a warrior and a man in my own campaign, in my own trial, in my own Forest, and my training was now complete.

That was what I said to myself before I went to sleep. So that I could sleep.

Defeat sleeps cold and alone, always looking for some excuse to snuggle under.

XXXI.
The Witch, the Amazon, the Cow

Island of the Holy Monastery, Thirty-fourth winter.
According to the Monk Eusebius.

We were approaching the second anniversary of Da-Ren's arrival at the Castlemonastery when we completed the first transcription of his story. Da-Ren waited in vain to see Baagh's trireme emerge from the waves of the open sea, together with the powerful Sorcerers of the Cross.

"There are no such men whom Baagh knows, only old hermits. Anchorites," the First Elder told me once after Baagh had disappeared.

No one came, and we didn't have any news from Baagh. We had only the first draft of Da-Ren's tale after nine hard months of writing. It was quite a sterile account of the events, written with a quick and abrupt style using the few words that he knew.

Monastic life had sucked the warrior out of the arms and eyes of Da-Ren. His frame had become leaner, and his weakness made him more acceptable—more like the rest of us. He now wore a brown hooded robe, without the embroidered cross. Not gray like a monk's. It made him look more like a merchant than a monk, as he had bought it, along with a pair of sturdy sandals, new from the ship that brought our supplies. The boots he had been wearing when he had arrived were suitable only for the island's harsh winters, and by now had become useless.

The only work that kept our thoughts away from Baagh and his empty promises was the storytelling, especially his. Baagh had ordered me to write down every detail, and Da-Ren, who wanted to get it finished as quickly as possible, was getting irritated during the first year.

"I want to understand more, Da-Ren. I'd like to know more about your tents, your clothing, your horses?"

"I have ridden hundreds of horses, Eusebius. Do you know the one thing they all said to me?"

"What?"

"Nothing. Horses don't tell stories. What do you want to know about the horses? Wouldn't you rather I spoke to you of the people?"

"I want to know everything."

"Have you ever ridden, Eusebius, hmm?"

"Only the mule down at the village."

"What do you think—that if I tell you about horse stirrups, you will understand me better?"

"I have heard about stirrups."

"We were the only tribe that had stirrups. Stupid when you think of it, but countless thousands of your empire's warriors died because of this. We could balance with our legs on the horses and use both hands to shoot the bow. They had never seen stirrups in the empire before we came."

These details would certainly be of interest to the Emperor and his Generals in Holy Thalassopolis, the reigning city of the Southeastern Empire.

"What other secret do you want to learn, Eusebius? That I kicked the animal's sides with my heels to get it going? That it grazed on grass two times a day? Tell me what secrets to reveal that Baagh's Cross Sorcerers don't know."

"You're mocking me, Da-Ren. If you don't want to, then don't tell me anything. The less you tell me, the less I have to change the next time we rewrite."

Only when we had finished the first transcription of the story, and I had read it to Da-Ren, from beginning to end in a pompous voice, did he understand that we had to do what I was saying.

"This is nonsense," he said about a description I was reading. "No, this is wrong. But, yes, it was winter. Didn't you understand that?"

Many times when he heard his story, he would say the worst thing: "I'm sick of this. I'm too tired and have forgotten."

It was strange, but when we wrote his story in short form, it was more painful. The scenes ran like bloodied arrows, stopping nowhere to rest. Only when we lengthened it did it become easier on the ear.

That was how Da-Ren was finally convinced, and I with him. We had to rewrite and rewrite. It would never be good enough, but we had to rewrite as many times as our patience allowed. If and when the wise men ever came to hear his story, it would have to be much better written.

"You should read the Sacred Books, the eternal ones," I said, "to see what you like about them. They might help to open up your mind and loosen your tongue."

I read to him all the new codices that the merchant ships brought to the monastery, even the old dying scrolls from the libraries of the South, and Da-Ren gave me gold coins to find even more.

And so we rewrote the story during his third year on the island. When Baagh still didn't appear, we had nothing else to do but retry a third time during Da-Ren's fourth year. Da-Ren's and Baagh's gold had run out by then. We did not have supplies to do a fourth draft and, thankfully, we didn't need to.

It was the third winter when we rewrote for a second consecutive year. We searched for the right words, and we took out those we didn't like. We added color on papyrus. We added horses. A few.

At this point of the story, when I learned that Da-Ren would not be Leader of his Tribe, I always asked him the same thing: "You didn't keep your promise, Da-Ren. You said the word 'why.' You had told me before that the whys didn't matter, but now you broke down and told me many times why you would not be Khun."

Unlike the many times he fooled me when I asked him about his soul's repentance, there were times like these when he had nowhere to hide.

"Do you know how many thousands will be massacred before the end of this story, Eusebius? To etch Malan's fate in red? How many tens of thousands perished in this tale that is just now starting to boil? But that is what the men and the First Witch of my Tribe wanted, the One Leader for the Final Battle."

"And that wasn't you?"

"A Khun looks down on us from the top of the hill. We are small to him, born only to die. He doesn't see the difference between animals and men. Not even between men of the Tribe and othertribers. He would feed them all to the fire of his Story. I didn't have that in me. That…gift."

"You didn't have Zeria in you either, but you found her. Why?"

"Are you going to start with the whys again? What do you know about women, Eusebius?"

It was obvious that I knew nothing. Nobody in the Castlemonastery did, and that gave me an idea. I had spent so much time writing, and I wanted to share some of it with all the monks. I asked the First Elder to read the story. He refused. I asked him if I could read it to the peasants. He said that would be blasphemy and no one would feel pacified listening to a tale of slaughters and infidels.

"Maybe I can just choose a few passages about their lives."

He thought about that for a while and said, "Only about domestic matters. These barbarians do not honor family or wife or sister. Tell that story to the villagers. It will water the plant of their faith to the True God."

I found that odd. I asked Da-Ren to sit down with me and write the story of the women of his Tribe. I read it to the villagers on a dark winter night in the stable next to the church. Most of the monks joined us as well. Many women were there, even the miller's widow who had claimed that Da-Ren had violated her. The unmarried twin sisters were there. They were the ones who worked the fields alone, and it was said that they were not even sisters, that they had just been orphans together since they had arrived at the island with the refugees. Even the mad old woman who never attended church came. She stayed away from the monks. The peasants would go to her for help only when the Almighty God refused to listen to their prayers. And that was more often than not.

Da-Ren had sat with me patiently to give me his account of the women of the Tribe, and I read it from the papyrus, for all to hear and renew their faith in our God.

The Tale of the Women of the Tribe

When I was born, Khun-Taa was the Leader of the Tribe. He had brought us to Sirol in the Great Valley between the Eastern and the Western Empires, in between the Endless Forest and the Blackvein River. During the first summers, Khun-Taa often went on campaigns to the South and looted cities and villages, but he never dared to go near Thalassopolis, the city my Tribe calls Sapul. The Southeastern Empire was all-powerful, and the Kings of the Cross Worshippers hid behind the city's indestructible walls and wouldn't come out to face us.

For thirteen bloody summers Khun-Taa raided the South and when he got tired, he camped in the Great Valley and concerned himself with the Change. We stopped moving every spring. The Story of the Change was the Story of Sah-Ouna, the woman he found under the full moon on the twelfth spring of his reign. The Blades captured her across from the Blackvein, between the bare willows half-naked—

The priest had left already. That man was not a monk. He was a man of God. As my faith waned in later years, he became the opposite of God, everything that I came to despise about God. He carried the burden of a thousand rules, rules that the Holy Books never mentioned. His own rules. The more of them he made, the more power he had.

The First Elder shook his head, and I understood that I shouldn't use another word like that even if it was written down. I would ignore that rule a few more times. He was right, though. The miller's widow had fixed her dreamy gaze on Da-Ren, her hand rubbing between her legs. I continued.

—and brought her to Khun-Taa. Sah-Ouna was meant to be fucked like a slave, but she possessed three unique gifts, and they were more than enough to transform her into the Wise-woman of the Tribe and the Guide of the Leader.

She knew the powers of each plant and every spell. She had a thirst for power. And everyone believed her to be sent by the Goddess because she spoke our tongue. She spoke our words without any difficulty, even though she had been born south of the river.

She was younger then, much younger and some say beautiful beyond what any man could resist. That wasn't even her name; no one remembers her real one. Khun-Taa became wet clay in her hands.

Sah-Ouna was a dark mystery for the men but a very visible catastrophe for the women of the Tribe and the othertribers. She insisted on separating the women, taking them from the men's tents and throwing most of them with the animals. She had understood that a warrior would either listen to the one Goddess of the Sky or to the one woman who shared his tent.

Even now, I don't believe that Enaka planted Sah-Ouna at the banks of the river to wait for Khun-Taa. Maybe she lived in her hut with one of our warriors who had gotten away from the Tribe, in love for many summers, until he died or she killed him. She then waited and planned her revenge. Maybe she had children or lost them to the Tribe's warriors.

One way or another, Khun-Taa made her our First Witch when in reality, she was only an othertriber slave of the South who spoke our tongue.

Whenever I tried to bring up this forbidden Story to other warriors as I grew older, I kept getting the same answer.

"It makes no difference. Enaka uses strange means to send us her Voice."

For as long as I lived, two things remained invincible against my blade: the frozen wind and the blind faith in the Witches.

But Sah-Ouna didn't just boil roots and herbs in her cauldrons; she plotted to create a new Tribe. To do that, she had to change only one thing. The women. She separated them into three groups from a very young age.

Very few women, the most fearless who stood out early in the Sieve and endured the training, became warriors. Always Archers. They could not become Blades to fight in man-to-man combat. Women like Danaka in the Sieve. Like Elbia. No, not like Elbia, forgive me.

I stopped to take a breath, to honor the innocent dead. Only Da-Ren and I understood.

The women. The Archers. None of them could ever become Khun of the Tribe, but some of them could become Chiefs of a Pack of women Archers and command forty of their own. They had their own Packs and fought alongside the men but never among them. Their Chiefs took orders from the Leader of all the Archers, and in battle, they were equal and, in some cases, even better than the men.

Fewer still were those who were born with a gift and were chosen from a very young age to become Ouna-Mas. Those with the long heads, pitch-black eyes. They were taken as newborns by Sah-Ouna. They had the gift, they learned the Stories, and they could read the signs of the Unending Sky and Selene. They—and only they—also had the privilege of fornicating for pleasure. At night, they would take off their black-and-red robes and reward the best warriors. Witch would ride warrior like a horse. Warrior would fuck Witch like a dog.

The First Elder approached and whispered to me to stop this at once. "This is revolting blasphemy," he said.

"I didn't write this. It is the words of the infidel. That's why I read it. It will disgust the peasants and make their faith stronger," I said, as my excuse.

Surprisingly, the First Elder let me continue. Nobody wanted me to stop. I could read their eyes.

The first, second, and third woman we had all ever lain with, after leaving the tent of the Uncarved, was one of Sah-Ouna's young Witches. If an Uncarved was to lie with a different woman first, the hut would forget him and cast him out of the Pride of the Sieve.

Every Ouna-Ma left a deep carving, not on the left arm but on the right breast just beneath the nipple, after the first coupling, to show all that he had come of age. A few drops of blood for all of us to remember that even if we didn't have the carvings of the weaker warriors, our fates would always belong to the Ouna-Mas. Although all were younger than Sah-Ouna, they were usually a few summers older than we were and never got with child. The roots they boiled and drank took care of that.

And then there were all the rest of the women, the endless herd of cows, thousands of them who were neither warriors nor Ouna-Mas. They had only one purpose, and that was to get with child and give birth. Always males, if the Sky allowed, or else they would end up eating whatever the pigs left over. They were always coupling with as many men as possible until their bellies were full. The warriors fucked them day and night. Only from behind on all fours. That was the order so they would conceive only boys. The men never spent an entire night with the women. Only a few breaths.

The other monks had long excused themselves and left the stable. It was time for prayer, and I imagined the prayers would be longer and filled with guilt that night. It was the third year after Da-Ren had arrived. I had spent a lot of time with his story, but less with the Holy Books. My faith had been challenged and found weak. Maybe because I knew the end of his story, or so I thought.

No one was permitted to own such common women for many moons. They could keep them for only a short while, as long as it took for the seed to quicken in their wombs. They succeeded, and the women left to give birth, or they failed, and had to leave and let some other Pack try. Most of them were used by many different tents each moon, and that was necessary. That way, no one concerned themselves with whose child belonged to whom. All and none of the children belonged to everyone, to the Tribe.

Rarely, some discovered the poison of love, even for a while, against every Truth of the Tribe. Or—another way to say it—someone's cock rubbed itself better in a certain woman's hole. These unfortunate men tried to keep a woman to themselves for one whole moon. Hardly ever for two. And I have seen the revenge of Sah-Ouna, half-rotted corpses of crucified women who had stayed more than three moons in a row with the same warrior without spreading for any other. Women in love. The Reghen and their two hundred eyes made sure to be everywhere and see these things.

That is the true story of the women of my Tribe, as I lived it.

It was deep in the night. The peasants around me sat with mouths gaping in awe. Maybe it was the barbarism of these faraway monsters. Maybe it was just the storytelling that someone had put on papyrus and read to them something beyond the Five Holy Books. Their own life stories were not that different.

There were only three fates that this world of ours had for the women of any tribe: the witch, the amazon, the cow.

Here in front of us was the crazy fortune-teller who lived in the last hut of their settlement. She read the leaves of the trees, the goat's shoulder blades, and the flight of birds. She had once been very beautiful, and it is said that she had taken many men to her bed. The priest was terrified of her and she of him.

Here in front of me were the fighters of life: two well-built, tall women, sisters some said, who harnessed mules to the plow, and kept every man who wanted to possess them at a distance. All the rest? Whether they were young or old or with full bellies like cows, they all had that same nauseating smell that came with feeding animals and children all day.

The peasants left, and I opened the stable door. The dawning light fell on us and the barren island.

"Do you understand, Eusebius? Zeria had been condemned by my Tribe from the first moment she had laid eyes on me."

I had understood something more. Men and women lived separately in Da-Ren's Tribe. I knew nothing about horses or women; that much was true. I turned the question back to him.

"What do you know of women, Da-Ren?"

XXXII.
Stake and Lard

Eighteenth autumn. Uncarved—Wolf.

Freedom. Those few nights, before they carved me and after my return from Kar-Tioo, were the only ones I found the bitter repose of defeat and the peace of indifference inside me. I sought nothing. I was never going to be Khun, I didn't know what I was going to be, and there was nothing I could do about that anymore. I had all but completed my training. My fears had been swept away. I didn't have to stand out or even to obey in the field of training anymore.

I was naked, unsuspecting, and careless. The wind and the rain passed through me as if I too were made of the same. I became invincible and invisible. Chaka decided to speak to me again finally, to guide me once more now that his guidance meant nothing.

He gave me a warning. "The Reghen say that Enaka always remembers us when we surrender to frivolous joy."

The pompous words of the Reghen.

"And what do you say, Chaka?" I asked.

"I say: 'Don't piss with trousers down and your ass facing the Forest.' Because that's when Darhul remembers you."

But I wanted, if only for a while, to forget the rivalries, the trials, and to take a break from the countless moons since that first night when I had been dragged by the hair into the Sieve. They wouldn't just let me enjoy it.

"Now you are Second," Bera told me, "but that is not a good place. You are closer than anyone else to the First's blade."

I was making more frequent trips to the Forest, which had opened all its fall colors: the wild, the bloodstained, the desperately brilliant. It taunted me to stay. I always went alone in the morning, but I could not stay there for the days that it would take me to get to Kar-Tioo and back. I hadn't seen her again.

A crazy thought stuck in my head during those aimless long walks: instead of Second, I would become First. The First who would cross the Forest. My Legend would say that I was the one who first found the secret path to the West, defying the Reekaal.

I wanted to learn everything I could about the Forest, even those age-old, sacred secrets that the wolves whispered to the Ouna-Mas. Every herb, every tree, every seed, and every path. I wanted to find who had hunted Rouba and me like wild boars. And yes, I pissed many times in there, just to prove Chaka wrong.

I waited patiently for the moment when the Ouna-Mas would order me to go back to Kar-Tioo and bring the precious belladonna. It was my only chance to fulfill my promise to Zeria.

Before that next moon came, the last of autumn, Malan became Khun. Witches, men, and stars conspired for that to happen before the end of winter, when the two of us would have to be carved. The weaver of the fates unraveled the events in one night. The Leader of all the Blades had died, and the Story that would be told was that a mosquito, huge as half the nail on his little finger, defeated him in a duel. Keral, the meanest and stupidest Chief of the Fifth Pack, asked Khun-Taa to make him the new Leader of all the Blades' twenty Packs. But Khun-Taa told him that he would not decide yet.

It would be Khun-Taa's last decision: to remain undecided.

Keral summoned his loyal Blades, attacked the sleeping Rods, and stabbed old Khun-Taa in the back in his own tent. For a few moments, he bragged about being the new Khun, defying our Truths and spitting upon the bloody body of Khun-Taa, who had remained standing for thirty winters on his throne and saddle.

The news slithered like a thousand venomous snakes from tent to tent and soon reached the Uncarved camp. It was a cloudless, windless night, and Selene's heart shone half of half in the Sky, her shape a curved blade. Maybe Keral saw the blade shape and thought the stars favored him. Maybe the Witch had whispered her false prophecy to mislead him, cloud his mind.

Malan gathered all the younger Uncarved who could fight like men, about twelve boys, and the few Guides and gave us his first order:

"The moon has come when we become Leaders and guide our Tribe, out beyond the Endless Forest and into the Final Battle. Follow me tonight, and know glory tomorrow."

What he really meant was that *he* would become Leader. But in those very first words, he had given us the vision, the mission, and the adventure. He had already said things that no one else dared say and shoved the scepter of insatiable imagination deep into our assholes. My first instinct was to run a hole through him that very instant. But it was futile. The Guides and the Uncarved youths already followed him with their blades and bows in hand.

I stood frozen, only my fingers twitching on the blade's handle, next to the horses outside of the huts of the Uncarved. Two Uncarved Eagles, one spring younger than us, stayed next to me.

"What?" I asked. "Don't you follow?"

One tried to mumble an excuse; the other looked away biting his lips. Their faces were identical, twin brothers, real brothers from same mother and father. I'd seen them many times. Handsome boys with broad shoulders, slim waists; brown-haired like myself.

I had to choose whether to follow or not, and that decision would determine how and when I would die.

"And you? Don't you follow?" the one mumbled to me.

"Tell me your names again," I said.

"I am Alian, that one is Olian," said the one who asked me.

I am thinking, Alian.

As Zeria had said, the moment decided for me. We heard first the trampling hooves of the horses, and then we saw Keral's warriors storming through the main gate of our camp. The Blades hacked two kids first, a couple of young Owls who were standing guard there. They came to murder Malan in the darkness.

"Are you coming?" I asked.

Alian had already grabbed his bow and quiver. Olian was stepping back to hide in the darkness.

The Blades wouldn't stop at Malan. They were coming too fast, the irons shining high. They wouldn't ask; they wouldn't see. They would have to eliminate every Uncarved. One more breath of indecision and my flesh would be the lamb, their blade would be the spit.

I had already reached Malan, Chaka, and the rest and stood right next to them.

"Stay close to me," I said to Alian.

"For glory and Enaka," he answered.

It was a stroke of good luck that we were fighting against Blades, the worst archers of the Tribe. Selene's light was weak and their arrows blind.

"Shoot now, the horses!" Chaka shouted.

I grabbed five arrows between the fingers of my left hand, and the others did the same. The shafts ripped the air, and we took down most of the horses and a few of their riders. They outnumbered us, and they were on foot now, yelling and chasing after us. I took out both blades and charged upon them with the younger Uncarved and the Guides. I cut through horse, leg, man, and parried irons, again and again. I kept swinging, and heavy bodies fell around me. I fought next to Chaka, Bera, and Malan himself. A tall bearded man was ready to hack Malan, but I pushed my long blade into his chest.

It was a night soaked in black blood, a night that came close to being our last. There were a dozen of us left, surrounded by about twenty of Keral's men.

"Stupid choice!" Alian said as our backs were facing each other to defend against the coming onslaught.

It was still possible. If I could take out three or four more. But I had boys around me and only two Guides, while Keral had sent strong warriors.

"We can't win here," Malan screamed in panic.

"Make for the gate. Now!" yelled Chaka. He had fought bravely to open a way out but his right arm was bleeding crippled and the short blade on his left hand was equally useless.

We were backtracking to get to the gate, whirling and swishing blades faster and higher. I killed seven men that night, fighting at the side of the next Khun. That in itself was Story enough to stuff down Enaka's throat once I saw her. Seven traitor warriors of the Tribe. Traitors like me.

We had opened our way and had almost reached the gate when we heard the beating hooves, and saw the torches of dozens of riders charging toward us. We were trapped in a pincer. I turned and smiled a bitter smile at Alian. There was no breath left for words.

"Yeah, we made the stupid choice, kid," were the words I never got to say.

But those riders were not foes. They were the Rods and the Archers sent by Sah-Ouna and Enaka to protect the One. The Goddess cared little for my deeds and my Stories, but I had chosen the right side. Keral's men were hacked to pieces.

Drenched in victory's sweat and blood, we all galloped toward the tent of Khun-Taa. The cheers and the shouts of praise and glory grew louder as we got closer to the Khun's tent. The rest of the Rods and Reghen were there, the Ouna-Mas next to them. The Tribe was honoring us. Us? Him.

Before we had time to rush into the tent, the Rods dragged out Keral's body, his bloodied mouth sealing his death.

"The crazygrass avenged the Khun," said Sah-Ouna, and she pointed somewhere in my direction and a little to the side of me where the new Khun stood. I wondered who had given Keral the crazygrass—who had put him up to murdering Khun-Taa. What Witch had whispered to him about the night of the blade-shaped Selene?

Malan dismounted, and we followed his lead. Sah-Ouna pulled him by the hand, like a mother pulls her only son, lifted his fist high, and shouted to all around: "The sixth Khun, Khun-Malan, the First Uncarved." Her words, her prophecy, the same as Malan's. "The One who will cross the Endless Forest."

Steal all my dreams away, bitch. One day I'll do the same to you.

The killing continued into the night in the camp of the Blades, or so I heard. I didn't go with them. The fighting stopped at dawn when the few warriors who remained alive and faithful to Keral were brought in neckropes in front of Malan and the rest of us. They had gathered all the traitors, and those who stood next to Malan at the Wolfhowl. The Tribe had a new Khun, and the traitors had to fall to his feet and plead for mercy. It was Khun-Malan's first decision, but there would be no mercy for them, as there would be no mercy for entire tribes and proud cities that were later to get in his way.

Chaka, the loyal Chief, found the right moment to ask Malan for a favor. He was allowed to return to the Archers and be a warrior again despite his old age. Even at that moment, with his one hand severely wounded, that was all he wanted: to have another chance to slaughter

Garol, Dasal, and whatever else he found in front of him. Meat. Horse. Woman. One Leader.

Olian, the Uncarved boy who had chosen not to fight next to us, was also brought in front of Malan.

"Did you think you'd become Khun by hiding? If they killed all of them?" Chaka slapped the cheek of the kneeling boy with his open palm.

"Carve me," the boy begged.

"Oh, don't worry, they'll carve you wide-open," Malan grinned.

Alian, his brother, was the one standing still and biting his lips now.

"I think your brother dies," I said to him.

Malan looked at Alian too.

"No, not this one. This boy fought bravely next to us," I said. "Even the other one, deserves some mercy. It was dark. He got scared…he froze," I said to Malan.

Malan leaned right next to my ear and whispered only for me to hear. "Are we still arguing here, Da-Ren? Your turn hasn't come yet." His nails were pushing into the flesh of my uncarved arm hard, and I could do nothing anymore. He turned his back on me. "That boy lives," he said pointing at Alian.

"So my brother dies," said Alian lowering his head. He lifted his eyes up again one last time and looked at Olian. "Stupid choice, brother."

"You wish he dies," Chaka said.

The next sunset, Khun-Taa was laid to rest in the funeral pyre, together with his finest hides, but without his bow and blades. These were sacred weapons bequeathed to Malan. Khun-Taa's slaves were put to death at once, so no one would ever hear a different tale about what had happened on that fateful night. The last raindrops of the Squirrel Moon were wiping out the funeral embers when Malan turned to me.

"You fought like a true Chief. The Tribe owes you, and you will be rewarded."

My witch, the blue-eyed one, had told me so: "There are no servants of the goddess or the demon. Only moments. One moment, you kill, and the other, you save."

How does one choose?

One doesn't. If I wasted my breath thinking, it would have been too late. Whatever I had decided wouldn't matter if I were slow, and Zeria, Malan, and I would all be dead now. When the moment comes, the Goddess has already planted everything. The hand will reach toward its fate on its own. If it moves the wrong way, an iron veil will fall down upon it and stop it. If it moves in the right direction, then it will get there faster.

That night, before any thought even began to run through my mind about what I did and didn't want, my blade had saved Malan, Alian and, with them, my ass from the stake.

It was the right moment for the Tribe. Khun-Taa had long lost his vigor and his judgment, and Malan had to bring the Change. The Change came the following morning. But not for me. Just like before, my life would hang by its last thread—day and night.

I have a strong preference of stopping this Story here. I did so, the first and the second winter we came upon the events of that night. But Eusebius would always ask me every time that we'd reach that point: "But, what happened to Olian and Alian?"

The monks of the Cross have a craving for such tales of torture and death. They blend well with their delusions of divine salvation of the weak and the innocent. "I'll tell you, Eusebius. It's not hard to bring back the images. The sounds...well, that's much tougher." But the ink is silent, and we are thankful for it.

The four of Keral's warriors who had been captured alive were impaled outside of the new Khun's temporary tent. And so was Olian the Uncarved boy. Their screams, the stink of shit, mixed with the lard slathered on the sharp, long stakes and the blood coming out of their assholes, reminded us for the three days it took them to die that we had a new Khun.

I found Alian looking up at the screaming stakes and the trembling faces of unending pain on the second morning.

"He still doesn't die," he said, staring at Olian, who would only mumble, pleading for death with the last of his strength.

"No, you see, they don't pierce the guts, the pointy wood just passes next to the spine and out the shoulder. Skewered. It will take another couple of days."

"Damn! Stupid choice," he said looking straight at his brother's body faintly twitching on the stake.

"Let's go, Alian, you don't have to see and hear this anymore. He was your brother."

"He still is. One of my brothers. So are you."

Alian had already turned his back on the identical twin whom he had just called stupid for the last time.

XXXIII.
Yes, My Leader

Eighteenth winter. Uncarved—Wolf.

The celebrations to honor the sixth Khun lasted for three whole days after Khun-Taa's pyre, and so did the torture of the traitors. Sheep, goats, chickens, rabbits, even horses—all Keral's best—were slaughtered and put onto the spit. The animals roasted slowly over the fire. The traitors were not so lucky.

The slaves milked the mares dry and poured the milk into buckets that they sealed tightly. They tied the buckets on the animals' backs and rode them around to shake the liquid until it fermented, taking on a bitter, stinging taste. If one drank a lot of it, it made the head dizzy and light. We called it milk-spirit. But it was not as potent or dangerous as crazygrass. The milk-spirit flooded the men's bellies and clouded their heads. Archers holding hands in circles danced wild war dances, and their shouts became a true devotional chant for the new Khun.

Ouna-Mas were constantly coming and going from the makeshift tent that had been set up for Khun-Malan. More of their sisters were outside singing. The Khun would not sleep under the same hides where his predecessor had been murdered. Sah-Ouna would not allow that. The ground was still boiling angry from the Khun's blood.

The milk-spirit wasn't helping me swallow this reality. Some were slapping me on the back, praising me for my bravery in saving the life of the new Khun. Some were ending their slap with a hug, out of gratitude or fear that I would become some important Chief next to the Khun. Others were slapping me softly on the shoulder. Slapping me farewell. I just wanted to disappear, the earth—or the Forest—to open up and hide me from everyone's stares.

On the third day of the celebration, I asked to see Malan, and the Rods led me to his tent. He was sitting outside on a coarsely carved wooden throne, larger than Khun-Taa's. He had put the West and the sunset on his back to sing his victory in bright dazzling colors of blood. Chiefs and Reghen were waiting in line in front of me to pay their respects and to offer simple gifts: an amulet, a bow, a dagger. Back then, my Tribe did not have much gold. Jewelry and fancy artifacts were considered signs of the weak and the demon servants.

Malan was holding a cup and raising it to everyone. A slave girl refilled it twice while I was waiting to speak to him. He had acquired the taste of the previous Khun's pleasures from the first night.

I knelt.

I knelt.

"Welcome, loyal Da-Ren. Are you here to claim victory's spoils already?" he asked, raising his cup again.

But I wasn't there to claim anything he could offer.

Wasting no time, I said, "I have to leave for the Forest. The Ouna-Mas asked for belladonna."

I did not ask for permission. I did not realize that from now on I would have to ask him where I could go and what I was allowed to do. He made an immediate gesture with his left hand as if he were saying, "Go wherever you want," but his hand froze midway. He looked at me for a breath; the skin around his eyes crinkling and questioning silently. As if he understood amid his stupor that I was talking total nonsense. What foolish liar would go to search for belladonna in the middle of winter and leave these nights of triumph and celebration?

I didn't wait. I thought he had let me go, and I disappeared. I hadn't brought any gifts.

Before dawn, as I was galloping for the Forest of Kar-Tioo, I heard the stomping of hooves approaching behind me. Six Rods were on my trail, and they stopped me at the edge of the Forest just before I managed to disappear inside.

"The Khun orders you to return to the camp."

"I have to…the Ouna-Mas…"

"He said to wait for his orders in your hut. He'll call you when it is time to carve your fate. Follow us back to Sirol now."

I had promised Zeria to return after one moon since I last saw her. Two had already passed, and I still could not fulfill my vow to her.

I returned to the Wolves' hut completely alone now, the last Uncarved Wolf, abandoned. The Tribe had a new Leader, and unless a tragic accident befell Malan, no other Uncarved would be needed anytime soon. The celebrations gave everyone a reason to stop and rest for a while. All of our Guides had died in the last battle defending Malan or had disappeared, except for Bera.

I was almost alone in what was now a camp of ghosts, the closest one to the Forest. I made another attempt to leave, but the Rods were patrolling the paths to the Forest, and I returned before they tried to stop me. I wasn't going to sneak out like a rat. That would only bring death to the Dasal and me if I ever made it there. I still hadn't found the Reekaal who had killed Rouba. I stayed among the few unfortunate younger Uncarved who would not become Leaders either. Alian and a handful of the rest were left fighting aimlessly with the pumpkins.

A few days after the festivities, I went out and started meandering about Sirol. It was the end of autumn, and the north wind was blowing strong. Not so strong as to stop people from working or send them for cover into their tents, but enough to quicken everyone's pace. Everyone was dancing to a frantic rhythm under the commands of the new Khun. Even if there wasn't anything important to do, they ran around looking busy.

"The Change. Finally, we are preparing," a Reghen who visited the Uncarved Camp one evening told us.

"What are we preparing for?"

"Khun-Malan leads."

The Reghen's eyes were glowing with pride and anticipation; his voice chanted the glory of the new Khun. The men needed the Change, even if it meant death for most. It was so much better than rotting in the same valley forever. The Change, the meat, the woman, the Story.

I rode all the way to the tents where the new Khun resided. The Rods recognized me and allowed me to approach.

The Change had begun.

"What are you building here?" I asked a Craftsman who, upon seeing the arm of an Uncarved, got excited and rushed to explain himself. He was a short man, but his forearms swelled, and his palms looked as if they belonged to a bigger body.

"Khun-Malan has ordered a new tent be built, bigger than any other before it. Six-sided and a frame made from wooden beams. It has to be bigger and sturdier than the bigger huts but covered with hides to look like a tent."

All of the tents were round, except for the wooden huts and those of the Ouna-Mas which were square, but no tent was ever six-sided.

What if I had been Khun? It would have never crossed my mind to ask for something like that.

"Why?" I asked.

But, like me, he wasn't good with the *whys*.

Night fell, and my hut became a freezing cave. The Carriers had forgotten to bring dung for days now, and the first snow had fallen earlier than I ever remembered. Outside, everything was slowly vanishing in white. The milk-spirit lying next to me was my only friend. When I drank a lot, it brought back old friends: Malan, Gunna, Lebo, and the ghosts of the seven children, the seven Uncarved whom we had lost in the pyre. Seven children, hand in hand, begging me: "Don't go. Stay with us."

The fading image of Zeria swirled around my head all the time, but it didn't warm me. In the iron valley of Sirol, under the light of the Sun and Selene, her magic of gold and green had no power. The Rods and the Reghen came to check on the camp every day. They would summon us outside the huts, together with Bera and the few young ones left, take a count, and then leave. They hadn't brought any news.

After a few days, I passed by Malan's tent again. White, brown, and black horsetails had been hung on the outside and fluttered in the song of the wind. The tails, more than thirty of them, hung vertically with bells and a red band tied at the ends. I remained completely indifferent to them, but those around me looked in awe to find the new Khun's face, the hope, the change.

To the right of the tent's entrance, four heavy wooden beams were raised. They supported the Khun's new emblem, a huge horizontal iron leaf.

"And this is what?" I asked the Craftsman.

"They say it stands for the Unending Sky," he replied, his face glowing with pride.

The metal plate had holes in the middle. Hanging from each were three spheres, each a different size.

"What are those spheres?" I asked.

"The Sun, the World, and Selene. It was what Sah-Ouna asked for," he answered.

"And why is the World a sphere?" I asked.

The Craftsman shrugged awkwardly.

"It is a magnificent emblem, though," he said.

No other tribe would agree with him, but I had to travel the world to learn that.

I wanted to go inside Khun-Malan's tent and learn my fate. I wanted to tell him about the Forest, the Dasal who had saved me, and the monstrous Reekaal who had attacked me. I wanted to win the admiration of all because I knew the secrets of the Forest better than anyone else. But distrust and envy were enough to keep me back, and I didn't do any of that.

When Malan became Khun, my fate was sealed. At best, I could hope to become Chief of a Pack, forty men under my command. But I had to learn what Banner I'd follow first. There were three real choices: Rod, Archer, or Blade. There were lesser Banners also, like Hunters, Trackers, Craftsmen, and even Tanners, but they amounted to deadly disgrace for someone with my warrior training and ability. Somehow, I always knew that I would never be an Archer.

"Have they told you where they will send you? How many carvings?" Bera asked. He had become the new Chief and only Guide of the few younger Uncarved, a useless honor that carried no importance anymore.

"No. I hope only one."

One carving would mean that one day I could be Leader of many Packs, all Archers, all Rods, or something else, getting my orders directly from Malan.

"But I'm afraid they'll send me to the Rods," I said.

"That will be great luck for you. The Rods are Malan's guard. They live next to him and drink from his power."

"I don't like to be stuck in that camp forever."

The Rods spent their whole life around Malan's tent. They could never leave for days and nights to roam in the Forest, or anywhere else.

"They taste the fresh women first, eat the good meat, even the cow, get the best share of the loot, and are the only warriors with five horses each. Even the Archers get only four."

The Rods were tall men with powerful thews who stood proud and fearsome, but their lives were bowed and dark. Dark because they were constantly in the shadow of the Leader, and bowed because they saw him often.

"They can keep their fifth horse, Bera. I don't want to become a Rod."

"Yes, my Leader," said Bera, bowing his head.

"What?"

"It is what they do all day and all night, those Rods. They bow to the Khun and say, 'Yes, my Leader.' You wouldn't be good at that."

It was the one thing that I hadn't been taught, having been an Uncarved for five winters. To bow. It would turn all my livers upside down. The reality of my training was that I wouldn't be good at anything. I had been bred to lead the Tribe or to die trying. Not to kneel.

For one and two and three more nights, I fought with those thoughts and the choices that I didn't have. Even worse, I fought to remember my naked body embracing and entering Zeria's in the pond at Kar-Tioo. If it had actually ever happened. Zeria, her legs wrapped around me, the feeling of her skin a dying memory…my downfall. That was how my nights passed: the dreams of her soft, warm flesh, the humiliation of my lonesome carnal pleasure, in the white exile of the snowstorm that had covered us.

My torture ended on the thirteenth night of the new Khun's leadership, when the frozen snowflakes of despair were falling heavier than ever upon Sirol. An Ouna-Ma with no other name rode alone through the white darkness and entered my hut uninvited. She had the most lustful eyes and the biggest breasts.

And she brought the fire.

XXXIV.
My Iron, Your Fate

Eighteenth winter. Uncarved—Wolf.

I got good at fucking quite fast, just as I had at riding and blade fighting. It was a useful revelation that the basic secret to perfection was the same in all three. To think with my body and not with my head, and to take control of my opponents by leading them where my body wanted to go. When I was in control, everyone, from women to fearless warriors, could be pierced more easily and sensually.

But the first time—the night I became a man on my eighteenth winter—wasn't like that. I can hardly remember what my body did that first time. I was lying still on my back most of the night, burning but incapable of movement like a heap of smoldering coals while the Ouna-Ma danced on me.

Whatever it was, it was what I needed. I needed this more than the Banners, prophecies, fathers, Legends, and Leaders, more than the life-giving fire of the winter night. The naked legs of a woman wrapped around me.

It was that moon of my life when I had just about washed the Tribe's Witch out from inside of me. She came back stronger than ever. The Ouna-Ma came as a woman but left as a demon and goddess, poison and water, death and life, curse and prophecy.

She walked into the tent, looked at me without saying a word, and knelt in front of me. The fire was between us. She started to take some things out of her saddlebag: two wooden cups, dried herbs, and powder. I kept stealing glances toward the tent's flap and expected the Reghen, the Guide, or someone else to walk in at any moment. She could not say words to me. Selene was not full, and I was not even the Chief of a Pack. She was mumbling a song to break the silence. The silence begged for words, and the song was an excuse to avoid uttering or listening to them.

Selene would have been bright, almost full that night, if she weren't hidden beneath the snow clouds. With the softest whispering song on her lips, she moved her head to the left and to the right to let me know that I shouldn't expect anyone else.

It is just you and I alone in the white darkness tonight, Da-Ren, was her silent promise.

She turned silent only when she started undressing with slow movements, a sacred dance ritual she had probably done a thousand times before. She let the black robe fall behind her. A thin tunic covered her breasts and the upper part of her body and left her dark, taut skin bare from the waist down. She took that off. Her small nipples rested high and proud on her full breasts like fresh winter flowers. Nipples that had never been suckled by a babe.

Her body was painted with red and black designs with the henna of the South. Designs that took whole days of careful crafting under a bright sun's light to make. They said that the Ouna-Mas spent a lot of their time painting one another's bodies. Her back was decorated with red henna in a pattern of spiral lines, four spirals connecting into a cross, feeding into one another. At the center of each red spiral was a black pattern: a mauler's head to the north, the two crossed blades to the east, the double-curved bow to the south, and the long skull to the west. Her hands were painted with red henna in intricate blood-red ornaments:

flower stems, blades, and arched bows, interlacing and curving like tendrils across the fingers and the top of the hand. They gave the illusion that blood had poured out from every nail and vein and was running everywhere, in harmony, representing with perfect shapes the cycles of life, the spears and the blades of death, and the roots of the trees.

Those fingers touched me and made Zeria vanish for one night. They were painted like the red veil on her long head, the veil that came off last and revealed that long, painfully sensual head with the very short black hair. Her full lips, her forehead was long as a deer's.

I didn't know how the Ouna-Mas came to our Tribe, or from where. But they were the most beautiful women I've ever seen, if only for those big eyes with the full iron-black iris that grew even bigger at night when they danced on a naked man. Even more than their rumps, it was their eyes that were trained for countless nights. She kept them fixed on mine as she moved on top of me.

Later in life, when I would take the Witches from behind, they would always turn their long heads to the side as they were on all fours. Even as they moaned, they never closed their eyes but kept them nailed on me, as if that was the trial they had gone through for five winters. I never regretted that night, although it ended in horror. As I never regretted any of my many nights with the Ouna-Mas.

In my life, I would take only one woman under the spell of eternal love, but as many times as I embraced and looked into her blue eyes, I never felt confused. Zeria's eyes were colorful forest birds. They were the green of hope, the gold of light, the blue of life. I wanted to hide them from all men before they flew back to some faraway forest.

The eyes of the Ouna-Ma were iron, fire, sweat, death, and a feast of fucking. That night, I truly became a wolf. I burned with unquenchable fire and shivered with the fear of the Sieve's night from my lips to my feet. I wanted to scream with desire and tear her apart.

When the end came, as she was writhing faster and more

rhythmically atop me, I lost myself inside the burning black water river of passion for the first time. I closed my eyes and tightly wrapped my arms around her dizzy. I traced the henna designs on her back as her heart pounded between the painted patterns of the blades and the skull.

She sealed my mouth tightly with her hand. I bit it hard. Her blood blended in with the red finger drawings. She wiped it off on my neck and dismounted me.

I wanted nothing else, not even to speak a word. She wasn't ready to leave, so she knelt and continued. She started her whisper song once more as she steeped the herbs and the powder she had brought with her in boiling water. She gave me a cup and filled one for herself. The Ouna-Ma had put on her robe, but her bent legs, still showing, naked, made her even more desirable to me. Now I knew what she had inside of her, and it burned my head.

A black horse with raven-black feathers rose from the fire in the tent, evaporated in front of my eyes, and disappeared through the smoke hole. I didn't want to lose my senses again like I had done the last two times that Sah-Ouna had given me a wooden cup. She had deceived me twice in the past with crazygrass. The Ouna-Ma drank again. I pretended to swallow it all and threw the contents of the cup into the darkness. I kept my mouth full. She drank again. I spat out the black water when her eyes were not on me.

The Ouna-Ma pressed her palm to the back of my neck, pulling me closer to her lips, stuck out her tongue, and pressed it even deeper into my mouth. She twisted it in a deep kiss that choked me. I had kissed Zeria, but it wasn't the same. The Ouna-Ma's tongue was fast and persistent, a worm determined to reach all the way into my mind and my heart.

Like a helpless child, I fell backward on the hides, and she climbed on top of me for a second time. She started rocking fast again, still kissing me as if she were slowly filling me with poison, as if she were trying to pull out my soul. Or to make me less careful.

Her knees were bent and locked around my body, her hand squeezed my neck even closer, and her tongue slid deeper down my throat. I came in the end, emptied for a second time, blinded by pleasure, my eyes shut.

That was when the tearing pain came. In half a breath, with one long, angry scream, I flew upward, uncoupling her body from mine abruptly. The two, sharp iron rings she wore on her middle fingers had ripped my skin with quick simultaneous slashes, leaving two carvings. One just below the right nipple on my chest. I had, after all, just lain with my first Ouna-Ma. The other on my left arm, ending my days forever as an Uncarved. A gift to remember her by and an eternal punishment.

I had thrown her off me. She was laughing hard now, almost growling like a satisfied beast at me, already victorious. She had stolen all she had come for. And against her vows, she spoke:

"This is how the boy dies, and the man is born. My iron, your fate."

Whenever I saw others being carved, it was shameful and reminded me of horses being branded with a red-hot iron. It was probably an honor that one of the most beautiful Ouna-Mas had come with the order to carve me. She had melted me, I had melted her, and the black water she had boiled had melted us both. She sat coiled next to me, looking the other way as if I were not there anymore. I was alone again. Sleep came fast and sweet.

I woke up much later but still in darkness, delirious and breathing heavily. The horses in my nightmare were frightening shadows, blood dripping from their hollow eye sockets. The black water, the cup. I was losing my mind in that hut, abandoned there, Uncarved no more. The night had begun with hunger, fire, and desire, but it turned into an unsparing nightmare. And that was how it would continue.

I had knives in my bowels. I curled up in pain. I had drunk crazygrass many times before. It had never burned my throat and my bowels like this. This was another kind of poison that swam inside me.

I pulled the Ouna-Ma by the wrist to make her face me. There was blood running from her nose, reaching the edge of her lip. She tried to wipe it off with the back of her painted hand. This blood was not from my carving or my bite. It was from her insides. The poison was burning her too.

She crawled to reach the waterskin. She took a sip but spat it out, coughing up green foam. She tried to stand upright. I went to help her, but my legs were shaking. She pushed me away faintly. The little white rim around her pitch-black iris had become blood red, and she stared, lost and desperate. She was trying to mumble, to speak, despite her vows to not say a word. She couldn't.

"What did you give me?" I asked, shaking her with both hands.

Gone was her lustful gaze of absolute domination. The gleaming tears of her eyes reflected terror and agony. She barely managed to stand up. She was still trying to utter a word, and she pulled the black robe like a cloak to cover herself. She took two or three steps backward and doubled over with a scream, holding her belly like it was hatching snake eggs that were biting to get out.

She crawled out of the hut, half-naked and barefoot in the snow. But on that one last breath before she disappeared, the Witch looked at me like a frightened girl who had just burst into tears and uttered that one word, the last word I heard from the lips of the first woman I had taken.

"Drakon…"

XXXV.
To Death

Eighteenth winter. Uncarved—Wolf.

Drakon. Solitary servant of Darhul, exiled to the North to guard the crossing of the icy rivers. A creature with indomitable power absolutely committed to protecting a priceless treasure. A mythical beast that spewed fire and couldn't be killed by any means known to mortals. Its poisoned blood could make a warrior invincible if he rubbed it on himself. Darhul himself, transformed.

Stories for children, women, and fools. I had the rest of my life, as many moons as I had left, to find out. Drakons were the stuff of Legends. None of the men whom I met had ever come across a Drakon. Only Bera had said once, "They had sent me up, very far to the North, on a campaign. I was young like you. Thousands marched, fewer than a hundred returned, and of those few, no one ever speaks of it: I saw him."

"Saw what?"

"I didn't see the Drakon; I saw his cloudbreaths of green and blue above his lair. Have you ever seen green clouds dancing and shining in the sky at night?"

"No."

"Those cloudbreaths were bigger than Sirol, moving, flowing like green rivers above our heads. They had taken the shape of the tongue, the body, the talons of the Drakon, the color of his cursed blood. He was there."

"You saw clouds only. Green clouds."

"He was there."

The Ouna-Ma disappeared half-naked in the middle of the night. She left behind only questions of Drakons and erotic hunger for me to warm in my hut like drakon eggs. And she left the poison inside of me, the crazygrass or whatever it was that she had given me to drink.

Alian sneaked into my hut at dawn, drawn by my screams.

"Are you in pain?" he asked in a worried voice.

"My bowels," I said. I was burning up.

"Boiled water and salt," he said. "I'll bring them now."

He had long brown hair, Elbia's brown hair. That I remember of him. He brought a cup of hot salt water. I drank it and spent the whole morning on my knees throwing up until there was nothing left inside me. I started slowly to feel better. I boiled herbs I had taken from the Forest and drank.

I stayed in my hut alone for days. Bera sent Alian every day with water and boiled meat. He was the only one who dared come close. He would leave them outside the entrance and disappear without saying much.

"The others say you got the sickness. Did you?" he asked me once.

"I wish."

When I had enough strength to stand on my feet again, I stepped out of the hut for the first time to let them know. I was alive, strong. I was also carved once. Finished.

It was time for me to leave the Uncarved, but no one had given me orders. I walked aimlessly around Sirol and looked among the hide covers and the tents, where the dogs mounted the bitches and the warriors took the women. Those acts were not sacred or hidden in our Tribe. Every woman belonged to everyone. That was our upbringing. I had seen it many times, and no one cared who watched or walked by. At some of the Banners, like the Blades, especially in winter, the public display was the main entertainment for the men. I went there now to watch the warriors and the slave girls.

Because now I had questions.

Had I done something wrong? Was I made differently? Why had there been so much fear in the eyes of the Ouna-Ma? Was it so obvious, when I was naked, that I was cursed? As much as I watched men and women sweat and rub against each other like animals in front of me, I couldn't see anything on the men that was different on me. I saw female slaves riding warriors, and I saw men salivating rabidly and taking common women from behind. The older warriors were more experienced than I, as with everything else, but that was all. But I had questions and no one to answer them.

Why had she uttered that word? *Drakon?*

I had a lot of time every day to be concerned with things like that, abandoned in my hut, alone, without any idea of what fate Malan was carving for me.

Drakon, the iron ring slicing my arm, disgrace, lust, the Ouna-Ma's fear, pain, the solitude of the hut as my only cloak, Khun-Malan, the Leader, the death of Rouba, the wolves tearing the flesh of brave Gunna, the screams of Keral's warriors as the stakes tore through their asses, the decorative horse tails hanging outside of the Khun's six-sided tent, a poisoned arrow stuck underneath my ribs in Kar-Tioo, Zeria putting me to sleep inside my slaughtered horse to keep my heart warm, another brutal winter descending, Archers, Blades, Rods, leeches sucking blood and giving me the kiss of life, the Ouna-Ma on top of me, falling almost dead afterward, her eyes red and black in fear, the Unending Sky of Enaka colored like the eyes of Zeria, Drakon.

The Guides of the Uncarved had nothing more to do for me, and Bera said, "I can't keep you here any longer. Chaka is gone, but I have sent word with the Reghen to Khun-Malan asking about your fate. I hope that luck will be on your side, Da-Ren."

"Why won't you look at me?"

"It could have been you. But for your mark."

The mark of the ninestar. As if the mark had had a will of its own and had bewitched me to disappear into the Forest for two moons. As if the mark had decided by itself to abandon the Tribe and had sent me to search for a Dasal girl. The excuses of the weak, that's what the birthmarks were.

Almost half a moon passed after the night of the Ouna-Ma before Malan finally decided. He sent four proud and strong-muscled Rods to summon me. They rode up to my hut, at midday under a hazy winter sun, and told me to follow them to the tent of the Khun.

I didn't recognize Malan's camp. The new Khun had raised, in a matter of a few days and nights, a new six-sided tent on a hundred-feet-tall hill. It was visible from a long distance in the flat valley of Sirol. All the animals and their smell were missing from the camp of the Khun, except for the horses. I had been in Khun-Taa's tent only once before, a few moons ago, when he had thrown us out with the certainty that he would not die anytime soon. The Guides used to say to us, "Enaka gave you a short tongue and a long blade."

The Khun's tent had a triple entrance, three sheets of rippling fabric falling heavy, each one five yards after the other. They were rich, othertriber spoils from the South and I had to push them aside with both hands. Two Rods were standing guard in front of each entrance. I finally found myself in the largest hall I had ever seen in my life. I was at the beginning of a corridor, at least a hundred feet long, across from Malan's empty throne on the opposite side. I looked so short and small inside this tent. Broad wooden beams supported a vast structure that rose twenty feet high. It was built as if the Craftsmen had connected many traditional tents together. Lighter beams notched into the top of the vertical ones and meshed to form the skeleton of the hide-covered roofs. The hides were sewn together, leaving smoke holes open. Torches resting on iron sconces illuminated the tent, but there were also many side openings for air and light, half-covered with horsehide flaps.

There was singing. To the right end of the hall, the torch flames trembled above their red veils. A few Ouna-Mas were in a circle, their knees on the hides, and singing. The animal skins hanging behind them were decorated with their unique henna patterns. I walked toward them. An unveiled girl rose to her bare feet and started swinging a black-horn knife, slicing the tallow smoke, over a body lying flat on the hides. The resting body was covered with a robe, and under the scant light, it looked like a black goat to be sacrificed or a giant coiled snake. It was neither. I had tasted her. She was the same Ouna-Ma, the first, the one who had mounted me a few days earlier. She was staring at me with glassy eyes, her body frozen. Her soul had left forever.

I was close enough to the Ouna-Mas that I could touch them now, and they all turned their eyes away except for the one who was holding the knife above the dead body. She moved her lips, glanced at me, and murmured the word "Drakon," while the rest covered their ears. I struggled to remember her face from long ago but before I did a Rod pulled me by the arm and pointed to the center of the tent.

"The Khun is waiting," he said.

Two rows of skulls defined the corridor that led to the throne. Skulls from big-sized oxen, bears, and wolves. They were all impressive in their own way, but the most fearsome were the two skulls at the end of the corridor, closest to the throne. They were almost human, narrow and long like that of the Ouna-Mas, but larger. Those had goat-like horns and the teeth of some wild animal. Wolf. Bear. Maybe both. Those were skulls from creatures of another world. They were not on the ground as the rest but atop waist-high columns, usually used to hold urns. There, in between the horned humanlike skulls, the Rod motioned for me to stop.

"When you address the Khun, keep your head high. When you bow, keep it low," he said.

"Wise advice," I said, trying to laugh at my own words. I shivered for a breath at the thought that I might join the Rods before the night was over.

I stared again at the long skulls with the horns and dog teeth.

The Rod came closer, eager to share his wisdom. "Reekaal." He whispered the word hastily as if the skulls were listening. A hand touched me on the shoulder from behind. I turned and saw Malan.

I hadn't seen him but for a few moments since the night I had fought next to him and saved his skin from the warriors of that usurper Keral. He wore a dark leather coat and had shaved short the sides of his head, except for two small ponytails that rose upward one in front of the other. The hair on the back of his head fell oily and straight almost reaching his shoulders. His short black beard had started to thicken, making him look older than I, maybe even five summers older.

"Don't you know the Reekaal, Da-Ren? Legend says that you have killed some of them."

"Yes, what…" I wasn't ready for this encounter.

I was still looking at the otherworldly skulls.

"Do you like them? I made them myself," he said with a smirk.

He walked up the steps that led to his throne. I remembered Khun-Taa's throne; an unremarkable carved single piece of wood with a narrow, straight back. Khun-Malan's throne was of othertribal craftsmanship. Its back was wide and unnecessarily tall, painted crimson to stand out from the animal skins hanging on the walls behind. It was framed by three curved bows connecting. Each arm ended in enormous mauler's heads, shiny black with jaws open and gleaming hazelnut eyes. The wooden beasts were carved to be almost twice their real size; their bodies strong and wide were forming the legs of the throne.

Sah-Ouna was right next to him. No, she wouldn't look me in the eyes. Rods, Ouna-Mas, and Reghen, four from each craft, followed and filled the steps leading to the throne left and right.

The horse-dung reek that fell heavy in the other tents was missing, as if the fire burned only wood and lard. Behind the throne and around the tent hung hides with drawings of dogs, bears, lions, and other hunters of the wild in thick, straight lines without too much detail. The animals were outlined in black lines, and their teeth, jagged and sharp, were in white. The Sun and Selene behind the throne were painted in blood red on the earth-colored hides. The Rods held spears taller than themselves at their sides. I knelt.

"You don't have to kneel yet," said Malan, sitting on his throne.

I had knelt to look at the skulls more closely. They were looking back.

Their dark and empty eye sockets whispered to me: "Kneel for the Khun."

Bone, glue, and horn, this is how we made our bows. Those fourcarved Craftsmen knew how to handle them well in my Tribe. That was the secret of these skulls unless I had really found the monsters that had killed Er-Ren, my father, Rouba, and me in the Forest. Before Zeria pulled me out of the caves of the dead. Bone, glue, and horn.

Malan was not resting on the back of his throne. He was sitting down but leaning forward, alert and ready to speak. Whatever he had had to drink that morning had done something to him. As I got up closer to him, I noticed that his eyes were cloudy and almost gray.

"I've missed you, Da-Ren. How long has it been since we had meat and milk-spirit together? Since the night you gave Gunna an Iron End?"

No. Since the night I fought at your side and saved your life.

The words still wouldn't come out. It choked me that we could no longer speak as equals.

"Da-Ren, the Witches here have marked you as a Drakon of the North. They have discovered the omen of your mark, the ninestar, they say. Your mother, rumor has it, was a filthy slave from up there. Your hair is the color of hay at the ends."

I should have cut it, but the truth was that I never took notice of my reflection on the crystal waters. Everyone else could see my hair and wonder.

"I don't know what my mother was. We both grew up in a tent with orphans. You know that. But if you want, I can tell you about my father, who—"

"I have heard the Legend of Er-Ren," he said. "Chilled my spine! Couldn't sleep." He showed me the two skulls of the…Reekaal to the right and left of me. "The Cyanous? You dared talk of the Cyanous Reekal in your tale."

"It is a Legend, not a tale," I said.

Sah-Ouna, the maulers, Malan, they all fixed their dark stares on me. I lowered my eyes. Sah-Ouna whispered words to one of the Ouna-Mas and the young girl descended the steps. She came next to me and she spoke softly in my ear.

"Be careful with your tales, Da-Ren. Speak them thrice and they'll find their own skin and bones. And then they'll rise alive."

I had spoken them exactly three times in the Forest.

Malan wasn't in the mood for fairy tales that morning.

"Enough with this. Do you want to serve your Khun, Da-Ren? You showed courage the last time. I have not forgotten. You know, if those jackals had killed me, then you would have been the only Uncarved Wolf and the next Khun of the Tribe."

"For a few breaths only. Until they killed me too."

"Oh, yes, yes, that's right," he said and burst out laughing so hard that he had to lean over and embrace the wooden armrest of his throne. "If Sah-Ouna had not sent the Rods, we would have all died."

Everything is funny when you're talking from your throne high above.

He asked if I wanted to serve the Khun. There was no other choice, not because they would slaughter me at once if I said no, but because I didn't know how else to respond. For a moment, I was filled with shame, watching my twelve-wintered self cheering with a skinned rabbit, a terrible and formidable beast. As much as it pained me, I was not the One, the undisputed Leader. But I had no urge to die.

"Yes!" I answered.

"Are you sure that you will be able to do it without betraying me? Otherwise, I will send you to the far-off outpost in the East and never see you again."

The far-off outpost of the East was on the other side of the world from the Forest of Zeria.

"No, great Khun, I will do it; I want to fight here."

"And what Banner fits you best, Da-Ren? What glory do you dream of?"

The Forest, the Trackers.

My thoughts almost escaped to the open. The Trackers were the only ones who dared explore the Forest, but they were not warriors. My mind returned to the dead Ouna-Ma who tried to poison me. I saw the corner of Sah-Ouna's eye watching me.

I won't tell you what I want.

"So?" he asked again when his patience was spent.

"Wherever you decide, my Leader. I had hoped to join the Rods, but—"

"Can't do that. I've already chosen my personal guard. They are far better warriors, even better than you."

I was tempted for a moment to say, "Bring any one of them here and now. Let's see who is better." But I didn't want to be in his personal guard. I could think of nothing worse than watching every night to see if some murderer was hiding outside of the tent or if he had poisoned the Khun's milk-spirit.

"You will go to the Blades. Chief! Hear that, everyone! I told you that you would be rewarded. Chief of the First Pack. Their last Chief died on one of the campaigns in the South about a moon ago, and they must get a new one as soon as possible. Your serpent cock's reputation will make it there before you do. It's not often that a Witch falls down helpless like this. She was green from pain, from the moment she left your hut. So they tell me. She coughed up bloody vomit to her end."

I wanted to tell him that I too had been in pain and vomiting and that it had been she who had brought the poison, but it would have done me no good. I thought that the rumors had more to do with my strong stomach than with what I had in my trousers.

"I don't know how that…"

Malan rose, walked down the steps, and approached me.

"Follow me," he said, and we walked down the skull path, away from everyone else. He stopped before we reached the exit, stretched his arm and grabbed my head in a lock and whispered into my ear.

"I don't know what happened either, but I will find out. Oh, believe me, I will. Enough for now with these bitches. We don't always have to listen to them. Now tell me, what did she tell you?"

"Who?"

"That Ouna-Ma, Sah-Ouna. What did she whisper to you?"

My Khun! You don't trust the Witches either.

It was the first thing I had found amusing since I had entered his tent.

"Nothing, some warning."

"You tell me right away." He was persisting and he had grabbed my arm.

I repeated the Ouna-Ma's words and his face softened.

"That's all?" he asked again.

I nodded with eyes wide to make him believe me. It was the first time I realized that the Witches were sacred to most, but for Malan, they were simply useful. The demon mania and witch faith would never rule over him. He would consult them and use them whenever the sheep had to be guided, but they wouldn't dictate his fate. And that would make him an invincible Leader.

I had become Chief of a Pack. Forty men. I still had only one carving, and that meant that I could one day be the Leader of all the Blades. About twenty Packs of them, all their Chiefs would kneel to me. I could climb to that onecarved honor. Not higher.

I wouldn't be forced to kneel every day. I had to kneel only now. The ritual was clear to us from many winters before. To be named a leader of men, I had to kneel and swear before the One Leader. Malan himself had knelt before Sah-Ouna to accept the ultimate honor.

I knelt before him, removed my blade and thrust it into the ground to speak the heavy words we knew.

"I swear to the Goddess, the Sun, and Selene to serve my Tribe and my Leader, Khun-Malan, to be a Blade, a worthy Chief, to tear through the othertribers till the end of the Final Battle."

The words were the same for every Chief. The words were easy. I had already betrayed the Goddess, the Sun, and Selene. I could swear anything, and their punishment would come someday. I had uttered many lies already. But now I had to say them kneeling before him. That was the difficult part. We were away from the others, the two of us, and somehow that made it even worse. It wasn't a ritual; this was a man to man battle I could not even fight. My head was at the level of his waist. I was naked of my Uncarved pride. At that moment, he was the second one of power to ride me in a period of only a few days. Instead of the fiery sweetness of the first time with the iron-eyed Ouna-Ma, the second time was shame and humiliation that strangled my throat.

"Go now, Da-Ren. The Rods have arranged a new horse for you."

He shouted once and the two Rods standing behind the first of the three entrances walked in to hear his commands. "The Chief's horse. And give him two flagons. Not wineskins, the bronze ones. From the new spirit that they brought from the South." My blood was boiling like bubbling hot wine. Wine was new and hard to find in the Tribe. The old men knew only the milk-spirit, and the boys knew nothing. I honored both flagons that night, my last night with the Uncarved, until I forgot my fate.

"Celebrate tonight, Da-Ren, and ride tomorrow for the Blades camp. I will send you another Redveil tonight. We have to see if your famous cock will be as potent again."

Our gazes drifted toward the few Ouna-Mas who were mourning over the dead body of their sister. I looked again at the one who had not covered her face, and I remembered her from a long time ago, from the rituals of the Sieve. Razoreyes, the one Ouna-Ma I'd always found more beautiful than all the others.

"Her," I said to Malan pointing to Razoreyes. "Send *her* to me."

He laughed again. He was drunk in the middle of the day; that I could tell. From the wine or the power, I couldn't tell.

The strong brown horse was waiting for me outside. It was mine, a gift from the new Great Khun. It was not a gray-white as those of the greatest Leaders of the Tribe. Its left ear had a short straight cut and his right a bigger one. The common mark of the Blades' animals. They had marked this horse a long time ago. It had never been a choice, no matter what I would have asked of him.

I tried to fish what I already guessed out of the Rod.

"This animal is half dead. Did you just run it here from the Blades?"

He was stupid enough to fall for it. Or he didn't care.

"No, they brought it yesterday. It has rested all day. We fed it and stroked it for you, Chief."

Chief!

Malan had marked me for the Blades long before I had entered his tent that morning. I descended the hill of the Khun's tent, the flagons strapped on the horse's sides. I, too, was now a leader of men, a Chief. I would lead forty men. He would lead more than thirty thousand. He was grateful enough to reward me for my loyalty.

But I would discover the inescapable truth on the next evening, when I passed the gate with the emblem of the two uneven-sized crossed blades welded together and I arrived at the small and filthy camp of the Blades. Malan had sentenced me, quickly and decisively.

To death.

XXXVI.
It Led Me to Both

Island of the Holy Monastery, Thirty-fifth winter.
According to the Monk Eusebius.

"Why did the Ouna-Ma call you *Drakon*? Drakons are cursed creatures in our faith, Da-Ren."

"I am sure. Almost everything is cursed in your faith. But it matters not what monster you were born, Eusebius—only what you become."

"And when did you decide what you would become?"

"No one decides. When the time comes, the false skin sheds and the true one is revealed."

I broke the rules a bit and took a sip of the wine he had poured into my cup. It helped. He had mocked me recently, asking me what I knew about women.

"What do you know about women, Da-Ren?" I asked him, reversing the roles.

"A lot more than a monk, for sure."

"That may be, but I am not sure you know enough either."

He may have lain with the Ouna-Mas and other common women and slaves, but was that enough?

"How many women have you spoken to, Da-Ren?"

"Many."

"Did you exchange more than a few words with them? How many did you sit with at sunset, to break bread and talk, as you are speaking with me now?"

"With one," he revealed to me as I now began to unravel the labyrinth. "But even with her, I didn't speak enough."

The Ouna-Mas did not speak, and he didn't speak with the slaves or the women Archers. He had never been married like the faithful and pious people. Had he fallen in love with Zeria because she had been the only one to give him the gift of a true smile? Or just because God intended it to be so?

I was searching for that answer that did not have a *why*. The *why* of the mad passion of love.

"When did you fall in love? The moment you first fell for that one woman?"

"A warming question for wintertime," he said. He went to the window and breathed in the violent breeze. "Look at the sea, Eusebius. Cold, unforgiving, blue, unending. Do you love her or hate her?"

"I mean when did you first fall—"

"I understand your question. But what difference does it make which is the first moment, Eusebius? We rarely choose the first of anything that will befall us. The only thing that matters is what the last one will be. What will be our last word when this Story ends?"

He gave me no other answer that day. But two nights later, he did.

"I am still looking for the answer to your question. I don't know. Was it the first time I saw her in the Forest? The second in the pond when I was inside of her?"

"The night when Sah-Ouna poisoned you in her tent?"

"Are you asking me about the love that conquers the soul or the hunger of the flesh, Eusebius?"

"Either. Whatever *first* means to you."

"Then the first times are many, Eusebius. The calling of Sah-Ouna,

Zeria, the Ouna-Ma who rode me for the first time, even the twenty-first night of the Sieve, when Elbia lay next to me and our fingers…when I saw Aneria for the first time, a different love…"

"Can you choose one?"

"Choose? How?"

"I don't know. The most important one?"

"I don't think I can."

I insisted.

"I know only of the love of our God. For us, the one moment that defines this ultimate act of love is His sacrifice on the Cross, the moment of life-giving death," I said.

He let out a sigh and looked away from me as if to remember.

"Life-giving death, huh? That I know," he said and paused for two breaths. "That was when the arrow pierced me in the Forest and Zeria took me into her hut. Because I died at that moment and came back only to see her."

"The moment you were hit by the arrow…" I murmured. An ancient myth fluttered for an instant in my mind. "So strange, I've read something exactly like this in the old scrolls."

During the next few weeks, I searched for days and nights to locate the papyrus in our library. When I finally discovered the unique manuscript, I flew up the stairs into Da-Ren's castle-wall cell triumphantly.

I unraveled carefully the papyrus that I had hidden under my robe. The books of the Faith were written in codex, bound together sheet by sheet. I was creating one codex book for each chapter we finished. But the myth I had found seemed to be truly archaic—a rolled scroll. It sang forgotten poems of solitude and abandonment as I opened it. It was only a few decades old, already succumbing to the damp. It had been copied many times by other monks, and even by me as well.

"I was granted permission from the First Elder to reread the forbidden texts of the ancients of the south, the idol worshippers. I had copied on this scroll, some years ago, a myth that I think I must read to you. I didn't pay much attention to it then, but yesterday, when I finally found it again, I had a revelation."

"A revelation? From the scrolls of the pagans?"

"Well, I don't believe any of this, Da-Ren. But it is so strange the…the similarity."

I began to read with a smile on my face and eyes wide open, as if I had discovered something incredibly joyful. It took me a long time to read under the scant light of the single candle. I wanted to enjoy it slowly. The wooden shutters were closed tightly against the screaming winds of winter, and the room stank of smoke and oil. I threw the woolen cape over my back and shoulders before beginning. These words could be read aloud only during winter or when it rained. Under the bright summer sun, all of this would sound frivolous: the conversations, the cell, our writings, and love.

As I read, Da-Ren lowered his eyes and sat motionless, his body bent as if frozen. Maybe because he had given me his cape. Maybe because he wanted only his ears to remain within the room. I read to him from the ancient gods.

"In the beginning, there were only two: Chaos and Gaea. And from them, Erebos, the Deep Darkness, was born. Deep within him, Nyx, the Night Goddess, left her egg, and from their dark and silent union came to be the God of Love, Eros, his wings sparkling silver and gold. The God of Love carries a bow. If his arrow strikes a mortal, he falls into passionate ecstasy. And then, as Love triumphs and conquers, it leads that man down to one of two paths. To Virtue or to Misery."

Da-Ren lifted his gaze and spoke the last words of the wintry day. "As for me, it led me to both."

XXXVII.
The Merciless Rain

Eighteenth winter. Chief of the First.

Not from a barren field afar
or from the fiery Sky above,
not as a coward in the dark,
or with the arrow's deathly mark.
I see the white fear of his eye,
the demon's heart when I pierce,
the sound of fury in crimson dreams,
the flesh that parries iron screams.

Sun, come and harden my long blade
to shine and burn in the dawn's raid.
Selene, lead me into the night
so I bring death under your sight.
O stars, I'll join your golden sands
with two red blades in my hands.

The Song of the Blades

Soaked in the sweat of a brave fight and a young man's sexual passion. Not in the blood of a beardless boy. That was how my five-wintered term with the Uncarved came to an end. It was not the end I had always dreamed of. But it could have been far worse. Gunna, Redin, Urdan, Akrani, Lebo, and the others. Sometimes, even defeat deserves to be celebrated. Especially when most of my comrades and adversaries were now but ashes swirling among the clouds.

I had become one of the most dangerous men of the Tribe, and that would make me for the winters to come one of the most desirable to the Ouna-Mas. For those who had fire beneath their waists and not ice in their heads, anyway. They were the She-Wolves of the Legends that bore us. For them, I was an otherworldly demon, a touch of death, and an insurmountable power. Not because I had some special gift of nature or talent—I had seen greater stallions in the tents—but because I had the word *Drakon* carved inside of me.

Their Stories claimed that I breathed fire from my mouth, released lava from my dick, and had saber-long blades for teeth that tore them apart at the moment of orgasm. I was carved only after the Tribe had a new Khun; I killed a Reekaal in close weapon combat in front of ten thousand men; I survived in the Forest alone for more than a moon and didn't die from a black fate's arrow or any other poison poured down my throat. It didn't matter if only half of that was true; they believed it all. When they entered my tent, they melted like white-hot iron at the blacksmith's forge before I even touched them. Or so I liked to think, and that had the same effect, at least on me.

The Blades whom I came to command knew a few things about women and would tell me the same. They claimed that the first ones to get with child were those they took by force in the heat of the raids.

"With the blade at their throat and the blood of their kin on the ground."

The fearless women didn't become pregnant easily. Those who felt secure were also impregnable. The ones who trembled were the ones who opened up first like roses.

Razoreyes, the Redveil, came that night as Malan had promised, and she did not meet death. Quite the opposite. She lived, even though I forced her to taste a drop of my blood to be completely sure. It might have cost me my life had she told Sah-Ouna or if she had died, but absolutely nothing happened to her. First thing I did was to turn her over. I didn't want these women to have their way on top of me anymore. I moved behind her and put her on all fours as I had seen the warriors do to the slave girls. I stuck her hot and sweaty buttocks to me and went inside her. She released a cry of surprise when she lost control. Many more moans of pleasure followed before she was to find it again.

When we finished, I realized that I hadn't really taken Zeria in the pond that night. She may have taken my mind from the very first moment, but I had never taken her as I took these red-veiled Witches. Nor did I even think that Zeria, with the eyes of the Sky and the hair of the black night, was the same as the Ouna-Mas. I didn't desire to mount her like a dog. I could wander through the Forest for seven nights just to be able to look at Zeria's eyes for a few breaths and hear her voice again.

In the morning, just after the Ouna-Ma left my tent, I strapped my blades, bow, and quivers and packed my clothes onto the horse that the Rods gave me. I left the small settlement of the Uncarved without any farewells and passed through the Archers' endless fields and tent camps where the young ones were being trained, the Tribe's greatest warriors.

I then turned east and took the wide road that cut Sirol in two. The road became busier with Rods riding and carts pulling supplies of hay and wheat as I got closer to the Khun's tent. I always wondered where the grain came from since there were no farmers in my Tribe. Not one.

I kept my head turned toward the north most of the day. Toward the south was the hill where Malan's tent rose magnificently, surrounded by all of his faithful and none of mine. I passed the few tents of the Trackers and finally reached the meeting point. It was a gated entrance that led to the camp of the Blades. A few more had gathered outside of it to report to their new Packs. Not Chiefs. Thrice carved.

"And here is Da-Ren, the young Chief of the First Pack, finally," said the Reghen.

"What's this?" I asked.

"We have been waiting for you to honor us with your presence all morning. I am to take you all to your new camp," said the Reghen, who approached me on horseback so close that our horses were sniffing each other's sweat.

"I didn't know."

"Now you'll have to do the waiting. We'll take all others to their new Packs first and drop you last."

He had a faint grin on his face, as if that would be some kind of punishment for me.

"Yes," was all I said and even that reluctantly.

"But first things first. You can't go like that into the Blades' camp," said the Reghen.

I was still wearing the skins of the Uncarved. The Reghen gave me a black ribbon to tie around my arm and show that I was a Pack Chief, leader of forty men. What a strange thing it was—the eyes of the others embracing me with admiration while I was choking on my own defeat. I took off the heavy familiar wolfskin that shielded me from the cold. The Reghen gave me a new, worse skin, like those worn by the Chiefs of each Pack, made of squirrel fur. Many squirrels. Archer warriors wore goatskins or sheepskins, Blades wore dog, and so did the Guides. The Uncarved wore wolf, the Rods bear, and the Leader of all the Archers was the most impressive, donning his deerskin.

I wondered what Malan wore. Khun-Taa had chosen wolf

throughout his reign, but Malan could have changed even that.

Wrapped in dead squirrels, I entered the camp of the Blades on horseback. The man who rode next to me, dressed in dog, was named Ogan and had just finished his training with the young Blades after five winters. He had known for a long time where he would end up. But he talked too much. He had so many questions. He would die early, without answers.

I knew that the Blades were about twenty Packs. Each one had fewer than forty warriors.

"Eighteen. They die faster than we can train them," the Reghen said. "We had to cut the Packs by two."

Still, the camp of the Blades seemed much larger.

Ogan kept his horse next to mine and never stopped talking. Sometimes he had useful things to say: "Slaves, Carriers, women they brought for this moon, their brats, old crones for cooking, Blacksmiths—"

"They have their own Blacksmiths here?" I asked.

"Yes, we do. We need many blades."

"How many altogether?"

"Huh. A lot." He didn't know how to count and just shrugged his strong young shoulders. "If we start now on foot to go fence by fence around the whole camp, we will be back here by sunset."

I looked at the sun and then started speaking as I was counting: "About five hundred tents. Six men to a tent, give or take. Not even a thousand Blades for battle. The rest for everything else."

The Reghen smiled. Ogan looked at me, lowered his head to one side, and squinted hard, as if that would make his head work faster. He didn't understand a word I said. I would see that empty stare in the common men I would lead from now on. I would speak plainly, using simple words, and they would understand nothing of what I said. One more thing the Guides had not taught me at the Uncarved, the best of the best: all the others had not been raised the same way. As I grew older, the stupid seemed to multiply around me. They died quickly, but they sprouted even faster.

We arrived at the tents of the First Pack.

The Blade warriors, those whom I would have under my command, were just returning.

"Training ended for today," the Reghen told me. We continued a slow trot on horseback in between a bunch of busy warriors, slaves, and women who were watering horses, carrying the wounded, yelling, and moving in a hurry.

"Did something happen today?" I asked.

"No, this is how it is every day."

I dismounted and walked my thirsty horse to the trunk-carved trough. I cut my eyes left and right watching everyone shouting and fighting over stupid things. These menial tasks that had never bothered me—cooking, watering, caring for the wounded—seemed so important to those around me. Somebody pushed me.

"You're blocking the path, kid. Move."

"Yes," was all I said.

"Are you a Squirrel?" he asked with a look of surprise. He left, shaking his head and mumbling before I had a chance to answer.

I am no squirrel.

There were no old men around. Everyone was young, but I was the youngest, and it showed. I was clean, better dressed, and moving more slowly than they were.

"Don't worry. I will help you during your first days. You have been sent here by Khun-Malan; they will obey you," the Reghen told me.

I wasn't at all worried. I had the cool composure of someone who had never thought, didn't expect, and was not afraid of being there. I was swimming in another man's dream. A bit curious I was, and that was all.

The First Pack, the one I was to command, camped in the southeastern corner of the settlement, near the river. At the edge of the fence. I had known that fence well since I was a boy, many winters ago. Across from there, if I continued toward the east, I would fall upon the first tents of the orphans. That was where Malan had sent me—across from the tents of the piss-carrying boys where we had grown up. So that I could see it every morning and smell it every night when the easterly wind blew all the way into my tent.

The Reghen gathered all of the men of the First in front of the evening fire and announced who I was. I received many hard looks and a few lifeless cheers.

"A worthy Chief! A worthy Chief!"

Whatever words the tradition dictated. The cheers faded fast.

I knew two of them. One was an unwelcome and forgotten face from the Sieve, Urak. No longer a twelve-wintered, he was bearded, grimy, and uglier than I cared to remember him. He lowered his eyes as soon as he saw me. The other was Ogan, who had just arrived with me and wouldn't stop turning his head in every direction and talking.

The men were gathered and waiting, looking at me, their meat, and the fire.

"Say something," the Reghen told me.

Say what? I didn't care to say anything.

"At daybreak, we'll have words, men," I said. A heavyset, long-bearded man greeted me with a drawn-out belch before I finished my words and brought a round of laughter.

It hadn't started well.

I didn't know what to do, and everyone could see it. The older ones were chuckling. I took a cup of the milky mush and sat next to the only one who had put a little spirit into his cheers.

"What's your name, warrior?

"Leke, three carvings, Chief."

I had already seen his carvings—thick, old, swollen, deep, unmistakable.

"And how long have you been here, Leke?"

"This will be my eighth winter. I am already a rusty iron."

He looked young and strong, but his words said his better days were behind him.

"Who is the Leader of all the Blades Packs here? I have to go and meet him in the morning."

"We don't have a Leader of all the Blades yet. The last one who tried to—"

"Yes, I remember. Keral. I was there. And still, there is no one?"

"They said that Khun-Malan will choose a new Leader for all eighteen Packs of the Blades before the winter is out. They are in no hurry since the raids have ended till next summer."

"Winter we rest. Spring is the fresh beginning," I said in a loud voice.

My head started to thaw, and I was beginning to think. I couldn't handle any damned Leader over me.

"Let's hope the Khun chooses a brave one," Leke said.

Oh, that he will, Leke, I promise.

I would be the next Leader of all the Blades, even if I had to swallow blades and shit them from my asshole.

I stood up to say some words worthy of a Leader. I passed my eyes for a breath over each warrior there. I took off my squirrel skin. I was alert for the first time that day because now I had a purpose, even if it was not a great one. I took out both blades, raised them into the air and crossed them over my head to honor the Blades banner. I lowered them ready to begin my first speech.

It wasn't necessary. Almost all of the men slowly stood up before I had uttered a word, and about forty pairs of eyes fixed straight at me. A few came closer, three or four paces away. They weren't looking me straight in the eye, but rather at my naked left arm. The mark of the ninestar triangle wasn't visible. My long hair hid it well. They would find it soon, but it didn't have to be on the first night.

With everything that had happened over the past couple of days, I had forgotten one strange detail. Above the black ribbon of the Chief, there should have been a deep carving—the one the Ouna-Ma had given me with her ring half a moon ago. As I looked at my arm, I could see the carving, but it wasn't deep. It had healed and looked more like a scratch. The carvings of our Tribe were scars that could not be missed. They ate through the flesh and swelled to a flush of pink, and hair no longer grew there. Not mine. Ten feet away from the nearest warrior, I looked as if I were completely…

"Uncarved!"

The word came out of a few mouths. It would no longer protect me. It would only bring death.

The Reghen rushed to end our first gathering.

"Tomorrow, men, the Chief will speak to you. Go and rest now."

Murmuring among themselves, the warriors started to make for their tents. The night was freezing, and it was best for everyone.

"Now be careful, Chief," Leke said to me, grabbing my arm softly just beneath the black ribbon.

"Careful with what?"

But he had already disappeared among the others.

Before I left for my new tent, the Reghen pulled me aside.

"I'll stay the first three days to guide you till you settle in."

"Yeah, but—"

"It is what the Truths require when a fresh Chief starts."

My new tent was small, the hides old and stinking of horse dung and made for someone much shorter. Every Rod, even if he wasn't a Chief, had a better tent. The hole where Khun-Malan pissed was bigger and probably smelled better. The Chief's tent was an angry slap in the face for an Uncarved. At least it was mine, I said to myself that night when I looked for more hides to guard myself against the frost. My little squirrels were shivering. But I was a Chief, and I had my own tent. I didn't go, like Leke and Urak, to sleep side by side with other men.

I would learn quickly that having my own tent didn't stop anyone from coming in and waking me whenever they chose to. The first man—I didn't even know his name—rushed in way past midnight when the rooster usually crows for a second time. Before he shook me awake, the blow horn was already sounding the alarm, and I immediately rose to my feet.

"Chief! Gather everyone!" the dark shadow of a man shouted at my face. A breath of worms and bile.

I crawled out of the tent flaps as fast as I could.

Even the Reghen was shouting and running. He was calling my name: "Chief Da-Ren! Chief Da-Ren. Hurry!"

Chief Da-Ren.

Ogan was next to me and armed for battle. Brave boy, born only to die.

"The Blackvein horn!"

"On your feet!"

Everyone was giving a different order.

Men with torches were gathering around me on foot. They had woken up but hadn't mounted their horses.

"What's going on?" I asked. "Did you lose a mare?" I even tried to smile at my stupid joke.

"Down at the Blackvein. They are invading. Ride now and stop them," said the Reghen. "I sent messengers to wake up everyone."

He pointed toward the south at the banks of the river.

"Then…let's go! Everyone on their horses!" I shouted.

"You haven't gotten such orders," said a much older man with a long beard and a half-shaven head.

"Who are you?"

"Sani, two carvings," he replied.

He had only two. He could make Chief of the Pack. If it wasn't for me.

There was no Leader above me to give me orders.

"We ride now! Bring the oil and the pine's blood for the arrows," I said, louder this time, looking straight at him. I was already on my horse.

The First Pack was ten tents altogether. One for me, one for the Reghen, and eight for the rest. The help and women were farther away. I could see the Second to the west. The two of us were camped closest to the river. The Reghen was shouting for us to make haste. I led the way. The Second had mounted but stood still. My men followed me with their horses and their curses. Not for long.

"To the hill!" shouted a rider in the dark, and they all turned left. I turned to follow them, screaming madly.

"Da-Ren, Chief of the Pack, you're following last in battle," Enaka whispered above my head.

We made it to the top of a grassy hill above the river.

"Who ordered that?" I shouted again.

"I did," said Sani.

Before I got a chance to strike him, the Reghen was next to me.

"Good! From here, we can see everything," he said. "Let's see how many they are."

"I don't see anything," I said.

I could barely see the river; I guessed where it was because the fires of our camp snaked around its north bank. I thought I could see some shadows by the fires down there, but not much. If only there were some light.

"There you see those men, the rafts," the Reghen said.

My sight was improving gradually, adjusting. A couple of torches.
But there are very few of them.

"Doesn't look like an invasion to me," I said.

"Light the arrows," ordered Sani.

Under the flight of our flaming arrows I saw half a dozen rafts approaching from the south coast of the Blackvein. More and more cries tore through the clear winter night air.

"We must burn the bridge. Stop them. They are invading," said Sani. "Fire, fire!" he was shouting.

"No," I countered. "Wait!"

"No time. Now!" he said again.

Six rafts invading Sirol of the thirty thousand Archers?

"I am not sure. Those men, to the east, running for the river? Are they Blades?"

"Who cares? Burn the bridge," Sani screamed.

He was no leader. He had panicked, I could see it.

I could count about twenty men running from our side of Blackvein toward the rafts. They looked unarmed.

"They are on foot," I said.

They couldn't be ours. When they reached the othertribers there were no screams of fighting.

"No, I think they are…prisoners," the Reghen said. "We gather them next to the Craftsmen camp."

I think your prisoners are escaping, Reghen.

"The kid doesn't know what to do," Sani cried to the Reghen. "By Enaka, we need to burn the bridge now."

I wasn't even looking at him anymore. I was watching below.

The raiders had overtaken the few of the Tribe's men who were guarding the bridge. But they were not invading. They were helping the prisoners board the rafts. And they carried lit torches.

They are trying to set the bridge on fire. They are too few.

"Save the bridge!" I screamed.

"They came to take their prisoners," the Reghen mumbled.

"Everyone ride for the bridge!" I shouted.

"If we lose the bridge, they will crucify us," said the Reghen.

I raised my Uncarved arm and motioned for my men to follow me. I started cantering downhill as fast as it was safe for the horse, to get to the riverbank. I stopped many breaths later. Ogan was next to me, but no one else. They all remained behind.

I turned and yelled, "What in the Demon?" I had to go back again and gather them.

"What are you doing?" Leke asked me.

"Da-Ren, protect the bridge!" shouted the Reghen.

"We wait for the Archers," said Sani, next to Leke.

My left hand grabbed the hilt, and I bit my lip with my upper teeth until I bled. These men I had been given were no warriors. More screams were coming from the side of the bridge. We couldn't see who they were, but we could hear. They were our guards who were falling.

The Reghen was pushing me with orders: "Save the bridge. We mustn't lose it. Attack now."

But my men were not my men yet. They weren't listening.

"We wait for the Archers," said Sani. "Always, everywhere."

"We never go first," said a man next to him.

I turned my head to meet their faces. Fear or mistrust? I didn't care much about any bridge. But it was right there that I knew that either I tamed these men or I would be dead in a few nights. The chilling breeze woke me. I had heard enough. The Archers were nowhere in sight. Their camp was at the other end of Sirol. It would be more likely that the orphans or the Tanners next to us would come before the Archers.

A few of my men were turning back up the hill.

I didn't have a cool head anymore, only rage that I had ended up there. I needed to kill someone. The othertribers. Sani. Anybody.

"Men of the First. Ride forward with me!" I shouted from the bottom of my guts. "Now, by Enaka. Last one gets five!"

Five carvings. I would send him to the Guides. He would never again see a woman or fresh meat. They understood that order.

About forty men followed me. No one overtook me. We tried to gallop wherever the slope flattened. Close to the riverbank, the terrain changed and became treacherous. Blind dark puddles and rocks spread in front of me. I pulled the horse back to stop before we both went tumbling down.

"Everyone dismount; on foot, we run!" I yelled.

Behind me, I heard the voices of my men raging.

"*On foot*, he says!"

"A crazy fuck of a Chief we got."

Othertribers and prisoners were setting the bridge on fire.

"You! Bring water. Lead 'em, Sani," I said to the men on my left, pointing with the blades in my hand. "Rest, follow me," I said to the men on my right.

I could hear more than I could see. I had to trust the blade more than the bow. Our blades came out to cut the heads and bodies of the othertribers; my long iron hit first to cut through the bewilderment and the objections of my men.

We took back the bridge. Blow by blow. Man by man. The prisoners who were running to escape were unarmed. I struck down three. Now, yes. This was what I needed. Life in their death. I wiped out defeat and rage. This was even better than a Redveil moaning on all fours. The screaming guts spilling out of them. Enaka lit more stars to guide our way. I could see three rafts loaded with prisoners heading back south. I leaped into the water. The stars were becoming brighter.

"Burn the rafts! Stop them!" I yelled.

"He's going to finish us all tonight," I heard someone saying behind me.

"No, Da-Ren. Back!" shouted Leke.

"No, forward!" I yelled again with the frozen water of the Blackvein up to my knees.

Ogan stood confused for a breath but then he charged first. He was even farther in than I was, and was hacking the othertribers that were trying to reach the rafts. With a roaring smile, he showed me three fingers after he killed his third man.

Few followed me. Most stayed behind and were already retreating.

I would kill Leke, the coward, as soon as this raid was over. But Leke was still standing there, shouting at me to get back. I could see around me clearly now. Enaka lit even more stars, so many that the night brightened in splendor.

Damn, these are no stars.

Hundreds of torched arrow shafts were coming toward us from the direction of the camp.

"Back, Chief, run!" yelled Leke.

I finally realized.

"Will they shoot?"

"They *are* shooting."

"Everyone, back now. Now. Now!" I shouted with every bit of strength I had inside of me. We were far from our horses. We were running on foot over the rocks and the mud.

The damned Reghen. I had sent my men to doom.

The flaming arrows of the Tribe's Archers were descending over our heads. Many arrows, like blind shooting stars from above. Some whistled above me, but I was one of the last. The cowards and those who had disobeyed me were out of danger. They hadn't even gone into the water.

As I was running out of the muddy water, I looked behind me. The raiders' rafts were ablaze in the river. To the left of them, the bridge stood strong. I had saved it, and the last of my men were retreating rapidly.

I turned to shout to them.

"Quick. They're shooting at us. Run!"

We were running uphill to get away from danger.

But who could outrun the Tribe's Archers?

"Oh, demons, Ogan. No!"

The merciless rain of arrows. Our arrows.

The first arrow found him on the arm. He kept moving, aghast. More arrows hit him. Two more of my men behind him. Why were they running so slowly? Their screaming agony as they were dying, one covered in flames, was the only answer I'd get.

I had killed the othertribers. I had killed my own men.

I kept running toward our torches. The Archers. I passed all of my men. They were spitting curses behind me. Some cursed the Archers. The rest cursed me.

"You snake! What are you doing?" I grabbed the Archer with the black ribbon, their Chief, with one hand and pulled him down from his horse.

His back hit the ground hard. He got up slowly and tried to attack me.

Many hands held us back.

"You didn't wait for us. I didn't wait for you either," he yelled.

"Those men you killed."

"They shouldn't be there. It's not for the Blades to tell me what to do," he said with a brazen look.

To him, I was no different from a rat.

I was looking at his left cheek. I pretended to calm down with his words. I lowered my head and nodded. I bit my lip and humbled myself. To show him that I understood. That I accepted. As soon as they made the mistake of letting me go, I surged toward him like a rabid mauler. I punched him hard, my knuckles crashing on his cheek. I didn't see him getting up again. The Archers attacked us. Punches were flying in every direction. One of the Archers landed a full one on my nose. Sani and Leke were next to me, fighting on my side. They dragged me away to safety.

"We're not finished," the Reghen said when things cooled down and the Blades separated from the Archers.

We had to attack again. That was the worst. I didn't have any desire left in me to do anything. I was tired of my own orders already. But now it was the turn of the Blades. After the Archers. We went back down the hill, this time to hunt and slaughter the wounded othertribers.

Dawn broke to carve the sky and the river with the same shade of red. Blood darkened the Blackvein and soaked our boots. The blood of the othertribers and the three men of the First Pack. My pack.

We kept going, mad with rage and exhaustion, until midday. We had to burn the bodies and stand guard as the Craftsmen fortified the bridge. The Archers and two other Packs of Blades, those who had never followed my orders, went beyond the river to hunt down anyone who tried to get away.

"Did you listen to that young fool? 'The last one gets five,' he said," mumbled someone to my left. He was one of the two who were carrying the corpse of a stout man. The dead man had legs crooked from riding all his short life, and more than ten arrow holes in him. Exactly three carvings.

I went back to the camp followed by my men.

"What crazy kid attacks before the Archers? And dismounts?" one of them was murmuring. I had been listening to that same voice all day. It was the one from the night before. He wouldn't stop.

"Who is he?" I asked Leke.

"Mekor? Be careful with him. He was pledged to the previous Chief. And he favored Keral."

"We will talk of this tonight after the pyre," I said. "Rest now, and tend to your wounds."

I had a scratch on my thigh from one of our own arrows. I was glad of it. The arrow that had found me had reminded me of Zeria. By now, she had become a mythical wind-ghost of the Forest. A dream that vanished as fast as it had come. She was now a thousand worlds away. Even the camp of the Uncarved, just a little farther to the north, seemed like another world—still close but completely unreachable. It had taken only one night for my old world to crumble to pieces, a lost dream chopped to bits by eighty blades.

Sani came by and gripped my forearm.

"You did the right thing, Chief," he said.

He gave me a slice of dried horsemeat.

He saw my surprise. I didn't feel proud. I wasn't eating.

"What happened here today, Reghen?" I asked. "Is this how it will be every night?"

"No, you were unlucky. And lucky in some way. Seems you got the trust of some men here."

"Some; not all of them. But what happened down there? I've never heard of othertribers raiding from the south."

"Last Harvest Moon, the Archers captured a General of the South beneath the river. He was of noble birth, they say, a nephew of the Emperor himself."

"What's a nephew?"

"Yes, anyway, someone important. We were holding him prisoner. Seems like he led an uprising. One of his men probably escaped before the rest and informed the Southerners, who came in for a rescue raid. He was too important."

"And if more of them come?"

"The othertribers had become very daring lately with Khun-Taa, especially the Southerners. Khun-Malan will change all that."

Mekor spoke again behind me as we watched the fire take our three comrades. "He lost three men on his first night. Within Sirol! Have you ever seen such a useless shit?"

The Reghen was next to me and held my arm so that I wouldn't make a move.

"It is difficult to be Chief, Da-Ren. Not to know what is the right thing to do. Should you have attacked first? Should you have waited?" he said.

"We should have attacked," I said.

"Yes. We should have. If we had lost the bridge, that would have been a disgrace and a disaster. A brave and wise Chief would have attacked. You made the right decision."

His words surprised me. I hadn't made a mistake.

It was a small pyre, barely worthy of warriors. The tongues of the flames engulfed the men who had obeyed me. The fast-talking Ogan would never say another word. He had been a brave kid. His Story was honorable. Short.

"That is why we Reghen always favored leaders like Malan. Like you. Young. Uncarved."

"What, why?" I asked, a bit dazed, my mind still on Ogan.

"Because you are not rotten. Old men rot. Out of jealousy, envy, and defeat. They creep. The young never stop. They haven't yet learned fear. The Truths and the Legends are fresh in their minds. They were raised that way, and they rush in without the weight of an old man's fears. We want new blood. The Tribe moves forward. It must not rot. Khun-Malan leads."

"Khun-Malan leads," I repeated.

It was the favored hail of the day around Sirol. Khun-Malan led, and I had to save his bridge.

The Reghen had never joined the battle; he stayed at the summit of the hill the previous night. That was the main reason I wanted his opinion. Not because he was a Reghen. Because he had chosen the best view, he had seen everything without anyone blocking his sight.

I said to him, "I had to attack. And the Archers should have waited."

The Reghen signaled goodbye.

"I leave you now. You don't need me anymore. So many things happened in one day, and you learned so much, things that I thought would take many moons to learn."

He had mounted his horse, and he spoke to me for the last time.

"The Archers shouldn't have waited. They, too, did the right thing. Just as you did."

Indeed. He had nothing else to teach me.

"A Chief of the Blades. Hear that!" Malan had said a couple of nights ago.

The Blades were the quickest way for Malan to send me to Enaka in the Unending Sky. Their Leader, the one who had charge over all eighteen Packs, died a moon ago. The Chief of the First Pack, the one I replaced, had fallen recently while backing the usurper, Keral. For all I knew, I could have been the one who killed him that fateful night.

I had thirty-five men left. I gathered them all around the fire.

"Speak."

Ask, and you shall receive. I asked for rage and pain and received exactly that. Their voices overlapped, fast, angry, and loud.

"It is always the same. If we attack in the raids sooner than we should, the Archers hit us. Blind. They don't care."

"When we delay, we don't get any of the loot."

I remembered Rouba saying, "The Blades are for slaughtering the unarmed and the women. They are vultures. The only true honor of the Tribe is the bow. The merciless rain."

"They don't respect us as their equals."

"We have to make heavy shields and learn to fight like the other tribes. In battle, only the Blades fall."

The soldiers of the Southeastern Empire beneath the river were not Archers. They were formidable sword fighters with armor of steel and iron shields with leather covers. In man-to-man combat, they had the advantage. If we didn't outnumber them massively, then we would lose more in battle. In the Tribe's victories, most of the dead were always Blades. The Tribe had yet to see defeat, but only because we had the bow of Enaka, the invincible weapon.

"We are the only ones who see the white of the enemy's eyes."

"We are the bravest but are always last to get the women. And the worst meat."

"Even the Craftsmen eat better."

"The Rods have five horses each."

All of them had miserable tales to tell, and none glory. I, too, had a tale, but I didn't tell it. I remembered a raid at the Garol in the North when I had gone there with Rouba. The Blades had gone into battle only when victory was certain. They had killed the old and taken the women violently before the others came. They had torn babes from the breasts and heads from bodies. All of this with just their blades.

Bloodthirsty warriors, cowards, and lesser in battle, who hid behind the Archers and yet managed to die faster than anybody else. I would fight for the rest of my life beneath the emblem of the two unequal-sized crossed irons that marked the scum of the Tribe. Together with those who wouldn't have great Stories to tell when they would meet Enaka. Only short ones.

XXXVIII.
Behind Me

Eighteenth winter. Chief of the First.

Loneliness. Not squirrel, nor dog, nor wolf. Loneliness was the unbearable new skin I had to wear. Away from Zeria, Rouba, Bera, and the other Guides, the Uncarved, anyone else I had ever known. A solitary boy Chief among older men who could smell my inexperience. Alone in my tent. Loneliness was the enemy they hadn't told us about in the Stories.

I had been trained at the blade and the bow. The most common trial of each Uncarved was to slice pumpkins with eyes closed. That training would make me the fear and torment of every pumpkin. But I knew from the first moment I joined the Blades that it wasn't enough.

My third day as Chief dawned.

"You are the youngest Chief we've ever had," said one of my men who had been there for three winters.

"They brought a fresh one like you five winters ago, but he lasted half a moon. You better watch out, Chief," added Leke.

"Watch out for what?"

Everything.

The cloudbreaths had parted before dawn. It was a clear-sky day, perfect for riding and shooting.

"We ride for the training field," Sani said, this time trying to help me rather than challenge me.

We reached a vast and empty field of shit-colored mud and snow-covered stones. The few poles were broken and there were no pumpkins or targets to shoot. I had no idea what to tell them, and I couldn't even imagine how someone could train there. I wouldn't even want to ride a horse through that. The men had already separated into smaller groups, each one having its own talk. One group was fighting amongst themselves; another was casually striding around with neckropes. In a third group, farther away, the men were taking turns drinking from a waterskin and from the laughter I guessed it was filled with milk-spirit instead of water.

"Start," I shouted.

"Start what?" asked a man close to me. He was a man with a long beard, the body of a bear and the eyes of a mad jackal.

"What you do every day."

"What are you going to do?"

I didn't answer; I didn't want a fight.

"Who is this?" I asked Leke, not looking at the man.

"Hey! You asked before. Learn my name. I am Mekor," the man replied, waving his wide-open hands above his head. Mocking me.

Mekor again, a name I had heard of a lot and would hear for a few more breaths.

"I want to see how the Blades practice," I said.

"I say you want to see the tit of your slave mother, shit hair."

There, too, I had the lightest hair color of all of them.

It was true that I wanted just to watch them train because I didn't know what else to do. I wasn't afraid of anything, but it was already too late. My first trial, and last if I failed, would be to finish with Mekor.

He took out both of his blades, and I did the same. Then I thought twice. I had already lost three men.

"Lower your blades, man. I am an Uncarved; you will die here. Don't be stupid," I said.

"You're no Uncarved anymore."

Smart thought, big mouth, fatal words.

He was wearing a chain-mail armor like nothing in the Tribe, each iron ring smaller than my nail. He had stolen the armor of an othertriber and it fell short and tight on him, almost to his navel and a bit below his elbows. I hated armor. It wasn't of the Tribe.

"Where did you find this fancy dress? Stole it from a Southerner?"

"Killed him. I've killed many."

"Oh! How? Running scared up the hill like yesterday?"

The men were laughing, the sun was falling bright, his blood was bubbling mad under the stolen helmet. It looked like an upside-down acorn. No Archer of the Tribe wore a helmet. "Blades are vultures; they wear whatever they find," Rouba had told me once.

Rouba, it's time to find out if you trained me well.

I took off the soft squirrels. I had nothing but a leather jerkin over my sleeveless tunic. I stayed across from him at ten feet. He motioned for me to come and meet him, but I remained still.

"Hungry again? Or do you always wear your gruel pot on your head?" I said to Mekor.

Leke was clutching his belly, laughing, on his knees.

Mekor sheathed his small blade and raised the long one with both hands. He charged, bellowing, to bring it down on my head, but I made a quick move to the right, and he missed. He continued to wield it high, but he was too slow, like a huge bear in chains. That armor would be his death.

"I still let you live if you quit now," I said. "You're too slow."

That was what had made the greatest impression on me when I had lost those three men at the river. All of them were slow on their feet. They lived night and day on their horses and had all but forgotten how to walk.

"Will you fight, you butt-fucked lizard, or are you going to the snakes without lifting a blade?" he said.

I had no intention of going to the snakes. I let him swing his irons without touching a hair on my head another three times. I was tall and a relatively large target, but I had the fastest legs of all the Uncarved. We kept dancing around, and I waited for the moment when he would have the sun directly in his eyes. Then, I closed the distance between us fast and tried a crazy move. I threw my short blade like a spear toward his face. He fended it off with his, but before he had a chance to stand firmly and parry again, my long blade had taken his fingers. Two, maybe three.

He screamed and tried to raise his blade again. I hit him, deep and hard, low in the bare forearm. His blade fell. I could have sliced his throat right there. But that wasn't necessary. Not yet.

His wounds were not fatal, but he wouldn't be a warrior anymore. A one-handed, crippled, burly man who would be fishing salmon from now on with the rest of the bears. He was on his knees, facing me, holding his maimed bloody hand, and screaming. The thirty-four men around us were silent, waiting for my final move. I turned my eyes away from him and shouted for all to hear.

"I am Da-Ren, the son of Er-Ren, who fought the Cyanus Reekaal and lived to talk about it. I wasn't carved on my twelfth winter like all of you Rabbits, and I am the one of only two who survived till the end Uncarved. The other is Khun. Any scum who wants to go to Enaka today come up here and talk lizards. Anyone?"

They listened, and all of them understood. Except for Mekor. My guess, he didn't enjoy fishing. I saw him with the corner of my eye as he pulled a third blade from his belt, a small dagger. The dagger flew past me, barely grazing my cheek, and my mood for talking was cut abruptly. I ran at him before he got up and, a breath later, opened his throat with the thrust of my blade. The First Pack had one fewer warrior.

"Continue, great warriors. I want to see how you train for battle," I said to those remaining. "Is there anyone else who wants to leave the Pack?"

Only one more did, the one who had been sitting close to Mekor on the previous two nights. He tried to stab me in the back that night after we gathered to eat outside my tent. Slow feet, stupid eyes. To my surprise Sani warned me from across the fire, his lips opening to "watch out" and his eyes darting quickly to my right. I turned with a sudden move and stuffed a lit tar-covered torch into his mouth. I was out of patience. Out of mercy, I opened his stomach with my iron to end his muffled groans. A quick death. I couldn't blame him. He was loyal to his friend and his old Chief. Good for him. Enaka would like his Story, if only he could tell it to her with burning tar in his mouth. Thirty-three...

"So? Watch out?" I asked Leke.

"Now everyone will be watching out," he said, laughing. "You did good. You cleaned up the Pack in two nights."

It was about then that I stopped killing my own men.

Chief of the Pack. Of brave men. I had to convince them, to trample on them like worms when they weren't convinced, and that was easy. I had to inspire them, and that was difficult—not to let them think for one breath that I could be afraid of them. I had to make them rip their own hearts from their chests, roast them, and serve them to me on a spit if I asked for it. If I couldn't do that, it would be they feasting on my heart that same night.

I hadn't learned that either when among the Uncarved. I had wasted five springs in trials with pumpkins and walks in the Forest. If I had lived one winter with the Blades, I would have been a better Chief now. I may have even been the One Leader of the Tribe. If I had lived.

Sani got up before the men started leaving and addressed everyone.

"I am with the Chief. This stops now. If anyone else tries to harm him he will have to kill me too," he said.

"Me too," Leke added and so did a few other voices.

Respect. Not bad at all after three nights. As we were sharing the milk-spirit around the fire to drown the horrors of the day and the night, I asked each of them, "How long have you been with this Pack?"

"Nine winters," said Sani.

"Three."

"Two."

"I came one moon ago."

"Eight."

All of them had come on their eighteenth winter, and none of them had reached their thirtieth.

"And where are the older Blades? Do they camp at another Pack?" I asked, thinking I had been put with the youngest.

"Yes…the big Pack," said Sani, the nine-wintered, showing me the twinkling stars above our heads.

With fortune on my side, I'd have ten more summers of life. But there was something I had learned with the Uncarved. The first Truth of the warriors of our Tribe. The first command any leader of men was taught to say: "Behind me."

Behind me meant that a Chief always charged first in battle and usually fell first. He did not pass judgment, as the Reghen did, from the summit of the hill.

Outside my tent, I noticed a pole and a wooden slate hanging on it. Small iron pegs were nailed into the slate. I knew from training that every Pack had a slate such as this and counted how many men belonged to it. I ordered Leke to take out five pegs for the five we had lost the past two nights. I would have done it myself, but I got confused. Underneath it, there was another slate. And a third. Many instead of one.

"Which one is our Pack?" I asked him.

"These don't count how many heads the Pack has, Chief. We are not Archers; we don't lose count," he answered.

"What do they count then?"

"It's a wager we play. They count—" he stammered.

"Play what?"

"They count how many moons the Chief of the First Pack has stayed alive. That is why it is outside your tent. They are for…you to know."

"Moons?"

He nodded silently.

Not even winters?

"So, what did you bet, Leke? How many slates before I bleed away?"

"I am with you, Chief. I wish you well."

"Five?"

Bleak silence.

I looked at the slates again. Most of them counted fifteen to twenty moons, some even had thirty, and others had as few as the fingers on one hand. And the last, mine, didn't have any.

"Throw them all away," I told him. "As of tomorrow, we will count only our victories, not our deaths. We'll carve the slates to count the othertribers we slaughter. Bring many slates."

"As you command, Chief. Tomorrow."

Tomorrow. The starless night had come once again, and so was her sister: loneliness.

Victorious in my small, stinking tent I closed my eyes and dreamed of Zeria. In my nightmare, the Reekaal had crucified me and left me nailed on a leafless winter oak. Zeria came to save me at dawn, her fingers pulling out slowly the pegs from my palms as her lips touched mine.

It was the only beautiful face I had seen for many nights.

XXXIX.
Silent, Holy Night

Eighteenth winter. Chief of the First.

The night was silent. The frosty wind of the North had stolen the voices of men, the songs of birds, and the howling of the dogs. The second full moon of winter, the sacred one that marked the end and the new beginning, was upon us. It was the night of the Story of Birth, the Genesis of the World.

It was a long-standing tradition that once every three full moons every Ouna-Ma was completely free. Once in winter, once in spring and so on… Her only duty was to choose a Pack of men and go there to recite the Story of Birth. But after that, she was free to sleep and speak with any man she favored. Her unique and sacred gift belonged to only one man, usually the worthiest, the Chief of each Pack.

Razoreyes chose to come to my Pack on that Long Winter Moon. Razoreyes, a name I had made up only for her. She was the same Ouna-Ma, the second Redveil I had taken, the one Malan had sent to me after I had made an oath to serve him. She came to our fire and sat among the men. She rode alone, without a Reghen or Rods, on a night when a full Selene had hidden behind the clouds and the black breaths of Darhul. Everyone sat around the blaze and waited for her Story. The only Story that the Ouna-Ma would recite every thirteen moons herself, not delivered through a Reghen's mouth. But afterward, she would be naked only with me. She had chosen me. This time, she had not been sent. For the men that was the only winter's moment where they could be so close to a beautiful Witch. Deep in their hearts everyone would kill to be in my place. But all they could do was huddle around the fire and try to listen.

To celebrate the Long Winter Moon, the Ouna-Ma always followed the same ritual; she recited the Legend of Enaka, the greatest Legend of the Tribe, the Story of the Birth of our world. Chills turned the warriors' skins to gooseflesh. The thought of the Ouna-Ma's legs wrapped around me made me even more formidable to their eyes—a giant and a worthy Chief.

These were the words Razoreyes spoke a little before she melted with me:

The Legend of Enaka
The First and Second Epoch of the World

Hear now, men, the most sacred of the Stories of the Tribe.

This is the Story of time before yesterday, of the world before the Earth, of the Sky before the stars, and of the Goddess before the birth of man. It is the breath before the breast, countless winters before the cold. An age when the only meadow, the whole world, was a thick slime, black and shiny. No solid earth or wavy sea existed, only the mud boiling hotter than the sun and colder than ice, a sludge that neither light, nor hope, nor even time itself could penetrate.

There in the slimy, shining darkness lived an eternal Demon, alone, the only breathing thing, the ancient, eternal, immortal Snake, Darhul with the nine heads, each dressed in a different skin of black. Ravenfeather, Woodstar, Charcoal, Onyx, Blackberry, Ebonetree, Stormcloud, Nightsky, and Despair were the nine shades of black and the names of the heads of Darhul with the even darker soul.

Then, in that Yesterday—endless for man but only a heartbeat for the

Immortal Goddess—as the heads of Darhul fought among themselves, Despair ripped out Charcoal's glimmering red eye. The eye rolled down from the Demon's head, covered in crystal tears, into the radiant black muck. A smoldering coal, the orphan red eye drank its own tears, and in the heat and cold of the mud, it transformed.

It became Light.

And thus, the First Light was born, and it took the form of a beautiful maiden, her bareness covered only with a blinding cloud of hope. And she was the Only Goddess, Enaka.

Enaka stormed on Despair, the most loathsome of Darhul's heads, and from that moment, the First and Final War between the Goddess of Light and the Eternal Demon began. The fiery rays from the Goddess's quiver and the icy tongues of Darhul fought until the dark slime that made up the entire world split in half. The one baked into life and became the golden earth of the steppe, and the other half melted as death and became the black sea.

The war had no end. No one could prevail. On one side, Darhul spewed black clouds from his nine doubled nostrils, and from the other side, Enaka threw screaming lightning bolts from her chariot.

Then one night, Enaka turned her milk-white winged horse, Pelor, who drew her chariot in the Unending Sky, into a brave, black-haired man and lay with him. From their love, she bore seven sons, the Seven Suns to light the entire world and burn Darhul, defeating the Darkness forever. A new world was born, and it would soon be ready to give birth to men.

Almost defeated forevermore, Darhul spat out his dying revenge. He cut off with his nine jaws his own nine heads and dipped them into his belly, steeping them in poison, making them deadly arrows. The arrows fell upon the Goddess's newborn Suns, killing all but one. Six heads found their targets six times and killed six sons, six Suns of Enaka.

To save her seventh Sun, the life-giving Goddess hid him behind her chariot and opened her mouth wide to swallow the other three arrows. But the heads of Darhul sprouted and kept doing so again and again. A thousand times his nine heads became deadly arrows, and a thousand times the Goddess swallowed nine of them, their venom in her body until she grew enormous, the size of the Unending Sky. Finally, with one giant explosion, she burst and shattered into countless pieces. These countless parts of Her shone brighter than ever before. They flooded the night and became thousands of stars and new Suns, and her heart became Selene of the night. Selene rides the dark sky whole and strong at times, broken in half from sorrow over the loss of her sons at others, and the nights when Despair overpowers her, Selene is no more than a faint sliver of hope.

That was how the Goddess defeated the Demon. With her sacrifice and that of her children.

The stars were now myriad gleaming specks in the Sky, and the Demon, blinded by the Sacred Light, knew that he had been defeated. Life had been born. The nine heads of Darhul, all screaming at once, dove and hid forever in the depths of the cursed salt sea, and there he still lives, in the bottomless abyss where the light has no space to rest and where our warriors cannot walk or gallop upon the black water.

Golden stones from the stars fell to the earth, and fed the soil to give birth to our men.

But other pieces of the Demon's flesh washed up on the barren shores, covered in pus and charred blackberry blood, and from them, our demon-bred enemies were created.

Reekaal, his firstborn sons; Drakons, his greatest curse; and the Buried Deadwalkers were the myriad warriors of Darhul. They were born from his wounds and his vengeful heart.

Archers from the stardust of Enaka rose to fight them.

And still, every day and every night, the war between Enaka and Darhul rages on. Their spirits are weakened now, but their offspring are stronger. Enaka prevails by day, and the Demon is triumphant by night, but there are still days when the Demon is all-powerful. With his nine breaths, the black clouds, he darkens the Sky and blackshrouds the stars, the Sun and Selene, the son and heart of Enaka. The Goddess fights him with her bow, *sending her fiery sun rays in the day and her terrible thunderbolts at night.*

And so the epochs and the winters passed with the children of Enaka caught in an eternal battle against the demons of Darhul, the Reekaal, and the other monsters.

But the Story has not come to its end. Here and now, in your generation, is the most fateful and glorious moment of its culmination. For the darkness has returned; unstoppable rivers of black slime run again and drown the rest of the world, and the Demon has poisoned, from end to end, everything in the lands farther away from here. Everything except Sirol.

Beyond the Blackvein, the Buried Deadwalkers, the undead, rule in the Southeastern Empire, servants of the old white-bearded Sorcerers of the Cross. They wait to be resurrected from their bones. Sapul, the city they call Thalassopolis, is their cursed palace and their heart.

In the Endless Forest in front of us, the Reekaal have sealed with horrors all roads to the West and have put the entire Western Empire under their command. That is where the hiding place of Darhul lies, in the seas after the West, and his tentacles reach all the way to the Forest and the tendrils of the cursed trees.

And in the white darkness of the North, the Drakons of the ice rest but never sleep, where the Sun is pale and frozen like a dead girl's touch and no one ever dares approach.

The Final Battle is upon us, the one where the children of Enaka and the scum of Darhul will fight till the complete catastrophe. Have no mercy for any demonseed. Do not stop until the last one is annihilated.

You will live forever,
as brave and worthy among the stars;
or as cowards melting slowly in the belly of Darhul.

Glory to Enaka, the Only Mother and the Only Goddess of the Unending Sky and the Light.

Razoreyes had finished her Story under Selene's silent, holy night.

My men stood up and walked away shaken and distraught, more so because she would be spending the night in the tent next to theirs.

These were the Stories I had been fed like black milk since I was a small child. When I was young and foolish, I blindly believed in them. Later, I spat on them. In the end, I learned to respect them. Their wisdom and their brutal truth. This unlikely myth of birth, struggle and love, is nothing but the most common Story of each man and woman:

Darkness is our mother. We are born in Despair, by a faint, unlikely ember; but we find Love, and Love transforms us to Light and Hope. We live our Love for only one Night like a cursed Butterfly, and then we die, still fighting the Darkness with our last breath.

I had been chosen by this Ouna-Ma, this winter, and this is how it was meant to be. Razoreyes was already walking toward my tent, and I followed. The gazes of my men followed us too, but they couldn't enter. She undressed and I marveled at the two magnificent snakes painted across her body. Their black heads on the left and right side of her shaved head, their red cloven tongues touching and hissing in her ears, the bodies of the snakes painted down on the back of her neck and to the sides of her spine, reaching her beautiful ass. Like the nine heads of Darhul, she wrapped her arms, her legs, and her henna snakes around me all night. Like the fiery scepter of Enaka, I went inside her and filled her loins with white-hot rivers of life. We wrestled ceaselessly, front and back, like two gods. One would dominate briefly and then the other, until we both lost ourselves together in the eternal end, a formless mass underneath the hides that covered us, as dark as lust and as shiny as sweat. I kissed her body a thousand times, she bit my flesh a thousand more. It was the one time she would be entirely mine, the sacred night of the winter full moon and the only moment when the Ouna-Ma could escape her vows and speak. Only to me.

My body had received nourishment and Truth. My mind searched for more.

I asked her, "The Legend says that the Archers were born from stardust?"

"That's what it says."

I remained silent. She understood.

"But who knows? If you fight bravely, it could say so about the Blades tomorrow."

I didn't much like her words, but she wouldn't grace me with more hope.

"Tell me, how can I tell apart the children of Darhul from those of Enaka?" I asked.

"Foolish question, young Chief. You can always tell apart the people of our Tribe from the othertribers. From their color, their tongue, and their ways."

"But I have the ninestar, the triangle of Darhul imprinted on my skin, and the pale-faced Sah-Ouna rules the entire Tribe even if she wasn't born in it."

She lowered her long head and crawled backward on her hands and knees, like an animal on all fours, wrinkled her brow, still looking at me as if she couldn't believe what I had said. Her words were a threat but not an answer.

"Hold your tongue, strong man, because the prophecy listens, it is a haunted spirit searching for a body. Do not ignore it but do not challenge it either. Forget your ninestar destiny. Or else, if you challenge it, it will find skin and bones and come to life. Do not awaken the spirits of the North."

That was not the answer I was looking for. The two lips I wanted to nibble again were spewing out nonsense. We had a few breaths left together before dawn would come again. For one more spring, summer, fall, and winter, she would not hold command over her own body. She had chosen me. Still, she was in a hurry to go, as if I had frightened her.

She lifted herself onto her knees and turned her back on me. I glanced for the last time at the two painted snakes on her back and then she put on her robe. She waited there silent and distant, before the robin and the rooster called her away from her heart's love.

I asked her one more question: "The Story of Birth, the Legend of Enaka that you sang tonight—"

"Yes? Haven't you heard it before?" she said, reluctantly turning her gaze to me.

"Countless times. And it always says that the darkness is stronger than the light. It existed before the light. Enaka was born from the eye of Darhul…"

And that meant that in the end, the Light, Enaka, and the Tribe would be defeated. There was no need for me to say anything else.

Razoreyes did not think. She answered immediately. She knew. Her eyes, wide open, stared into nothing, their pupils giant black suns. Boundless was their magic. The otherworldly words escaped her lips of love.

"The Nothing always engulfs, precedes and follows. It existed before Something, and will after it. The Something always dies, even if it is born. It is an unequal battle that the Eternal Goddess fights for us. But have faith. The Nothing never dominates."

"The Blades?"

As if she had guessed what I wanted to know, she continued.

"Blades, bows, horses—they do not go to battle alone. The Stories guide them. Believe. We will triumph. You will all sacrifice yourselves for Enaka's victory, but you'll rejoice and receive your reward beside her."

"And what about me?"

"You…you, Da-Ren, are the blade of the Khun, the one who will rip first through the othertribers. Spare none of them. And when the Goddess calls you into her arms, accept your sacrifice as she did. Remember, she sacrificed her children for us. The prophecy says you will be First there, Da-Ren." She said my name very slowly with her tongue inside my ear before her love faded abruptly. She had come alone, of her own will, to lie with me on the most sacred night of winter. "The Final Battle begins. That is what Khun-Malan sent me to tell you."

XL.
Armor

Eighteenth winter. Chief of the First.

I hated armor. Metal plates or chainmail, armor always meant certain doom for those who wore it. It was death foretold.

"There, above the iron rings, below the beard, to the side, where your veins are still pumping. That's where my arrow will sink."

"A polished chainmail but it stops at your waist. I'll have to thrust my iron into your groin."

I suffocated each time I tried on the dark iron rings woven like impenetrable tunics. It slowed me down and weighed heavily on my joints as if the ghosts of the condemned pulled down my arms and begged for a quick death.

I hated the winter because it, too, was a kind of inexorable armor. It descended from the north and covered everything around me like a white linothorax. The rivers wore their own wintry armor, fat slabs of ice, and when they broke, rarely and with difficulty, they sounded like Darhul grinding the bones of our warriors between his teeth. The ground wore its own armor too, countless blue-white icy needlesheaths, one for each dead blade of grass.

And the men, it wasn't only the dogskins but also the cold itself that swathed them tightly. It numbed and made arms and legs hard and unbending like their own skin had become a panoply of death. The winter winds punctured our bones and filled them with rust to the marrow, making them creak with every move. The cold slid inside the ears and made every command feel like an icy-hot needle piercing the ear hole. Every hope and song was cut in mid-breath upon bleeding gray lips. The armor of winter prevented them from reaching our heads.

The horses, unable to graze upon the burned grass, wore for armor their skeletons and their weakness, the armor of mercy. The weaker ones were left where they fell, only their legs visible in the snow, protruding upwards. The fish were lost beneath the frozen river, and the swans had disappeared. Hunting them was forbidden, and the last ones were taken to Malan's tent.

The men wanted to scream for new raids, but their voices crashed against their crystal-frozen rotten teeth before even reaching the ears of the Reghen. The Truthsayers wore their gray hoods, their only armor for winter and summer.

He found me by the fire in my tent as I was taking off the unwanted armor of frost that was torturing my hands. With slow, careful words of winter, the Reghen spoke.

"Khun-Malan demands to see you in his tent tonight. A council will be held."

I stepped reluctantly outside my tent's scant warmth. The earth was sleeping under the white layers of fallen snow. The sun and the sky were hidden too, under white layers of clouds. More snow was coming. A valley of white emptiness above and below. Only in the middle, where gray men and brown-skinned animals toiled, a faint sign of life remained. As the lifeless sun descended on a bleak sunset, I took four Blades with me, to look important, and started out, covered in skins and fur hats.

"What is a council?" asked Sani, one of the four.

"Don't know. My first one," I answered. It was difficult and stupid to exhale many warm words in the frosty air.

I had never been to a council before, and nor had anyone else because Khun-Malan was the first to call for one. We arrived at the foot of the hill. At the top of it, the new wooden structure that we still called "the Khun's tent" dominated, fearless of wind and cold. The Rods stopped my companions and forced them to give up their blades and dismount there, in the snow, far from a fire or tent.

I walked up the hill alone. The path to the Khun's tent was marked by hundreds of poles to my left and right, painted a gleaming black against the white landscape. Iron sconces were mounted on the poles and most of them flickered weakly as I ascended the main path. To warm what? Nothing. The three spheres of the Sun, the Earth, and Selene outside Malan's tent shined as the dew dripped from their curved surfaces. The Rods were keeping them warm. I looked back down at my men. I could recognize them from their hides and their hats, as if those were their only names. Their faces had been hidden for two moons now.

Thick felt covered the sides of Malan's tent except for the three-level entrance with the heavy draping fabrics that stopped the freezing winds three times. The Rods to the left and right of every entrance looked even taller than the last time, well-fed and proud. I slowly strode down the aisle with the skulls. The ox skulls were my favorite. As stupid as the oxen were, their skulls looked wise.

There at the end, on the urn columns, they stood still, just as I remembered them—the two skulls, elongated like quivers, humanlike except for the horns and dog teeth.

"Bone, glue, horn," I reminded myself. It was the ancient art of our bow Craftsmen. There are no monsters.

It is a lie. Don't be afraid, Zeria. There are no monsters; you know that.

I breathed my escaping thoughts toward the smokehole to send them to the Forest. Her memory was the only armor for me, a shield to protect my hope—not my flesh. I would seek that memory every day and much more at nightfall.

It was warm inside Malan's tent, as the heat of many scattered hearths emanated from every corner. The throne was in front of me, ahead of the skulls. Laid out were many sheepskins, rich and abundant, enough to warm three Packs. They were the armor that covered the dirt. To my right, there was a large circle of burning coals resting in a narrow trench. In the middle of the circle three Ouna-Mas, Sah-Ouna's entourage, sat kneeling on the hides. They wore their short sleeved, torn black-ribbon, summer dresses. Razoreyes was there and turned to say something to the rest covering her mouth with a hand. She didn't turn to look at me, but the other two did.

I approached them with slow steps, and some of their escaping whispering words made it to my ears.

"Evil."

"North."

The two Rods were quick to stop me and show me the way.

"Not here. The council is there," one of them said, pointing to the opposite side of the tent.

I took a careful look at the glowing coals that surrounded the Ouna-Mas. The fires smelled like the Forest itself, blurring my mind. They were burning oak wood, not horse dung. I kicked the smoldering trunk with my boot just to be sure. There were rules. Wood was for coal, what we used to feed the bloomeries which made the iron. The Blacksmiths had to burn wood to separate the iron from stone, as horse dung would not do. Wood was valuable, especially since the Forest was cursed. Wood was for the bows and the arrows, for the carts and the machines of the Craftsmen. Wood was not for warming men or naked Witches, or for cooking meat. Rules since forever, created by the Khuns and the Reghen.

The Rod tried to push me softly to the other side where the council had started.

"No need. I am going," I said and walked to the small group of men.

"And the Chief of the First of the Blades arrives last," Malan greeted me.

Everyone was sitting cross-legged, except for Malan, who was standing. He motioned for me to sit when he saw that I wasn't doing it voluntarily. I sat and lifted my head to look at him. I was one of the two Chiefs of the Blades he had invited to the council. Druug, the Leader of the thousands of Archers, was there too, as well as Sah-Ouna, two Reghen, and a man I had never seen before. He had the brown ribbon around his arm, and I guessed he was a Tracker. All Leaders.

Most of them gave me only one quick glance. Druug's eyes stayed a bit longer on my face. *A great honor for you to be here, a fresh Chief ruling only thirty-three men.*

The oldest of the Reghen continued as if the council had been going on for a while and I had interrupted.

"The men are hungry. For meat, for campaigns, for pillaging, and for young women." He spoke loudly and sternly, addressing himself to Malan, and that woke me up immediately.

"We always start the campaigns in late spring with the Redflower Moon. And the loot comes in the fall. There is nothing we can do in this frost," said the Leader of the Archers.

"Khun-Malan promised that we would cross the Forest," said the Reghen.

Sah-Ouna motioned for the two Rods to approach. They brought trays heavy with slabs of raw meat.

"Roast meat. Want some?" Malan asked me.

Not horse or rats. Fat beef. Each of us grabbed a small spit, passed it through a thick piece of meat and held it over the fire. The charcoal gave a mouthwatering smell to the meat, so different that, for a while, I completely forgot what we were talking about. Every bite I chewed melted in my mouth and melted my fear. The beef juices were dripping from my jaw, talking with the crackling fire. They reassured me that somehow we would make it, despite the rage of the Drakons of the North. Some of us, anyway. Meat and wine soothed the minds of the men, and with their bellies full and warm, they talked without restraint.

"You, Tracker," ordered Malan. "What news of your missions to the Forest?"

The skinny young man jerked his head back twice, trying to swallow a large piece of meat quickly before speaking. He probably knew that he would be thrown out after saying what he had to say.

"We sent many scouts there into the white darkness. An evil demon wanders among the trees. In the beginning, my men went in but didn't return. We sent more, and they found the first lot, or whatever was left of them, pierced with arrows."

He showed us one of the arrows that had struck his men.

"So they are men, not monsters," said the older Reghen.

"Dasal?" asked Druug.

I looked at everyone around me, but my gut told me to play deaf and dumb at this great council. No one spoke of the obvious. Those were our arrows. Who had shot them? Were they the sons of the Ouna-Mas, as Zeria had told me, or our own Archers? Or was he just a scared Tracker spewing lies? I waited for the other Chief of the Blades, but he didn't dare speak. As the silence continued, I reluctantly voiced my thoughts.

"The Dasal have small bows," I answered. "And their arrows don't have such iron heads."

"How do you know?" asked Malan.

"They don't have arrows like that."

The Tracker spoke again. "No, I did not say they were Dasal. The ones who survived spoke of demons of the night. They heard their evil screams, and it froze their blood. Those creatures, they're not men like us, they laugh and scream at the same time. Otherworldly monsters, like that over there," said the Tracker, pointing behind me at the long, horned humanlike skulls.

"So they have horns now, do they?" teased Druug.

"Pheasants again," Malan mouthed with his lips, looking straight at me with a disappointed chuckle.

Malan sat down next to us, as if the foolishness had fallen heavy upon him.

The old and wise Reghen started speaking. "It takes only one day for you to take the throne, Khun, but for thousands of moons, the Forest has remained untrodden." He had a hundred heads, two hundred eyes and ears. He counted the livestock, and he could smell the hunger of the men and the footsteps of the Forest. It was his way of telling the Khun that he was young and this was not a laughing matter. A mistake.

Sah-Ouna motioned to the Tracker to continue.

"Demons, big as bears and with teeth like sabers, are the Reekaal. The trees come alive as their allies."

The fear filled his mind, and the Tracker started telling us about the horrid names his men had given the trees. He spoke of the "Embrace of the Reekaal," the "Hundred Skeleton Hands," the "Sword in the Heart of the Sky," and the "Hair of the Old Crone Witch."

Malan was no longer laughing.

"No one shall ever speak such nonsense, or else I will gather all the Trackers to the middle of Wolfhowl and let the maulers loose."

The men sat frozen as if the winter chill had slid inside and thrown an armor of silence over everyone. Only one dared to break it.

"Enough with all this. You will follow me, and we shall cross the Forest, now," said Malan. Large, wide eyes looked at him. "Now, in the heart of winter."

The men were speechless and the Khun's words sounded wrong in my ears. He had promised to cross the Forest, but not now, when Enaka's Sun was weaker than ever.

"It can't be done," said Druug the Archer.

Malan's slap found him on the ear, the one that wouldn't listen to the commands. Druug was twice our age, but he wouldn't dare challenge the One favored by Sah-Ouna and Enaka. The One surrounded by Rods in this tent.

"You can stay here if you're afraid. We don't have enough food to last for thirty thousand men till next winter. We will cross the Forest now. I will go in front," Malan said.

We also had forty thousand women, children, and slaves in Sirol. And another ten thousand in the outposts of the east and the north and a few south of the river.

Four gleaming eyes appeared from the darkest corners of the tent, and two black dogs jumped next to Malan. I hadn't seen them until then as if they had been buried beneath his red throne and just sprouted out of it. A Rod threw each a piece of meat. I had little left on my spit and was still hungry.

Sah-Ouna spoke for the first time, her eyes fixed on the Tracker. "With the air, not with carts and horses. That is how Stories travel. They cannot be caught, and no arrow can stop them." She spat her disgust at the feet of the Tracker. "You spoke loathsome tales for weak men. As soon as the Forest embraces your men, they lose their hearts."

"Have you ever gone into the Forest?" I asked the Tracker.

I had interrupted Sah-Ouna.

The Tracker nodded quickly, his eyes darting once to Sah-Ouna and back to me. He was telling the truth. He had been in there. He had seen something. I had had the same look on my face a winter ago when the Forest had swallowed me whole and alive for the first time. Only one winter ago I was First of the Uncarved, the hero of the Wolfhowl. It felt like so much longer.

"Say what you saw," Malan commanded.

The Tracker, as if he had kept the worst for last, opened his mouth again: "Khun-Taa sent us in there the last two summers. Both times we returned before the winter began. I never made it to the other side. The

Forest never ends. There is nothing at the end of it except the foot of a vast mountain chain, frozen and impossible to climb. When I found a pass to reach the top of the mountains, all I found was again—"

They rise again. Mountains. Forests.

"…mountains higher. Forests larger," murmured the Tracker.

Rouba had told me the same, long ago. I nodded with eyes closed to the last words of the Tracker.

"What do you think, Da-Ren? Do you agree with this?" Malan asked me. "You have gone many times."

"I have gone, but a few times only. I am not afraid of the Forest like the others. We will have to stay on the southern side. The north, where the Dasal live, is sunless, and the ghosts do not melt in that area."

"And how do these Dasal live there?" asked Malan.

"No, we have to go everywhere, even farther north to bypass—" the Tracker cut in.

I interrupted before he spread the idea any further.

"The Blackvein is frozen, hard as a rock all the way to the south. If you go north, the wind will become a breath of death and will burn our lungs. Khun, I will go with a few Blades ahead to the northern Forest, to find out what I can from the Dasal. You stay south where the cold is bearable and the horses can pass. I will meet up with you soon."

"The young Chief is right," said the Reghen. "The horses cannot go north."

Sah-Ouna nodded in agreement.

I imagined myself run through with a stake after every lie which came out of my mouth. I wanted all those men far away from Zeria. I was a despicable traitor, and it had happened so fast again.

"We will start in two days. Everyone must be ready," Malan said.

Malan motioned for me to stay.

The others left, even Sah-Ouna.

"Talk," said Malan.

"We should wait," I said.

"We cannot. I want to find the prophecies before the Great Feast of Spring. I will not wait for them to find me."

We were not alone. Sah-Ouna's entourage had stayed behind in the tent to my right, resting leisurely on the sheepskins. The three Ouna-Mas had not followed her. Their tongues and their legs were the armor that would wrap around Malan.

The Khun motioned me to join them.

To the armor of their young skin.

How much night had passed in this tent? My men had probably left their last frozen breaths outside by now. I grabbed the last spit with meat on it and exited through the draped entrance. I raced down the hill to reclaim them from the unforgiving night freeze. They had been standing all night outside in the snow without a fire.

"Eat up well because soon we will be hungry again. Come dawn, we ride for the Forest," I said as I passed the pieces of roast beef to them.

A Rod followed me, yelling for me to give back the spit that I had taken.

Glory to you, Malan, for exiling me to the Blades.

Eternal praise to you, my Khun, for not letting me fall to the lowly fate of a Rod, chasing after spits.

I threw the piece of iron which was burning cold in my hand between his legs and mounted my mare. She was weak and too old to last the winter; before spring I would need a new ride.

None of the men I had with me praised Khun-Malan. No one had anything good to say about him. Only the hanging horsetails and the size of his tent impressed them. But I knew that if they were ever to set foot inside the tent, if they saw the wood-burning fire, the horned skulls, and felt the warm legs of the Ouna-Mas wrapping around their bodies, they would fall to their knees at Malan's service and offer their hearts to him.

They followed me with admiration because they believed that I was one of Malan's men, his trusted servant and a faithful dog. One of those dogs he shared his meat with. "What irony!" I would say much later when I learned that word. But even that did not prevent them from whispering among themselves on the road back.

"Where did he say we were going? Did he really say it? Into the Forest?"

"We are doomed."

"No one ever returns from there."

"You'll see; they will send only us Blades. No Archers will come with us."

That was all I heard behind me as we were trotting the horses back to the Blades camp. I said nothing. I waited for the dawn, for the sun which came out so rarely, to sweeten the moment and breathe some hope down their chests. I gathered all thirty-three of them together and said, "I'm going into the Forest. Khun-Malan will go, too. And if, by Enaka, you want to be called men and warriors, you will follow. Behind me."

Fearless the Leader rushes toward the demons first.

That is the only true armor for a warrior.

XLI.
Rowan

Eighteenth winter. Chief of the First.

We set off two dawns later. For the Tribe to cross the Forest for the first time. Witches, Truthsayers, warriors and the Khun. To battle our monsters. With Enaka and Sah-Ouna at our sides.

More than a thousand warriors and slaves and a handful of Reghen and Ouna-Mas followed Malan into the Forest. I had managed to convince him to let me lead a separate mission. I took the First Pack and galloped north. We rode parallel to the Forest so that we could enter much later.

"Why do we go north, all alone, Chief?"

Those who asked questions were to be trusted more, those who didn't, hated me beyond words for leading them there.

"So we can have all that we hunt to ourselves," I said smiling.

But I had faith. If they saw no terror in my eye, the men would hold. I didn't lose any men; I only won their respect in the Forest. There, where all others trembled, I was walking surefooted. I knew the paths, the trees, and where to stop to make camp.

"By Selene, you are truly the son of Er-Ren," said Leke. The rest agreed with silent nods.

I had answers to their questions, even the lesser ones. I knew why some oaks still had their leaves in winter and others did not. To the men, I was a wizard in there. Nothing less. I did remember some of the paths, tried to guess the rest, and I followed my instinct to get as close as possible to Kar-Tioo. Close enough for the Dasal to spot us.

The only thing I didn't know was what I would do when we made it there—when my fearful men would come face to face with the Dasal, the ones they believed to be servants of the Demon. Was I so strong a wizard to spread my arms and separate the world into two to protect one from slaughtering the other? I could just about manage that with the First Pack. But if Malan with his thousand warriors ever came north, there would be no Dasal left alive—man or woman.

On the fourth day, I saw the footmarks of the Dasal and heard the light-footed shadows among the trees.

"Someone is following us," said Sani.

We were not far now, perhaps only one or even half a day's road.

"We make camp here, and I'll go to them alone," I said to Sani.

"What? No. Why?" he replied.

"If they see us all charging in, they will panic. They'll fight or run away, and I don't want any of that in here. They rule trees and animals," I said.

"It's madness to go in alone," said Sani.

"We will come too," said Leke.

I took only two men with me, Leke and Temin, who was young and didn't ask much, and moved north.

I knew we were close to the camp, I'd seen the Dasal's shadows watching us from a distance, I'd walked through the same rivulets and glades with Zeria a few moons ago.

"Are we far away?" asked Leke. "We shouldn't venture far from the Pack."

"We are here," I said, that same afternoon when I smelled the fires of the Dasal. "Take your blades and bows out, drop them here together, and make a fire."

"Is this wise?"

"No. But it is how it must be done."

I started shouting Veker's name, eager to find the Dasal before nightfall. Not much later I saw him coming out of the woods, six men following him.

"I told you never to come here again," he said.

I had to find a good excuse. The one about herbs, crazygrass, and exchanges made no sense in the ice of winter.

"If I didn't... I must talk to you, Veker. Alone."

They led us back to their settlement. I spoke with Veker in his hut and told him the truth. Or at least a bit of the truth.

"A thousand men have entered the Forest. I kept them away from here but you must help me. Our Tribe is looking for the road toward the West. You have to show me. Better for me to find it than the others."

"There are many roads. If you go way south or far, far north. Not here. That is why we chose to live here."

"How far south?"

"Before your river and through the mountains. It's a treacherous footpath."

"North?"

"Very far. You'll never get there now, but—"

"But what?"

"Why do you want to go to the West? The Forest protects you."

"From what?"

"From them—the other side."

"Have you seen...them?"

"Yes, I have seen them. The Western Empire. Their damn One God. The Empire is invincible. Only the Forest could stop it. That was why my ancestors hid here, to be free."

"You came from there?"

"We..." he hesitated. "What do you want here, Da-Ren?"

"Can you lead us?"

"The Dasal live by an oath, and that is to never go back to the West. I would come with you—only dead. Now that your Tribe made it in here, we cannot go east or south either."

"I can force you."

"I told you before, if you step outside of the Forest to the West, the Empire will raze you. I have seen both of you in battle."

"You will come with me."

"No. Leave now. Before spring, the paths are impossible to cross. I wouldn't even try."

"I'll leave, but I'll take Zeria with me."

"Are you mad? It's only three of you. I had told you never to come back. I make one sign and your men are dead. This is my last word."

"I have to see her."

"The only reason you are still alive is because you freed me that night from the cage."

I never freed him.

"I never freed you. I saved your daughter but not you."

"A hooded man unlocked the cage. He spoke your name. And his voice was young—"

Made sense. That was how he would do it. Not that it mattered anymore.

"Like mine. And he wore the same clothes."

"Who was he?"

I swallowed my anger in two breaths and managed to lie. "Someone I sent. Now I must see Zeria."

"I won't bring her. Know that Zeria is already—"

I was ready to smack his head against the cut stump he was sitting on and take him with me, tied up if necessary. Instead I pounced on him and knocked him down with a punch. I grabbed his knife and held it close to his throat.

"I am losing my head, Veker. I can't help you if you don't do what I say. Call your men. Have them bring Zeria here."

Veker was on the ground, and I was on top of him. His eyes were fixed on mine as he shouted. Immediately two men came in, holding my blades. I was not scared of them. They looked at each other and to Veker, uncertain of what to do.

Veker shouted something to them, I only grasped Zeria's name and the men walked out.

I gave him back his knife and he stared at me, wide-eyed. I was at his mercy.

"The rest of my men are close by," I said. "Kill me and you all die. I am the only one who can save your people."

He ran out of the hut, leaving me there unarmed. A few breaths later he came back in with Zeria. The corners of my mouth painted the faintest smile. A stream of frozen wind entered the hut with her. I desperately searched for a warm smile.

"Da-Ren, come with me, I beg you," she said.

She whispered something to Veker, and when he seemed to disagree she raised one hand, silent, to him. Her open palm almost ordered Veker to listen.

Before I turned to leave with her, I said to Veker, "I don't mean harm. I am trying to protect you."

I didn't give a damn about Veker or the Dasal. Save one.

"You come back with her before dusk or your men die," said Veker.

I grabbed Zeria by the hand and we stepped outside into the gray, bleak wood. She was pulling me away.

"Not here, it is not safe," she said.

There were many Dasal men around us, watching, and approaching. One of them, young and fair looking, was trying to reach me, while two more were pushing him back.

How I wish you'd let him free. Bring him to me. I know who you are. Come, claim her.

Zeria was pulling me away from them, but I kept looking at the danger. Leke had left Temin with the horses and was coming my way to help.

"Hide your eyes. My men must not see the blue," I whispered to Zeria.

I ran to stop Leke before he came closer.

"Leke, I have to speak to their witch. She knows the secret paths," I said.

"What of us?" he asked.

"You wait here. Don't do anything stupid. I'll be back soon. Promise me."

He nodded without a word.

A few breaths later I had disappeared away from all eyes with Zeria. She took an uphill path and I followed. Mud and dead leaves, silence and a cold hand. We kept walking fast without words, trying to find a moment of peace away from the rest. When we reached a slope that cut our way abruptly, she stopped. We were about a hundred feet high. In the void stood one tree alone, clawing with its dark branches on the rocky cliff. Its gnarled body was the only thing that broke the fog below our feet.

You don't belong here, tree.

"*You don't belong here, boy,*" it whooshed back.

Zeria cut my thoughts, only to say the same thing. "It's late, Da-Ren."

Late? Dusk was falling fast. I hoped that's what she meant.

Four whole moons had filled from the time I saw her last. The day I promised that I would be back for her in one moon.

I tried to come back for you.

She wasn't looking at me, and when she was it was even colder.

Where is your smile, girl?

"I tried to—" I tried to explain.

"Saim said that you would not come back for a while. Much longer than four moons," she said.

She kept walking carefully close to the dropping cliff, more to avoid my eyes and words rather than to get anywhere. I followed, I tried to say my Stories, about Gunna, Malan, the Blades. Not about the naked Ouna-Mas.

The farther away from the huts we got, the more she talked of trivial things. "We gathered enough supplies last summer. This winter is dark and heavy in snow, but we are well-protected from the winds here."

I didn't care about any of that. I wanted to steal a night with her. A real night, like the one I'd had with Razoreyes.

We were descending through the winter woods and after a while we miraculously reached the pond, where the arrow had hit me. Around my feet, the leaves had frozen red, gold and some even green, like the colorful tongues of monsters that didn't manage to finish their words. Everything was still, sleeping, to rise again much later.

"You chose a bad moon," she told me.

"It chose me. I could not come sooner," I answered.

"Why did you come here again, Da-Ren? Our story died with the autumn flowers, moons ago. There is no hellebore or cyclamen anymore. Our light no longer shines."

I took her hand.

"Since you left, the black hellebores… The snow killed them now, but when they blossomed, they made me think of you," she said. "Dark roses, so dark, so different and beautiful. Sad."

"What are you saying? I left to find the monsters. Only when I defeat them will you be safe here with me," I told her.

"You should have stayed with me the first time. Now it's too late. We are leaving for north, come spring. Before you hunt again."

"You must wait for me."

"I had to defy the men to save your life once more. My people were cursing and asking Veker for your death when they first spotted you alone from the Pack this morning. Are you mad to come here only with two men?"

I am mad.

"They know what you bring, Da-Ren. This is the last time I will ever see you. I promised them; you'll leave and they'll spare your life."

"No, I will come back. In seven nights after the first moon of spring."

"We will not be here."

"Damn them! You will be. You'll meet me here." My eyes searched around for a mark. "There, by the fallen oak that touches the pond. The fallen oak will be here, and so will you."

"We'll be far away by then. If we stay here, we're prey. You, those monsters that hunted you, anyone can come and—"

I pulled her closer and kissed her lips. She did not resist, but she did not embrace me either. An icy cloak, the armor of love lost, covered her.

I am going to kiss your lips just once. A burning kiss as if you were my Ouna-Ma. I am going to kiss you a thousand times just once.

Her lips were a red of chafed flesh and frozen blood; her tongue was warm but lifeless. The winter kiss lasted only two breaths. I ran the fingers of one hand through her hair, and with the other, I instinctively grabbed my blade, as if I needed to protect us from whatever was coming. But nothing came, not even a smile, not even a second kiss.

"Go. Find peace and forget," she said. She put her hands on my shoulders as if she wanted to point me in the right direction. Away from her. "My father has forbidden me from seeing you ever again," she said.

"Veker doesn't matter. No one does. Seven nights after the first moon of spring. We will be together here, Zeria."

She took her gaze away from me. We walked back to the huts in silence.

"One moon, Zeria. I won't leave until you say yes."

"Then...yes. I beg you for the last time. I can't save you from the dead again, Da-Ren. Go, now."

She turned her back and reached the huts alone. I followed her, until I lost her in a group of Dasal who protectively gathered around her.

I motioned to both of my men that we were leaving.

"There is a pass. South, through the mountains, but no one can cross it until the third moon of spring. We have to tell Khun-Malan. We gather our Pack and we ride to him," I told them. I wasn't lying. Just choosing my truths.

We left the wood behind and led the horses to the vast frozen meadows under the open sky. We could move much faster there, and five days later we reentered the Forest in the south and caught up with Malan earlier than I expected. It wasn't difficult to track an expedition of a thousand warriors who were afraid of Forest demons.

Malan called me immediately to his tent. This one was a campaign tent and barely fit six men. We all nearly had to bow. He had abandoned the glorious abode of the Sirol camp and was in a hurry to get this campaign over with.

"What did you learn over there?" he asked.

"There is a passage in the south. That was what the Dasal told me. But ice and snow cover it in winter."

"We will continue until we find it. You will be in front."

"It's a very small pass. The horses can go through only one by one," I said. "No carts can follow." The lies were crawling of their own will, like roaches out of my mouth.

"If the supplies and the war machines can't get through, we cannot go to battle with the West," said the Reghen.

"It wouldn't be wise. I've heard words of a Western Empire. And they say it is very powerful," I said.

"How do you know all of this?"

"The Dasal told me."

"Did you torture them or ask them with your honeycomb voice?" Malan asked.

I didn't answer, so he continued.

"Can you tell me why you haven't brought even one captive to show us the way? Are you stupid?"

It was the first time he called me that since the Sieve. I swallowed my rage and my words. Whenever I was forced to tell so many lies, I truly sounded like a fool.

"Those Dasal always seem to get away from you, Da-Ren. But winter is almost over, and then we'll round them up all. I will make a forest of stakes at the Blackvein and stick their heads there. I'll boil their light eyes and throw them to the dogs."

I didn't say a word.

We continued forward and southward into the Forest. I tried to stay away from Malan so he could forget me, forget them. He kept calling to me and asking me questions. Most of the others couldn't tell him anything about the Forest. Not even the Ouna-Mas.

Not only were the Ouna-Mas not helping us by clearing the paths with some magic spell, but they were also slowing us down with their rituals, which raised the men's fears. If there was a willow tree in front of us, they forbade anyone from touching it. Willows were considered the protector spirits of the Blackvein, revered for keeping the Cross Worshippers of the South away.

"It is the ancient willow pact, made by Ouna-Ma, the Blind, the First. We don't touch them, and they protect us," a Reghen said.

How did the Blind know of willows? Again, I chose not to speak. I so much wanted to be Reghen for one day only, just to find out if they truly believed all that came out of their mouth. *So many lies, for so long, so many times, Reghen. They multiply like the roaches of the Undead.*

If it was oak or birch, we were free to cut it to bits. If it was a walnut tree, then the Witches would stop anyone from even passing by it.

"Sah-Ouna asked for green walnut leaves," a Rod said to me one afternoon. "But she cannot touch them herself. Bring them to me so that I can take them to her."

"I can't either, unless I wait underneath the tree for three moons." Some of the young Rods had spent every day of their lives in Sirol, guarding Malan's tent. They didn't know anything about anything else. "Walnut trees don't have any leaves in winter. Are you sure that Sah-Ouna asked you this?"

"Yes."

"I will speak to her."

"No, you don't need to."

Walnut leaves were necessary ingredients for many spells, and many Ouna-Mas wanted them. This was not the easiest of routes in the Forest, with the false stories of the Ouna-Mas being our only guides. It wasn't enough that our men were attached to the magic and stupidity, but inside the Forest, their horrors came to life. If we came across a hazelnut tree, we stopped for a long while because an animal had to be sacrificed. We didn't have many goats with us, so it was whatever we could find.

We dismounted and walked with our horses for seven long days and covered a distance that, alone, I could have traveled in one night. Eventually, we were south enough where the snow patches melted and some brave trees even spurted their first green. We were warmed by false hopes. Each small glade and each large clearing was succeeded by stone-covered hills and crags, and then the wood rose again, denser than before. The Forest would end many times only to thrust its next tentacle.

Three days later we thought that we had come to the end of our journey, but it was only the end of our patience. It was early morning, and I was riding first. The meager dawn's light passed with difficulty through the thick fog and branches, but a crisp westerly wind was breathing against my face. By noon I had made it to the end of the Forest where the sun rays beamed plentiful and unhindered. The trees thinned, and ahead of us rose hills and mountains, black stone at the bottom and white snow on top, just as the Trackers had foretold. The course stopped, and the men camped at the foothills.

Malan ordered me and twelve other men to move forward with him. We climbed a hill almost two thousand feet tall. We descended and ascended an even taller one. And then a third, which was a treacherous mountain that tried to swallow us. We lost three men in the gorges and blind cliff drops. It took more days of climbing and nights of sheltering to reach a spot where we could have a clear view of what was ahead of us.

I finally reached the summit. Not the tallest one, but one where I could see the whole of the West. Malan was behind me. I rubbed my eyes, which had remained half-closed against the cold wind. There, across from us, spread the undefeated Empire of the West. Her warriors were nothing but giant firs, arrayed and evenly aligned, still and fearless, countless and endless. They wore their black and white armor, that of frozen wood and snow. The firs grew closely together, like an army of immovable giants, thirty feet tall, their icy spears even taller. Yet another forest. The forest ended somewhere to the north and south, where the clouds, fog, horizon, and snow all became one white nothing. Farther back rose a great mountain chain, like a black stone castle, thousands of feet tall, its invisible summits tearing through the gray clouds. Mountains that ended all paths to the west.

Mountains higher. Forests larger. The words of the Tracker and of Rouba.

I turned to look at Malan. He wouldn't look back at me. He had just been handed his first defeat by the West's army of firs and stone mountains. That which no horse could pass through, and that could swallow any rain of arrows we showered on them only to spit back hunger and despair. We were trapped.

With all the strength we had left, we turned back to the thousand men who were dying slow deaths in the land of the invisible Reekaal. We ran like hunted prey and the thorny branches marked us all with countless scratches, like tiny demon swords that remembered us from the Sieve.

They welcomed us back with cheers and bellows that died fast when they saw that Malan had no words for them. He shut himself in Sah-Ouna's tent.

"What do we do, Chief? Did you see them? The demons of the West?" asked the men of the First Pack as soon as I returned.

"Yes, this campaign is dead. We will soon head back to Sirol," I said.

I was wrong. We would continue our search. Malan refused to believe his fate.

"We continue farther south until we find the pass," he ordered.

We wandered toward the south for many a dark night and days that felt even darker, parallel to the foothills, without daring to climb the mountain again.

Malan was pushing everyone forward. He rode first, a blind man, a Khun in search of his foretold fate.

At the council of the fourth night after our return, the First of the Trackers spoke, "I sent men ahead and they are back. They didn't find any path through the mountains. As I told you, my Khun."

Those last words sounded stupid in my ears. Those men didn't know Malan as I did. The Tracker continued. "I say we get on boats and go up the river to the West, to find a way later, after the mountains."

Boats. Another folly.

The Tracker stood with arms crossed, proud and confident for knowing so much more than all the rest, without even guessing that those would be his final words.

"So our best Tracker here says there is no path through the mountains," said Druug, looking at me. "Where is your stupid path, Da-Ren?"

"Boats?" I replied. That single word was enough to save me.

Sah-Ouna whispered something to Malan, and before she even finished he continued with an angry, impatient voice: "Where the horses don't follow, the Tribe doesn't go. Never will I put the fate of our men upon the black water." He nodded to the Rods. Two of them stepped forward and caught the Tracker by the arms. "Carve this useless dog and send him to the Fishermen," Malan shouted for all to hear.

"You'll get your little boat there," the Rod said to the Tracker, laughing at his own half-brain joke.

"Someone has to stop this madness," murmured the Reghen, shaking his head.

Malan looked at the old man, ready to carve him too. But he couldn't punish a Reghen. There were things that even the One Leader couldn't do.

"We are cursed. One among us is unworthy, and Enaka does not favor this campaign," said Druug.

It was what I'd expect Sah-Ouna to say, but she wasn't looking at me. All that was missing was for someone to recall my ninestar mark. Then everything would suddenly be my fault. I took two steps back to hide. I didn't offer any wisdom, let alone the truth. I had figured already that one shouldn't say much in these councils. Their only use was for the weak and the old to shout their terror and despair. And to find a scapegoat to lose its head faster. Nobody ever decided anything in a council. A Khun knew better than that.

"Da-Ren, tomorrow you ride forward with the Rods and me," Malan ordered. "You lead until we find the path, and if we don't…"

I kept riding first for three more days, waiting for each one to be my last. In my sleep, I saw Zeria, her back turned to me, and heard Rouba's voice behind my ear. "The Forest Witch. This is her wood. Fear not, Da-Ren, you are safe here." Once more the old Guide was right.

On the fourth dawn, as I trotted next to Malan and Sah-Ouna, the First Witch raised her hand and stopped. She dismounted and approached a tree. I had seen this tree once before. Bunches of crystalline red berries like drops of clotted blood against the white forest.

You are the tree of my death. You had charred branches, and now they are frozen white. I have seen you in the caves of the dead; you were the one draining my blood. I remember you, tree.

At the sight of the red crystal tree, Sah-Ouna fell to one knee and covered her eyes with the back of her hand.

"Back!" she screamed.

My horse, which had not complained for two tormenting moons, rose on its two hind legs.

Rarely did the Witch speak, and never before had she screamed in front of us, not even at the pyre of Khun-Taa, the one who had named her First. The thousand-warrior horde quickly gathered everything, and we broke camp, running before anyone had a chance to wonder what had happened.

We turned eastward, stopped only for a brief sleep, and returned to Sirol without even paying much respect to the rituals required for each tree. Everyone marched back in silence for days. When one sets out for the unknown on a journey of hope, the road seems endless. When one returns home after defeat, the road blessedly shortens and ends quickly. It still took more than half a moon until we finally made it to Sirol. The Blades welcomed the frozen shithole that was our camp like a warm nest of rest and plenty. All things I loved had died in that winter but the cold was finally dying as well.

Eighty thousand, hungry and weak, waited for us to tell them what we had seen and when we would move out of Sirol for the West. None of my men said a word because no one knew what to say.

"What did you find? Do we move out?" asked the other Packs of the Blades.

"We found only curses and blood," I answered. Only that.

Malan held another brief council from which Sah-Ouna was absent. Only a Reghen and three more of us, Tracker, Archer, and Blade, were there. And quite a few Rods, as there were already rumors of traitors wanting to assassinate the young Khun.

"We shall await the Truths of Enaka to guide us at the Great Feast of Spring," said Malan. It was the briefest council we had ever had.

Someone spoke out. It was the elder Reghen, from the previous council, the wise one with the calm voice, still trying to teach and guide the young Khun. This time he decided to point his finger to the Khun.

"It won't be the best of Feasts, if—"

Before the Reghen finished his words, Malan took out his small blade and plunged it into the old man's chest with a sudden move.

"You, a wise Reghen, most of all, should have more faith," Malan said as he twisted the knife deeper. A big red circle, another one, expanded on his gray robe. I had never seen a Reghen fall. I bent over him. I touched his neck and then his shoulder.

"He's gone," I said to Malan, but he wasn't listening. He was punching the air around him with both fists like a madman.

"Useless traitors, all of them!" he yelled.

The Rods ordered us to get out of the tent, and we left Malan alone with his skulls.

"That was a rowan tree," one of the Rods said to me in confidence as I was walking out.

"What?"

"The oracle. Rowan, the bloodtree."

I had never seen nor heard of rowan trees before in Sirol. But soon afterward, their fame spread. Without a doubt, we had to turn back. Everyone understood that, especially those who had no idea what a rowan bloodtree was. They agreed because Sah-Ouna screamed and that was enough. Of the endless fir forest and the mountain chains that pierced the sky, not a word was spoken. That was the end of Malan's first campaign, where the only blood we saw was the prophecy of the red berries of the rowan.

We were days away from the Great Feast of Spring, the first of Khun-Malan's reign. It would be a miserable and inglorious Feast. Instead of prophecies of tomorrow, Sah-Ouna had only Legends of yesterday. The wolves, our ancestors and brothers, had summoned her in the Forest's night and had given her the omen. They told her to turn back if she ever reached the rowan trees that dripped blood in the middle of winter.

There had been no word of the rowan tree since ancient times back when the men of the Tribe dwelled in the tall mountains of the East, before they had taken to the steppe. Not even the very old Reghen could remember tales about them. Wherever the rowan took root was a mark of the end of the world—the Tribe should go no farther. A new old Story sprang up for the occasion, a Legend of the Witch that she had been cooking up for some time. On the last night of the Great Feast, Sah-Ouna told us of the rowan.

Know this, men.

A long time ago, in the age of the First Leader, in the dead of winter, the proud eagles gathered—unheard of—in flocks for the first time and flew south, toward the Sun's warmth.

Greedy and foolish were the first people of the Tribe, without the words of the Ouna-Mas to guide them. In their madness, they shot the eagles with their arrows and killed them. As the beloved birds of prey of the Goddess began to fall from high in the Sky, the blood flowed like rivers from inside of them. The red drops watered the soil and gave birth to the rowan, the bloodtrees. Cursed, they stand and bear fruit in the death of autumn to remind us of the wrongdoing of our Tribe. And of the rage of Enaka that awaits us if we take the forbidden path.

A path that is guarded by the rowan is one that we cannot ride upon.

I was watching all this next to the other Chiefs of the Blades. Not everyone was so impressed with this Story and I heard words of doubt repeating back at our camp.

"That's a horseshit Legend if I ever heard one."

"I overheard the Reghen talk. They said there's no such tale."

"Worse, I heard that it is a Legend of the Southerner othertribers."

The meat and the milk-spirit were not abundant at the Feast and the men resorted to the worst of habits. Pondering. Questioning. Thinking.

"You know, Khun-Malan killed a Reghen. Khun-Taa ruled for thirty winters and he never—"

The Story of the rowan was the only armor Sah-Ouna could offer against Malan's reckless decision to send us into the Forest in the dead of winter. Many winters later, I would find out that this was truly a Legend of the ancient southern tribes who worshiped the thirteen gods.

Sirol was boiling, angry and hungry once again.

"I heard that Druug called for a secret meeting. He summoned some of the Blades' Chiefs," said Leke.

"Any Reghen or Ouna-Mas?" I asked.

"Don't know, I can find out."

"Do."

Leke came back the next day, and it was as I expected.

"No, none of them."

They were all under Sah-Ouna's claws and spells.

"Then Druug and those Chiefs are doomed. Stay away from them," I said to Leke.

As I had guessed, the Ouna-Mas and the Reghen united again and on the same night they came to the camp with more Truths.

"It has been decided that we cannot go to the West now. We'll need to get stronger first, get more weapons and gold."

It was one of the rare times that I had heard the word "gold," and it sounded important to be next to weapons. Spring and summer were coming, but they would not bring a great campaign, only limited raids to the South and to the East.

Not everyone blamed Malan. Most of the men slept easy on the night of the Great Feast when Sah-Ouna warned them of the bloodtrees. The cold began to weaken further in the next couple of days, and even more men praised Sah-Ouna for that. The fools were trampling on my mind.

"We must do something," Leke said. "There will be a war here."

A war where I would be either a servile dog on Malan's side or a dead dog because everyone thought I was.

Yes, I must do something, Leke. It is about time. I have promised her. Seven nights after the full moon. I either leave tomorrow, or I betray her once again.

Spring was coming, with the carefree innocence of a child ignorant of the evils committed by its father, the black winter. There was still another path, a way out, to leave all this behind.

I was no longer in the Sieve. I was no longer with the Uncarved. Ouna-Mas had ridden me, I had taken others on all fours, some had fed me poison and others honey, some desired me and others were sent by the Khun. I had slaughtered armed and unarmed men, brave ones and cowards, othertribers and brothers. I had led men, blind and wise, faithful and jackals, to victory and to death. I had endured and cast off my armor. Before I entered my nineteenth spring, I had done it all.

I had seen so much death that I was dying to drink a little life.

My patience and curiosity about everything to do with my Tribe, which I had carried since childhood, had died.

My eyes had lost their light.

The stupidity and the false magic smothered me.

My mind traveled elsewhere.

I had to make a decision that night or suffer forever.

I asked Sani, "Did you say you've been here for nine winters?"

"Yes."

"And?"

"And what?"

He didn't understand what I was asking.

"What are you waiting for? What do you want?"

"A good Story. Because I'll be up there for all the other winters. The countless," he said, showing me the stars.

Maybe he was right. But I couldn't live only to die.

Stars of my Goddess, you can wait, I'll find some other way to you. My skin craves to bathe in her blue waters once more.

Kar-Tioo defeated the night. I had heard Sah-Ouna's Stories of sacrifices, blood, and demons for one final time. I'd had enough. If I did not start at that moment, I would betray Zeria for the second time. I told her to be there. Seven nights after the full moon.

"I am going to be away for a while," I said to Sani.

"We'll talk tomorrow," he answered. He thought I was going somewhere in Sirol. I mounted my horse before he had a chance to ask me anything more.

This time, the Rods didn't stop me. They were busy looking out for traitors around Malan's camp. I kissed the neck of my old horse, held its long mane gently, and it gathered its strength to carry me as fast as it could. I left it to graze in one of the new outposts Malan had established on the fresh spring meadows just outside of the Forest. The few Archers there welcomed me and looked with awe as I entered the wood alone on foot. They had heard the Legend of Er-Ren at least once. I was soon lost in the trees, running toward Kar-Tioo for three days. No one had ever made it faster.

I arrived at dusk, exactly on the night that I had asked Zeria to be there. She had told me she would not come, but we men hear what we want to hear when the women we love are talking. Kar-Tioo was deserted; the few huts of the Dasal lay ruined and burned. There were no bodies anywhere. The monsters couldn't have found them. The water in the pond was crystal clear once more, and trees all around were turning green.

I waited for Zeria until dawn. I had made my decision. I would stay with her, far from Witches and Khuns. Even now, I want to believe that her eyes were watching me from somewhere, hidden behind the trees. Every freezing breath down my lungs made me more certain that she would come. She would slip away from Veker and run to me.

I had defied death and disgrace; I had left my heart at her pond. I had turned the world upside down to get to her. She would come. I had asked it of her. I had been fast, made it on time. I had taken off my only armor, the Chief's skins, and untied the black ribbon from my arm. I had denounced my Tribe and Story, Goddess and Witch, Legend and Father, to be with her. I had run for days to steal only a few breaths.

She would be here any moment.

Everything would end. And everything would begin again this spring.

I was now a man, a warrior, but I would never become Khun of the Tribe. I would thrust my blade into the ground. Any moment now she would appear in front of me. I would live there forever with her.

She is still not here. Maybe they ventured far away. I have to wait for her.

I waited all the next day, dawn, noon, and evening until night came again. And then I waited for her, standing on two feet for a second night, like a cursed child of the Sieve.

She is trying to escape from her father. I can't sleep, what if she doesn't see me and turns and leaves? I have to stay awake.

That was all I could do: stand proud and tall and hope.

I count to forty. My last farewell to my brothers, my Pack. I left them forever. I open my eyes and she'll be standing in front of me.

I count to forty. Her smile will be here.

I count to forty. My farewell...

That night passed without meat, just seeds and water, but that was the least of my torment. A tremor across my whole body. That was all. A tremor of nights without sleep, days without food, a tremor of love and betrayal.

I count. I can't...

The sun had cleared the horizon for the second time and was rising high, a dancing, bright spring sun, when I started my way back to Sirol.

I hate the winter and its armors. Desperate love drowns in its embrace. Impossible love does not stand a chance in the snow. It cannot bloom in the ice, it cannot take its first steps in the frozen soil, it cannot leap numb, and it cannot dive where the water cannot flow. It will shrivel. It will sleep cold, with violet lips shut, and it will already be too late.

Before it awakens again, the careless feet of spring will trample upon it and crush it triumphantly.

XLII.
Brown

Island of the Holy Monastery, Thirty-fifth winter.
According to the Monk Eusebius.

Da-Ren never changed his story. He had come here to the Castlemonastery to save the lives of his wife and daughter. The women in Da-Ren's story were exactly what unsettled me the most. It was the part that stirred sinful thoughts within me and the one I understood the least of all.

During the first year, I insisted that we avoid the lustful parts of Dar-Ren's stories, with the Ouna-Mas and his carnal encounters with Zeria. The salacious transcriptions of these acts would not be looked upon with mercy by the wise monks who would eventually read them. The second year, I changed my mind. I didn't want to geld his true story. The tallow candle of my faith had started to die out by then. The third year, I made an honest effort to understand. But I wasn't faring well.

It was a night that we had run out of firewood, and the hearth's warmth was dying. We started talking again, faster, trying to find an answer to those questions.

"How many women have you been with, Eusebius?"

"None."

"It is difficult to explain to you certain things. How many times have you fallen in love?"

What could I say to him?

"Never. We have been trained to defy these demons that torment the mind."

Da-Ren filled both of our carved cedar cups with wine even though he knew I wasn't going to drink that night.

"I thought that your god was the god of love."

"That is a different kind of love, Da-Ren. It is the love of your neighbor, of someone weaker than you."

He shook his head, wrinkled his chin, and bit his lip disdainfully.

"You and your neighbor hunt the same meat, Eusebius. If he eats, then you won't."

"But you gave meat to your men from Malan's spit."

"That was different."

"How is that different?"

Da-Ren got up and filled two bowls with chickpea soup. I dipped my spoon into the pulp that was long cold. A cockroach slipped out the door to seek heat elsewhere and left us to our licentious quest.

"I shared it with them because I respected them. They were strong. That was different."

"And if they were weak, what would you have given them?"

"Hmmm? A kick in the ass?"

This story would not live long in the libraries of our saintly fathers. The fire in front of me had no life left in it either so I abandoned my efforts to make more progress that night. I was still to understand his love for Zeria, and I kept coming back to it until the very end. We reached an impasse for the third straight year at precisely the same spot before I found the papyrus of the so-called ancient god Eros. "I never understood why you betrayed your Tribe for Zeria. What was special about Zeria? Why didn't you do it for any other woman in Sirol?"

"Are you starting with the *whys* again, Eusebius? I have the luxury of time now to recount everything that happened and rethink carefully every word so that you can write it again, better. But back then I was young, not even twenty. I did whatever my head and my legs were burning to do. Do you think I thought of or counted the *whys*? The moment decided on its own."

"The moment decided. But the moment never tells me why it decided that and not the other."

This conversation had happened about a dozen times, and he only gave me a suitable answer in his last year on the island.

"The same question again. Tell me. What colors do you see three winters now when you write this story? The Tribe, Sirol, the Sieve? Tell me."

"I see mud and shit."

"Yes, good. Brown. Of dirt, leather, and horses. Gray and brown mud. What else?"

"Red."

"Yes…"

"White. The snow and foam coming out of the mouth. I don't know why I see white foam. You never mentioned it."

"White, the snow. What else, Eusebius? Close your eyes. Don't look around this cell here; look at the story."

Da-Ren started to become more interested and stood up as if he, too, had made an important discovery.

"Nothing. Black, gray…"

"That's it. Brown, red, gray, black, and white. That's how it was, Eusebius. You know, there was no other color allowed in my Tribe. No one wove or colored any of his clothing green, blue, or yellow. Even the sky was rarely blue. It was the gray of cloud in winter, the dust of the horse hooves in the summer. Our women wore no jewelry. Never. Malan later changed all of that. The only colors when I was young were brown, red, gray, black, white."

"But in the Forest…"

"Yes, tell me, Eusebius, you understand what I am saying."

"Green. So much green, each a different shade. Golden rays of the sun, the designs that were embroidered on Zeria's dress. Green, gold, and—"

"And blue. Do you see it? I can't explain to you why I fell in love the moment I saw her. I didn't even know what love was then. But, yes, you see now, it was impossible for me not to fall in love with her. She was the other half of the whole world—the missing colors."

XLIII.
Legs

Nineteenth spring. Chief of the First.

The night my mother bore and condemned me.

The moment when Sah-Ouna cursed me with the mark of the ninestar.

That cloudy morning when Elbia flew away.

Each day that Enaka protected Khun-Malan.

That most humiliating night when I waited in vain for Zeria.

How? Why?

Why was I still standing?

When love bleeds from the sword of betrayal.

When glory scatters away like ashes in the demon wind.

When death becomes a dark cloak of flies covering meat.

Why do the legs hold?

Don't they remember all this? Did the Sieve give them an iron heart, to mercilessly beat for Nothing, to be scorned?

Or do they remain strong exactly because of this? Because those legs have the memory of the entire Tribe within them?

They have walked the steppe of our ancestors. They have fought all the demons and were victorious over and over again. They have crossed the steppe, the mountain, the rivers, and the valleys, and they remember.

They remember that the one invincible demon is the one whom our ancestors left inside them. In their minds, their souls, their hearts. And their legs.

Spring was in full blossom when I walked out of the Forest. I reached the outpost where I had left my horse on foot.

This is where I saw him for the first time. He was the most beautiful male I had ever laid eyes upon. His mane so long, rippling and shiny, his eye looking so inviting and proud at the same time, almost female. All the warriors simply stood around and admired him, pointing and gaping; dreaming. He was galloping unsaddled on the young grass, the earth trembling to a distance under its hooves. I wanted that stallion the moment I saw him. I had never had a stallion before; the Truths proclaimed that a man had to reach his twenty springs to claim one. As if the strength of any man could dominate that white and gray-speckled beast of Enaka.

The few Archers who were there turned their gazes away from the stallion when they saw me approaching. I was starving and exhausted, my skins dirty and covered with mud and leaves.

"Bless Enaka. We were looking for you all over," said the oldest of the pack. Hollow cheeks, a bit of drool at the left end of his lips.

"You can use some milk, hey? Not much meat here, but I'll boil some gruel," added the second. He had the rheumy eyes of a madman and was holding a knife. Its blade was slick with blood.

Archers tending after me; this was not to be expected.

"We thought, you, son of Er-Ren and all, would come out of the Forest with a deer on your back. Uh, no luck." The first Archer was now mocking me, giggling like a little girl with his comrades.

"I need to get my horse and get back to Sirol," I said.

I wasn't even certain if I would head back to Sirol, or steal a horse and ride all the way to the North away from all I knew. I just needed to get away from men and talk.

"His horse?" said the one with the knife looking at his companions. He scratched the back of his head and wore a stupid smile.

"Ah, you better wait for the Reghen, Chief."

"Who?"

"They just made it here this morning from Sirol. A Reghen, a whole swarm of Rods and a couple of your men."

"*My* men?" What was a Reghen doing here, looking for me? Nobody knew I had left for the Forest.

"Yeah, they won't be long now. They said that they'll be back before noon. They would go hunting or searching for you, or hunting you, that I didn't get." A grin spread across his face. "I don't ask much. But they said that if we saw you to make sure you stay here."

"And if—"

"I hope you don't make trouble, Chief. I must keep you here; those Rods were not joking. Have you seen them? Those lucky oafs have meat every night, that I can tell," the Archer said.

He kept talking words that didn't make sense to me. He was an older man; a couple more springs and he would be sent to the Guides. He had shaved his beard very short to look younger and his thinning frame helped in that. A man loses his broad shoulders very fast in a starving outpost.

In the distance, I spotted a large group of Rods coming out of the wood from a southern direction. Their dark bearskins were unmistakable. A Reghen. Leke and Temin to the right of them. All galloping faster as they were coming closer, as if they had recognized me too. I just wished I could steal that brave stallion in front of me and get away. I needed to know at least.

"That stallion. What is that beast?" I turned and asked the Archer.

"Oh, you noticed the Northern Boy here? I didn't think that Blades cared so much for such a horse. Haven't seen a stallion like that in all my life."

"Have you put a saddle on it?"

"Yes, but nobody has ridden it for long. We were keeping it for Druug, our Leader. Now…I don't know."

"You don't know what?"

The Reghen was already next to me and the Rods dismounted and encircled me. They stood at a few paces away, neither friendly nor threatening. Dull and solemn looking as Rods always were.

"The Chief is asking about Druug, wise Reghen," the Archer said. "Better you tell him."

The Reghen's squinting eyes showed that he hadn't come after me for good. "Don't you know about Druug, Da-Ren? About those other Chiefs?"

"Know what?" I cut my eyes toward Leke; he looked worried. "I was in the Forest, searching for the Dasal," I said. "What about Druug? Something happened?"

"Many things. In time. Did you find the Dasal?"

"Are you questioning me, Reghen?"

He nodded a slow, confident, smiling *yes*. "Or we can go back to Sirol and let the Khun question you. He is less patient than I am. Did you find the Dasal?" the Reghen insisted on his question.

"Yes…no. I found traces, their huts, but they have headed south. Now that spring is here. I found a couple left behind but couldn't speak their tongue. They tried to show me; I made sense of their hand signs. Their kin have gone south to reach the West. Through the southern pass."

I was making up lies I hadn't even thought of when I started my words.

"And why are you back, Da-Ren?"

The Reghen continued his relentless questioning. Leke's silence was not helping me decipher his intentions.

What do you know, Reghen?

"Who asks?" I said.

"Sah-Ouna herself."

What do you know, Old Witch?

"Are you deaf, Reghen? I was tracking down the Dasal. I can't hunt them alone; I came to get more men and let Malan know."

"But why did you leave Sirol in the first place? Who gave you such orders?"

"I had—"

I had run out of lies. The Reghen's silent stare was trying to enter my mind like a dark worm, seeking the truth.

Leke walked his horse forward and talked.

"Darhul's nine heads, what are we doing here? Don't you see that the Chief almost died, trying to save your skins? Didn't I tell you that much in Sirol? Chief Da-Ren was in shame after we didn't find the pass last time."

I shut my gaping mouth as Leke continued.

"The Chief made an oath to walk in the Forest alone and without food until he found the south pass, to lead our Khun back there. This man is no traitor."

At least that part was true. I was no traitor, only a fool.

Leke even managed to look outraged. He threw me his waterskin and shouted to the Archer. "Fetch the Chief some gruel. Be quick now."

The water woke my face and my mind up and I found my words again. "So, Reghen, what else do you want to know?"

"Don't you know anything about Druug? Don't you know why we flayed that dog in the middle of Sirol?"

"Along with those three other Chiefs of the Blades?" the Rod closer to me added, talking for the first time.

It had all started to make sense now. I could very well guess why Druug was lying flayed in the middle of Sirol. I could still remember the day when Malan—a boy half his age, the One who had beaten out Druug's own son Redin—had slapped him in front of the council. The only thing that didn't make sense was how did Leke know what to say and why did he? What had I done to deserve such luck?

"No, Reghen. Tell me."

"Forgive me, Chief. Your men were right." The Reghen's voice lost all its arrogance and his tone changed to wise and calm. "You did a brave thing going alone in the Forest. And when you came out of it alone, I knew you were no traitor. Just had to be sure." He continued explaining what had happened, adding the details about flayed bodies, rabid maulers, decapitated Chiefs and crows that nibbled off the eyes of the traitors. "Malan asked us to question all the Chiefs of the Blades. There could be more traitors. When we heard that you were gone…"

"Let's head back for Sirol. We need you there, Chief," Leke added, eager to end all this.

"Yes, we are all needed back," the Reghen added.

It was not meant to be, and I wouldn't escape to the North alone. If I tried now, Malan would send a thousand men to hunt me.

"My horse," I turned and shouted to the Archer who had made fun of Er-Ren's Story. "I left it here for you to look after."

I had to repeat the order a couple of times until he replied.

"There," he said, and he pointed me to the hooked pieces of horsemeat drying flayed and bloody. A ribcage, a haunch.

"You stupid dog."

I didn't have much strength to fight or even shout at him.

"That old mare was useless, Chief. It had a quick death, and we can use the meat."

"So, you kill my horse, for…meat and you offer me some…gruel? It was the only horse I had."

It was a good horse and you, Archer, are going to find the same death someday. I owe you that much.

"All Chiefs get four horses. Even Blades. That can't be your only horse," he said.

"Not anymore. No one in the Blades has four horses."

"Give this man another horse," the Reghen said. "We need to get back fast."

A persistent and rhythmic thumping sound had followed all this exchange of words. It hadn't stopped since the Reghen started talking. I could hear his hooves beating. The most magnificent horse I'd ever seen. I turned to him, and then to the Archer.

"You said that you were keeping that stallion for Druug," I said with a wide grin. He turned pale then red with fury in the same breath. "Does he have a name?" I asked.

"Arrow..." he said, mumbling half a word.

"Arrow what? Speak up!" I shouted.

"Arrowind." His face turned sour.

I waited for three long breaths, laughing silently at his face, and scratching my left temple, just to prolong his torture; my enjoyment.

"Fuck Arrowind. His name is O'Ren," I said. I was already walking toward the animal.

"That's a stallion, you fool. It was bred for the Leader of ten thousand Archers. You have to be twenty springs old to ride it." The Archer had turned crimson and purple by now but couldn't do much more than that.

"Oh, yes, I am twenty. Twenty springs and three days old. You know how I know?" I pulled my hair to the side and showed him the ninestar mark. "Ask Sah-Ouna; she'll tell you about me. That's why I can roam the Forest alone, unharmed."

No one dared say much when I talked of the ninestar mark and mentioned Sah-Ouna as if it were a laughing matter. Still, there were a couple of meaningless complaints.

"I thought you were only eighteen. Same as Khun-Malan," the Reghen said.

"Truth is I am nineteen. But today I feel like twenty. This is decided;

those men owe me a horse, and the Truths also say I get to choose one of theirs."

"You have to have legs of iron to ride this one," the Archer said.

No, you don't.

I had had enough of the Archer and didn't even reply to him. I was next to the stallion that had stopped his stride and was resting, as if he knew that it was time. I stroked his neck softly and he lowered his head. The gray speckles painted a silvery color on his back, his rump and hind legs were a darker gray. His tail and mane were long and gold-white. *Legs of iron.* No man's legs were strong enough to rule this beast. He either wanted me riding him, or he didn't.

Let's get out of here, boy. Are you with me, O'Ren? Are your legs strong enough to keep me going? When love bleeds from the sword of betrayal? When glory scatters away like ashes in the demon wind? Are you with me to the end?

I was riding first, challenging the stocky Rods and the frail Reghen to keep up. To make it back to Sirol, to listen once again to the Legends of the Ouna-Mas, to taste their flesh, to lead my loyal men. They had been the one surprise against all that was betrayed.

"Slow down, Chief. What a horse this is! Don't let Khun-Malan see you riding it." Leke was trying to keep up with me as a blood-red sun was descending on our backs behind the Forest.

"How did you know, Leke?"

He didn't say anything at first, and I insisted.

"How did you know I had left for the Forest?"

"Know? I still don't know. It was a guess. I was with you when we went up to the Dasal, all alone, when you left with that Dasal witch. I saw your eyes when you walked away with her and when you came back. All alone, again and again? That is madness, Chief," he said shaking his head left and right slowly, his horse trotting next to mine.

"So, how did you guess? You read eyes, is that your claim?"

"*Madness*, Chief. Only one thing can drive a young man to madness. And don't ask me how I know."

"Have you? A woman in Sirol?" I asked.

"Some other night, Chief. Some other day. This one has brought enough."

Forward, O'Ren. Forward, my brave one. Sirol awaits us.

It had been eight agonizing nights since I had left for Kar-Tioo and I was back at the camp. Only the eagles, the hawks, and the other birds could have done it faster.

Sani was surprised to see me, and he couldn't hide it. The men were training while he was giving orders.

"We thought you were lost forever. Don't ever leave alone again, Chief," he said.

"I thought you liked being Chief," I said.

Many men stood in front of me, but only nine heads, like those of Darhul, smiled as soon as they saw me. "I had to find the road to the West. I had to go into the oaks." Nine heads lapped up my lies. "Don't worry. The Forest doesn't scare me."

"The Reghen asked if you had died, Chief. Some even called you a traitor. They wanted to bring someone in your place. You haven't seen the Chiefs of the other Packs. The maulers are better than most of them," said Sani.

"How come they didn't choose you?" I asked.

"They don't seem to trust us," he laughed.

But Malan trusted me, or wanted me close to him, and that was proven a few days later when the Reghen brought new Truths.

"You, the First, and four more Packs of Blades will stay to guard Sirol. Summer and autumn. The rest of the Blades leave for raids immediately with the Archers. To the South and to the East."

Not to the West.

Not all of the men were on my side, and they showed it at once—some more vexed than the others.

"The other Packs will get loot and women, and we will starve here all summer."

"If you hadn't left for the Forest, they would have sent us too," said a second.

Maybe they were right. But I didn't care. Betrayal. Loyalty. I knew that now and even the Khun did so. These were the only words worth something. Neither glory nor love. Betrayal and loyalty. Death and life. My patience had ended, and I would take no more whining.

"How many of you want to go on the raids with the other Packs?" I asked uttering every word slow and loud.

No one dared raise his hand.

"Weren't you just now mumbling? I won't punish you. Speak up."

Sani understood and raised his hand. More hands followed.

"And how many of you would rather stay behind with me?"

Half of the hands went down. Sani's and Leke's stayed up. They would stay with me.

I wasn't about to beg or drag anyone like a corpse on my back. We still didn't have a Leader of all the Blades, so I rode alone to find the Chiefs of each Pack who would be leaving for the raids. Every Pack had to have forty men. But all were short a few men. Some two. Others three.

"I have a few strong men. I'll let them loose. They want to go raiding. Who wants them?"

I went to all the tents until the light was gone for that day. I was giving away my men. Strong, brave, capable men, who didn't want to stay with me. The other Chiefs looked at me like a welcome fool and took whatever they could.

The strength of any leader in the Tribe was always and everywhere measured by the number of warriors under him.

The One Leader, the Khun, commanded over thirty thousand men. All of us.

The Leader of the Archers, more than ten thousand. Except for the rare day when he was lying flayed on a pole in the Wolfhowl, with the flies kissing his long-gone lips.

The Leader of the Blades? Whoever was finally chosen by Malan would rule almost seven hundred men.

A Pack Chief could lead up to forty men.

A thrice-carved warrior commanded his two legs and his horse, and nothing more.

And a lunatic like me, who was giving away the warriors who didn't believe in him anymore, had nineteen men. Those who chose to remain with me.

The more the men, the more important a leader was. Or so everyone believed. But not I. The men who follow without believing make the heaviest yet most useless armor. Men without heart, without soul, without legs or eyes. Blind unbelievers. Their apathy and disdain spread like the deadliest poisons and corrupt even the few who remain true.

The nineteen who remained close to me questioned, even doubted, but believed. Those who left were grateful. I never looked behind my back again.

When I made it to the Thirteenth Pack an old friend from the Uncarved approached me. It was Noki, the one who had kissed the Ouna-Ma when we were still kids.

"Can I come with you?" he asked.

"Don't you want to go on the raids, Noki? Are you scared?"

"All this riding in the heat of summer bores me. And I can't stand that Pigface Chief."

He had been unlucky enough to get the worst Chief. Noki had once been an Uncarved and the best of the Sieve. He wouldn't fall easily. I offered Pigface two men and asked for Noki. He refused. I gave him a third, Urak, the one I cared the least about, and Pigface agreed.

Back at the camp of the First, half of our tents stood empty and abandoned. Those who had left had stripped all the good hides from them. The few torn skins hung over the wooden skeletons and billowed like angry ghosts in the winds. I parted with my tent to sleep with the rest, offering my hides to mend their tents.

"Don't do that. They will not respect you," said Sani.

"The ones who stayed behind respect me already," I said.

There were fewer mouths to share the scarce meat, but I needed more blades.

"You have to find young ones for our Pack. Very few of us are left," Sani told me.

"Where?"

"Go to the young Blades. The training fields."

The Sieve had finished six moons ago, and the next one would begin in seven moons. We were way past the time of the first spring moon when I could take new blood.

"The other Chiefs will never allow me to break the rules and steal the best," I said.

Summer found me with a handful of men fighting the mosquitoes and the flies of Sirol. Those under my command started patrolling, as Malan had ordered. Supplies were running out, and men killed each other over a dead rat. Thousands of men of the Tribe, hungry and impatient, were left behind for the few of us to whip into order.

One sizzling summer afternoon, we were inspecting the large camps of the help. The stench of the Tanners and the smell from the Fishermen invaded my nostrils and blanked my mind. But they kept going about their work, untired by the heat and the misery of their fate. The Blacksmiths were farther away, covered in soot, carrying coal wood in the heat of the day and feeding the bloomeries to milk the iron of the land. They hammered their anvils to sing and shiver like young maiden slaves.

A crazy thought came over me the next morning, a little after the sun began to burn relentlessly. I was looking only for twenty to fill the First. Men of iron. Unbreakable.

"Sani, Leke, everyone. Mount your horses, and spread my word. To the Tanners, the Hunters, the Fishermen, the Craftsmen, the Blacksmiths, and the slaves."

"You want us to take a message to the slaves?" asked a man with a huge gash where his eye used to be. His name is by now long lost from my memory.

"Not the slaves. Forget I said that. But go to all the others of our Tribe. Tell them that whoever dares may come, and I will choose twenty new Blades for the First Pack tomorrow."

"It cannot be done. They have four carvings," Sani told me.

"Do you think I don't know that? Bring me only those who don't remember how many they have."

They brought me exactly twenty.

Blacksmiths most of them, a few Tanners, three Fishermen. They came on foot to earn their first war horse. They looked at me as if I were the son of the Goddess, the Sun himself, who had come to redeem them. No Hunters or Craftsmen had come.

"Those who have meat to eat didn't even look at me. The ones who came have been living on scraps and roots for many moons now," said Sani.

"Why are you here?" I asked a Blacksmith named Rikan.

Rikan and those like him would be the Pack that I would forge. I remember him still, as I remember few others. His mustache was two black bending iron blades. The short hairs of his beard were shavings from the furnace, black as coal dust. His arms and sweating shoulders were shiny metal slabs, smoothly welded together. Brutally forged with a uniform roughness were his nose and forehead. His eyes, two black holes filled with hot melting ore. They wrinkled half-closed against the hard summer sun rays. There was never much light in the Blacksmiths' caves, where they forged the metal. They had to get the color right—the gold, not the red or the white hot and ample light was their enemy.

His voice rose and fell heavy as a hammer. "Chief, I came because I want to see the West. And the South and the East."

His eyes wanted to see the world. His eyes commanded his heart. To abandon the darkness of the forge. To see.

Those whose hearts still traveled like children also came. If the heart travels, it will give wings to the legs.

"You? Kuran?" I said, recognizing the unlucky scorpion-struck Kuran from my Sieve.

"I want to change my fate."

Even the unlucky scum of the stars had come. To the One Chief they deserved, a ninestar.

Leke was trying desperately to count the men, old and new, with his fingers again and again.

"What is it?" I asked.

"You were wrong, Chief. We could have brought one more. You can rule forty men," he said.

"I am the fortieth Blade, the last and one of you," I answered.

He nodded silent. Embarrassed, honored?

Truth is I had counted them wrong. But a Chief needed to find his words fast, to rule over so many men. Even his false words. Men, warriors who face death, hate the truth as much as they hate a Chief who is wrong and still rules over them.

"Tomorrow, we begin training!" I shouted.

"I will pass out horses and blades," said Sani.

"You won't pass out anything."

He didn't understand.

At dawn, before the sun began scorching us with vengeance, I started making the changes in the training routine of the First Pack. I had meant to do that for some time after the battle at the Blackvein and after our winter march through the Forest. The Blades fell. They were the weak link of the Tribe.

We still didn't have a Leader for the eighteen Packs of the Blades. The post had been widowed, and Malan still didn't trust anyone. No one could forbid me anything. I had only one chance to become that Leader of all the Blades, and I meant to seize it before it was lost. Two men, new recruits, Blacksmiths, stood around the morning fire, drinking milk and showing off the chainmail armors they had brought. They were making those for the Rods now, but each had the foresight to grab one for himself before joining the First.

"Those will be useful to us," Sani said, as he felt the weight of the armor with both hands.

The armor was truly magnificent—as a decoration for Malan's tent. I sent him both as a gift. I whistled for them to stop talking and said, "Throw away all your armor. And I don't want to see any shields or looted helmets on your heads. You will strap only two swords. Long and short."

They threw away the rest of the stuff, but a second surprise was awaiting them. I dismounted my horse.

"Forget your horses. We won't ride again for four moons."

Rest, O'Ren. Rest your legs, be free of any rider until we meet again later.

Some of the older beards began to laugh. Heads moved, chuckling with disbelief left and right. Even the recruits turned pale. I repeated my words many times until the last man took me seriously and dismounted his horse.

The most difficult thing I had ever done. Because, when the big words were over, I knew that everyone was there for the meat, the women, and the horses. The Tanners and the Blacksmiths had never had any horses, and they had come to change that. My older men had been living on horses, so they could hardly walk, let alone run fast for a few hundred paces. They fought, trained, talked, slept, and ate on their horses. The horses were part of their bodies. They dismounted only to sleep, shit, and fuck. If I had asked them to cut off their balls, cook them in their barley mush, and eat them, they might have obeyed me. But four moons without horses was something that their minds could not get around.

"What are you doing Da-Ren? Don't torture us."

Even Leke called me Da-Ren, not by my title.

"Who's with me?" I asked again.

Leke and Sani said yes, but even they did it with their heads down. Most of the recruits were with me because they had no choice. The other Packs had already left for the raids. Everyone was with me, whether they liked it or not.

"Maybe I am wrong, but you are going to bust your heads proving it to me. Who disagrees? Let him wear a shiny pot over his head. Let him wear an iron-ring coat."

Some were looking at the beautiful armor.

"And then he can come and fight me like Mekor did. Inside his iron coat, I will roast his bones. His helmet, I will fill with his ashes." When no one moved, I continued. "Khun-Malan said that we will cross the Endless Forest."

I repeated it so they could picture it in front of them.

"The Endless Forest. It is as dense as the beard on your face, and men's boots have never stepped in there since Enaka bore the Sun. No horse gallops in that Forest; no man carries a heavy shield up the gorges. You have only your legs. You will run, and run, and run. Without horses."

And so they learned to run.

To run with a blade in each hand, to run in the thick mud of the swamp, to run up and down the rocky hill four times each morning, to run next to the dogs with manic fury, to run through the undergrowth, on the perilous stones, and over fallen trees. Without losing their eyes. Without water. With one hand tied behind their backs. With one leg lamed. Carrying baskets full of stones on their backs.

They would run in summer and beyond, while my mother, the slave, the witch, the northerner, southerner, or whatever wretched dog she was, gathered, every day before midday, more curses than she had in her entire life. They ran in the height of summer when the heat was unforgiving. They ran in the autumn rains.

Whoever saw us would point to us and sneer.

One night, one of the most simmering hot of summer, when the mind surrenders to the damp heat and the sweat flows down a river from the brow to the asshole, the Reghen came and gathered us to tell a Truth. Instead of a Truth, he told us things that even a seven-wintered child knew.

The Truth of the Seasons

In the frozen winter, the warrior and his horse take cover. To escape death. Nothing else. The horses cannot survive the cold and the icy grass. Without horses, the Tribe will perish.

In the spring, the warrior trains, he readies himself. The animals must mate in the spring. They do not go to battle. The horses must feed, rest, and regain the lost strength of the winter. Without horses, the Tribe will perish.

At the end of summer, in early fall, the warrior will go to battle. Before the great rains begin. Those rains crook the bow, destroy the soil, lame the horses. Without horses—

I raised my hand before he finished his words. Two things I hated: the heat and his stupid Truths. They were both melting my brain. I put my body between the Reghen and my men and interrupted him. He didn't like it. He was a young and tall Reghen.

"Thus declared the—"

He tried to continue.

"I thought you were finished, Reghen. Why are you telling us this? Even the seven-wintered know this."

"The Truths are eternal and easy to remember. But it seems you forgot them, Da-Ren. What do you think you are doing here?"

I took him to the side, away from others' ears.

"Are you talking about the training? Without horses?"

"Your training…is for the maulers, not for men. The Tribe knows only the bow and the horse. And, no, we don't care about your training. But how dare you defy the greatest Truth of the Sieve? Who do you think you are?"

"Is this about the Blacksmiths and the Fishermen?"

"Any man with four carvings can never be a warrior. Enaka decided thus, and the Sun cannot turn backward."

"You can tell Enaka that we ran out of Blades. I need men."

"I will tell Khun-Malan. You will send them all back where they came from. Today."

"No."

"It is the Truth."

It was a bunch of lies.

"Listen, Reghen, with your two hundred ears. Come back on the first moon of winter when all the other Packs have returned from the raids, and we have the Competitions of the Goddess. If you can tell the ones with the four carvings apart, I will let you take them."

I knew how to spot a coward. This one, who was even taller than I, kept his chin up high when he was talking.

"We will not accept this. It is a mockery of all our Truths," he said.

"I took free men. Not slaves. You do not command me—not me or them. What does Khun-Malan say?"

"Khun-Malan has far more important matters to deal with."

I laughed.

"Do you know what the Reghen used to say?" I asked him.

"Huh? What?"

"A Reghen told me once that the Tribe favors young Leaders like Khun-Malan and like me. The old ones rot inside. The young will lead the Tribe forward. They will bring Change. That is what the Reghen say. I brought Change."

That shut him up.

He would speak only to have the last word.

"The Blacksmiths and the Fishermen you took are missing elsewhere. Who will fish?"

"Go find a couple of lame slaves to do your fishing."

Leadership. Everyone wants it. Few can master it.

I had been raised with the Uncarved, three dozen of young men who were supposed to become leaders. Most of the youths I had grown up with would have died in two days if they had been sent as Chiefs of the First. Not because they were slow with the blade, but because they were arrogant and, at the same time, afraid. Each one believed himself to be unique. They walked the same. With one foot in front of the other. As they had been told. Before they bled to death.

Malan had sent me to the First to die, but Malan's triumphs had made me far more dangerous and fearless. Invincible in defeat. Elbia's death had made me impervious to pain. Then came Zeria's betrayal, and that had made my heart as cold as iron buried in snow. Those three shielded me. They were my own three mythical, identical Reghen brothers.

I continued with the changes, though a few nearly cost me my life. I slept with half an eye open every night, but I survived.

"A black luck found me," said Noki, laughing, while the sweat ran rivers out of his body. He was the fastest in every run. Second only to me. Each trial they did, I did with them. The baskets of rocks, the hills, the swamps. Otherwise, they would have drowned me in the Blackvein by the third night.

Leadership. Everyone wants it. Few understand it.

Each birchwood saddle weighed about as much as a three-wintered boy. I cut off the front and back arches of the wooden frames. The frames supported the Archers when they rode using both hands for the bow and arrow. But I wanted the Blades to mount and dismount with speed, and a heavy, rigid saddle was a hindrance.

"You go to the Tanners, you bargain, and you get lighter clothes; exactly the same for everyone," I said.

"Why the same?" Leke asked me.

"Because *same* is what we are. Same clothes, same life, same rules, same right, same wrong. When you are all dressed the same, the others will not see a scattered useless mob but one monster with forty heads and twice as many blades. We dress as one, fight as one, live as one."

Finally, I asked them all to trim their beards very short. They thought I was joking, but I was dead serious. We didn't cut our hair, only so that they wouldn't confuse us with the shaved slaves. We just had it tied with a band. So that the ninestar mark of their Chief would show unmistakably.

"I don't want anyone to be able to grab you from the beard in the mayhem of battle. You must slither away like snakes."

When the other Packs returned, they made fun of us. "Blade girls on foot," they would shout down to us from their horses. We heard much more, along with sneers and laughter every day. We stood out from the other Packs as the one-breasted female Archers stood out from the thousands of men.

Before the desperation of the winter frost, came the Squirrel Moon, the last of autumn, and it brought the Competitions to honor the Goddess. The victorious warriors would receive generous amounts of booty from the great Khun. Horses and women. All other activities stopped during the trials. It was the season of Changes, after the raids and before the snow. Everyone was there either to participate or to watch the best. Wild and reckless festivities flooded Sirol from end to end. Milk-spirit, roasting and feasts as if it were our last moon. Slave girls with legs wide open, winners and losers, thousands of men and women became one wild orgy looking for that last ember of warmth before the winter swallowed them.

And that's when the ridicule stopped.

We competed against all other Packs of the Blades.

In man-to-man combat with unsharpened blades, on foot, the First Pack came in first. Noki, Sani, Rikan, Leke. Faster than demons on their legs, capable of bringing down ten men each. I persuaded Malan to add an event: running in the Forest. The First came in first.

At the horse-riding competition, the First came in first. I rode O'Ren faster than the best of the Archer horses.

"Pelor's iron balls! How did we win this one? We hadn't ridden horses for so long," Leke said to me. No one was better than he was on horseback.

"Now you are two ironstones lighter each, and your horses were hungry for this, well rested for so many moons."

At the bow, the First came in third among the eighteen Packs. But the Blades didn't do much shooting in battle.

In the neckrope, the First came in last.

Pigface found only that single opportunity to take a jab at us.

"When you go into the Forest, Pigface, take your neckrope with you. And go hang yourself from a tall branch to feed the bats," Noki answered.

We attracted the yellow-green eyes of jealousy. And the eye of the Khun.

"That horse of yours," Malan said when he found me resting at the end of the last trial. "Where did you find it?"

"Oh, that? A crazy beast. Not safe for a Khun," I replied with a dead-serious face and a shit-scared heart.

He sneered at my fear and dropped the talk. "I am not here for the horse. I have been watching your men all these days. Do you know what you are doing?" he asked.

"Yes, the Blades need faster legs. We don't fight man-to-man in shield walls like the Southerners. We chase those left behind at the end of the battle. Or they chase us. Or we climb mountains and hills. Those with slow legs and heavy armor always fall first. I have seen it from the first day."

"Not one Reghen or Chief agrees with you."

"But Enaka agrees, and that's why I am victorious."

Khun-Malan was just. He cared for the strength of the Tribe first. He had no jealousy for anyone. He knew he was the One Leader. The just Leader. He was as smart as the son of the Devil, I said later in life, after I met the Devil herself. Almost as smart. Just and brilliant. And a madman. His Story would be better than mine if he, too, were ever to write it.

"The First is the best Pack," Malan announced. We had first choice of horses and women.

"By the Goddess, you are the Chief I have been waiting for all this time," Leke said to me. They lifted me up in their arms.

"Everything you said came true. About the horses, about the legs," Sani said.

That is not why I had won, though. It was not about legs. I won because I had by my side hungry, bloodthirsty, faithful men—not whiners.

The Blacksmiths and the Tanners took the horses and the women they had been dreaming of all their lives. We left Noki to choose the fresh slaves for them. If those men believed in me a little before the trials, they were mine forevermore after. And they were the only ones I wanted.

When the competitions had ended, I gathered them again. We

roasted the best meats, and I told them, "Here, you will grow old and you won't fall by any othertriber. We will keep on running and get faster than the wind until we become ourselves Enaka's arrows. The First Pack of the Blades will be the glory and honor of the Tribe, and we will lose no warrior in battle. Not one."

Big words that caressed the ears before the bloody campaigns begin that crush all promises.

When I was finished, I drew my knife and carved my left arm deeply in front of all, to end their doubts once and for all. I was the Chief of the First Pack—nothing more, nothing less. I was among brothers, and I shared with them meat, pain, women, and sweat. And in all these brief pleasures, I was trying to drown the memory of Zeria. I slept alone in my own tent again. The men had made a new one, just for me.

I became brothers with Sani, who was the oldest and strongest; with Leke, who was the most faithful but never servile; with Noki, who opened the legs of the women, and they screamed so loud they could be heard in all of Sirol, while we stood back to watch and learn from him. With Rikan, the Blacksmith who wanted to see the West; with Kuran, who wanted to change his fate. These men had become my Pack and replaced the Uncarved. I slept easily with both eyes shut among them. My men would go into the jaws of Darhul with me, and that was exactly where Malan would be sending us after all.

But I was still deceiving myself about one thing.

There were those moments, when I rode O'Ren head on to the sunset, when the sweat was running burning rivulets down my spine, and the cheers were loudest, or when my men lifted me up in their arms, I was at the top of the sky. Then night fell and my small tent strangled me.

Leave for the North, Zeria. Find peace.

I had delivered my heart forever. To the First and to the Last. The one with the blue eyes. I was enchanted, and every night, the magic took me away.

Leadership. Everyone wants it. Few can endure it.

Twice, in between all these moons, once in autumn and once in the dead of winter, I rode O'Ren north to Kar-Tioo. I told Malan I was looking for the hidden Forest paths. The first time, I found nothing. No one. No woman. The second time, I went deeper into the snow-covered trails all the way to the northern slopes. I made it to mountain caves I had never been to before. Two Dasal were guarding the entrance of a cave, and Veker came to stop me.

"Don't ever go in there. Those caves are cursed, and no man can enter," he said.

"What is in there?"

"Nothing good. Why are you here again?" He was walking ahead, and I followed without answering. Another winter was coming down hard in the Forest. "We'll be heading farther north," he said.

"Why?"

"Come. I want to show you something."

We had reached a rare wood of magic; all the oaks were alive with leaves though we were past the first moon of winter. He showed me two Dasal bodies hanging from a branch with their legs cut off.

"As if someone took only the meat they needed."

"This wasn't done by us," I told him. "Our Witch has forbidden us to enter the Forest. The Reekaal did this."

Veker spat in the snow, went into his hut, and brought out some arrows.

"These are what killed them. You! And you dare to come here?"

They were arrows of my Tribe. He wasn't lying.

Zeria was nowhere to be seen. I had to know if she was all right. When I had lost all hope, patience, and honor, I asked him.

"Zeria doesn't want to see any of you—you or your Tribe. She has taken a man," he told me.

"What does that mean?"

"They have exchanged eternal rings."

Rings of what? That meant nothing to me. I wanted only to see her. My heart was beating like O'Ren's crushing hooves in my chest.

"If you wait, she may return in a few days. With her man," Veker said when he saw I was not about to leave.

I could hack all the men there into pieces, make eternal rings of their guts. Become a Reekaal.

My eye caught the saddened gaze of O'Ren. There was a faint blue around the pupil.

Let's go back, Chief. You are dying here. The brave wait for you at Sirol.

Boot on stirrup and I was on the back of my horse. The evening sun had descended low, unleashing a sea of gold among the trunks, painting the shadows darker. Could that faraway shadow be her, standing like a frail wood spirit among the eternal oaks? She was not going to come any closer. Next to her was a man with short hair and weak legs. Was she holding an infant?

Stay away from me, my love.

They were looking at me. I was holding an arrow of the Reekaal that Veker had given me. I snapped it in two, on my knee.

I am not bringing death, Zeria.

I knew as I had the first time, as I had every other time, that I wasn't going to kill anyone. Even her dark shadow in the distance was enough to melt my rage.

Betray me, Zeria.

I'll still protect you with my dying breath.

Abandon me a thousand nights.

I'll save you from death a thousand times.

Deny me a thousand kisses.

I'll come to find you to steal only one.

I kept one of the arrows to remind me of the two mutilated bodies.

Veker was right. I had the skins and the quiver, same as the monsters, strapped around my body and my saddle. How could I demand to reap the fruit of peace and love? In the Forest, the monsters hunted their prey, and I had to find them before they killed all that I loved. The last and only way for me to be near Zeria was to find the creatures who threatened her.

Or, as it happened soon enough, they would find me.

XLIV.
The Ssons

Nineteenth winter. Chief of the First.

Monsters spreading death. Black, gray, and brown, with six legs, their bellies glowing full of the red blood they sucked. As big as my nail. Mosquitoes. They had annihilated thousands of the Tribe's bravest warriors, but no one spoke of them. Enaka did not frighten them. Always on our skin. But it was the Reekaal, those mythical invisible bloodeaters, who haunted our nights. The Reekaal who no one could yet describe.

The abominable beast, the most dangerous of them all. The marshy stagnant water of the Blackvein swamps. But it was the Black Sea that scared us the most, the lair of Darhul, the dark waves of the east that we had yet to lay eyes upon.

So many other monsters, impossible to count. Othertribers, Drakons, Sorcerers of the Cross, Buried skeletons, Deadwalkers, all had but one purpose in our Legends: to exterminate our children, the seed of the Tribe. And I had seen many of our children perish. All perished at the hands of our own monsters. They were the ones with the most hideous faces: ours. We hid them behind red veils and gray hoods so that we wouldn't see them reflected in the crystal-clear waters.

The Stories honored the warriors who had fallen bravely in the fights against the monsters. Who wants to lament and praise the one who battled the mosquito and the plague? Was he victorious? Did he die yellow from an insect's bite? A Story worth a stallion's fart.

All men wanted to be the lucky ones. Those to be torn apart by the nine jaws of Darhul while naked Ouna-Mas wrapped their slender henna-painted arms around their knees and sang their Story.

I was still standing after nineteen winters. If there were monsters, then sooner or later I would find them. Sooner.

On a chilly winter morning, I saw for the first time the Tribe's only monsters, the ones we would come to call the Ssons.

We had been summoned to the Ceremony of the Brave and I was trotting with my Pack toward Wolfhowl. I saw Khun-Malan's procession walking the horses carefully through the tall birch trees. The Ouna-Mas around him looked taller than ever on horseback, floating like ghosts embraced by the fog.

This was the one day every winter that was customary for the Khun to make all the Changes. He would order more carvings for Chiefs who have proved unworthy, and he would choose younger brave men to replace them. The new Chiefs had to be in place before the boys finished their five-winter training in spring.

Only a few days had passed since the victories of the First Pack in the competitions. Inside of me nested a blazing hope that Malan would make me Leader of all the Blades. That day, it was the ceremony for the Blades only. The Archers were too many, and they had already completed their Changes. The eighteen Chiefs stood in a circle in the arena, each one about seven paces apart, and their men a few steps behind them. Malan commanded that only the First, the Fifth, the Seventh, the Thirteenth and the Fourteenth come with all their men.

"The others shall send only their Chief and three more men to witness," the Reghen had told us.

"Darhul's jaws! He's only going to make changes to our Packs," said Sani. He had seen more ceremonies than anyone else among us. "He has brought all the men from the worst Packs here. That is not a good sign."

"He also brought the First Pack," I said, with a tone of voice that faked confidence.

My fingers ran up my left arm feeling the one carving that ripped straight through the skin. I would not bear it if the one scar became three.

The Khun's place was always higher up in the stands, in a designated seat of honor. But Malan had ordered the Craftsmen to rebuild the Wolfhowl ahead of the coming Feast of Spring. The stands were not ready, so Malan had decided to come to the ground next to us and took his place at the head of the Chiefs' circle. He was flanked by a handful of Ouna-Mas and two Reghen. About a dozen Rods surrounded the whole entourage. I looked at the Ouna-Mas again. I always tried to guess if I could recognize them just by their movement under their robes. Those were taller figures that I'd swear I've never seen before, wearing gray hoods, not veils. An agonizing silence prevailed as the men waited for the Reghen to speak. The only sound came from a few men coughing from the cold; the only movement were the breaths of about two hundred men evaporating slowly and mixing with the gloomy morning.

A flock of blackbirds crossed Wolfhowl's silent sky. Instead of their flapping wings I heard a child whispering. Such gatherings of hundreds always brought Elbia's face back.

"A morning of death. Like that one long ago, when you didn't save me. Remember, Da-Ren?"

I had tried to get rid of that memory the night before, but I had chosen the worst of all ways to do it. Milk-spirit and a sip of crazygrass. A stupid mistake.

The Ceremony began with a young Reghen reciting praises to Enaka and a brief thousand-told Story about Packs of wolfen brothers and sisters. Then, the Reghen called for the Chief of the Fifth to go to the center of the circle. He was a man two times my age, who had taken the place of Keral after the night he had murdered Khun-Taa. The Fifth Pack had been cut down to half its size that night. I could count only twenty or so men behind him, and they were following him. The Fifth was about twenty paces from the center, another twenty from Malan. My Pack stood exactly in the opposite spot of the circle from the Khun, about forty paces away.

Why are they following him?

"They always begin with the disposal of the unworthy Chiefs," said Sani.

"Are they supposed to follow him?" I asked Sani.

"If the Khun decides to name a new Leader of all Blades, that will be done at the end of the Ceremony," added Leke.

The fog was not helping, but those men had quickened their pace and had unsheathed their blades.

She whispered again, closer to me now.

"This is it, Da-Ren. You are here again. Will you save him? Him?"

The men of the Fifth charged toward Malan and his personal guard, shouting and waving their knives. The boy Reghen was massacred in the middle of the Wolfhowl before he even had a chance to scream for help. More Blades from the other Packs joined in the ambush. About forty Blades, eighty knives, were running, searching for Malan's throat. Against them stood twelve Rods. Malan saw the jaws of Darhul in front of him. The next Khun would be someone even younger. Even less worthy than Malan. Someone much worse than I.

I was running as well, not even knowing why, whom I was going to defend, save or slaughter yet.

The oddly tall shadows who stood around Malan took off their hoods and their robes with one sharp move. They were not Ouna-Mas. They weren't even women. Were they human? What makes us human? Or monster?

That was the first time I saw the Reekaal—the ancient servants of darkness who in our Legends sealed our path to the West. In the tales of Zeria, they were the sons of Ouna-Mas, their hearts locked with silver chains. Those who had killed my father, Rouba, Er-Ren, in the Endless Forest and who had even killed me before Zeria brought me back from the serpent's belly. But the Reekaal were just another fairy tale, same as that of my father. The human truth of our Tribe that existed in the place of the tales was far more horrifying.

The four monstrous men who protectively surrounded Malan had the unique long heads of the Ouna-Mas. They were taller than anyone else I had seen in my life, taller than I, with long fingers, as if they were talons on birds of prey. A short blade in each of their hands, a loud scream out of their mouths. A scream overlapping with an eerie laughter at the same time. One laughing, two screaming? Their leader silent. Underneath their robes, they wore nothing but loincloths that covered the nakedness between their legs. Their bodies were all muscle, bone, nerves, like skinned wild beasts. The naked legs looked strong and fast, as if they always roamed the Forest on foot rather than on horseback.

No one would ever pronounce the names of these four men without fear and hesitation. They would be called the Sons of Ouna-Mas, but the first *s* would sizzle and simmer and stay like a sleeping serpent in the mouths of all who ever saw them, as if its own sound was a slithering spell. *The Ssons* would be their name.

They did not look sacred like the Ouna-Mas but were still awe-inspiring. Their long quiver heads were those of monsters painted with fearsome black and red designs. The back of the skull of one of them was painted with a wolf's face, the second one's skin was done to look like a skull with fangs, a third one was an abomination of hundred eyes, and the last one, the silent leader, had drawn flowing red lines out of every crevice of his face. His arms had blue painted ornaments, and a memory from Sah-Ouna's camp returned to my mind. It was all painting and shouldn't scare great warriors like ourselves, yet it was so masterfully done that one couldn't understand from a few paces away what was eye, jaw, bone, teeth, scar, curse, fangs, skin, blood, and where each feature belonged. Fake eyes were painted in the wrong places, looking straight—and so fighting them was confusing. Their own eyes were completely hidden among all the painting, stretching thin like tiny knives. The iris covered most of the eye, and the whites were veined red like those of men who have never slept. Most of their hair was gone or shaved, with only a few tufts remaining on the stretched painted skin that covered their skulls.

"Death to the worm Malan!" screamed the Fifth. Revenge had been boiling inside Sirol all summer.

The traitors were getting closer to Malan. I was running; my men following behind me to intercept the traitors. As they saw the unhooded Ssons they froze and hesitated for a moment in the face of terror. For a few breaths both sides stood watching each other, the traitors trying to believe their eyes. I had made it to the right of the Fifth, the left of Malan, forming a triangle of death. I still hadn't chosen sides, and my men just followed my steps, waiting for an order. Malan's eyes fell on me. Was he scared? I couldn't say for sure from that distance, but he was staring at me, with eyes wide open pleading silent. Faster than any Archer I've ever seen, the Ssons nocked their bows and brought four men of the Fifth down. The Fifth charged with screams; they had no choice anymore. They had already made their move and still had the advantage.

Forty Blades. Against twelve Rods and four monsters.

It was only after the massacre when I counted the traitors lying dead in the dirt. It was only later when I saw clearly the color in the eyes of the Ssons, their paintings, and their features. When the Fifth attacked, all I saw were gray shadows falling on gray shadows in the fog.

Malan would fall. A new Khun would come to command me. The other Blades would then come for us. I was considered Malan's faithful dog, and I would have no luck with them. At one corner of the arena, one could still see the remains of Druug and the stakes that carried the rotting bodies of his fellow traitors. This would be my fate before the end of the day.

It was only later when I thought about what I saw, what I did, the *whys*. When I was washing off. That first moment in the fog, I let out a battle cry that escaped my chest.

"Save the Khun!" I shouted, and I was already running to shield Malan. The First Pack of the Faithful, the Blacksmiths, and the Scum of the Stars fell on the traitors like swarming wasps on meat. If we had been a few breaths late, the Khun would have fallen.

The knives have twice the rage when they strike within their own Tribe. I would fight with othertribers many times later in life. There were battles. Bloody and savage, but my mind was there. I knew. I knew that I had been born for this. It was what I prepared for every day: to slaughter the unbelievers in the name of our Goddess.

But that morning in the fog, I had to bring down my own. Brothers. The men of my Tribe. Children of the Sieve and Blades. "By Enaka!" screamed the First, as our short blades went straight for the throats of the traitors.

My enemies claimed the same Story. "Glory to Enaka!" The Fifth was charging against us with their long blades.

Only pure hatred remained, glittering in the fog, adorning it with red. Everyone struck their brothers without mercy. In the face, until that face of the enemy came to look like something totally different. Othertriber. Monster.

We had the four Ssons among us. It was easy for the loathing to blossom at their sight.

We, of the First, had made it a custom to tie our hair in ponytails and that proved a wise trick. That girlish mark distinguished us from the traitors.

I fought shoulder to shoulder with the Ssons, so close that I smelled their skin, a smell of forest and freshly skinned meat. I saw one of them bleeding from the arm. Just a scratch, but his blood was the same as mine. They were nothing more than tall, fearsome men, those Ssons. They were not Reekaal.

Not a single traitor survived to be put on the stake that day.

The whole Fifth, every one of the forty traitors, were slaughtered there as a spontaneous sacrifice to the Ceremony of the Brave. Eight of Malan's Rods fell, as did two of my men. None of the Ssons. Two of my men lay bleeding to death on the day of my greatest glory. One throat, one kidney. Not even two moons ago, I had promised them that no one would ever fall under my command. We say foolish things in our youth, as if there are thousands of autumn rains left to wash them away, winter snowstorms to cover them—to hide the skeletons of our foolishness so that they don't gawk at us with terror.

Malan was trembling behind us. Fear. Shock. Rage. Everything. What difference did it make? He was trembling. He hadn't raised his own blade. He was holding it cleaner and shinier than all the others. And that was exactly how it remained. Spotless.

Sable! Finally, I had found the answer to my question. The Khun's winter coat was made of sable. A rare animal living by the rivers beyond the steppe. It was a thick golden-brown fur with blue undertones. I remember the Hunters had brought such skins to the Uncarved a couple of summers ago. Sable, spotless without a speck of blood. The Khun stood stronger than ever before as the Ssons knelt before him. My men knelt too. Before him.

Enaka parted the mist to throw ample light on the bravest and the traitors. Who was who? Who was looking at me? Who was praising me? No one. Even my own men had turned their stares toward the four blood-covered Ssons. The monsters were chopping and tearing the heads of the traitors with raging fury and throwing them high into the air. More and more men from other Banners and Packs were gathering in the Wolfhowl to witness the spectacle. Darhul's Reekaal had finally risen from the bowels of the darkest caves and now stood only a few feet away from us.

Reghen, Ouna-Mas. They would weave new Legends for this morning. What would their Story say? That night, the fires trembled and sang about this day, the first time that the Ssons appeared before us. The Reghen ran all afternoon, after the Ceremony, from fire to fire to spread the Stories before the warriors made Legends on their own.

"Were they Reekaal?" my warriors had asked that afternoon when we had gone back to our camp.

The Reghen had the answers: "No, they are our best, the sons of the Ouna-Mas. For many winters now, Sah-Ouna secretly chose a handful of children, the most beautiful girls and the biggest boys, immediately after they came out of their mother's bellies, to be raised by the Ouna-Mas. They breastfed on crazygrass, that we know. Very few have survived."

"Do you believe that, Chief?" Noki asked.

"Do you want Zeria's tale or Rouba's?" I answered.

"Who are they?"

My men had gathered closer; everyone wanted to learn more.

"Rouba's it is. Do you know why they have those long heads? The Ouna-Mas, the Ssons?" I asked, looking at all faces for an answer.

"Who can know the ways of the Goddess? To see the—" Sani replied.

"Before he died, a Guide told me that he had seen such babies, girls. Early after one of them was born, the Ouna-Mas wrapped cloths around its head tightly. The baby slept and sucked from the tit with the cloth always tied. Every few nights, they changed the cloth and washed the skin. After many moons, the soft skulls had become long like our quivers for the rest of their lives."

"I don't understand. What are you saying?" asked one of my warriors. A couple more who were listening had turned to their most sour face.

"I'm saying that this is why their heads are shaped like snake eggs. The Witches tied them that way when they were babies. They're not born like that."

More shook their heads as if I were a liar or a drunk. Some started walking away.

It was a simple truth. So simple, it made them feel stupid. Few believed it. Nobody opposed it, yet their silence said a lot more.

Lead us, torture us, rule us, but don't take away our monsters. Because when our monsters die, so does our Goddess and our Story.

Give us Witches who dream Enaka's whispers. Not mad, plain mortals with banded heads.

My men needed the monsters. No one liked my Story.

The Reghen did not stop me. He didn't even need to say that my Story was false.

"If those creatures are sons of the Ouna-Mas, then they should be wise. But to me they look like the sons of a drunken Witch fucked by a pack of maulers," said Noki, his stare fixed on the Reghen.

It took the Reghen a few breaths to believe what he heard before he replied. "The females with the long heads are wise. The Ssons have the spirit of the She-Wolves and the strength of the Tribe's bravest warriors."

My men wouldn't let the Reghen leave. They kept attacking him with questions.

"Will they go into battle with us?" asked Leke.

"They are a handful and take orders only from the Khun of the Tribe," the Reghen said.

They wouldn't.

"What Pack do they belong to?"

"These men are very few, and they have been raised in the Forest. That was where they hunted, living off the meat of the deer and protecting us from the Forest demons."

The Reghen said the word "men" with great difficulty.

"Who gave them orders? Did they kill many demons?" I asked.

He didn't answer. He knew.

"How long have they been hunting?"

Still no answer.

"How come no one spoke of them for so many winters?"

"Most of them died. Some would not obey, and some went crazy. The Rods took care of those. The ones today are the four who made it to twenty winters. Sah-Ouna trusts them, and they will serve Khun-Malan."

Khun-Malan. I had saved his life.

"And how is the great Khun?" I asked.

"He is stronger than ever. I came for you, Da-Ren. He ordered that you go to him after sunset."

I left most of my men behind whispering tales about the Ssons. I rode around Sirol for a while before going to Malan's tent. Noki and Rikan rode next to me. Passing through the training fields, we fell upon a handful of women Archers who were returning to their camp. With them was Danaka from the Sieve. She recognized me and called out to me.

"They want to know. Let's stop and talk to them," I said to Noki.

The women had gathered proudly on horseback around me. I ached to tell them the Story of the day. My eyes searched in vain for Elbia among them. I had heard her ghost once more, after such a long time, only that morning.

"Were you there today?" asked the woman with the Chief's ribbon around her arm.

"Yes, we fought alongside Khun-Malan. We—"

She cut me off.

"Did you see them? The Ssons? Are they what everyone says?"

"Who says what?"

"They say that the four of them brought down forty men," she said.

I exhaled too tired and angry to say anything more.

"They are strong warriors. Almost as strong as we are!" Noki shot out.

I bade them goodbye and signaled to my men that we were leaving. Noki stayed with them. He wanted to tell them other Stories.

"I have to explain a few things to these Archers here," he said.

I reached the tents of the Sieve. I had not returned to my first brutal winter camp since the day I had left it. The Guide in charge tried to stop me.

"We came to bring the Stories of the Ssons," I said, and he let us inside. Rikan started talking to him about the Ssons. I approached the tent of the winners and took a peek inside. Four twelve-wintered children were chewing meat around the fire. They were mumbling, and I heard them uttering the word "Ssons." One of them was a girl. She was drawing with her rosy lips the smile that I had lost in the Sieve. She turned, and I thought she looked at me. Her lips were shut, I could hear her. "So, you saved him. Him! Not me."

"Let's get out of here," I said to Rikan.

"You are pale, Chief."

"Last night, I had a sip of crazygrass. Haven't tasted that demon for a long time. Only a taste, but that's all it takes. It's been a strange day, today."

"Crazygrass! Ha, give it to me next time."

We rode side by side.

I preferred to have him next to me rather than the Ssons. A loyal man with iron heart and arms.

"How did you end up with four carvings? You can bring down four Blades on your own," I asked him.

"Leave it. I have never talked about this."

"You never had a Chief who gave you a horse before. Tell me."

"The first five nights of the Sieve, I was in the winners' tent every time. And then I caught the sickness. They had me for dead; I didn't even leave the sick children's tent. I puked my guts out every morning and night. I wouldn't eat anything for days," he said.

"And you survived."

"A miracle before the end of the Sieve. When the Witch came and made me swallow the crazygrass. That thing cured me. No one could believe it. I crawled back out again on the last day, to the trial with the rabbits."

"Yes, I know."

"They gave me four carvings. What else could they have done? They were right. Bad luck."

"You don't look sickly to me."

"No. I never got sick again."

"Your luck has changed now."

I entered Malan's tent unarmed. The Rods had really gone mad after that morning's attack. They searched us until they found and removed every weapon we carried. The bodies of their comrades had been laid to rest on the funeral pyres to the right of Malan's hill.

Malan was drinking. Neither men nor women were with him in the vast room. Only lifeless skulls and the monsters that guarded him. I approached, and he put his hand on my shoulder.

"Da-Ren, you really proved your worth today. No one else moved."

"Maybe they couldn't see in the fog, Khun."

"Yes, right. Some saw only what they wanted to see. Our days are numbered, Da-Ren. We have to leave for a campaign; else they will slaughter us all soon."

Sah-Ouna was not there, and Malan and I had become *we* and *us*.

"This is your big day, Da-Ren," he said.

"I don't deserve your mockery," I told him.

"What do you mean?"

"You are high up on your hill here, but you don't see around you, Khun. You are too far away to hear. Everyone, everywhere, is talking about them. Only them." I gestured to the two Ssons who were standing still as leafless trunks on each side of his throne. They were Malan's only companions in the tent.

"The Ssons never utter a word," the Reghen had said. For the rest of my days and theirs, I would never see them eat, drink or touch a woman. And yet their presence next to the throne felt stronger than a hundred bellowing Rods.

Malan offered me a wooden cup full of wine. I touched my lips to it but didn't drink.

"The Tribe will sing about you, Da-Ren. You will find your Story when our campaign begins. You will lead first among the brave. I promise it. We will both find our Story. Our Legends are going to be unveiled together."

"The Goddess despises warriors who grow old," I said.

"Yes, Chaka used to tell us so in the Uncarved. Remember? Not even two winters have passed," Malan said.

"I will die in a few moons anyway, Khun-Malan. I have seen it on the pegs the Blades hang outside my tent," I said. "There is only one thing I fear: that I will not live in even one Story. My ashes will scatter in the darkest corners of the night sky, and no star will warm me with its light. I can't breathe here."

I was gasping for air without Zeria, without glory. My failure had simmered too long in the cauldron of the Witches, the Reghen, and the Ssons.

"We are leaving," Malan said.

"When?"

"Soon. Very soon. The greatest campaign that ever was."

"I will come. I will no longer stay here."

"As of now, you are the Leader of all of the Blades. All eighteen Packs will be under your command. You will kneel only before me," said Malan.

"Seventeen."

The Fifth was no more.

"First thing you'll do, change all the Chiefs who were in the field today and did not fight by my side. And whoever else you suspect. Carve them, Da-Ren. Send them to the Guides. Clean them out. From now on, you are my Firstblade."

I must find a new Chief for the First to take my place.

"And take a wineskin. Celebrate tonight!" Those were his last words. And so it was.

A decision. A sip of crazygrass, a whispering ghost, a man consumed by love lost, a man running in the fog of Wolfhowl. Choosing sides. The blue-painted ornaments on the arms of the tallest Sson. Had I seen those or did I dream them? One battle cry.

"Save the Khun."

Without ceremonies or any other kinds of celebrations, in the nineteenth winter of my life, all the Packs of the Blades had come under my command. The worst cutthroats of all the world would ride behind me, even into the belly of Darhul.

Firstblade.

When I reached my tent, I wondered for the first time. I would never know why Malan had called the whole First Pack that morning. Had he been planning to carve me three times and dispose of me, or to give me the leadership of the Blades anyway?

I had no answers. Only a new title. And a wineskin.

XLV.
Hunger

Twentieth spring. Firstblade.

The Legend of the Annihilation
The Fourth Season of the World

Darkness. First. Light. Birth. Enaka. Battle. Demon. Darhul. Sun. Men. Victory. Domination. Birth. Tribe.

All this came and passed, and then began the Third Luminous Season, that of Birth.

From the fragments of the Goddess, the first-ever men and women were born. They were not warriors; they had no enemies. They lived off the hunt, and the food was plentiful, always from the hand of the Goddess.

Until the Black Autumn of the Annihilation, when Darhul came to take his revenge. There in the black sea depths, he had hidden for hundreds of winters. He emerged stronger than ever. With vengeful fury, he cut and unleashed his most gruesome head, the Cloudarken.

It was the beginning of autumn, only six generations before, and it all came down on midday so fast. The Cloudarken, a white-headed snake with a red tail of fire, tore the Sky with ominous speed. A tiny speck at first, it grew as high as the tallest mountain before it crashed into the land. The Earth shook and trembled for countless breaths. Valleys opened in half and became desolate crags of fire and dust.

And then the Sun was gone.

The Cloudarken had covered him with a cloak of ash and poison.

Blind and blinded, the first male Sorcerers of the Tribe scarred their faces with knives in the faint light of the torches and called him back, but the son of the Goddess was lost, wounded for ten and five moons. A thick black cloud, which rained death, soot, and brimstone, swallowed him. As the Sun, so Enaka too was lost.

Thus began the Fourth Season, that of the Annihilation, which lasted only ten and five moons but was the deathliest of all. The Season that Enaka abandoned us.

It took only a few nights for the sun-orphaned autumn to turn into black winter and frozen death. The frost burned the grass. With cudgels, fists, and the warm entrails of the dead, the people tried to break the ice in the dark, if only to uncover a little grass for the animals.

The animals died first. In the beginning, only those that were to be eaten. Then in the days to come, our ancestors were forced to slaughter most of the horses as well and eat them on their way south. The raging warriors stoned to death the powerless male Sorcerers and abolished them forever. Never again would our Tribe honor a false Sorcerer.

Few of our Tribe saved themselves by fleeing south. From countless thousands, only three times a thousand were left alive. Some say fewer. They wandered around like demented wind-ghosts. Some began to beg for mercy in the name of the cursed Darhul, forgetting the Goddess. Ten and five moons passed traveling under the clouds of darkness. But the day and the night had become one, so no one could know how long the Season lasted.

The Goddess had not abandoned us. One night, she rushed with the chariot upon the celestial cloudbreaths of Darhul and separated day from night once more with lightning fire. Then another bright star appeared— hers, next to the Sun and Selene. Day and night, the star ran furiously toward the West with a tail of fire. Our warlords followed this first sign of Enaka and so were saved, leaving the black cloud back in the East.

It was six generations ago when the first men of the Tribe burned their lifeless children, women, elders, and mothers, all who had perished. And they gathered close around the fire, to savor the heat of the dead. The living continued until they finally came upon the other tribes of the South. That was the beginning of the next and greatest misery. Hunger was the agony that had prevailed until then, but it was followed by despair and rage. Because the othertribers they came upon were servants of Darhul. They had taken control of the lands of the South, where the fertile soil could still feed many. This was the only way open to them, as Darhul had placed the Reekaal in the West and the Drakons in the North as guardians.

Everyone, now listen carefully to these words, because the remembrance of yesterday will be tomorrow's salvation: Never allow yourself to be fooled by the false words and gifts of the othertribers. Only their deaths will breed a future for our Tribe. Annihilate the othertribers however and wherever you may find them. Show no mercy because they bear no such mercy for you. They are servants of the One Monster. They are not human. Their souls have been long lost.

The othertribers whom our ancestors encountered were ruthless, green-eyed, and evil. Our people pleaded for mercy but were murdered and enslaved. Our people pleaded for food, but the othertribers demanded the flesh of our children. What can one expect from the servants of Darhul, the abominations who bury their dead unburned with clothes inside the worm-infested soil? How can one ever live in the same land with the Deadwalkers?

Outside the walls of their most prosperous cities camped two-thousands of our ancestors to beg. The last survivors. They had lived that long by opening the veins of their horses' necks and sucking the blood of their animals. Whoever had many children in our Tribe lost some of them to the Deadwalkers' slave market to buy millet for the rest.

The First Ouna-Ma, the daughter of Khun-Nan, shed rivers of tears and cried to the Unending Sky for Enaka to hear: "Enaka, Enaka, why have you forsaken us?"

And the Goddess appeared before her, in her golden brilliance and rage.

"I have not forsaken you, and I will lead you to victory. You journeyed south and saw the servants of the Demon. Now you will become warriors and defeat them. Listen to me:

"Your father will become the First Leader of the Tribe.

"You will be my Voice, the Voice of the Sky.

"Keep only the strong and head north. First, you must defeat the Drakons; then, the Buried; and last, the Reekaal in the West."

And so the Fifth Season of the Leaders began.

Thus declared the Ouna-Mas, the Voices of the Unending Sky.

Six hundred and forty-nine men of the Blades I counted as mine.

I had gathered all their Chiefs in front of my tent. This would be a quick conversation; the evening north wind pierced our bones. They were all men older and more experienced than I. I had earned the respect of some of them because the First had triumphed in the trials and because they knew I had been an Uncarved until a few moons ago.

I had won the leadership of all the Blades by stepping over the older Chiefs, those who commanded the other sixteen Packs. They hated Malan and the hunger he had brought, they hated everyone who was Malan's favorite and younger than them. One more reminder that they were closer to death. That's all I was to them. I had to get this over with fast.

"Do not challenge them all at once because that could turn all the Packs against us," Leke said to me. "Be just."

I decided to listen to his advice.

I stood on the westerly side of the fire with my most faithful, forcing the Chiefs to take the opposite side. The wind was blowing that way, and they would have the warmth but also the smoke in their faces. Their eyes would water and hurt; they would pay much less attention to how young I was.

"Chiefs of the Blades, I will speak to you plainly. The Reghen came this afternoon and told me that the supplies here will last for a few more moons. After that, it's death or living on the blood of your horse. I give you a choice. The Reghen said that a thousand of our men are already moving far north and east to command the outposts there. They have grain, flax, sheep and women and they gather more. I must send a few men as well. Go there. You will be free to do as you please, far from my orders."

"We have heard those words before, and then whoever turned to leave was butchered," said one of them.

"By Enaka's glory, I will keep my word. We need brave men in the East. Whoever goes there will no longer be a Chief of his Pack, but his belly will be full."

"And if we refuse?"

"Or you can refuse, and stay as Chiefs here. And learn to live with hunger. You will endure hardships without complaint and remain faithful to the Khun and me. You must have enough faith to last for all the forty men each of you commands."

One Chief got up to leave without giving me an answer.

"Hey you, wait! Listen to me," I cried and ran after him. I didn't even know the name of some of them yet. At my signal, Noki, Leke, and three more of my men followed after me.

"What is his name?" I asked Leke.

"Korban of the Eleventh."

Eleven will be the breaths you have left, Korban.

One. I caught up with him when he was well out of sight of the other Chiefs.

"Korban, I plead with you. Make your choice but don't leave like this. This is not honorable," I said, my hand resting softly on his shoulder. *Five.* I tapped his shoulder. "Are we good?"

I lowered my eyes, and so did he with a dejected sigh. *Eight.* He was still shaking his head. I hadn't convinced him.

"Eleven," I shouted to him.

He cut a confused stare at me. I kneed him in the groin with a fast move. As he curled in pain, I grabbed him by his rich long hair and plunged my dirk in his neck vein. Gurgling sounds and blood spurting. The rest of my men followed with the blades. I ran back to the other Chiefs who were arguing among themselves trying to choose a fate. They had come all alone without their warriors. Leke was behind me holding Korban's dangling head from its rich long hair. He threw the head and it rolled awkwardly close to the feet of the Chiefs, and I repeated myself.

"I praise you for your silence, and I will say it again: you have only two roads before you. Either you leave now for the East, or you stay here and do whatever I say. Whoever wants to stay here only to spread fear and curses will meet a similar fate." Once again, the head of the Eleventh chose not to listen. It had already closed its eyes wearily as it lay on the dirt, warming by the dung fire.

Three Chiefs chose to abandon Sirol and leave for the East. I ordered my men to supply them with good horses and dogs.

"No one is to lay a hand on them. You give them strong horses and dogs," I said for all to hear.

The other twelve remained.

"Tell us what to do, Firstblade," said one of them.

First, I'd better learn their names.

Every Chief wanted me to know that his patience was exhausted. They all wanted to join the next campaign away from Sirol.

But where could we go? To the ice mountains of the North?

To the endless wooden forest walls of the West?

"The sign of the rowan cannot be ignored. We cannot go West," added another.

To the East, the steppe of Nothing and dust?

We had raided and burned the South many times and had taken all there was to take.

"The South is deserted."

"Only if we reach the great cities with the impregnable walls."

"To Sapul," said one of the Chiefs.

Sapul. The name my Tribe had given to Thalassopolis. The mythical capital of the Southeastern Empire. With walls built by giants. We didn't have siege machines to bring down those walls even if it took us a thousand summers. There were many cities farther south and east, but the only land passage was through the reigning city of Thalassopolis.

"This is the third moon of darkness," said the Chief of the Sixth Pack.

It was the third full moon in a row that remained hidden behind thick black clouds.

"Enaka cries and hides her face from us," the Chief of the Sixth said again. He was a short and ugly man who had the reputation of being a great horseman. One of his arms was scarred from battle. Half of his teeth were missing, and half of his beard was white.

"The darkness of Darhul returns," added yet another.

"It is winter. The clouds cover the sky and hide Selene. Don't speak foolish words as if you are talking to twelve-wintered boys of the Sieve," I said.

"We are too many for Sirol to feed us all. This cannot go on."

"Tell Malan we should leave for the campaigns on the first day of spring."

"I will do so, but we are still in Sirol. You will lead your men and give them courage," were my words to the Chiefs. "We will go where we are told. Khun-Malan has promised me that we will begin our campaign in the spring."

This was how I was earning respect and admiration. By admitting that I was Malan's most faithful dog, the one who knew ahead of the others.

Whenever I was in danger of losing my faith, I would go watch the Sieve of the twelve-wintered. I usually got there before nightfall to see who would remain standing. I wanted to find the strength that could withstand anything, the kind that I had stolen from the Goddess in the Sieve. The children were looking at me as if I was a Legend come alive. So many winters had passed, but it seemed like only one breath since I had been in their place. Everything was the same. Except for the meat. The meat they got was much less than what it had been in my time.

"That makes them stronger," I said to one of the Guides.

"They look like skin and bones to me," he answered.

"Stronger," I said to him again.

Hunger spread from the belly and became a sickness of the mind. False prophecies had poisoned every dung fire, every tent, and every Pack. The hungry men fed on rumors and curses.

"The Ssons steal children from the tents and eat them."

That is why the children were fewer. Not because there was not enough milk for them.

"Khun-Malan was an orphan, paler than the men of our Tribe. Who sent him here?"

Darhul. Who else?

"This Khun-Malan, he has put up three tents, and outside each one of them he has three spheres as his emblem."

Nine demon heads altogether.

That was what was seeping through ears all over Sirol.

I couldn't stop the rumors. Malan called me and put the Blades in charge of keeping the order across Sirol. We strove all day to stop the stealing, to ration the supplies that arrived from nearby settlements, and to stop disputes before they became bloody.

Sani told me, "If anything happens to you, Firstblade, or to Khun-Malan, they will pounce on us and eat us alive on the same day. I have never seen such rage and hunger in the Tribe."

Fortunately, that winter passed surprisingly mild and magnanimous in its mercy.

"Tell Khun-Malan that our days are dwindling," I said to the Reghen a few days before the Great Feast of Spring.

"Sah-Ouna will speak at the Feast," he said.

"If we make it till then. If the ten thousand Archers revolt, I will not be able to stop them with a few hundred Blades."

"They won't. Their last Leader, Druug, was not a man of great faith. Sah-Ouna chose a loyal Leader to replace him. One who kneels to the First Witch, and is afraid of Enaka's rage," said the Reghen. "Sah-Ouna will announce the new campaign at the Great Feast of Spring."

The word soon spread everywhere and gave Malan some time. The sharpened blades were sheathed, and the dung fires glimmered with faint hopes one more time. I was sure that Malan would announce the new campaign. He had told me so himself. The days of being trapped in Sirol were over. But where to? That, I could not imagine.

The Feast of Spring arrived. Every worthy man was summoned to the Wolfhowl that had been rebuilt under Malan's orders. I made it to the arena from the eastern entrance, along with the rest of the common warriors. The Wolfhowl rose huge to fit all the men of the Tribe: the strong, the worthy, and the few women Archers and Witches. The Craftsmen had worked night and day for many moons and had created a miracle. The ring field was a big hole dug into the earth, a thousand feet its perimeter. All around were rows of seats to fit over ten thousand warriors. Seated upon stones placed on the dirt, thirty round rows filled with warriors from top to bottom. The best from each Banner. Archers, Blades, Trackers. We were stacked next to each other.

"I don't think these stands will last the rains. They will collapse by next spring," said Sani.

"I think the Khun built it just for tonight," I said. "We won't be here next winter."

In the center of the Wolfhowl, was a round, wooden platform with Sah-Ouna alone on it. Malan was on the steps that led to the platform but not next to her. The four Ssons were all on one knee, each one on a corner of the platform.

Around the platform in a wider circle, eight stunningly beautiful Ouna-Mas stood on the ground. They were too far away for me to see their faces but there were two in front of each Sson, so they looked beautiful to me. I counted again. Eight Ouna-Mas. And Sah-Ouna. Nine Witches altogether. The weak at heart and mind would blabber again about secret dealings with the Demon.

Another circle of men, twenty and four Reghen, enclosed the Ouna-Mas. They were just ten paces in front of those of us watching from the front stands. Each Reghen was about ten paces away from his identically dressed brother. They were the tongues of the Khun and the First Witch, and had to recite the Truths that Sah-Ouna would reveal.

After that, an even larger circle. Countless Rods, almost two hundred of them, with tall spears, looking straight at us from three paces away. Ready to open wide anyone who dared threaten the Khun again. No man had been allowed to bring bow or blade into Sirol.

A torch flickered next to each of them: Rod, Reghen, or Ouna-Ma. Two torches to the left and right of each Sson illuminated their monstrous-looking heads that spurted out of their robes. About two dozen torches around Sah-Ouna, lighting the platform brilliantly as if the Witch was Selene herself, and everyone else around it a star. And thirty rows of men; all the Tribe's warriors waiting. For their fate and their Story. Everyone had encircled everyone else, as the Red Sun, the greatest circle of life, was setting.

Selene of the spring came out gold and perfectly round from the east and started to rise. Not the slightest shadow of a cloud obscured her. The men who were seated in the western stands, across from Selene, were the first to see her and filled the Wolfhowl with cheers. Cheers and screams of joy from the other stands joined in and rose to a deafening cry that reached the four corners of the Earth.

Sah-Ouna slaughtered a white goat, its long hair hiding the weakness of the skinny animal.

She raised the liver that trembled on the edge of her fingers and looked at it.

She listened to the Sky.

She sang with her most solemn voice, alone among ten thousand men.

O Goddess, sweet and beautiful…come listen…we beg you…I will bring as sacrifice…a heart of my own…

All eyes were on Selene. No man breathed until she was finished. The Ouna-Mas joined in the hymn repeating the words. Only when they stopped, the men began murmuring.

"What is happening?"

"What now?"

Each was anxiously waiting for Sah-Ouna's life-giving and death-bringing Truth. The ceremony had never unraveled like this before. Sah-Ouna had not revealed the prophecy. And she said nothing that night. She stepped down, took Malan by the hand, and then ascended to the platform together.

For the first time, the Khun stood next to the Witch on the Feast of Spring. He was the center of the whole Tribe, and all of us revolved around him. The Khun would not be listening. He would be speaking. Sah-Ouna hugged her favorite son softly and turned him to face the southeast, with Selene ascending valiantly on his left. The Forest was to the back of them.

Sah-Ouna stepped down again. In silence.

"Isn't she going to speak to us?" Leke asked me as if I had seen this sight many times and knew what the outcome would be.

"She has spoken," whispered a Tracker behind me.

Malan, with his eyes open, began to speak.

With the Voice of the Khun. The one that lifted Sirol to the Sky. He stopped after each phrase and the twenty-four Reghen, ten paces in front of us, repeated his words loudly for us to hear. Malan shouted with both arms raised, the palms facing inward.

"The First Witch spoke to me.

"The one who has heard the Unending Sky.

"With Selene, silver and gold.

"She heard the words of the almighty Goddess."

The thunderous shouts of thousands. Would I have thought to say the same? If I had become Khun? No.

"The magnificent Selene shone upon us, and the Sun will also shine brighter than ever at tomorrow's fateful dawn. Because the Goddess hates the traitors."

Wild cries. For the traitors who had been slain, all forty of them. "By the Ssons," was the Story everyone favored.

"The traitors will no longer be hidden in the fog or in the darkness. The Season of the Golden Light is coming, the Season of Victory, where no enemy of the Tribe will survive. Men, listen to me. We march on."

The women Archers were there too.

"The campaign for the Legends, the one that will bring life back to our Packs."

The Reghen echoed, stentorian.

A standing, deafening ovation. The monster with the nine thousand heads had awoken to swallow the faraway ill-fated lands. Malan took a breath and waited until the crowd settled.

"There."

There! Finally, we knew.

He pointed to the southeast. I was watching Malan sixty paces in front of me, and the Forest was behind him. We would ride in the opposite direction, he said. Not toward the Forest. Far away from her. East. South.

"To the seven cities of the South."

The seven cities of the South. The faraway edges of the world and the Southeastern Empire. The first, the greatest of the seven cities, Thalassopolis, was the only way, by land, to the other six. Otherwise, we would have to cross the Black Sea and then the Pelago of the Thousand Islands. Malan, with both arms raised above his head, and with his voice gushing out of the lungs of twenty-four Reghen, was sending us to the opposite end of the world.

"We cannot do that," Sani said to me as soon as the Reghen repeated the words. "Can't go southeast. We'll need ships."

"Or conquer Sapul, the cursed Thalassopolis."

But we would not attack Sapul, which connected the two seas with her straits.

My Tribe had no ships and would never build any.

Malan was still shouting.

"I will ride first, and you will follow me on the once-traveled trail of our Ancestors."

A murmur of thousand whispers multiplied fast and died faster around me. *The trail of our Ancestors?*

"Oh, fuck!" a man behind me screamed, and we all turned to see the face of a dejected Tracker. "Fucking dog fucker! He is taking us to the damned pits of the earth."

"We will head north for many moons. Then turn east past the great rivers and then through the steppe of our Ancestors for many more moons," Malan continued, and the Reghen repeated, too far away to care about the words of any Tracker.

The cheers died down. We were going to the steppe, back to where we had come from.

"And then south, through the salt lakes. We'll gaze upon but not cross the Black Sea of Darhul, and finally head straight through the belly of the Southeastern Empire. We will reach the six cities of the South. Conquer them one by one. And finally, last, we'll ride north from there to Sapul. To Sapul!"

Malan's shouts were feeding the men's screams.

"To Sapul we march, brave of the Tribe!

"To overthrow the Emperor of the Buried Cross Worshippers. We will avenge the evil deeds that weigh heavily upon them. We'll take revenge for the children of our ancestors, six generations before."

The Sapul of dreams. Louder than ever, the shouts rose again. The men next to me were asking whatever came to their heads, but I couldn't hear a word they were saying. Thousands of men were embracing one another in a mad celebration around the arena.

We were going to make an enormous circle of a journey to reach the other side of the world. First north, then east, then south, and then west until we reach the six smaller cities of the Southeastern Empire before ending in Sapul. Ride around the whole world of men just to avoid attacking Sapul first. The other cities were smaller. Maybe we could take them, but no one had ever set foot inside Sapul.

The Tracker behind me was not celebrating. I moved closer to him to listen to his words.

"This cannot be done," I heard him say as soon as everyone quieted down.

"What do you mean?" I asked.

"Go where? Do you understand what he said? North, next to the forests, east through the endless steppe, and then through the treacherous passes, over the stone hills and along the salt lakes? To cross the deserts of fire and reach the southern edges of the world? And conquer six cities, six armies after all of that? And then what? Head north from there to Sapul? How? And come back? No, it's not possible. Not even in seven summers. Not even with one hundred thousand men," said the Tracker.

"We have fewer than half of that."

"Seven summers," Sani mumbled next to me.

Malan continued.

"The Age of Hunger began before me, but it will end with me as Khun. The Change that the Goddess has promised is now.

"You will follow me. We will find gold there. Glory that you cannot imagine. Horse, meat, women!"

He was screaming now.

"You will have Legend and Story. For the revenge. For the promise of Khun-Nan and the First Ouna-Ma. For Enaka. For the end of all traitors and all othertriber demons. Follow your Khun. There. Forward. Our Brave. For the Goddess."

He was pointing in the exact opposite direction of the pond of Kar-Tioo.

The greatest, most thunderous Feast of Spring had ended and yet the noise will not subside. The rings of men broke and became long slithering lines, dragging themselves like hungry snakes on the earth to find their fate in the campaign. We were still pushing one another to get out of the Wolfhowl when I stopped and turned. Why was I rushing? Why were we pushing each other?

Are we men or sheep?

Malan was still standing alone on the platform. The Rods and the Ssons had assembled around him with the torches and formed a large shining ring of fire in the center of the field. The other torches in the stands and at the edges of the plateau were slowly dying out.

I turned back to go talk with the Khun on the night of his glory. I had to say something. But what? So he wouldn't forget me. So he would take me with him. I had to leave. Twenty winters now, my heart had rusted. In the land of Elbia and Zeria, of the Ouna-Mas and the Drakon. I wanted to go to the other side of the world. In the desert of fire. To let it burn everything inside me.

I never made it to Malan. The Reghen stopped me, with an Ouna-Ma at his side, before I climbed the steps.

"Great Truths the Goddess has given us. This campaign will last many summers," the Reghen told me.

"Yes, I got that."

"You have to go to the Forest to gather belladonna and crazygrass. As much as you can find. All of it. The Ouna-Mas will need to summon their visions when they are away in the campaign."

The Reghen and the Ouna-Mas had found a fitting Truth again. To get rid of me. But the trap they had set was much too sweet for me not to take the bait.

"I will go," I told him. "With fifty men. So the Reekaal won't dare to come near me."

I looked at the Sson who was closer to me, but he didn't move or utter a word.

"Be quick about it. We leave before the half moon. You have nine days," said the Reghen. "And bring that stallion of yours. The Khun asked for it."

Asked for what?

The Rod next to the Reghen smiled, staring at me and rocking his fists as if he was holding reins. "Easy now, boy," he said.

I ran away trying to forget or not to think about what the Reghen meant. As I was coming out of the Wolfhowl, I bumped into Chaka, who had been Chief of the Uncarved Guides for five winters.

"How are you doing, old man?" He was just a plain Archer now. I could call him anything I wanted. I was the Tribe's Firstblade.

"The Khun. He will save us," he answered.

He had found the One whom he had been seeking all along.

"The campaign? What does your heart say?"

"My last, Da-Ren. Your first."

"Do you believe this is what Enaka wishes? That Sah-Ouna saw our fate in the Sky? Or is the Khun taking us where he wanted to go all along?" I asked.

"Yes."

"Yes to what? I am asking you about the Witch. Does she have the eyes of Enaka, or is she playing with our fears?"

"Yes."

This could be the last time we see Kar-Tioo, O'Ren. But don't worry, no one will take you away from me.

I started out for the northern caves of the Forest that night, with fifty of my best men. Sani stayed back at camp to keep things in order while I was gone.

"Be careful," I told him.

"Careful of what?"

"Everyone."

By now I expected a trap whenever the Ouna-Mas or the Reghen sent me somewhere.

It took me four days to reach the northern settlement of the Dasal. I was lucky enough to find the Dasal before they left for farther north as Veker had warned me. It was one spring ago from that night that Zeria had not shown up.

We reached the huts but there were all deserted, though I could still smell the fires and the fresh sheep shit.

"They must be close by," I said.

We soon found the Dasal, about two hundred of them, all gathered in a clearing not far from there. They were all in a circle; their backs turned to me. Another ceremony of circles was unveiling in front of me, another ceremony to end the old and bring the new. I dismounted O'Ren and approached with care to remain unnoticed, urging my men to stay farther back.

I was not sure what I was watching. A tall old man was at the head of the circle, and I recognized him as Saim, the shaman. His mantle was a mesh of felt, leaves and feathers, made of the Forest itself. He was holding a flask and he gave it to a short-haired man in front of him. A woman, dark-haired and slender was next to the man. The hands of man and woman were tangled together, a hemp rope, coiled multiple times around them.

The circle of men, women and children were watching. There were four girls outside the circle in the four points of the horizon. One of them was waving two giant wings behind Saim and that made him look like a fearsome mythical bird ready to fly. Another girl to my right was holding a torch. On the opposite side, yet another one was spreading handfuls of earth in front of her. A fourth girl stepped out of the circle holding a flask and started sprinkling water with her fingers toward the direction of the trunks that hid me. The moment she spotted me, she dropped the jar and left with a scream. She was young, much younger than Zeria. At her scream, the circle opened, the Dasal turned, and they stared at me. I walked toward them, completely naked of fear. I had seen only the back of the girl in the middle of the ceremony, yet I had recognized her figure before I met her eyes once again. She turned together with the man, a couple with their hands tied.

I was surrounded by the Dasal. They were surrounded by fifty of my men, with shaft on ear ready to shoot. Veker ran toward me pleading and waving both hands up: "Don't bring death on such a sacred day. In the name of the children. Whatever you want. She is here. She is here; it is her sacred day. I'll give her to you."

"Ready, Chief," shouted a young lad from my fifty.

My men were ready for blood, and all these green and blue-eyed women were making them mad and hungry.

"Stand down," I shouted to my men. "We have orders to trade with those savages, not to kill." I turned to Veker. "Give her to me," I said. "All the belladonna you have. And all the potent herbs you've gathered. Bring it all."

"You want me to find belladonna in the early of spring? I will give you whatever we gathered from many moons ago."

The Dasal had broken the circle and had all huddled together around the couple, making the target my men needed easier to find. I had to get my men out of there before anyone from either side lost his patience.

"We'll camp for the night close by and leave by dawn. Bring as much as you can. And more herbs—crazygrass, whatever you have gathered," I said. "Continue with…with, whatever you do here."

"You see, Da-Ren, Zeria has already given—"

I cut him short. "I don't want to know."

She had broken the circle and was next to him. A white dress, as if of a pale ghost forever lost to me.

"We are leaving," I said.

"Da-Ren! Do you rule all these men now? I beg you to bring no harm to my people."

Tears? Hold the tears back in your eyes. You will never have to beg me. I would uproot my Tribe from the earth before I saw you harmed.

"You don't understand. We're leaving. For good. This is my last night here. You will be safe," I said looking at Veker now.

He shook his head as if he knew I was lying. I was lying even if I didn't know it.

Zeria opened her lips silently for me to read and no one else to hear. "I'll come find you."

I hadn't seen her so close and so clearly for so long.

We camped next to the Dasal huts for the night. The kettles and the flutes of celebration pierced my ears all night.

"Here, they gave us one of their pots with meat and greens. And wine. You want some, Chief?" said Noki who had come with me.

My breath shortened, and my stomach was tied up in knots.

"So there will be no bloodbath here?" Noki continued as I stood silent.

"No, none of that," I said.

"Good, I am in no spirit to hack children and old men. A couple of their women I'd like to spend the night with, but…," Noki said, and he stopped to gulp down the wine.

"What?"

"Nothing. I like you, Da-Ren. You're not a crazy fuck of a Firstblade. I'll follow you in any damned campaign they send us."

Damned it will be.

I didn't sleep or eat all night. It would prove a terrible mistake on our way back.

Veker came at dawn with his trusted men. They had gathered all that they could, and he offered it to me in sacks with a fake smile and cold sweat on his brow. We mounted our horses and walked them away from the huts. There was nothing more to take from the Forest.

We had been going for a while, and I had remained last, as if I still hoped. As I was gazing to the west, I saw a little girl signaling me silently with her hand, her body hiding behind an oak trunk. I turned O'Ren to follow her. She kept retreating farther away, hiding from one tree to the next. I lost her a couple of times among the woods, but she stopped and signaled for me to follow. I kept after her on horse for a while until I saw her jumping over a fallen trunk. I didn't see her again for a few breaths and I thought she was hiding in the thicket behind. I dismounted and ran to her but as I was about to reach her, Zeria appeared out of the green. The little girl was running away from us and didn't look back again.

"We had to be alone," Zeria said.

I stared at her, hands fidgeting, unable to find the first word. *Or would it be the last?*

"You are leaving," she said.

"I am."

"Do you want to go there?" She pointed toward the east.

Even the darkest black of her hair shone an outer ribbon of gold as the early sun fell on her head. At night, the same ribbon would have the silver-blue of the moonlight, but I wouldn't be there to see it anymore. I would be riding hard, far and away from her. I would ride so far that there would be no thought, no struggle, no pondering of coming to see her again and again every moon. Because I desired her more than anything else in this world. So far that she would become a dream, a long-lost spirit, an image that would clear up only when I closed my eyes.

She was wearing a forest-colored dress, the luminous green of the wet moss and the faint yellow of a dying Selene. The fabric was torn high on the right side, and I could see the soft skin of her leg as she was moving. I remembered her skin burning the first night I touched her. The perfect lines of her nose, the lips, the eyebrows, the work of an evil god who had brought my eternal doom. Her soft voice, so different from the shrill, agonizing sounds of the women of our camp. Touching her face and then her neck and down her breasts, a journey now far more impossible than the one I was about to embark on. Her breasts were fuller, full as a young mother's. Everything around her, the leaves, the shadows of the birds, were trembling slowly in the morning breeze. I was trembling. *Was this anger or fear?*

There was nothing to say, to touch, to kiss. I turned my back on her and put my boot on the stirrup. At least I could hide the tremor of my hands, grasping the reins.

Let's go, O'Ren, there is nothing more to do here.

He took very slow steps as if he wasn't sure.

Don't worry, O'Ren. I will keep you with me forever; you are safe. We must leave now.

"Do you want to go there, Da-Ren?" she repeated.

Anywhere.

The gray-white stallion refused to take another step away from her and I turned to say goodbye. And yet the opposite words came out of my mouth.

"I will come back, Zeria," I said.

"I know you will come back. The branches of our lives have been growing on the same tree since we were children."

I always came back. To both. I came back to the Tribe, and I came back to the Forest, torn between two worlds, to weld my pieces together. I always came back when it was too late.

She came close and stretched her hands to touch mine. She placed between my fingers a silver amulet I'd never seen before. It had the shape of a double-headed ax hanging head down by a leather cord. Each edge had a row of wolf's teeth carved into it. Two silver fangs at the ends and six smaller ones in the middle. Eight teeth on each edge, sharp enough to make a finger bleed at the touch. Two silver snakes embracing each other and coiling around the haft, their heads resting on the ax's cheeks.

"Do you still seek the magic, Da-Ren? I brought all the magic I possess to protect you," she said. "There is no other amulet like that. Wear it, and death will not touch you. My mother had it. Her mother had given it to her, and it saved her from your Tribe. I had it on me when you saved me."

"I can't wear this," I said. *You are not mine, Zeria.*

"Take it. You saved my life first. But you will promise me."

"What?"

The humiliation we accept in life. Another man was holding her every evening, making her his own. Yet she was asking me to promise, and I wanted to listen and say yes.

"Whatever you do, wherever you will go, you will not bring death upon a woman or child."

I was already wearing the amulet around my neck; the silver snakes coiled next to my heart and the wolf's teeth sunken into the skin. It still had the warmth from her hands.

"Promise," she said louder as her hands covered mine.

"I promise," I said and reluctantly pulled my hand away.

"Don't forget me. Remember me when you hear the wind singing through the wheat fields," she said.

How did she know?

Wind and wheat fields were all I would find for a thousand days and nights. And women. And children.

O God of the Cross Worshippers. Why?

The children.

The Story continues in
Drakon Book III: Firstblade

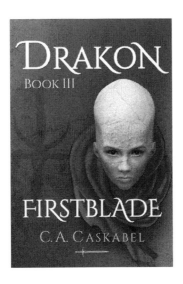

A bloody campaign to the ends of the earth, fierce battles against the armies of the Cross, a thirteen-moon siege of a great city, and an undying dream to return to the Forest.

Book III is the turning-point of Da-Ren's story as the Tribe invades the seven cities of the South. Myths unravel and legends drown in the blood of the innocent. Da-Ren learns of new gods, none as powerful as gold. He pays for victories with nightmares, for wisdom with loss. Empires crumble and cities are reduced to ruins, but there is no glorious story to guide him to the stars. Only a faint hope that metamorphosis awaits at the end of the journey.

Firstblade is a book of poisons: the legends of hatred, the words of the witches, the scorpion's sting and the Drakon's blood, the hunger of a mad leader for power. Love. One poison will prove stronger than all others.

About Drakon

Drakon is one completed story which consists of:

Drakon Book I: The Sieve
Drakon Book II: Uncarved
Drakon Book III: Firstblade
Drakon Book IV: Butterfly

You can find our newsletter, my journal and more information about the book at:

www.caskabel.com
journal.caskabel.com
www.facebook.com/CaskabelAuthor

Thank you for reading and reviewing

Till next time,
C.A.

About the Author

C.A. Caskabel started writing *Drakon* in 2013 and completed the 350,000-word epic fantasy novel in 2016. He split Drakon into four books which he will release within 2017, he promises. After all, he is eager to start working on the next novel. C.A. is also the founder of an indie publisher of picture books and fantasy fiction.

Before 2013, C.A. was a serial technology entrepreneur. He studied at Boston and Brown University. He calls Boston, New York, Providence, San Francisco, London, and Athens (and in general Planet Earth) home.

Printed in Great Britain
by Amazon